CYCLE OF EVIL: BOOK 3

SPEAKING EVIL

JASON PARENT

Speaking Evil

Cycle of Evil™: Book 3

Red Adept Publishing, LLC

104 Bugenfield Court

Garner, NC 27529

https://RedAdeptPublishing.com/

This is a work of fiction. Names, characters, places, and incidents either are the product of the author's imagination or are used fictitiously, and any resemblance to locales, events, business establishments, or actual persons—living or dead—is entirely coincidental.

---
1. http://StreetlightGraphics.com

PROLOGUE

S*eventeen years ago.*

The acrid air stung Jocelyn's lungs as she walked into her two-story home just outside the city. Smoke grated at her eyes. The fire alarm in the kitchen blared.

She coughed and waved away the haze in front of her face. "Honey? Something's burning!" Her husband was not the best cook, but lord, how she loved him for trying. And with her often-late hours, she could stomach a casserole filled with undrained tuna or a hockey puck burger in exchange for all his miraculous help around the house. She snickered. *Looks like it's burger night tonight.*

Her humor tempered when she noticed the unnatural quality to the smell—a chemical odor of something burning that had no business being over a flame at all, like plastic or rubber, noxious and overwhelming. She pulled her shirt over her nose.

A tingling came to her arms, a tightness to her chest. Sweat slickened the hair above her ears. "Honey?" *Maybe he can't hear me over the alarm.*

Jocelyn dropped her bag on the sofa and hurried into the kitchen. Thick fumes rose from the stovetop, where a pot had been left unattended. A flash of anger quickly transformed into worry as she rushed to turn off the burner. Sliding the pan over, Jocelyn cried out as her palm sizzled against the steel handle. She dashed to the sink and ran cold water over her fresh burn. A line of blisters and smooth pink tissue formed over her lifeline, erasing it from existence. Her eyes already watered from the smoke, but she bit back her pain and kept her tears from falling. *Where are you, Peter?*

1

Her palm felt as if it would tear open if she stretched out her fingers, but slowly, the pain dwindled with the smoke. After she wrenched the smoke alarm off the wall and removed its battery, the house went quiet. She returned to the mess on the stove, her short, quick breaths the only sound. The eerie stillness offered her a moment to catch them.

Jocelyn examined the saucepan. Its bottom still glowed hot red, but the billows of bright orange and black clouds had shrunk to asthmatic puffs of charcoal gray. Keeping her nose covered and blinking away the sting in her eyes, she peered at the charred remains in the pan. A plastic bottle and rubber nipple clung like melted cheese to the pan's sides and bubbled like swamp gases at its bottom.

Adrian's bottle? But it's after five. Peter, her husband, was like clockwork. He always gave their six-month-old his bottle at four o'clock sharp. All the water had long since evaporated out of the saucepan.

Did he fall asleep? Jocelyn shook her head and fidgeted. *Not with that alarm blaring.* Fighting back her worry, she grabbed a dishrag and used it to lift the pan and douse it in the sink. When she turned the water off, she again paused to listen. The house was eerily silent. No SportsCenter. No shower running or toilet flushing. No giggles from the baby to light up the house or cries to draw their family together. No life, no Peter, no Adrian.

"Peter?" The alarm would have sent Adrian into a fit, at least when it first started to blare, but she heard no bellowing and wondered if he was all cried out. She hurried back to the living room and rummaged through her purse for her phone, then plodded back to the kitchen while dialing her husband. "Come on. Pick up!"

Maybe he doesn't have it with him. But Jocelyn didn't need to be a detective—five years on the job, and several more as an officer preceding—to know she was fooling herself. Peter was safe and sturdy, perfectly solid when it came to their child, her calm through every storm. He didn't forget things like bottles on stovetops, he didn't miss Adrian's dinner time, and he didn't misplace his phone. *But he does leave it on vibrate so as not to wake up a sleeping baby.* The thought offered a smidgeon of comfort.

She studied her kitchen. Chairs were pushed in tightly against their small, circular table. The mail sat in a stack upon its surface. Adrian's high chair shined as if spit-polished, and it had been moved back into the corner. Dishes dried on the dish rack. The floor shined as if it had been waxed, not a Cheerio or macaroni noodle in sight. Other than the ruined saucepan, the kitchen looked clean and orderly and utterly norm—

Jocelyn gasped. She pressed a trembling hand hard against her mouth to hold back a scream. When she removed it, her shirt fell away from her face. "No... no, no, no, no." She paced the length of her floor, her thoughts a jumbled mess as she squeezed her temples with her thumb and forefinger.

A bloody handprint smeared the wall near the hallway leading to the bedrooms. Heart racing and mind screaming with terror, she struggled not to let her emotions conquer her. Jocelyn battled back images of worst-case scenarios not yet supported by hard facts, knowing too damn well that she would be no good to her family if she lost her mind. She took long, deep breaths to steady her nerves then drew her gun.

"Peter?" She crept toward the hall. Her pistol out in front of her, she peeked down the hallway before entering. Seeing no one, she edged forward. Her chin quivered as her foot landed with a squish. *Blood?* Her heart told her so even before she looked down. A tear fell down her cheek. More battered at her dams as her emotions threatened to unravel her. All her worst fears, spawned from a career of making enemies, had come to fruition. A piercing blizzard racked her insides, and she shuddered violently as if the icy bleakness of space had filled the hollowness inside her.

She swallowed hard, trying to choke down her rising despair. Re-dialing Peter, she slipped her phone into her pocket and listened for a buzz.

An electronic vibration came from her bedroom. Following the sound, she found a bloody streak as smooth and even as if it had been left by a paint roller over the hardwood floor. She turned the corner into the room. Blue-suede shoes—the pair she had given Peter last Christmas—peeked out from the end of their bed. His legs lay motionless, the rest of his body hidden behind the bed. The tone coming from his direction died.

Grief flooded her, carrying with it waves of guilt. It convinced her that her career choice had led her family to that day, that moment—their undoing. Biting her knuckle, her body jerking as if she had the hiccups, she let out a low moan. Her knees buckled, and she would have fallen had her shoulder not caught the doorframe and posted her upright. She raised a hand over her mouth to stifle a sob. Tears poured freely, obscuring her vision.

Across the hall, a giggle came from the darkened nursery, where the shades were drawn for naptime. *Adrian!* She snapped up, a renewed vigor pulsing through her, wild and enigmatic. All her fear and hopelessness succumbed to a mother's intrinsic need to protect her child. The jerky-hiccupy sensation—the sobs and moans and tears—was gone. She held her breath, tightened her grip on her weapon, and forced her disassembled mind back together through sheer will and the desire to annihilate whoever threatened her boy.

Still, her training kept her cautious where others' resolve might have broken. After peeking around the doorframe, she swept the hall then proceeded toward Adrian's room.

It's him. Jocelyn's lips curled into a snarl. Somehow, she kept silent when all she wanted was to scream. She'd faced off against a hundred or so of the worst felons New England had ever known, but it was the one who got away who terrified her far more. Even after four years and half a dozen sightings many, many miles away, she knew it was *him*. It wasn't due to anything rational but instinctive—a hunch, an inner voice, a mother's intuition, she didn't know—something that had always served her well as an investigator. *And if this is him...*

Her service pistol clacked as it rattled in her hand. Facing that monster alone was the stuff of nightmares. She needed her partner, Bruce.

She rounded the corner. A man dressed in black stood with Adrian cradled in the crook of his arm. In his other hand, he held a large steak knife, twirling its point under her son's chin. Adrian giggled and drooled, grasping at the spinning object just out of reach. The man's face, shrouded by a hood, was familiar but different—older, altered. But his eyes, those were the same: glossy black but with something behind them shining like a sharpened spear point. Those eyes could belong to no one but *him*.

He smiled, the dull light from the hall glinting off large canines, the teeth of an apex predator. "Hello, Detective. So nice to see you again."

CHAPTER 1

P*resent day.*
     Screaming again.

Tessa sprang upright in her bed, tucking her knees against her chest and clamping her hands over her ears. But she couldn't block out the sound or shut off her mind. *Whose room is it coming from this time?* It sounded like a boy, a young one, maybe Mitchell or Grady. *What do they want with him?*

Perhaps if she knew who *they* were, maybe then she could begin to answer her thousands of other questions. *They* were the monsters that scooped children out of their beds at night and the boogeymen who haunted her dreams. And beyond any doubt, one night, *they* would come for her.

Tugging at her hair, her lips trembling, she realized she'd been a fool to think herself safe, even after killing that horrible man, her stepfather. All the years of abuse, of being constantly afraid, over with the stroke of a knife, or rather, many strokes. She didn't resist her freedom being taken from her, had done all the doctors had asked of her. But in a place where she was supposed to be healing and kept safe, she was always afraid.

She rolled her shoulders, trying to loosen up the tall, slender yet curvier frame she'd only recently become comfortable in despite having stopped growing at least a year ago. She wished the self-confidence and self-awareness exhibited by some of her teachers or all those doctor-and-lawyer-types on TV had flowered in her with acne's decline and increasing cup sizes, but she had yet to learn the art of being a woman, if there was such a thing.

Her teeth gnawed and tugged at a hangnail. Maybe she was over-reacting. Patients screaming was a fairly regular occurrence at Brentworth Hospital's psych ward, something to be expected, not feared. And sometimes, those taken away would come back, acting as if nothing had ever happened. Other times, they didn't come back at all. Tessa wasn't sure which was worse.

A *thump* came from down the hall, and the screaming stopped. Heavy footsteps clomped then dragged down the threadbare carpet outside like a dull, dry razor blade sliding against the grain.

She slipped one leg off the bed then thought better of it. The sounds grew nearer, louder. She held her breath as a shadow blotted out the light under her door.

Without thinking, she dropped onto her feet, but fear kept her soles glued to the hardwood. Whatever had driven her out of bed in the first place had been forgotten. She couldn't possibly want to see what was happening outside her room in those dimly lit halls. She'd always been too scared to look before; it was so much easier to turn a deaf ear when *they* were taking someone else.

Coward. So be it. She'd faced more than her fair share of adversity and had a lifetime's worth of trauma packed into one decade with her abusive stepfather—her *murderous, psychotic* stepfather. She was nobody's sister or mother or caretaker. She wasn't the police. Let the rest of the world fend for itself just like it had left her to do.

And yet, Tessa took a step toward the door.

The sounds were fainter then, moving farther down the hall. Soon, they would be out of earshot. One step, then another. Closer and closer she crept, all the while telling herself she shouldn't be doing it. *Stay out of it. It's not your concern.* Her body paid no heed to her mind's pleas. She pressed on, remembering the line from an old poem. *Until they come for you.*

She had to know who *they* were, so she could know who not to turn her back on. The doorknob twisted in her hand. It clicked as the catch retracted. The floor creaked beneath her weight as she leaned against the doorframe.

The hall fell silent.

After a few seconds, which Tessa spent like a fossil in amber, the *stomp stomp rustle* continued. She pulled open the door a sliver, just enough for one eye to peek out. Gasping, she stumbled backward then fell onto her butt. Another's eye had been peering back.

She scrambled away, heels catching in her worn pajamas until she'd placed several feet between herself and the door. It swung open.

A curvy woman in her mid-to-late twenties with heavy eye shadow entered. The thick black bob hairstyle and white hat pinned to her head were reminiscent of days well before Tessa had been born. The hat matched her all-white lab coat and white slacks. Francine, if Tessa remembered correctly. One of the nice ones. But at that moment, Francine had a vacant look in her wide-open eyes. They locked onto Tessa's.

"What are you doing up, dear?" The nurse's smile went no farther than her lips. Her black lipstick stained her teeth. She walked the few steps over to Tessa, crouched, then threw an arm around her shoulders. "Come on. Let's get you back in bed."

Tessa shrank from the contact and resisted being pulled to her feet. "What's going on? Where are they taking him?"

"Who, dear?" Francine's smile was unwavering, her eyes unblinking.

"The boy—" Tessa pointed at the door. "The boy I heard screaming."

"Screaming?" Francine cocked her head as if she were a dog hearing a far-off whistle. But the hallway had gone silent. "I don't hear any screaming. Perhaps you were having a nightmare." She again tried to pull Tessa to her feet.

"It wasn't a nightmare. Mitchell or-or-or maybe Grady... he was screaming, and then he just stopped. Like he was suddenly cut off."

"Oh, yes, yes," the nurse said, standing up straight. "Mitchell suffers from night terrors. That's probably what you heard, dear. The poor child." She chuckled. "Anyway, don't you worry a smidge. They've given him a sedative. We won't be hearing a peep out of him for the rest of the night."

Tessa flinched. "And Laura from last week? What happened to her?"

Francine put her hands on her hips. "Well, you *are* an observant child, aren't you?"

Tessa huffed. "I'm not a child."

"Laura was discharged last week. All healed and happily back with her family." Francine cast her a sidelong glance. "Your turn will come. You'll be out soon enough." She extended her hand. "Now, come. Let's get you back in bed."

Hesitantly, Tessa took the offered assistance. The nurse pulled her to her feet and ushered her back to her bed. Tessa climbed in and allowed Francine to tuck her in as if she were seven, not seventeen.

She lay back, the knots in her muscles slow to unwind. The nurse's explanation made sense. A poor child screaming from night terrors—any screaming, really—yes, that was all normal.

Francine tugged on the comforter and ironed out its wrinkles with her hands. The wrinkles in Tessa's forehead, though fewer, persisted. She couldn't shake the hollow pang in her stomach and the nagging at the back of her mind. Something weird was going on.

Laura had been a cutter who couldn't be next to anything sharp. She was way more screwed up than Tessa. She stared blankly at her comforter. *No way they let her out already.* She squinted at Francine, trying to parse the truth from lies in her face. Her eyes fell on the necklace dangling from the nurse's neck—a shimmering sun pendant, appearing sometimes gold, sometimes silver, depending on the angle of the light.

The nurse smiled her plastic, manufactured grin. "That's it, child. Close your eyes."

"I'm not a—" Tessa yawned, stretching her arms over her pillow where they pressed against the headboard. As if under a spell, her mind began to cloud with fatigue. Her body sank into her mattress, her head into her pillow. Her eyes closed then opened again. Francine stood over her, grinning, the medallion at the end of her necklace still swinging slowly. It twisted in half turns, clockwise then counterclockwise, bouncing soft light into Tessa's eyes at the mid-point of each rotation.

Children weren't discharged from Brentworth in the middle of the night. That's what logic told her. Her eyelids closed again. Her breath whistled through her nose. She struggled to maintain that thought. Something about kids... yes, kids... disappearing in the dead of night.

CHAPTER 2

S am knew she was dreaming. Her partner's face, an apparition hovering over her bed, smiled then turned haggard, old and bristling—how he'd looked just before he'd been murdered. Then his murderer's face appeared. It was cruelty hidden behind a mask of decency and piety, sadly handsome, and altogether unassuming. It brought to mind photos of those clean-cut, all-American fifties crooners like Buddy Holly.

Evil, shrouded by innocence.

With the sound of her alarm, the malicious grin of Carter Wainwright—aka Darius Jefferson and countless other known aliases and probably infinitely more she would never know—dissipated. Only the cracked and peeling gray paint of her bedroom ceiling remained.

A small black spider traipsed across it. Wainwright was like that spider, skulking in the dark as he caught his victims in his webs, except the spider killed to live. Wainwright killed for fun.

And he was still out there, no doubt plotting his next sprint of depravity and atrocity. Over a twenty-year span, he and his followers had been credited with at least as many confirmed murders. He'd been linked to scores of others, his aliases appearing as suspects in cold cases across the nation and beyond. Sam remembered her father's relentless calls when those cult murders were happening all over Bristol County in the early 2000s. She'd been a newly badged officer with the Fall River Police Department with no direct connection to the case. Then came the Montreal fiasco with the FBI, followed by the San Diego sightings. Agent Frank Spinney—*dear Frank*—had followed Wainwright there after the original agent in charge was found eviscerated and strung up on an elementary school's flagpole.

For Sam, it had all been just headlines with her morning coffee, nothing more. Someone else's problem—like her late partner and mentor's. She grunted. *His obsession.*

Until Wainwright came back to Fall River, Sam had no personal stake in his capture. Not until Jocelyn, her baby, and Bruce.

Sam swallowed down acid and swatted her alarm clock. She groaned, the dull ache in her shoulders reminding her that she wasn't as young as she used to be, and rolled out of bed. A month's leave filled with a road trip and two weeks in the Caribbean—the whole time spent looking over her shoulder for the next attack—had failed to have its intended rejuvenating effect.

And now, dreaming of Wainwright.

She sighed. *At least Michael seemed to enjoy the time away.* An entire month of escapism and Michael only had one vision brought on by the close confines that came with flying coach. Sam had paid extra for the two-seat exit row upgrade to avoid a repeat on their flight back.

But Michael had to return to school and begin his sophomore year. *Soon, he'll be eighteen and off to college.* She frowned. She'd kind of gotten used to having him around, having someone to talk to, someone not just to care for but to care about. The foster system had turned a blind eye to their arrangement, and she wondered what he would do once he was on his own. Of course, he was welcome to stay with her as long as he wanted. Like her, he had no one else. Two loners alone together. She hoped he knew he would always have her.

But responsibilities called them to separate paths, and Sam had to return to work. She couldn't hide forever from whoever had attacked her. Letting Michael out of her sight would be the hardest part. At least for the foreseeable future, a detail would be posted at the school and at her house, but Wainwright had a knack for circumventing or killing details.

She didn't know it was him, and she had no real reason to think it was. It could have been any of a thousand people holding a grudge or even some random crazy. She wiped the crust from her eyes and blinked. *Why assume the worst?*

Because few people, not dead or already in jail, had the audacity to attack an armed detective in broad daylight. She remembered it as if it had happened yesterday, not six weeks ago—a man in a strange Indian mask charging at her in the hospital parking lot, dark eyes peering through circular cut-outs, sudden pain in her stomach, then falling. Michael protecting her. The man holding a stun gun. From her review of Bruce's files, she knew that Wainwright had a history with the weapon. He would stun his victims so that he could kidnap them and commit unspeakable, gruesome acts upon their bodies in some despicable den of roaches and vermin like him.

But Wainwright had never worn a mask before. It haunted her dreams despite its absurdity, a caricature of a Native American chief wearing a headdress thick with red, white, brown, and yellow feathers, all made of plastic yet with the veneer of a wooden cigar store Indian. Wainwright had been flamboyant, theatrical even, but he always wanted people to know that he was the cause of their pain. He wanted his victims to see the gleam in his eyes as he cut into them—a narcissist and sadist in every sense of the words. Everything had happened so fast that day, she'd barely gotten a look at her attacker. Other than the male body type and proportions that might have matched Wainwright's, she didn't have any clues by which to identify him. Michael said the man had laughed at him, taunted him even. Wainwright was nothing if not arrogant. But Sam had been reeling from the shock when the exchange took place and couldn't remember hearing any of it.

All she had was a hunch. And her hunches were just as often wrong as they were right—not the stuff from which any real cop should draw conclusions.

She dragged herself to the bathroom and blasted the hot water in the shower despite the muggy, stifling morning air. Steam filled the bathroom as she sat on the toilet long after she'd finished urinating, just letting her mind go blank. Her bruises from the beat-downs she'd received over the prior months had vanished, but the aches remained. Stepping into the tub, she let the water cascade over her for several minutes, her skin turning pink then red, the heat massaging her muscles, coercing them to work for her yet another day. In theory, she could retire with a full pension at fifty-five, a partial pension in just a couple years, but she knew she wouldn't unless her body made the decision for her. Until the last year, being a cop was 95 percent of her identity. From then on, it was split fifty-fifty with being a parent to Michael.

Maybe sixty-forty.

In reality, the pendulum had swung so far the other way that being a parent to Michael had been all that mattered over the last few months. She laughed and snorted, remembering how uncomfortable Michael had looked with that seal smiling over his shoulder at a Jamaican waterpark. He hadn't stopped complaining about how bad its breath had been.

If only that was their sole worry—marine mammal halitosis. Wainwright or not, *someone* was after her. She just prayed whoever it was wouldn't use Michael to get to her.

After washing up and shaving her legs, she climbed out of the shower and dried herself. Wrapping one towel around her body and another around her hair, she stepped into her living room. "Michael! Bathroom's all yours!"

A groan came from his bedroom at the far end of the apartment. The teenager was even less of a morning person than she was. When he'd moved in, he'd chosen the spare room the farthest away from hers. At the time, she'd been thankful for the space, but sometimes she wondered if the gap represented the distance between them—one she had spent every day since trying to close. They'd come a long way, but they couldn't change the fact that he was a troubled teenage psychic and she a curmudgeonly middle-aged cop.

And yet, she loved him. She'd never thought herself the motherly type, but life had a way of placing people where it felt they belonged. Sighing, she headed to the kitchen to brew a pot of coffee, guessing they both would need a cup or three. Michael had taken to the drink on their road trip when he realized he could get it really sweet, flavored, and sometimes with whipped cream on top.

He stumbled out of his bedroom, wearing only a white T-shirt and green-and-purple Riddler boxers. He was either becoming more comfortable with his living arrangements or too tired to care. He zombie-walked, eyes half closed and short brown hair spiking in all directions, into the bathroom and shut the door behind him.

Sam smiled. "The coffee will be waiting when you get out."

For all he'd been through, Michael acted as if he didn't have a care in the world. But Sam knew him better than that. She could see his trepidation about the attack, her going back to work, and his returning to school. His mouth twitched slightly just before he shrugged off a question about any of it, and his brow furrowed for half a second every time she mentioned Tessa or Jimmy. He needed to be around more kids his age, and as much as she hated to think anything bad about Tessa or Jimmy, both of whom had had it tough, he needed to be around less damaged kids his age. Maybe she would encourage him to join a sport. That would keep him social and surrounded by people, where he would be less likely to be kidnapped or attacked. Maybe she would encourage Robbie Wilkins to talk him into going out for football.

She shook her head. *Duh. Full contact sport, just asking for more visions.* She listened as the last trickle of coffee dropped into the pot, its strong aroma calling her to it. The shower pipes groaned as Michael closed the faucet with a *clunk*, another one of his infamous two-second scrub downs completed. She poured herself a cup of coffee, black, and fixed one for him with cream and lots of sugar.

As he stepped out of the bathroom, towel around his waist, toothbrush jutting from his mouth, she asked, "How do you feel about cross-country?"

"Huh?" Without another word, he grunted and went into his room and closed the door.

Sam sighed. *As if the kid hasn't done enough running.* She raised an eyebrow. *Maybe tennis is the way to go.* She carried the two mugs to her kitchen table then sat beside yesterday's paper, sliding Michael's coffee across from her. Steam rose from her cup and tickled her cheeks as she thought about getting Michael a racket. She'd tried tennis for a little while herself and had liked it despite not having been terribly good at it. Then she remembered that his school didn't offer tennis until the spring.

She huffed and sipped her coffee. *Maybe I should just let the kid make his own decisions and stop trying to be such a mother.* She rolled her eyes, realizing she was giving voice to his expression—that half-cocked eyebrow and smug smirk he gave her every time she showed even the slightest concern for him.

"I'm not doing cross-country," Michael said, startling her from her reverie. He wore a long-sleeved shirt, jeans, and carried his gloves. His sneakers sat by the apartment door where he always left them. His hair still looked wet and disheveled, and she couldn't tell if it had been what he called "styled" or if he hadn't combed it yet. At fifteen, he'd come a long way from the child she'd rescued from his parents' murder-suicide all those years ago. With Caribbean-blue eyes, some lucky girl—*or guy?*—was sure to get lost in and his still-smooth baby face. He was still a boy but starting to shed the awkwardness of childhood.

If his ability ever allows him to experience intimacy. She winced and coughed, quickly looking away so he wouldn't see the pain that had washed over her. The two of them made quite a pair, Sam reflecting on her own walls—her career, always her excuse—keeping her from anything meaningful with someone more age appropriate. Dismissing the thought, she looked up.

Michael smiled in that way that made his eyes sparkle—the way he always did when he wanted to say something bratty or clever but usually fell short of either. "Running for the sake of running has got to be the stupidest way I can think of spending my time. Other than *thinking* about running for the sake of running. If I do anything, it'll be soccer. At least then there's a point to all the running."

"Soccer!" Sam slapped her palm against the table, sloshing her coffee. "Why didn't I think of soccer?"

Michael laughed and pointed at her cup. "Maybe you should go easy on that." He sat at the table and drew the coffee closer, then pulled on his long knit gloves. He frowned, his eyes going a darker shade as the mirth vanished from them. "A lot of contact in soccer, and you're only wearing a T-shirt and shorts. I'd have to buy stock in spandex, and in case you haven't noticed, I don't have a job."

"School is your job. Do it well. You can worry about work when you get out of it." She smirked. "I'll get you some spandex."

"About that—not the spandex, but the school thing." Michael stared at her with deadly seriousness. "I was thinking of dropping out once I turn sixteen, and—"

"You're just full of jokes this morning, aren't you?" Sam rolled up her newspaper and threatened to swat him with it. "You'd better finish getting ready, or you're going to miss the bus. Want me to make you some eggs real quick?"

"You sure you know what those look like? White oval things"—he held up his thumb and forefinger, spreading them two inches apart—"about this big."

Sam ruffled her newspaper and frowned. "Do you want them or not?"

"Nah," he said, getting up and heading to the cupboard. He pulled out a package of Pop-Tarts. "These will do just fine."

"Michael," Sam said, standing. "Don't forget—"

"I know." He pulled the new cell phone she'd purchased for him out of his back pocket and held it up. "If I see anything strange, you'll be the first to know."

She walked over to him as he twisted his feet into his already tied sneakers. "Two officers will be following the bus—"

"I don't like taking the bus."

"Well, take it this morning, will you? Officers are already outside and ready to follow it. They'll be patrolling the school all day. If you need them—"

"Yeah, I got it," he said, Pop-Tart jutting from his mouth as he straightened the back of his shoe and yanked it over his heel. He pulled his breakfast out of his mouth. "Anyway, I'm not sure it's me who we should be worrying about. That guy definitely seemed to be after you." He raised the Pop-Tart for another bite but paused before chomping. "Still not going to tell me any more about it?"

"I don't know any more than I've already told you. I have no idea who attacked me. Just a gut feeling." She shook her head and looked away. "Never mind."

"Right." Michael stepped closer. "Whelp, you're the boss. I just hope you're doing even more to keep yourself safe than you are with me." He looked her in the eyes, no trace of a smile lingering. "Seriously."

"I'll be fine." She waved a hand dismissively. "Go catch your bus."

He pulled the tip of the glove off his forefinger. "You know, there's an easy way to find out—"

Sam grabbed him by the arm, turned him around, and hustled him toward the door. "Will you get going already?" She pushed him out of the apartment, chuckling. "Have a good first day back." She shut the door in his face and hoped he hadn't forgotten to comb his hair.

"You too!" he shouted through the wood. "At least it's Wednesday!" The sound of his hurried footsteps clamored down the stairwell.

Since her hours varied, she didn't have the short week he had, so the nearness of the weekend meant little to her. She tucked her hair behind her ears, conscious of the nervous tick. At the very least, she worried like a mother, and it was only the first of many school days to come. She had plenty of worrying to look forward to.

Checking her watch, she saw that she, too, needed to get a move on. She'd spent enough time hiding. If some villain was looking to take her out, she was ready and willing to do whatever it took to get him first.

And Sam had a feeling she knew exactly where to start.

CHAPTER 3

"Empty your pockets, please," a burly security guard said after Michael had set off the metal detector.

If he'd thought of school as a prison his freshman year, his sophomore year was off to a more confining start. He pulled his *Batman* keychain with its lone key from his front pocket and placed it in a dish atop the conveyor belt. He glanced back at the line forming behind him, chuckled nervously, then started to walk back through the metal detector.

The heavyset guard held up his hand. "Any belt?"

Michael thought about it, then pulled up his shirt to check. No belt.

The guard waved him through, and the detector buzzed again. He heard the mousy girl who was next in line sigh melodramatically and turned in time to see her eyes roll behind tortoiseshell glasses. Shrugging, he lifted his palms.

"Step over there, please," Metal Detector Man said as he pointed at a four-foot-nothing woman. She was chewing gum with her mouth open and holding one of those wand things TSA sometimes used at airports. She instructed him to spread his arms, then performed tai chi with the wand, waving it over every inch of his body. Whatever she thought he might be hiding behind his ears was a little disturbing. The buzzer went off at his groin.

"It's... I..." He lifted his shirt again and gazed downward, unsure what to say. The wand hovered over his crotch, and for an awkward moment, he and the guard stared at each other in silence.

"Button," the woman said with an air of such disinterest that Michael was almost offended. She handed him his keychain and threw a thumb over her shoulder at his backpack at the end of the rollers. "You're all set."

After grabbing his bag, he headed to his locker, hoping he remembered the combination. The halls had been painted during the summer, a blue so light it was almost gray and as drab as it had been before the paint job. The fresh coat failed to hide the divots and scuff marks, or the notch made by a bullet fired at Glenn Rodrigues—the one that had missed. Even the floor, newly stained and smelling like gasoline, held the markings of hundreds of dirty shoes. It clung to his sneakers with every step, his soles peeling off it with fart-like rips as he trudged through the start of his first day.

No one else seemed to notice the bleakness of their hallowed halls. The corridor was awash with bright clothes and brighter smiles, the teenagers happy to reconnect with friends and catch up on the latest gossip. Michael kept his head down as he walked, never raising his gaze to see who might be watching him and judging. He let out a breath as he reached the relative safety of his locker, then stared at his lock as if concentration could will it open. It only took him two tries to recall the numbers and a third go because he forgot to bypass the second number on the counterclockwise spin. Students were supposed to empty their lockers at the end of every school year, but he'd left the rock band poster up. It had been there when he inherited the locker, had been there for who knew how many previous owners, and was there awaiting him on his first day back. Seeing the poster made him smile. It was a token reminder of what was his—a narrow enclave all for himself in hostile wilderness.

A meaty hand clamped down on his shoulder. "What's up, nerd?"

Michael tensed, then relaxed when the voice's owner registered. He turned to face the over six feet and growing junior star center for the Carnegie High Hurricanes, Robert "Robbie" Wilkins. Robbie was one of three friends Michael had made at the school, and the other two wouldn't be showing up any time soon. *If ever.* Yet Robbie was all he needed to keep the rest of the population—the ones who whispered *freak* every time he passed them or *fairy* at the sight of his long, effeminate gloves—in check. Michael couldn't prove that was so, and Robbie never hinted as much, but since their friendship had become general knowledge, no bully gave Michael so much as a second glance.

But there were the others too—those who wanted to know all about his gift, wanted him to touch them and tell them their futures. Will Tyrese get into Harvard like his parents want? Will Becca get what she deserves for stealing Rhonda's boyfriend? Will so-and-so make varsity, pass her driver's license exam, get away with blowing up the toilet, or win a fight? The list was long enough even with Robbie's hulking presence to dissuade them. Michael could only imagine how many soothsayer seekers he would have if he had to face them on his own.

They didn't know what they were asking of him, what he would be forced to see and share with them. Best case, he would see nothing, and everyone would leave dissatisfied. Worst case, he'd have a seizure—something every one of the askers seemed A-okay with—and end up witnessing some horrific event that either the person requesting his help would commit or be a victim of. That was how it had all started with Tessa. When he touched her and had seen what she would eventually do to her murderous turd of a stepfather. Like he didn't already have enough drama in his life with a detective for a foster mom.

"Relax, man." Robbie flashed his big sloppy bulldog grin. Then he frowned and squinted, bending closer to Michael's face. "Hey, are you okay, bud?"

Michael looked up and forced a smile. Robbie could be a bit of a goof, but he had a big heart. Seeing the concern in his friend's face turned Michael's smile genuine.

"You thinking about her?"

Michael's eyebrows shot up before he could plaster on his poker face. Robbie was more perceptive than his grades or his speech let on. Sometimes, Michael thought he purposely dumbed down the way he talked to fit in more. Not that anyone at the school didn't like their football phenom. Michael shrugged. "Maybe a little."

"You see her lately?"

"Not since before I left for my cruise." Michael ran a hand through his hair and sighed. "And that time, she was... confused. She kept talking about weird things happening at that hospital. I don't know if she was drugged or whatever they're doing to treat her in there. Physically, she looked okay."

"Yeah, I bet you noticed that." Robbie punched his arm and laughed. "She is cute, though. Red hair—"

"It's strawberry blonde."

"Whatever. *That* color ain't really my thing." He guffawed. "You know what they say about red hair. A little bit of crazy goes a long way." When he noticed that Michael wasn't laughing, Robbie shoved his hands into his pockets and blew out air. "But you got enough of that in your life already, Superdude. Things like she's been through—abuse like that, then what she did to her own father—"

"*Step*father."

"You know what I'm saying." Robbie clicked his teeth. "People don't just bounce back from that."

Michael crossed his arms. "I don't know. People can surprise you. I bounced back all right from what you and Glenn did to me."

Robbie looked away. Michael could tell the barb had stung him.

"Sorry. I'm just a little on edge, I guess. First day back and all." He scrubbed the memory of Robbie dunking him in a toilet last year from his thoughts with a cleansing breath. "Look, I'm just saying she's gone through a lot but has been making progress. The time before last when I saw her, I thought for sure she'd be out soon, but—"

"But now you're not so sure if she's taken a turn for the worse?"

Michael sighed and his hands fell to his legs. "I really hope not."

"You truly care about her, don't you?" Before Michael could decide how to answer, Robbie added, "What kind of weird things did she say was going on?"

"She wasn't really all that specific. We didn't get a lot of time together, and-and... I didn't want her to be down, you know? To focus on the bad. The time before, she looked..." Michael bit into his lip as his eyes blurred. "She looked almost happy."

Robbie opened his mouth to speak, and Michael expected some quip poking fun at his feelings for Tessa. But Robbie clamped it shut with surprising tact. He tapped his chin, his gaze venturing toward the drop ceiling tiles. "Jimmy's in there, too, right? Why not just ask him if he thinks anything weird is going on?"

"That's... that's actually pretty smart." Michael nodded. "Thanks, Robbie."

"That's what I'm here for." The big guy stuck his hands back into his pockets and shuffled his feet. "And, when you go see him, can I go too? I'd like to, you know, apologize."

Michael inhaled through his teeth. "I don't know if that's such a good idea. Everything he's been through has really toughened him up. Glenn was only the first bully he took down. I'm not sure he's ready to just forgive and forget. I know it's been almost a year—and I don't say this to sound harsh, but—look where you're standing and where he's at."

Robbie's cheeks reddened. He stared down at his feet.

Michael sighed. "Look, let me talk to him first, okay? The gesture would mean more coming from you, but—"

Robbie threw up his hands. "Too soon. I get it." He shook his head. "Well, I know he's the reason for the new metal detectors, but those cops outside, they're here for you, I bet."

Again, Michael was surprised at Robbie's perceptiveness. "It's just a precaution."

"Yeah, I've seen the psychos you and that detective mom of yours cross paths with, and I ain't too proud to admit I hope to never see them again."

"Masterson's dead, Robbie. No one's going to see him again."

"Except in our nightmares. The dude's like Freddy Krueger. I can't imagine how it must be for Tessa." Robbie pursed his lips then glanced at his watch.

"Bell gonna ring?" Michael asked.

"We still got a couple of minutes. Anyway, who's got Detective Reilly spooked? She's mean as a—"

Michael shot him a warning look.

Robbie gave another sloppy smile. "—really mean person."

Michael crossed his arms. "Don't know." He stood up a little straighter as a cute girl fiddled with her combination two lockers down from his. She caught him staring, smiled and nodded hello, then looked away shyly. He blushed as he faced Robbie and his knowing grin.

"Anyway," he said before Robbie could comment. "We were attacked by someone with a stun gun the last time I went to see Tessa. He wore some cheap plastic Indian mask and was after Sam, I think." He shuddered, remembering the attack with vivid detail. "I think Sam knows more than she's letting on. The cops should be protecting her, not me."

"She'll have plenty of cops with her every day, I'm sure."

Michael ran his fingers through his hair. "I hope so."

The bell for first period rang. Robbie cursed then shrugged. "And so it begins. Well, I guess I'll see you later, Superdude. Come find me at lunch." He entered the stream of zombies shuffling through the corridor on waves of white-noise chatter.

A few feet away, he called back, "And don't forget you promised to help me with math this year!"

But Michael barely heard him, stuck in thoughts of Sam back on the job, wondering what she might be hiding from him. Wondering if she was safe.

I hope so.

CHAPTER 4

Tessa scanned the rec room for an ally. Other than the one they called Dizmo, a thirty-something-year-old with dissociative identity disorder—and only some of his personalities liked Tessa—she didn't really have any allies. Most of the children liked her, and she still visited their play area from time to time. But ever since she turned seventeen and had already proven she was no longer a danger to others, she'd been allowed free range in the hospital's community areas. The adult rec area quickly became her favorite spot, where she could whittle away time by completing a sudoku without getting caught up in a game of tag. She still slept in Ward C, the kids' ward, as the hospital had a policy—or maybe were required by law—to separate those eighteen and older from the rest. Tessa assumed it had something to do with sex. Different wards were probably a smart idea, not that she had any interest in the drippy-drooling men she'd seen there. But as far as she could tell, the adults were just down a different hallway, with no discernable barrier or security between them.

In any event, while the adults were kind to her or else paid her little attention, none were her friends. She'd only really ever had one friend, Michael, but he was on the outside. He could do nothing for her, not even with a cop for a foster mom.

Looking at all her fellow crazies, dressed in all white and gray cotton tees and sweatpants without drawstrings, Tessa felt more like she was part of a cult than a patient in a hospital. *A hospital for loonies*, she qualified, never missing a chance to tear herself down.

She grabbed a crossword puzzle book and a black crayon then took a seat at a plastic table. Opening the book, she stared at a very detailed drawing of a penis. She had to flip through several pages before the notorious penis artist had apparently gotten bored and left her a clean puzzle to work on.

As she considered a seven-letter word for nervousness, the hairs on her neck began to tingle. The room seemed quieter, the only sound Manny's spastic moaning. Raising her gaze without lifting her head, Tessa took a closer look at the morning crowd. In addition to Dizmo and the much older Manny, who only spoke Portuguese when his strange ailment allowed him to speak at all, the usual patients were in their routines—baby boomers Jordan and Harriet were playing chess, chins resting on hands as they focused on their board; Monica was scribbling furiously in her sketch pad, her long bangs always hiding her eyes but exposing a thick scar running along the side of her head; Dirty Terry was reading a sleazy romance novel, his hand rubbing the front of his pants; and the bridge club, all of whom seemed entirely normal, was, of course, playing bridge. Other patients were doing those heartbreaking little things—the rocking, the staring blankly, the muttering to themselves—that helped fill the hours of their days and reminded Tessa of where she spent hers.

But Link's eyes were on Tessa as he leaned against the wall in the corner, presiding over his subjects. She heaved in a sharp breath and averted her gaze from the orderly's, tapping the crayon against the side of her head as if in deep thought.

Actually named Jeb, Link was six feet seven or thereabouts with a skull that seemed too big to be human. That, together with the ridge of bone protruding under his eyebrows, his prominent cheekbones, and his right-angled jawline had earned him the nickname "Missing Link," or "Link" for short. In her peripheral, Tessa saw him watching her with beady eyes set deep in his orbital sockets. Catching her looking back, he smiled as if to say, "Yeah, I see you."

She refocused her attention on the page in front of her, her hand jerking and marking a black line across the clues. Taking a deep breath, she kicked off her slipper then bent over to put it back on. While leaning over, she checked the rec room for other staff but saw none and no one looking her way except... Her breath hitched as her gaze landed on another freakazoid, a fellow patient who the other kids called the Bandage Man. Despite their usually creative imaginations, the psych ward children failed to offer the man anything more than a descriptive nickname. Gauze and medical tape chaotically wrapped most of his head, with tufts of gray hair sticking out at the top and at his chin. His eyes, almost feline in shape and shadowed by eaves from the tape, peered out with seemingly vicious intent. A narrow slit over his mouth allowed him to breathe.

Tessa had heard at least half a dozen reasons for those bandages, most of which entailed fire and severe burns, but the most outlandish of them rumored that he'd carved his own face off. He never spoke and always scowled, but his deep brown eyes revealed a sinister mind at work. A mind that, at that moment, had turned toward her.

"How are you this morning, honey?"

Tessa jolted upright, whacking her head against the table. She rubbed it even though it didn't hurt as she looked up into the watchful eyes of Nurse Francine, which were circled with so much black eyeliner and shadow that she resembled a raccoon.

The nurse grinned. "Were you able to get some sleep after all?"

Tessa hesitated, searching for the right response, then nodded.

"That's good. Good." Francine smiled wider. "If you continue to have trouble sleeping, I can talk to your doctor and see if we can't get you some pills that'll help." She threw a thumb over her shoulder at Link, who was leering at them. "I'm sure good ol' Jeb there would be happy to bring it to you tonight. Would you like that?"

"N-no." Tessa fidgeted with her crayon. "No, thank you. I'm sleeping okay now."

"Good. Good, dear." Francine leaned closer so that her mouth was only inches from Tessa's cheek. Her breath reeked of eggs and her skin smelled of too much lotion or perfume. The overpowering lilac scent reminded Tessa of home, a place she would happily never return to. It smelled like the potpourri Father used to keep in the bathroom and something else, like disinfectant, maybe ammonia.

"I know you were worried about Mitchell last night. Well, I just saw him playing with the other children, looking happy as a clam." The nurse straightened, crossed her arms, and chuckled. "I don't think you'll be hearing him screaming again tonight."

Tessa didn't know how to respond to that, so she kept her mouth shut. A wicked gleam twinkled in the nurse's eyes that made Tessa want to run and hide. She thought she'd been locked away from the horrors of the real world, but she didn't feel safe there anymore. The people coming in from the outside would always be dragging their dirt in with them.

"Well," Francine began with an exaggerated sigh. "I have to get going—you know, places to go and people to see. But remember what I said. If you need anything, Jeb and I are happy to help. We're always around, and we're always happy to lend a hand where needed."

She turned on her heel then sashayed toward the double doors leading into the hall when a redheaded, freckle-faced teen about Tessa's age entered. Francine stopped mid-stride to avoid colliding with him. He smiled and held the door open for her. She nodded curtly, smoothed out her uniform, then walked out without a second glance.

The boy stood just inside the door, sizing up the rec room just as Tessa had. A tingling in her lizard brain told her she should know him, but she didn't. His gaze swept the room, eventually landing on her. Apparently taking her stare as an invitation, he offered her a warm smile before approaching.

Her heart pumping just a little faster, Tessa slid out of her chair as he came within a few feet. The boy slowed his approach, his smile shrinking. He took another step forward, and Tessa stepped back. He stopped and extended his hand. "Hi. I'm Jimmy."

Tessa hugged herself tightly and flinched away from his touch. The boy lowered his hand and frowned.

"Jimmy!" Tessa blurted, her eyes exploding open with sudden realization.

The boy's frown grew with the wrinkles in his forehead. "Your name's Jimmy too?"

She let out her breath then giggled. He must have thought her one of the gibbering crazies. "No-no, I'm Tessa." She smiled and looked away, her cheeks flushing with warmth. "We have a mutual friend. Michael told me all about you. In fact, he says he wants to visit you."

"Really?" Jimmy scratched the back of his head and smiled awkwardly, his dimples childlike and endearing. "Well, I guess it's good someone out there still cares, but he's sorta the reason I'm in this place."

She arched her eyebrows. "Oh."

"Though it beats the hell out of prison, I guess." He tapped his foot and huffed. "Well, then I guess there's no use in pretending I'm not as nuts as everyone else in here." He chuckled, apparently realizing his gaffe, then sighed and studied the floor. "Sorry."

Tessa laughed. "No offense taken." She took her seat, and he flipped another around and straddled it, resting his arms over the back. "Forgive me if I don't shake hands. I... I don't like to be touched."

"No worries." Jimmy's dimples returned. Just looking at them somehow made her feel a little less anxious. But she swallowed hard as she glanced at Link. He glowered at the two of them as if he hated them just for the sake of hating.

"So," Jimmy scratched his head again and blushed. "What exactly has our good friend Mikey told you about me?"

"He told me all about what Glenn Rodrigues did to you both. I was still in school when you shot him, so I already knew about that. Seems to me like he got what he deserved." She rested her fidgeting hands in her lap. "Other than that, not much else, really. Just that you were in here now, too, and he said you might be someone I could turn to if I ever needed a friend."

"Really?" Jimmy sat up straight. "Michael said that?" His body shook as he laughed. "That's really cool of him after all that happened. Did he tell you anything about the Suarez gang or his kidnapping—"

Tessa shot up from her seat. "Michael was kidnapped?"

Jimmy threw his palms out. "Woah! He's fine. Don't worry. He's back, safe at home. For a little while now."

Tessa slowly sat back in her chair, confused why Michael would have kept that from her, why, after all they'd been through together, he would feel the need to keep anything from her. "I guess I haven't talked to him in a while," she said, barely audible. She thought back to the last time she had seen him, when she'd tried to tell him about the screams she heard at night. Jimmy had come up then. "Oh crap."

Jimmy's dimples vanished. "What's wrong?"

"I just remember I told Michael that you didn't want to see him."

Jimmy's entire face seemed to scrunch, freckles closing in on his nose from all directions. "Why would you do that?"

Tessa studied her book, ashamed. "I don't know. I guess I was upset. We don't get to spend a lot of time together, and I was trying to tell him something important, that I was scared. All he wanted to talk about was Jimmy this and Jimmy that, and—no offense—I couldn't have given two shits about you at the time. I wanted him to shut up and listen. Urgh. Michael can be so oblivious sometimes."

She looked up at him, pressing her lips together tightly. "I'm sorry. It was dumb. I'll explain it to him the next time I see him."

"All right." Jimmy frowned, then sighed. "I kinda owe him and would love to see him. He and that detective helped me out a lot, especially since I didn't deserve it. Got me in here when I could have been looking at real time, maybe even tried as an adult. Mikey's a good guy. That detective isn't so bad either."

"Detective Reilly." Tessa snickered. "Yeah, she's all right, I guess." She met his stare for a second then looked away, the conversation falling into awkward silence.

He shrugged. "Well, I'd ask you what you're in for, but somehow that doesn't seem polite. Instead, I'll ask what there is to do for fun around here. The doctors have just declared me fit to join the general population. I'm no longer likely to stab anyone with those dull, curved-ended scissors or snort jelly up my nostrils or whatever else they were afraid I might do in here." He rubbed his hands together. "So, up for a riveting game of Yahtzee? I think I saw Monopoly on the shelf over there too. But if we play that, I get to be the car."

Tessa glanced again at Link, who was still staring their way. She faced forward, closed her eyes, and rubbed her temples. "You might have been better off where you were."

"What do you mean?"

She leaned forward over the table, her face less than two feet from his. "Is it true what Michael said? Can I trust you? Are you a friend in here?"

Jimmy shrugged and showed off his smile. "Look around. I don't see anyone else our age in here. I think that makes us friends by default."

Tessa pouted. "But you don't even know me."

Jimmy's shoulders drooped. "I've done some pretty awful things. Whatever you've done, I'm no one to judge."

"I killed my stepfather."

Jimmy started. "I'm... sorry?"

Tessa smirked. "Don't be. He was a real asshole." Her mirth was fleeting, drying up like a mirage in the desert. "A bully, like Glenn Rodrigues." She tapped her crayon on the crossword puzzle book.

"Anyway, it's not that." She sighed and spent a moment trying to figure out how to say what she wanted to say. "You're not going to believe me. You'll just think I'm crazy."

"Try me." His words said one thing, but his narrowing eyes and pursed lips suggested he had his doubts at the ready.

She picked at her fingernail, wondering how best to start. "Don't look, but do you see the orderly to my right with the giant head?"

"Woah." Jimmy rocked backward. "That *is* a big head."

"I told you not to look."

"Right. Sorry." Jimmy scooted his chair closer. Tessa winced as the back of it *clacked* against the table. He rested his forearms on the table edge. "Anyway, what about him?"

"Is he still staring at us?"

Jimmy started to turn his head.

"Don't look!" she said in a loud whisper.

"Then how am I supposed to know if he's staring at us?"

"Well, look, but, you know... do it discreetly."

Jimmy pretended to stretch his neck, first left then right. "Yep. Staring right at us. You want me to say something—"

"*No.*" Tessa reached across the table, grabbing his fingers before she knew what she was doing. They both stared at her hand around his. Embarrassed, she yanked it back. "Sorry, just... I'll explain. Now, how about the guy to your right, the one with the bandages covering his face. Is he staring too?"

Jimmy stood up, turned to his right, then walked straight up to the Bandage Man. Tessa nearly shrieked, biting on her knuckle to block it. She wanted to scream at Jimmy to stop. Her mind raced as she thought of all the horrors she might have just exposed him to, her wildest imaginations as vivid as if they were reality.

But Jimmy passed the man and headed for a bookshelf, which he pretended to peruse before grabbing a copy of what looked like *Time* or *People*. He headed back to the table with the magazine rolled up in his hand.

Sitting down, he said, "Yep, he's staring too. And he looks mean as hell. Kinda gives me the creeps." He wrapped his knuckles against the table. "Okay. Anyone else in here I should watch out for?"

"Well, those two are the worst, but I don't really trust any of them." Tessa gave him the rundown of all the Ward C regulars, staff and patients alike.

Jimmy listened as she spoke, guffawing a little too loudly when she explained why they called him "Dirty Terry." He folded his fingers in front of him and lowered his voice. "You ready to tell me what this is all about?"

"Are you in Ward C?"

"As of tonight, I am." Grinning, Jimmy almost looked proud. He must've been in Ward D, where they kept the dangerous and often violent patients. Ward C was for the still-crazy-just-not-violently-crazy residents.

"Sometimes at night, I hear screaming. Kids are taken from their rooms, maybe adults from the other hall too. I know because they pass by my room. I don't know where they take them, but sometimes they don't come back."

Jimmy frowned. "We are in a mental hospital. Kids screaming at night has gotta be common."

Tessa felt heat rise up her neck. "Don't you think I know that?" She looked away, hoping she hadn't drawn more eyes upon them.

Jimmy's eyebrows pinched together and a slimy, flat worm of a smirk slithered on his mouth. "What are you thinking? That some mad scientist is performing experiments on people here like they do in the movies?"

"I don't know." Tessa's lips quivered. "I don't know what's happening, but I know I'm scared. Last night, I peeked outside my door as I heard them dragging someone down the hall—a kid I think, one of the younger ones—until his screams were cut off. I didn't see who it was, but Nurse Francine—that's the one you almost bumped into when you came in—spotted me at the door. She was acting really weird and talking funny. Today, too, and she's usually really nice. I mean, she's still being really nice, but it sounds... fake, I guess.

"Anyway, she said it was Mitchell, who's like eight or nine, who was screaming. I'm worried about him, and I'm worried about me. Link and the Bandage Man—that's what the kids call them—haven't taken their eyes off me since I came in here."

Jimmy leaned back, folding his hands behind his head as if he were completely relaxed and totally unimpressed. "Seems easy enough to check. We can just go talk to Mitchell and see if he's all right." He shook his head. "Except I'm not supposed to be talking to those kids, I don't think."

"I can. I've been in with them for a long time, so they all know me. Francine says Mitchell is happy and playing, but I don't know." She pressed her index finger into the table. "You don't think it's weird that people are being taken from their rooms at night? The ones that don't come back—are they being discharged at, like, two in the morning?"

"Okay. I see your point. But if something funny really is going on, I think our best bet might be to stay as far away from it as possible."

Tessa's eyes blurred as she drew a long breath. "That's just it. I think I'm already deep in it. I saw them doing something I wasn't supposed to see, or at least they *think* I saw them. I'm afraid that tonight or some night soon, I'm the one they're gonna drag out of bed, and no one will ever see me again. It's not like anyone would even miss me."

"That's..." Jimmy chuckled and shook his head slowly. He let out a long sigh. "How the heck do I get myself into these messes? I just walked over to say hi to a pretty girl, and—"

Tessa's lip quivered again. "I'm sorry."

"No, I'm sorry. If you're really in trouble, then you can count on me to help. All these people with power over us coming after one girl? That sounds like bullying to me, and as you've already noticed, I really don't like bullies." He leaned across the table, sliding his hand toward her folded arms. She didn't flinch or pull away at his touch.

"So?" He looked her straight in the eye. "What can I do to help?"

Tessa ran her fingers through her hair and averted her gaze. "Where's your room?"

CHAPTER 5

The mention of Carter Wainwright always conjured painful memories. Even Sam's promotion to detective—a day she had thought would be the happiest of her life—had been tainted by her department's Public Enemy No. 1. The killer cult leader had been unstoppable, his undeniable charisma luring lost souls, even at least one within her own department, to his sadistic cause. She wondered if there could be others still looking out for him, keeping hidden in shadow the most despicable and successful murderer her city, and maybe all of the country, had ever seen.

Headlines had compared him to Ted Bundy and the Zodiac Killer, but Wainwright was more like David Koresh or Jim Jones blended with Leatherface from *The Texas Chainsaw Massacre* and topped off with a healthy helping of Jeffrey Dahmer. His face had been everywhere—on television, in newspapers, and in police files in more than a dozen states—yet he'd changed it like a chameleon. He'd popped up here and there to spread terror across North America with alterations to his appearance each time, like lighter skin pigmentation or a smaller nose. Born to a Liberian minister and an Irish missionary, Wainwright had originally looked as though he hailed from one of the Mediterranean countries. Back when Sam had followed his killing spree, he was like a slightly darker version of a young Fred Rogers right down to the cardigan sweater, except nobody wanted to be his neighbor. She'd never actually crossed paths with the monster herself.

A car honked behind her, and she looked up from her dashboard to see the light had turned green. She crawled into the intersection and hit her left turn signal, which prompted another honk and an angry shout from the car squeezing by on her right. As she waited for a break in the oncoming traffic to complete her turn, Sam's eyes blurred. She inhaled through her nostrils, steeling herself against the burgeoning grief as she remembered her mentor and friend.

While Wainwright's killing spree ran rampant through Bristol County, his primary opposition had been two Fall River detectives and partners, Bruce Marklin and Jocelyn Beaudette. Not long after, Special Agent Frank Spinney and the FBI had joined the fray. Wainwright came out way ahead in the war that had ensued, killing two of his adversaries and the career of the third.

Yeah, Wainwright had eventually killed Bruce, but he'd done so spiritually a few years earlier when he'd killed Bruce's partner. Jocelyn's death had meant Sam making detective. She cringed at the bitter irony. Jocelyn had been the one who'd recommended her for promotion.

After all these years, Sam could still see Bruce's face when he'd called her into his office.

"SHUT THE DOOR." DETECTIVE Bruce Marklin didn't look up at Sam as he spoke. His office, and Sam bet his clothes and breath, reeked of alcohol and cigarette smoke. His wrinkled shirt and bent collar were uneven as though he'd missed a button. One sleeve was rolled up to his elbow, and a light-brown stain flaked off the fabric. The sports coat and loafers that completed his typical California-casual look lay in a heap in the corner. His jet-black hair, usually slicked back, looked matted like the fur of a stray dog. The man looked like a bum.

"Take a seat." As he stared at Sam, his eyes flashed with that steel glint that unnerved so many of her fellow officers, a flicker of the intellect that should have made him a neurosurgeon or quantum physicist or even president, anything other than an underpaid cop in a city full of crime and criminals.

But Sam would not be shaken, having stood her ground with many men both on and off the force, figuring what was one more. She kept her gaze even as she sat, crossed her legs, then folded her hands on her lap, as confident in her blues as any officer had a right to be. After a moment, Detective Marklin cleared his throat and flipped through a file on the desk in front of him. In that moment, Sam saw just how broken Jocelyn's death had left him as he shriveled into the old man he'd become.

Her superior officer's gaze diverted, Sam took the opportunity to acquaint herself better with her surroundings. She'd never been in the office before and was surprised to see that, for a man so anal in his police work, his base of operations was as disheveled as he'd become. Files in manila folders and storage boxes filled the corners, papers jutting out of them as if haphazardly thrown together. His Harvard diploma hung crooked on the wall, its glass frame cracked. An unwrapped grinder sat on his desk, though it didn't appear to have been touched, its roast beef shimmering with that on-the-verge-of-rotting rainbow hue.

"I suppose you know why I've called you in here," the detective said, flapping a hand as if her mere presence was an annoyance. He didn't bother to look up from the file.

"I wouldn't make a very good detective if I didn't," Sam answered with a smile, then fearing that came off as glib, added, "sir."

Detective Marklin did look up then, eyebrow raised. He stared at Sam as if he were looking into her, searching for whether she was made of muscle and bone, grit and smarts, or just a whole lot of stuffing with window dressing. He grunted. "Well, I guess we'll see about that soon enough, Reilly. You've had twice as many arrests as the average officer out there, and I have no doubt you've made the masculinity shrivel out of the balls of more than a few of them. But being a detective takes more than nabbing purse-snatchers and breaking up bar fights."

"I play nice with—"

"Save it, Reilly. I'm submitting the paperwork for your promotion. The chief will, of course, have the final say. And lest you think otherwise, I'm not doing because of your record, your gender, or any other reason that might be going through that young, untested brain of yours."

He leaned forward, a vein in his forehead pulsating. A steely gaze had returned to his eyes, this time with a glimmer that almost looked maniacal, and he wasn't backing down. "So, let me make this abundantly clear to you, Reilly... Sam, is it?"

"It's Samanth—"

"It's whatever I deem appropriate to call you, if you want to work homicides." He slammed his palms against the desk. "This is my turf, and we do things my way, which means you do what I say when I tell you to do it." He sat back in his chair, his boil dying down to a simmer. "How's that work for you?"

Sam sat up straight and didn't hesitate. "Works perfectly, sir."

"You've shown great aptitude and probably deserve to make detective, but you weren't my first choice or even my second. Metcalf and Rogers both have seniority. A dozen others understand precinct politics better than you do. But you don't go in for that sort of thing, do you, Reilly?"

"I—"

"It was a rhetorical question." He fixed his terrible glare on her, his mouth set into a scowl. "The truth of the matter is this—*I do not want another partner.*" He tapped his finger against the desk to emphasize each word. "I'm only recommending you for two reasons. One, Jocelyn—" Detective Marklin's voice broke on his former partner's name. He swallowed then cleared his throat. "Detective

Beaudette would have wanted me to. She saw potential in you. Me, though, I think you're an arrogant SOB, kind of like that fucking Fed you've probably seen taking up our precinct space with his holier-than-thou attitude." He muttered something Sam barely caught, "A whole lot of good he's been."

She kept her face expressionless even as she considered how many officers in the precinct thought Detective Marklin was an arrogant SOB. Figuring even a modest defense of her character might come off as too proud and offer affirmation to his opinion, she clamped her mouth shut.

"To boot, you've got a chip on your shoulder as big as the Rock of Gibraltar. Think the whole damn world owes you something. Well, the world doesn't owe you or me or any one of us a damn thing." His eyes glazed over, and he looked past Sam. "Nah. We want something, we've got to do what it takes to get it."

The room fell silent. Sam shifted in her seat, her confidence wavering just a little as she tried to figure out the point of his tirade and how she was meant to respond to it. Deciding no response was probably the best response, she drove the conversation back to its genesis. "And the other thing?"

"Huh?"

"You said you were promoting me for *two* reasons."

Detective Marklin glanced over her shoulder at the door, then leaned over his desk but without any of the hostility he'd shown earlier. "Yes. Yes, I did." He puckered his lips and steepled his fingers like some B-movie criminal mastermind. Apparently catching her eyes on his hands, he cracked his knuckles one at a time before interlocking his fingers.

"We don't," he started, then scratched his chin and stared at the ceiling as if the words he wanted to say might be teleprompted up there. "To hell with it." He sighed. "*I* don't take kindly to cop killers, but especially not to one that murdered the best and brightest of us and kidnapped her little boy."

He squeezed his eyes shut and rubbed his forehead before offering her the most empty, deadpan look she'd ever seen on anyone living. "I have every intention of bringing in her murderer or taking him out by any means at my disposal, legal or otherwise. Any means necessary. Am I clear?"

Sam felt a slight twitch in her cheek and struggled to keep her poker face. Detective Marklin had always been one of the good guys, the by-the-book guys, the guy who officers went to when they wanted to ensure their actions would hold up in court. What he was saying didn't comport with the little she knew of him or the lots she'd heard about him. Her own philosophy had been that procedures were well and fine in a textbook setting but flew in the face of common sense when they blocked an officer from executing justice. Rules weren't only meant to be broken but shitcanned entirely when it meant putting some piece of crap rapist or murderer behind bars where he belonged. She smoothed out her pants, nodded once, then said, "Crystal."

Detective Marklin's gaze narrowed. "Given your arrest record, I trust that won't be a problem?"

Sam did her best not to smile. "No problem at all, sir."

"Good." Detective Marklin stood. "Congratulations on your promotion, detective. You'll be in Major Crimes, but we'll start you on vice, since with that Billings cocaine bust last month, you've already shown a nose for it. No pun intended. Still, I wonder if you have the stomach for it. Prove yourself there, and we'll bump you up to homicide. Any questions?"

"I'm ready to prove my worth, sir, but..." Sam sighed, her body slumping and for the first time truly projecting something other than confidence. She hated herself for it.

Detective Marklin squinted. "What is it?" He glanced at his watch. "Spit it out."

"Won't the men out there see my promotion that way, even if it's not the real reason? That I was promoted to replace a woman because I am one... sir?"

"Do you care?" Before she could answer, the detective rolled his eyes. "Look, do you want the promotion or not?"

"Yes, sir."

"Then screw 'em. You're qualified, have taken all the necessary exams and training, and I can easily justify a bypass. Metcalf and Rogers, some of the others, might give you shit, but they suck, and you can tell them I said so." He sneered. "For some reason, I get the feeling you're no stranger to adversity. Suck it up." He leaned forward onto his palms, instantly looking old and small again as if his body had just lost the fight against gravity. Sam could see he was doing his best to maintain his tough exterior, but its interior supports were crumbling.

Without a lash of anger or any trace of insincerity, he said, "Know this—you have some very big shoes to fill. Detective Beaudette was more than just a good detective. She was everything that was good and right about this department. And, she was my friend, which is why I don't take her recommending you lightly. If she believed in you, then I believe in you."

After a moment of awkward silence, Detective Marklin recovered his composure. He cleared his throat and offered his hand. "Congratulations again, Detective Reilly. Things will get a whole lot hairier for you from here on out."

Sam shook his hand, noticing how bony and frail it looked before feeling the strength in its grip. "Thank you, sir." She couldn't stop herself from grinning anymore.

"Now, get out of my office. You'll be notified and reassigned once everything's official." Detective Marklin returned to pouring over the files on his desk.

SAM HADN'T FAILED ANYONE. Well, no one except Bruce. He'd never let her close to the Wainwright case even as she got closer to him, to the point he'd become like a second father. He always said the Wainwright investigation had gone cold, that all leads had run dry, but Sam suspected he'd just been protecting her or maybe himself, afraid to lose another partner. Had she only been more compassionate back then, less concerned about her ambitions and more about the obvious fractured mind who'd promoted her and taken her under his wing, she might have been able to stop Bruce from going after Wainwright, broken him from his obsession.

"It's not your fault," she whispered as she pulled into the precinct, a tear running down her cheek. The dingy stone-gray building with a pale-green roof stood silent and gloomy. It reminded her of a mausoleum and added to her melancholy. *It's not your fault. Wainwright was his Moby Dick.*

Enough of this. She parked her Toyota in her usual spot and got out. If she wanted to know about Wainwright, there was only one guy to talk to. Lately, he was always babbling about a mysterious killer club somehow connected to the Suarez gang. *Could Wainwright be part of that club or connected to Hector Suarez?* She walked through the front doors and through the precinct, grunting in response to the many greetings and welcome backs that dared disturb her thoughts. *Not really his mo.*

She hurried to her office, a desk sergeant blabbering something into her ear the whole way. *So that's what I'll do. I'll talk to him, get him on the line or go out to the Boston office to see him if I have to. If*

Wainwright is back and someone knows about it, that someone would be—

"Frank?" Sam gaped at the tall, graying federal agent standing in her office, flashing that cocksure smile that, once overconfident, had softened over the years.

"Sam!" Frank's face brightened as he stepped closer, arms out for a hug. He reeled in his enthusiasm quickly, though, one arm falling and the other settling for a shake as the gap between them had nearly disintegrated. "Welcome back."

The spark that had blossomed the last time they'd worked together, that undeniable chemistry, had not petered out. Though nothing had come of it, she could tell that he, too, felt it by the redness in his cheeks. Yet, neither of them had been brave enough to make the first move. She supposed it was the age difference holding him back. She couldn't put a finger on her own reason—

"There's someone from the FBI waiting for you in your office," the desk sergeant blurted.

Sam snapped out of her stupor. "Yes, I can see that. Thank you."

Slowly, the liveliness drained from Frank's expression, leaving his cheeks sallow and mouth drawn. Any romantic inclinations he might have felt had once again been placed in check. "May I have a seat? We need to talk."

CHAPTER 6

Michael scrambled into fourth-period English five minutes before the bell rang, hoping to claim a seat in the back. He'd had to sit in the front row in Algebra II thanks to his morning conversation with Robbie but had managed back row in Spanish and the second to last row in Biology, which had assigned seating.

Score! As he entered the room, he spotted only one other student, a girl with magnifying bifocals sitting in the front row probably because she had to. He smiled politely at her and headed for the desk in the back-left corner. He'd have the best seat in the house so long as the teacher didn't assign them like Mr. Lukens. There, he would be dissecting frogs with a cute but shy girl he hadn't the courage to speak to. At least he'd gotten her name through roll call. *Jasmine, like the... fruit? Flower?* Whatever Jasmine was like, Michael had spent the entire class trying not to look at her.

She probably thinks you're a freak. He sighed and dumped the textbooks from his overloaded backpack alongside his chair, sat down, then checked the underside of the desk for gum, happy to find none. Rumor had it that the janitors scraped it all off with putty knives every year, and at the end of last year, they'd had enough to jam the trash compactor in the garbage truck, but Michael had no idea if that was true. A smiley face had been carved into one corner of the desk, and he smiled back at it before arranging his notebook and pen at his desktop's center.

Looking to his right, he gasped. Someone had materialized in the seat beside him. The boy, who Michael had never seen before, dressed like he was trying to impress his grandmother—wrinkle-free button-down, green sweater vest, dress pants, and suede boat shoes. His hair was light brown, combed to the side and shaved on the other where the part would have been. He looked clean and neat; Sam would have said he belonged in an Old Spice commercial, not at Carnegie High. Too perfect, too preened, a lot like Tessa's stepfather had been. He must have been new to the school and had no idea who Michael was, or he probably would have avoided sitting next to him.

His prettiness made him stand out in a school where everyone expected conformity. Sure, some of the girls might take a liking, but that would only make him more of a target for the boys. Michael instantly took a liking to him for that. The boy was different, like him. *Alone.*

"Sorry, didn't mean to scare you," the boy said, flashing a smile full of metal.

So he isn't perfect after all. Michael laughed. "Not scared, just surprised. Damn, you're quiet."

The boy shrugged. "Sometimes it's nice to go unnoticed, don't you think?"

"Dressed like that?" Michael scoffed. "I think you're going to be noticed."

The boy frowned. "What's wrong with my clothes?"

Michael's cheeks flushed. "I... I didn't mean..."

"Relax!" The boy laughed and slapped Michael on the arm. "Yeah, I know, I'm a bit overdressed. First day, new school—I never know what to wear." He stuck out his hand, which Michael found an oddly fitting greeting from his prim and proper new classmate. "I'm Dylan."

Michael stared at the hand uncertainly, then slowly took it. "Michael. Most of my friends call me Mike." He had, at most, three or four friends he could think of, stretching the definition of the word to its boundaries, and they rarely called him Mike. He wasn't sure why he'd lied. It had just spilled from his lips.

As they shook hands, Michael watched Dylan's gaze lower to his glove briefly before he let go. If he thought anything strange about Michael's fashion accessories, he was kind enough not to say anything.

"So, you're new here?" Michael shook his head. "Stupid question. You just said that. Were you at Durfee before this?"

"What's Durfee?"

"Another Fall River school. I'll take that as a no." Michael clicked his teeth. "Okay, where *did* you come from?"

"A little place called Barranco. It's in Peru. We go where Dad's business takes us, you know?"

"Wow, Peru. Really? I only left the country for the first time—just got back, actually." The classroom filled as they talked, all the seats taken but the one next to the quiet girl with the bifocals.

"My..." Michael tilted his head, wondering how best to describe Sam to a stranger. "My foster mother and I just got back from a cruise to the Caribbean. It was pretty amazing. I've never seen anything like it, except on TV. So when we're all done with this," he said, nodding to the class, "and I start making my millions, I think I want to travel 'just about everywhere.'"

"Well, traveling is fun, but take it from someone who really hasn't had a home—it's nice to have a place where you fit in."

Michael flinched. Being a foster kid, he'd never had a place he fit in. The Plummers had been nice enough, good foster parents, but not *real* parents. Tessa's stepdad had ended all that. Sam tried to make him feel like her apartment was his, but often he felt like he was just a freeloader or in the way. He wasn't so dumb as to not know the apartment had been hers alone before he'd taken over one of the spare rooms. She liked things her way, and he noticed her masked sighs or the twitch of a frown when he left his shoes by the door or carried food into his room. She was kind and patient enough not to say anything, but a thousand words laid in her expressions, and he was beginning to know how to read all of them.

Sam never invited anyone over the whole time he'd lived there, not a friend or boyfriend or girlfriend. He knew she cared for him, but sometimes he felt like he must be the biggest inconvenience in the world.

I mean, what did she have two spare bedrooms for anyway? He stared down at his long black gloves as an awkward silence settled between him and the new kid despite the hum of chatter and laughter of his classmates.

When he looked up, Dylan appeared to be watching him. Michael sighed. "So... aren't you going to ask me about the gloves?"

Dylan snickered, showing off his braces, a flaw Michael thought made him easier to talk to. "That's none of my business. I figured you'd tell me if you wanted to tell me."

Michael soured. He looked down at his hands. "I'm sure you'll find out soon enough." He sighed again, then inhaled, recalling the taunts some of the jocks had made about his gloves before Robbie had put a stop to it. "I-I-I'm not gay if that's what you're thinking." Warmth rose in his cheeks. "I mean, it's cool if you are."

Entirely deadpan, Dylan said, "That's too bad."

They stared at each other for a few seconds as a giant smile slowly crept up Dylan's cheeks.

"You dick!" Michael shouted, and they both busted out in what Michael thought might have been the best laugh he'd had in a long time. Sam was great and all, but humor was not one of her gifts.

They were still laughing as the bell rang, and a surly middle-aged woman wearing ugly beige pantyhose—the kind that Helen Plummer used to wear and came in an egg—entered and closed the door behind her. Her presence was undoubtedly commanding. The entire class quieted, all eyes on their new teacher.

"Hello, all, and welcome to English II. For those of you who didn't have me last year, I'm Ms. Alvarez. I hope you like your seats because you'll be sitting there for the rest of the year unless I have to move you. Believe me when I say that you won't like it if I do." She held up a copy of a paperback book with what looked like an old ship on the cover. "Your first day is going to be easy. You're all going to begin reading Herman Melville's classic, *Moby Dick*."

A few of the kids in the class snickered, and Ms. Alvarez rolled her eyes. "Yes, yes, and I suppose I should tell you now that Moby Dick is a white sperm whale."

A few more kids laughed, and Michael thought he saw the trace of a smile on Ms. Alvarez's lips. "Get it out now because we are going to be saying Moby's name a lot over the next month. Your assignment today is to go pick up a copy from the library. Ms. Armstrong has a stack ready and waiting for all twenty-four of you. Read the first four chapters and be ready to discuss for tomorrow. You may use the rest of the period to begin reading."

When no one moved, the teacher flapped her arms. "Well? What are you waiting for? Get moving."

Dylan stood, rolled his eyes at Michael, then giggled. "Shall we?" he asked with a slight bow and wave.

Michael smirked, finding Dylan's formal mannerisms quirky but in a good way. He rose, grabbed his backpack, then curtsied. "Yes, I do believe we shall."

CHAPTER 7

E*ight years ago.*
Sam chewed on her nail as she answered the call. "Bruce? Where are you?" She lowered the volume on her television, the screen depicting all sorts of carnage in Presidio, a Texas border town whose small population had just taken a serious hit—and that wasn't counting the dozens of federal agents and officers from adjoining communities who'd been killed.

"Bruce!" she yelled again, briefly leaning her elbows on her counter before resuming her steady pacing the length of her kitchen floor. She tucked her hair behind her ears and looked down at her cell phone to check if she still had a connection when a voice came over the line.

"We've found him, Sam!"

She let out a breath, relaxing just a little as she heard her partner's voice, alive, still alive, thank God. "Bruce! Where are you? Tell me, and I'll get on a plane right now." She glanced over at the little boy sitting at her kitchen table, a hand propping up his cheek and pouty lips on his face. Sam had promised to take him to the trampoline park that had just opened for one of their monthly playdates, but as so often happened, work took precedence.

He'll understand when he's older, she told herself, turning away from the boy and wasting no more thoughts on him.

"It's an absolute disaster down here, Sam." Bruce sounded exhausted, his voice lacking the confidence that had made him a terror in the department but also the recent alcoholic slur.

"I know. It's all over the news." Sam gaped at her television screen again. Bodies in uniforms and ATF bulletproof vests, which either hadn't fulfilled their original purpose or hadn't provided enough cover, lay lifeless over dried and cracking earth. Across from them, in the compound's courtyard, zealots in white bathrobes were equally dead beside their assault rifles and IEDs, larger components of their military-grade arsenal strewn about like kids' toys in a sandbox. The scene looked like something out of the war on terror with a touch of Hugh Hefner. A news camera zoomed in on what appeared to be stinger missiles.

"We're in El Paso now," Bruce said.

"We?"

"Frank and I. We saw Wainwright slip out, using his followers as shields. The son of a bitch started a whole new religion down here, and all the crazies that follow him are willing to die for him. We chased him back to his church in El Paso. He's holed up inside. I'm covering the front, and Frank's got the back, but we're going in."

"Bruce, *no*. You can't go in. Wait for backup!"

"Backup? Sam, you've seen the news. There won't be any backup. They're either still in Presidio or dead. And there's no way in hell I'm letting that monster slip away again."

"Just wait!" Sam hadn't realized until then that she was crying. "I can be down there by morning. I'll call in the cavalry. He's too dangerous. Who knows what he has waiting for you inside there?"

"Can't wait, Sam. You know it, I know it, and Frank, God bless him, he knows it. Wainwright will slither away like the snake he is. And there may be innocent people inside. I'm going in. I just wanted you to know in case... in case this doesn't work out so well, and I need you to pick up the trail."

Sam raised her arm, a flash of anger overpowering her so quickly that she nearly smashed her phone against the counter before she could check herself. "Don't be a freakin' idiot. Wait for help. You're too smart not to. Is Frank pushing you into this? That arrogant—"

"Sam."

"I'll kill him myself if—"

"*Sam.*"

Her breaths came hot and fast. His voice, calm and quiet, settled her just as it had all those times when she thought she'd screwed up on the job and let some perp walk. He'd never let her fail, had always reassured her she'd done the right thing when she couldn't be sure of it herself. Even in his worst moments, during his hardest struggles, Bruce had always been there for her. Until that damn Agent Frank Spinney had called with a lead on Wainwright and asked for his help and expertise. He was gone, just like that. Bruce had packed and headed south to settle an old score still ripe as a fresh wound without a second glance at his current partner, the one who was still alive and needed him.

His sigh whistled through the receiver. "Promise me, if this doesn't end now, you'll finish it."

Sam took a deep breath. "Bruce, I'm not—"

"Can you do that for me? This guy needs to pay for what he's done. Promise me you'll take him down if I can't."

"I wish you'd stop talking like—"

"Enough!" he snapped. But when he spoke again, his anger was gone. "Just promise, will you?"

"Yes, all right!" At that moment, Sam hated her partner. He had no right to put that on her. If he and Frank and a whole squadron of feds couldn't take down the bastard, what was she supposed to do in their stead? Still, she muttered, "Yes."

"Thanks, Sam." Bruce sounded resigned, and she wondered if he knew what he was walking into and what he was asking of her.

She sniffled. "Call me as soon as it's done, okay?"

"You got it, partner."

"WHAT ARE YOU THINKING about?"

Frank's voice snapped Sam's mind back to the here and now. Seeing Frank had always made her think of Bruce, but lately, memories of him were playing through her head so frequently she felt as though he might be trying to tell her something from the grave. One man's obsession was another man's game. *Has the winner come back to play a second round?*

Frank seemed to think so. He drove them in his black sedan to Forty-Two Dwyer Street, a condemned lot with the foundation of a run-down tenement house. It was the spot where Hector Suarez of the infamous Suarez gang, largely deceased, had exploded into tiny bits just over a month ago.

Every so often, Sam would catch Frank glancing over at her through the corner of his eye, his lips parting as if he wanted to say something, but his tongue could not form the words. Her view out her window kept her somber. Big houses, once homes for single families during the textile city's heyday, had since been subdivided into smaller and smaller units, bodies crammed into homes like cargo containers packed with refugees. Weedy lawns and broken sidewalks surrounded the tenements, while shady figures lurked in the cracks between buildings.

Sam rested her forehead against the pane and sighed. A bombmaker getting a taste of his own medicine? Even while lamenting the dreary neighborhoods of her city, that thought threatened to put a smile on Sam's face.

"How do you know he didn't die in Texas?" she said absently, thinking aloud.

"Wainwright?" Frank's voice again pulled her out of her reverie. "We never found his body. We saw him go in, but we never saw him inside. The whole thing was a trap. He must have slipped right by us."

She fixed Frank with a pointed stare. *You always said you thought he had help on the inside. But you and Bruce were the only ones there, and Bruce is dead.* The uncharitable thought lingered a little longer than she wished, but she eventually dismissed it. Not Frank. He'd always been one of the good guys. Even back when he was too headstrong and pigheaded, he'd always been exasperatingly fixed on doing things right, more so than she'd ever been.

"That blast and the chemical fire incinerated almost everything. You didn't find much of Bruce either."

Frank's jaw tightened, but he said nothing. Sam looked away, content to ride in silence as heat rose in her cheeks. She knew she'd struck him another blow, a hollowness inside her filling with shame.

A few minutes later, Frank's hand appeared in front of her face, pointing out the window. "We're here."

As they pulled up to the curb, Sam eyeballed the mostly vacant lot. The remnants of a foundation had been covered over with boards. A No Trespassing sign stood in a patch of brown grass. Broken bottles littered the sidewalk. They crunched under Sam's boots as she exited Frank's car.

"So?" Sam smoothed the wrinkles out of her long overcoat. "What is it you wanted to show me?"

Frank walked onto the crabgrass lawn, ushering her to follow. Though all of the large debris had been cleared, shards of charred wood, some no more than toothpicks but others as big as her forearm, speckled the property.

"There's nothing here," Sam said, reluctantly following. "Any evidence of who killed Hector Suarez went up in the explosion."

"True, but coming back to the scene helps me remember the details. The camera watching us... here." Frank pointed at nothing, indicating where it had been. "Tripwires... Suarez tied to a chair and rigged to blow."

"You act as if I don't believe you." Sam's hands dropped to her legs. "Even if I didn't—and I have no idea why you would think I wouldn't—Sergeant Montgomery told the same story."

Frank's eyes lit up. "But that's just it. It's not the first time I told that story. Or at least one pretty damn close to it."

"What?" Sam's nostril's flared as she inhaled. She cringed at its car-exhaust odor. "You mean Wainwright? I thought you said this was connected to that killer club you're always trying to convince everyone exists."

"It's called the Four Pi, and you know that because I've tried to convince you at least half a dozen times as well."

Sam scoffed. "Only every single time I see you, it seems."

Frank crossed his arms. "You said yourself the Suarcz gang must have had someone backing them. I'm telling you, Hector Suarez, Carter Wainwright, the Four Pi—they're all connected."

Sam also crossed her arms but added a sneer. "You know, Frank. I'm going to give it to you straight. Maybe if you spent more time trying to catch one killer instead of all of them at once, your career—and *my partner*—wouldn't have come to such a dead end."

Frank's brow furrowed, and he turned away.

Sam approached. She didn't know why she was being so harsh. All her dreams and thoughts of Wainwright and Bruce's death must have been wearing on her, and her patience was thinning. Frank didn't deserve her hostility—Bruce had known better than to go into that church. He shouldn't have had to die like that. He shouldn't have had to die at all.

Vision blurring, she put a hand on Frank's shoulder. "I'm sorry. That wasn't fair of me. I guess even after all these years, what happened that day still stings. But Bruce knew what he was doing when he followed you to Texas. He made the call to go in that church. It wasn't your fault."

His jaw set, he shot her a reproachful stare. "Look at the facts, Sam. Officer Reynolds was tied to a chair, just like Suarez. He was surrounded by booby traps that, if not for Bruce, I would have set off. When we entered that church, Wainwright had all but vanished into thin air. Reynolds was shot and bleeding out, explosives wrapped around him and wired to blow at the slightest tampering. The comparisons to Suarez are not definitive, but they're certainly striking."

Sam tossed her hair out of her eyes, softening as she considered Wainwright's young victim. "You know, Reynolds works a desk up here now, right? He had nowhere else to go after the El Paso PD laid him off. He got so big after not being able to do anything—after his injuries hindered his ability to sit up straight without pain. The man suffers so much in the line of duty, and El Paso PD drops him like some deformed Spartan baby." Sam shook her head. "Did you know some of the officers call him Porkins, after the fat pilot in *Star Wars*?"

Frank gritted his teeth. "If they understood what that man has been through... I have no doubt Wainwright tortured him psychologically as well as physically before leaving him there as bait. If Bruce hadn't shielded him from the blast—" He cleared his throat, his hands on his hips while his eyes studied empty air. "It was all Reynolds and I could do to get out of there before the whole building collapsed on us."

"Okay," Sam said, feeling the need to be somewhat more agreeable to make up for the unnecessarily mean things she'd said. Though they'd been enemies at the outset all those years ago, she knew Frank and Bruce had grown close in their mutual pursuit of evil. In turn, she'd become close with Frank too. She tucked her hair behind her ears and forced herself to give Frank the deference he deserved. "So maybe what happened here is a bit similar to what happened in El Paso. Assuming I accept that Suarez was one of Wainwright's lackeys—and we both know his terrible skill to cultivate a following—that implicates one man or maybe even one man and his cult.

Are you saying Wainwright is the leader of this Four Pi? What evidence do you have that this group and Wainwright are even connected?"

"I don't know if Wainwright is their leader." Frank sat on the rotting plywood covering the foundation. The cellar wall only stood ten to twelve inches above the ground, so Frank, tall as he was, folded into an M between his legs, his knees bending near his chest. His lips shrank into a pucker as they shifted over toward his cheek. "I don't think he is. Rumors about the Four Pi have existed since well before Wainwright was even born. Manson, Berkowitz, and others are linked to the group. Even Stanley Baker, you know—the guy who ate the heart of one of his victims out in Montana—was said to be Four Pi, and that sounds a lot like Wainwright long before he was even old enough to hold his first knife. Whoever they are, they're well-funded and prefer to keep to the shadows."

"Still sounds like a fairy tale to me. What would be the purpose of such a group? All I can think of is Blofeld stroking a cat as he thinks up elaborate ways to kill 007." She smirked. "Do they want to take over the world?"

"As far as I can tell, chaos for chaos's sake, the total worship of evil."

Sam smiled goofily, then laughed despite her efforts to hold it back. "Oh, come on!" But her smile shrank under the gravity of Frank's stare. "You're serious? Then let me ask you this—if they're so connected and so well hidden, how would you know if they had anything to do with Suarez's death?"

"A signature, among other things. A Greek symbol." Frank pointed to the wooden boards covering the foundation. On it, someone had spray-painted in red something that looked like "Π^1" four times, making a square in one plywood corner.

---

1.   https://en.wikipedia.org/wiki/Pi_(letter)

Sam traced a smiley face carved into the wood beside it. "Cute. Still, how do you know that's not the Roman numeral II or—"

Something fast whistled by Sam's ear as she bent over to take a closer look at the nearest symbol. A golf ball-sized hole appeared in Frank's car window. She hit the dirt, shouting at him to do the same. Fumbling her gun out of her holster, she aimed it in the direction the shot had come from. A plastic cigar store Indian mask stared back at her from behind a parked car nearly forty yards away. Its wearer aimed a silenced pistol at them.

"It's him!" She struck the ground as bullets made divots in the dirt ahead of her. "The one who attacked me."

Frank threw himself over Sam. His chivalry might have been appreciated had she not been readying to fire back. "Get off me!"

"Sorry." He rolled to his left, taking what little cover he could behind the exposed foundation. More bullets whizzed by them. Their attacker was a terrible shot, but he was bound to get lucky sooner or later.

"We need to find better cover," Frank said.

Sam glanced over at him, and he must have realized what she was about to do.

Frank's jaw went slack, and his face turned ashen. "Oh no."

She pushed off the ground and exploded to her feet, then she charged at the shooter. The masked man fired twice more as she closed the distance between them. His gun clicked empty. He dropped it, shuffled on his feet, then took off running.

"Stop!" Sam sprinted after him. "Police!"

The man ignored her and kept running. Sam dispensed with any additional warnings in favor of saving her breath. Her heart pumping fast, her legs pumping faster, she reveled in the fact that she was gaining on the man, wondering if this could be it—her chance to lay her hands on the man who'd killed her partner too many years ago and so many miles away.

The shooter hopped a fence into someone's backyard. Sam was on his heels. On the other side, some kind of terrier had latched on to his sweatpants and wouldn't let go. She reached out to grab him when her sole slipped on what she immediately knew to be dog crap, its freshly broken open aroma accosting her senses. Her leg lunged forward, and though the muscle in her thighs stretched farther than comfortable, she managed to keep her footing. The man, however, had kicked the dog free and was already climbing the opposite fence. Whimpering, the dog paid her little attention as she renewed her pursuit.

The masked had man turned a corner around a tenement up ahead. Sam heard a car honk and hurried after him. She spotted a car idling in the middle of the road as she rounded the house. Across the street, the man was bent over, fingers clutching under his ribs as he caught his breath. His chest heaved as he stared at her through his plastic mask. She darted toward him. Once again, he darted away.

He only made it another block before Sam tackled him into a re-cycling bin. As she pinned his hand behind his back and cuffed it, the man giggled. Sam furrowed her eyebrows.

He began to sing. "Ten little Indians standing in a line. One toddled home, and then there were nine."

Like a broken record, he sang only those two lines, repeating them over and over again. It sounded to Sam like it might be a nursery rhyme, but not one she'd ever heard before. As she yanked his other hand back to cuff it, the man's voice grew louder as he sang.

"Shut. The fuck. Up." Thoughts of her late partner had already soured her mood far worse than even being shot at could have. When he wouldn't stop, she elbowed him in the back of the head a little harder than intended. His face bounced against the pavement, and he went quiet.

Frank pulled up in his sedan beside her, his window rolled down. If he'd seen what she'd done, he didn't say anything. Leaving his car idling, he got out and casually strolled over.

"Nice of you to join us," Sam said, smirking.

"Looks like you have everything under control." He crouched. The smile vanished from his face. He placed a hand on her shoulder. "Are you okay? Are you hurt?"

"I'm fine, I'm fine." She waved him off.

"Well, let's turn him over and see who we've got."

Sam's stomach tingled. The man seemed a little too short and round to be Bruce's killer, but Wainwright could look vastly different after eight years without a confirmed photo. Together, they rolled the shooter onto his back.

"Shall I do the honors?" Frank pointed at the cracked mask.

"Be my guest."

Frank tore off the man's mask and laid it on the ground beside him.

Sam studied their suspect's face—Caucasian, squat nose, and ruddy cheeks. A big round babyface, the youthfulness of which was amplified by the fact that he was peacefully out cold. "Well?"

Frank frowned. "I've never seen this man before in my life."

CHAPTER 8

As the final bell rang, Michael sighed. *One day down. A hundred eighty-four more to go.*

He plodded to his locker through a murmuring crowd, the hum like a shallow wave endlessly rolling to shore. Most around him likely felt the same way he did, awkward in their own skins after another day of trying to fit in and of exhaustively being conscious of what others were saying or thinking about them. Everyone could relax just a little with the day finally over, shuffling to the locker rooms, the bus stop, or the parking lot, wanting to forget school but taking with them homework that would not let them.

At his locker, Michael unloaded his backpack, only to stuff it again with all the books he would need to take with him. The last to go into his heavying burden was his worn copy of *Moby Dick*. He ran his thumb over a plastic sleeve that protected what little remained of its cover. *Who names their son Ishmael?* He'd gotten as far as that line before goofing off with the new kid. With another sigh, he dropped the book into his pack, zipped it up, then grunted as he threw it over his shoulder.

He closed his locker and turned just in time to see Robbie run by, heading for the locker room.

"See you tomorrow!" Michael shouted, feeling invisible as his friend kept on running. Invisible was good, much better than being the subject of gossip. The day had gone by quietly, with Michael not noticing a single person whispering to another while looking or pointing in his direction. He wondered if he'd already become old news and was back to being inconsequential. Yeah, invisible was good, but sometimes it was lonely.

I'm still not doing cross-country, he thought, silencing Sam's voice as it chimed up in his head. With another heavy sigh, he hunched under the weight of his pack and headed for the exit.

Outside, his detail waited. He waved, thinking he saw Officer Tagliamonte in the passenger seat. He considered asking him for a ride home, but in spite of his load, he opted to hoof it over taking the bus or a personal escort. He'd walked to school his freshman year and had always enjoyed the time to let his mind go blank. Sam's apartment was farther than his last foster home had been, a good three miles away even if he cut through a couple of yards between parallel streets. His entourage might have a problem with his route if not because trespassing was illegal then because they couldn't follow him. Turning to leave, he wondered if the cops would trail behind him the whole way. And as he began to walk, they began to roll.

Still, Michael didn't want to go home and sit in an empty apartment, waiting for Sam to return with some greasy fast food or pizza. He certainly didn't want to start his homework or read a book about whaling. He didn't have to be a psychic to know he'd be Googling the plot of *Moby Dick* in his near future. The walk was a dramaless way of killing time, and he had time to kill.

Before he'd reached the bottom of the bus lane, someone called out to him. He turned back to see Dylan hustling down the hill toward him. Despite it being a rather warm September day, the new kid wore a navy blue North Face jacket that looked brand new. An EMS backpack, looking conspicuously lighter than Michael's, was slung over one shoulder.

"Where are you heading?" he asked, showing off his metal mouth.

Michael shrugged. "Home, I guess. You?"

"Work. Mind if I walk with you?"

"Cool by me," Michael said, sounding more eager than he would've guessed he felt. He pointed to his left. "I'm headed that way. What about you? Where's work?"

"Brentworth Hospital. My dad works there too. He got me a job in the daycare center. Basically, I play hide-and-seek with four-year-olds while their parents get colonoscopies or radiation or whatever treatment their wrinkled old sick bodies require."

"That sounds... fun?" Michael laughed awkwardly, then kicked a pebble along the sidewalk. He thought about mentioning that he knew a couple of patients there, then thought better of it. He shrugged, shifting the weight on his back to a more comfortable position. "Well, at least you've got some money to spend."

"Oh, my dad gives me plenty of money." Dylan shook his head, likely attuned to Michael's sudden rise of anti-snobbery feelings. "That sounded wrong. Sorry. What I mean is, my dad doesn't have me do it for the money. He says it builds character or some crap like that. I think he just likes having me around."

Michael studied the sidewalk, looking for another rock to kick. Having a father who wanted him around was not a problem Michael could relate to. He chewed on his cheek, countering the burgeoning self-pity with the knowledge that sometimes having a father was even worse than having no father at all, like in Tessa's case.

Tessa. "I've got a friend at that hospital," he said quickly, anxious to fill the silence that had formed between them and landing on the one topic he'd already vetoed.

"Oh, yeah? Is he sick or something?"

"She... well, there's a *he* too. And yeah, they're sick. Sorta." He looked up at this stranger who'd become his friend in less than a day—*that's what we're becoming, isn't it? Friends?* Michael didn't know. He didn't know how to make friends, at least not with anyone normal. He pushed away the thought. "Maybe you know them. Tessa Masterson? Jimmy Rafferty?"

"No, sorry." Dylan adjusted the strap over his shoulder. "I don't really interact with any of the patients." He flapped his arms. "I mean, I may recognize a few faces, but I don't really know anyone staying there... or in this city, except maybe you now."

"Believe me, if you knew anything about me, you'd be walking in the opposite direction."

"I don't know." Dylan smiled warmly. "You seem all right to me. I'm guessing maybe a little hard on yourself sometimes, but otherwise, you know, normal."

Michael guffawed. "Normal? Me?" He shook his head. "I'm anything but normal."

They fell into a silence. After crossing a main road, they took a left at the bottom of the hill into suburbia. A lawnmower roared, out of sight behind one of the mismatched houses—a cape here, a Victorian and a raised ranch over there. The scent of freshly cut grass tickled Michael's nose and made his eyes water. On the other side of the street, a pit bull barked as it followed them along a chain-link fence, its nub of a tail wagging. As the sounds of both dog and mower faded, the soft rumble of an engine reminded Michael of his escorts, having previously tuned out the sound before it had been drowned out by the others.

Dylan threw a thumb over his shoulder. "Does what you mean about being normal have anything to do with the police car that's been following us since we left the high school?"

"So you noticed them, huh?" Michael asked in a hushed voice. He chuckled. "They're my bodyguards." He blew on his fingernails, then mocked tossing his hair back. "They keep all the ladies from swarming me. Maybe you haven't heard yet, but I'm kind of a big deal at Carnegie High."

Dylan smiled, his braces glinting in the late afternoon sun. "Big enough to get a police bodyguard? You sure you're not some serial killer they just don't have enough evidence yet to put away? Maybe after you kill me and toss my body in a river, they'll have enough to hang you."

"Nah-ah. There's no death penalty in Massachusetts. You'll have to get yourself murdered by some other badass back in South America if you want that to happen, assuming they've got that there." Michael frowned and continued his search for rocks to kick. "That's me—regular badass. The only kid in the high school to have almost drowned in a toilet."

Dylan stopped and fixed Michael with a grave look. "So what's the deal, really? Are they harassing you? If you want, I think I know a way we can ditch them."

"No, no, nothing like that." Michael searched for the words to explain. Just talking with Dylan, someone his own age who wasn't locked up or—and he knew the thought was unfair as soon as it occurred to him—*Robbie*, was something he thought he could get used to. Talking like a kid with a kid—even though Dylan didn't talk too much like a kid—just *being* a kid was something he hadn't had a lot of time for before.

"They really are"—Michael blushed and looked away—"like bodyguards. My foster mom is a detective. About a month ago, someone attacked us. Attacked her, really. But now she's all paranoid and thinking I need a babysitter twenty-four seven."

"Wow!" Dylan's eyes widened, and he poked Michael's arm. "That *is* serious. They didn't catch the guy? Do they know who he is?"

"No idea." Michael tugged on his lip. "I think Sam—that's my foster mother—has some idea who it might be, but she isn't telling me anything. So yeah, I can't go anywhere without the boys in blue. Except—" Michael sprinted across the next property at the curve in the street, slowing only to climb the stone wall in the back. When he saw Dylan keeping up, giggling, Michael said, "Let's see them follow me this way."

The boys laughed as they ran through another yard, this one with a swing set in the back. They listened to the police car's engine rev then speed away, Michael knowing it would be back in less than a minute.

"Well," Dylan said, backing away in the opposite direction Michael needed to go. "The hospital's this way. I'll catch you later."

"I'll probably be heading there on Saturday. Maybe I'll see you if you're working."

"Seriously?" Dylan raised his arms out to his sides. "Won't I see you tomorrow in class? How else am I going to know what happens in the first four chapters of *Moby Dick*?"

Michael smiled. "You could try reading it."

"You first, Badass." Dylan pointed at him. "You first." He waved. "See you tomorrow."

"Later." Michael watched him go for a moment, still smiling, then turned as he spotted the police car heading up the road toward him. Finishing his walk home, he thought about how much better his first day as a sophomore had been than as a freshman.

CHAPTER 9

Wearing only light-blue pajamas with yellow rubber duckies all over, compliments of some generous do-gooder who'd donated them, Tessa tiptoed to her bedroom door. In Ward C, essentially a prerelease ward, security was minimal. If there were any hard and fast security measures to keep the younger and older sort-of-sanes separated from the children beyond a bend in the hallway, Tessa couldn't see them.

Nevertheless, she had her own room, cubbyhole that it was, and could do pretty much whatever she wanted within the confines of Ward C—which equated mostly to zoning out in front of the television in the rec room—so long as she took her meds, attended group sessions and all roll calls, and met individually with a doctor every other day. She was not a danger to society, maybe not a danger to herself, but she wasn't healed, whatever that meant, and doubted she ever would be. No one ever said anything about the hospital being a danger to her.

Maybe I am crazy. Maybe it's all in my head. She recalled Jimmy's furrowed brow and squinty eyes when she'd told him her suspicions. She shook her head. *It doesn't matter if he believes me. He promised to help me anyway.*

She creaked open the door and peeked out. All clear. The dimly lit hall shrouded many of the stains on the worn, lime-green carpet. She swung the door open and slipped into the corridor, closing the door quietly behind her.

Jimmy's room was a left down the hall, first right, five doors down. Tessa repeated the directions over and over again in her head, a mantra to keep her moving as her heart fluttered against her ribcage. On bare feet, she stepped lightly, her fingertips sliding along the wall, ears attuned to every creak in the floorboards.

Thud, thud, thud, thud.

Tessa froze. The noise grew louder, footsteps coming her way from around the next corner, heavy and plodding like Link's. Hands trembling, she looked around for a place to hide, the hallway empty except for doors. *Think!* She turned around, sprinted for her door, and turned the knob. Locked.

Her breathing quickened, coming in short gasps. She didn't remember locking the door before she'd left. *Doesn't matter! Hide, you idiot!*

Voices carried ahead of the approaching steps. "The doctor gets who she wants when she wants them," a woman said.

Tessa sprinted past her room to a small alcove on the left where a laundry chute was built into the wall. There, she crouched and placed a hand over her mouth. She had to get her breathing under control, her panting as loud as a dehydrated dog's.

Another voice, this time male and much louder, echoed down the hall. "She's just a skinny girl. What good would she be for anything?"

"Shhh! Keep your voice down," Francine scolded, her tinny voice unmistakable even without the sickening syrupy sweetness to which Tessa was accustomed. "Do you want to wake up the kids?"

The sound of footsteps died. They'd stopped somewhere in the hall, but Tessa didn't dare peek around the corner to look.

"Besides, it's not our place to question the doctor." Francine's voice was clear, close. They were outside Tessa's room. She'd been right. They had come for her.

Francine knocked. "Tessa, dear. It's Nurse Francine. I'm coming in to check on you."

Tessa heard the rattle of a doorknob. "Shit!"

"What is it?" The male voice asked. Tessa was sure it was Link.

"It's locked, you moron. Give me your keys."

"Use your own keys."

"I don't have my—" Francine groaned. "Just give me your damn keys!"

Tessa heard a jingling, then Francine said, "Tessa, honey, I'm coming in now." The door squealed as it swung open. Link's heavy feet thudded on the hardwood floor inside her room.

"Well?" Francine asked. "Where is she?"

"She's not in her bed?"

"Do *you* see her in her bed?"

"Maybe she's underneath it. Or maybe she had to go to the bathroom?"

"Well?"

"Well what?"

"Check, you freakin'..." Francine grunted in frustration.

I need to move. They'll be looking for me now. Tessa chanced a quick look around the corner. Link's back filled the doorway as he stood just past the threshold of her room. He disappeared farther inside.

Hand against the wall, Tessa rounded the corner and crept closer to her room. She paused and leaned forward to look in, her eyes exploding open and mouth clamping shut when Nurse Francine's back appeared no more than a couple of feet away from her. Link was farther into the room, on hands and knees and peering under the bed.

"Find her!" Francine ordered, her shrill command stopping Tessa in her tracks but jumpstarting her heart. "The doctor does not like to be kept waiting."

Tessa moved painstakingly slowly, one step at a time, until she thought she'd made it far enough past her room to sacrifice complete silence for haste. She hustled to the intersection ahead, turned right, and sprinted to Jimmy's room. As she raised her hand to knock, she heard Francine's voice again. "Check the halls. She's gotta be around here somewhere. You go that way. I'll check this way."

Tessa *rat-tat-tatted* Jimmy's door, a series of short, rapid, quiet knocks she hoped he could hear. She could feel sweat pooling at her hairline as she bounced on her feet. Again, she knocked, this time just a little louder. *Please, Jimmy! Come on!*

The door swung open and she flung herself through it, pressing herself into Jimmy and her finger over his lips. The door closed on its own behind them.

Thud, thud, thud, thud. Link's heavy footsteps plodded by as Jimmy and Tessa stood still as statues.

Jimmy's eyebrows were raised and his mouth hung open, but he blessedly waited for her to say something before he so much as twitched a finger. The rise and fall of his chest against hers was strangely comforting, an ally close to her when she desperately needed one. As the hallway quieted, her heartbeat began to slow.

When her panic had mostly subsided, her face flushed with warmth. She stepped back and swayed. "Thanks." Her hands behind her back, she nodded and gazed at his knees.

Jimmy crouched to meet her eyes, his own containing a playful sheen as if he didn't quite grasp the severity of her situation. "Who was it?"

Tessa nibbled on her lip. "That was Link. He's looking for me. Francine is too."

"So... the guy with the huge melon head and the nurse I almost bumped into today?"

Tessa nodded.

"Do you know what they want?"

"I ran before they could see me." She rocked on her feet. "But I heard them talking. They said some doctor wanted to see me and that she won't be happy if she doesn't get to tonight."

Jimmy huffed. "What doctor? We all see plenty of doctors."

"I don't know, but I have a feeling I don't want to find out." She looked over his room, which was a small cubbyhole just like hers. "They're looking for me. They'll be checking all the rooms soon. I'm not safe here."

Jimmy's boyish face lacked fear or perhaps the intelligence to know when to be afraid, the glint in his eyes remained hardened and indifferent.

"And now you're not either. I'm sorry." Chin against her chest, she turned and headed for the door. "I'll just—"

Jimmy grabbed her arm and spun her around. "I promised you I'd keep you safe. If they'll be coming here for you, the way I see it, we have two options—run or hide."

"We can't get out of Ward C. Those doors are locked at night."

"A window maybe?"

Tessa shook her head. "You seen any without bars over them? We may not be in chains, but this is still a prison."

"Then we hide you." He darted about his room, tossing around his clothes and examining his belongings, quickly ruling out options, a sort of battle between hopefulness and defeat playing out on his face. Like hers, his room was empty except for his bed, a small dresser, and some books. There was no place to hide. It had been a mistake to go there.

He raised a finger, then pointed at his bed. "What about between the mattress and box springs." He jammed his fingers under his mattress and lifted it. "You're thin enough that you just might be able to squeeze... huh."

"What?"

"No box springs."

A knock came at the door.

"Oh, God." Tessa chewed her thumbnail. "We're too late. I'm sorry, Jimmy."

He grabbed her by the elbow and put his finger over her mouth just as she had, then led her to the door. *He's handing me to them?*

Too stunned by the betrayal to react, she allowed him to guide her to the door, then alongside it, where he pressed her shoulders gently against the wall. He mouthed the words, *Don't move.*

Swinging the door wide open, he startled Tessa, who barely resisted the urge to throw up her hands to block it. She winced as the uneven wood at its bottom scraped over her big toe, turning her head sideways and biting on her knuckle to hold back even the slightest utterance.

"Hello?" she heard Jimmy say, the sound of his voice dulled by the solid mass between them.

"Uh, hi," Link said. "Random inspection. Please step aside."

"Oooo... kay?" Jimmy's left side came into view. He was standing in front of the door, shielding her. "Um, isn't that something the guard usually does?"

"Yeah, well, I'm helping out." Link's voice oozed sarcasm. He grunted. "Doctor's orders."

"What are you looking for? And why would it be under my bed?"

"Look, kid," Link said, the floorboards groaning and his voice straining as he picked himself off the floor. "You want to shut up? I'm just trying to do my job here, all right?"

Tessa squeezed her fingernails into her palms. *What are you doing? Stop provoking him.*

Jimmy sneered. "Well, I don't know what you're looking for, but it ain't here."

Link snorted and plodded closer. His breath, warm and stale, seemed to permeate through the door. "You know, you may be here a while, so you might want to learn how to watch that mouth of yours."

"It's attached to my face, so pretty hard to see without—"

Tessa registered the groan a split second before the door hit her in the head. She yelped, her eyes exploding open with panic when she realized what she'd done.

"What was that?" Link asked.

"I didn't say anything," Jimmy answered, his words hissing through clenched teeth.

"Yeah? That's what I thought." Link's plodding footsteps headed out into the hall where they paused. "You squeal like a bitch. Lights out, asshole."

Jimmy slammed the door. His face was redder than his hair as he paced, arms swinging. "That guy—"

"Might hear you," Tessa whispered more forcefully than she might have liked.

"I'm..." He ran his hand through his hair, then pressed two fingers into each temple, making small circles. "I'm sorry. I just have this strong hatred—"

"Strong hatred for bullies. I know. You mentioned that." She put a hand on his forearm. "But you have to keep your cool. We don't know what we're dealing with here. Antagonizing Link like that makes me... well, it makes me afraid they might come for you next."

Jimmy smirked. "I can take care of myself."

"You promised to take care of me, too, remember?" Tessa sighed then smiled. She liked his temper—so much raw passion, so much fight. Michael never had a harsh word, never raised a fist to defend her. He was always treating her like she was delicate, a flower that would die without just the right amount of sunlight, water, nurturing, and love. She'd killed a man, stabbed him more than a dozen times. She wouldn't be abused again. She would not be a victim. And she wouldn't be treated as if she were one either. Because she knew if she were pushed far enough, she'd push back fast and hard.

She didn't need Jimmy's protection. She needed a friend, but if he wanted to play at white knight, well, that was sort of nice too. "Thanks." She smiled then blew a strand of hair out of her face.

"For what?" Jimmy frowned, perhaps thinking her insincere.

"For letting me in here. For hiding me from Link. For keeping your promise." She crossed her arms. "I don't know." She bumped him with her shoulder. "For being the only friend I've got in here."

Jimmy smiled back. He shrugged. "Never had a girl back to my room before."

"You jerk!" They both giggled, covering their mouths to keep their laughter quiet.

Then, they waited.

They turned off the light and sat side by side on the floor, backs leaning against his bed, listening as the hall traffic died down, then sitting in silence long after. At some point, Jimmy fell asleep beside her, his head lolling back and his mouth hanging open, wind whistling through his nostrils each time he blew out air.

She had no idea what time it was but figured the hospital would be waking soon. The daytime staff would be arriving. She could rest around her medication and treatment schedules, so sleep wouldn't be an issue, but she had no idea how she could keep dodging the people snatchers who came at night. They would be on to her, and Tessa had gotten lucky with that door trick Jimmy pulled. She doubted she would be so lucky again.

She needed a more permanent solution. She needed to escape.

And what about Jimmy? He didn't stir as she kissed his cheek and rose to leave. She would have to be back in her room before the day staff found her and pray that Francine, Link, and this doctor they'd referred to were all she had to avoid. If they were up to something shady, and she was convinced they were, maybe they couldn't be up to it when the rest of the staff was around.

Maybe she could tell the daytime staff. Her eyes watered. *Yeah, and who will they believe? Three of their coworkers or the teenage girl sent to the loony bin for killing her stepfather?*

She was on her own. Looking at Jimmy, Mr. Hot Temper, Mr. Gonna-Get-Himself-Killed, she needed to remember that. She slipped out of his room without saying goodbye.

As she took the left into her hallway, a hand closed over her face, blocking her airways. Its owner spun around her as lithe as a dancer, keeping his calloused hand in place while the other secured her around her shoulders. But she'd gotten a good look at her attacker before he could get behind her, before the purple spots formed in front of her eyes—the Bandage Man, glowering at her through his mask of gauze, perpetual cruel scowl on his lips.

Darkness took her as she gasped for air. *So much for boys and their promises. So much for their lies.*

CHAPTER 10

Sam had dropped her collar in a holding cell and had him booked for attempted murder. The whole time he'd raved and cried and professed his innocence, even to her and Frank, as if they hadn't been there when he'd pointed a gun at them and fired. Either she'd knocked the man into a state of amnesia, or her assailant was stuck in one of the strongest cases of denial she'd ever seen. *Or he acts better than Meryl Streep.* He didn't seem to know where he'd been, not just earlier that day, but for the last several months. Disorientation manifested in his darting eyes, overactive sweat glands, and frantic thrashing, all of which made it easy for her to order a tox screen. None of it, however, made him ripe for questioning.

At least the man had a name, or one he'd given them anyway—Harlan Bowes. With no identification on him and no fingerprints in the system, Sam had only his word to go on. So she let him spend the night in a holding cell, assigning Officers Pettigrew and Mollicone to background checking, figuring her perp would still be there in the morning.

She needed a chance to sleep on the man's apparent madness. Everyone feigned innocence in the face of charges. Harlan Bowes just did it so well that he shook the sanity of one who had him dead to rights. *Perhaps a psych assessment is in order.*

She chuckled as she left the precinct for the night, figuring her thought could have applied to Bowes or herself. After picking up a pizza for her and Michael to split, she ate dinner with him mostly in silence. Asking Michael about his day had resulted in a non-committal grunt—maybe something about Herman Melville—in return.

And when he disappeared into his room after, it was fine by her. She was struggling for the words to tell him she'd been attacked again, not wanting to worry him. After all, they had caught the mask-wearing turd, hopefully bringing an end to their constant looking over their shoulders. She would know more in the morning and could fill Michael in then.

She kicked back on her sofa with a cold beer and her feet up on the coffee table to watch a few cooking shows. She liked them despite never cooking. At one moment, it occurred to her that she'd been shot at that day. She shrugged, finished her beer, and went to bed.

Sleep came easy, but it didn't keep. Her dreams played out scenarios around Harlan Bowes that her mind had been too tired to consider in her waking hours. He hadn't been one of her past collars, had never even been arrested as far as she could tell. Maybe he had something to do with one of Frank's cases. That familiar mask he'd been wearing suggested otherwise.

Who are you, Harlan Bowes? Sam twisted herself up in her sheets. She envisioned herself dolled up like General Custer, mustache and all, as a Lakota, Cheyenne, and Arapaho army swarmed around her, and she recalled Bowes's words. *Ten little Indians standing in a line. One toddled home and then there were nine.* The tribesmen circled her on their horses, drawing closer and kicking up dust until all she could see were dark shadows in a suffocating cloud.

She awoke with a start, her alarm blaring on her nightstand. Bowes's chant was probably just the ravings of a mad man. She rolled to the right and swatted the alarm off, then propped herself up on her elbows. *Or maybe he just really likes Agatha Christie.*

Her bed head flopped over her face, a matt of frizzy brown kinks. Her lips cracked as she yawned, and she picked white crud from their corners as she scanned her nightstand for a water bottle. Not finding one, she threw her legs out of bed, stood, then grabbed a pair of jeans she'd left on the floor for... *three? No, four days?* Sniffing them, she concluded they passed inspection. She stepped into each leg and hopped to tug them over her hips.

An old scar on her belly itched as if it were still healing, and she ran a finger over it. The narrow line of raised and rugged flesh from a slash to her bicep, compliments of Tessa's stepfather, still tingled when she thought about it. The bruising to her head from her fight with Rex Billings, a violent drug lord with a heavyweight boxer's build, had vanished, but her jaw and forehead still throbbed and cracked with the freshness of waking up. She'd been shot only a fraction of the time she'd been shot *at*, which was becoming far too many. It had been a crazy last two years.

After throwing on a T-shirt from the pile on the floor, she opened her door and stumbled out of her room. Michael sidestepped her with a muffled grunt, toothbrush jutting from his mouth, hair wet and wearing nothing but the towel around his waist.

"Good to see you up already." Her voice croaked as she shuffled along the wall, still not fully awake. She squinted and threw a hand up to block the sun pouring in through the blinds.

Michael grunted again and disappeared into his room. *Anxious to go to school?* Her eyes opened a little wider. *Maybe it's a girl?* A twinge of guilt hit her in the gut as she thought of Tessa. Sam liked the girl just fine—well, maybe not just fine—but thought that, given her history, maybe Michael would be better off staying away from her. The verdict was still out on how messed up she might be. The twinge grew into a pang when she reminded herself that Tessa had been a *victim* of her stepfather, someone for whom she should sympathize, not distrust.

She was acting like a mother. It was her job to look out for Michael. As she listened to him slamming shut dresser drawers and closet doors, hastily getting ready for school, she laughed. *I only want what's best for my boy.* She nodded. That much was true.

After a cup of coffee, she headed for the bathroom, the ache in her joints fading with each step. A nice hot shower cleared her head and got her moving, though she stayed in too long again to let the water pressure massage her muscles. By the time she got dressed, Michael was gone. She looked at the clock and figured she'd better get a move on too. Finally feeling like a whole person, she locked up and headed out.

FRANK WAS WAITING FOR her outside of the precinct. "Are you going to question him now?" he asked, dispensing with all the usual pleasantries and idle chitchat, which Sam appreciated.

"Yeah." She put her hands on her hips, her long gray coat billowing in the wind. "You want to sit in?"

Frank nodded. Clean-shaven and wearing a dark suit, he reeked of bitter coffee and cheap aftershave. His prominent chin with its small divot was a focal point to his face. That and his height made him hard to look in the eye without refocusing. "He wasn't just shooting at you, you know."

"What's your take on this guy?"

"I don't have one. He's... not what I was expecting."

"What were you expecting?"

"I'm not sure." He stroked his chin. "Maybe someone more menacing or more—"

"Cult-oriented?" Sam fixed him with a cold stare. "Maybe it's time you told me everything, huh? This is twice now that someone—hopefully the *same* someone—wearing some kind of hokey Native American stereotype mask has attacked me. And it all started right after we took down the Suarez gang."

Frank grunted. Under his breath, he muttered, "Hector Suarez certainly seemed their type."

"See? That's what I'm talking about. You came down for more than just the Suarez gang. And I hear you when you say you think Hector Suarez was part of some dark criminal enterprise. Fine, and maybe so, but what links him to the guy in the mask, and more importantly, what links all of them to Carter Wainwright?"

Frank set his jaw but could no longer meet her gaze. "Sam, I wish I could tell you more. Suffice to say, I have strong intel that suggests Carter Wainwright is operating out of this—"

"What intel?" Sam huffed. "Who's your source?"

"You know I can't reveal the name of my CI. Please don't ask me to. I wouldn't ask it of you."

Sam studied his face. He looked pained, his eyebrows crinkling up his forehead, wrinkles showing their dialogue running through his mind. There was so much he wasn't telling her, so much he wanted to but couldn't. "Frank, you and I have been through a lot together. Sure we had a shaky start when you first showed up, but I thought we'd come a long way since then. Now you're here, and it's like we're right back where we started—me giving you full access while you keep your dirty little secrets."

"It's not like that. It's just—"

"I'm on your side. You know that, right?"

He nodded but still couldn't look her in the eye. "I know."

Annoyed, Sam concluded she would have to seek her answers elsewhere, starting with the mysterious shooter, Harlan Bowes. Sam extended her arm toward the entrance. "Shall we?"

Frank nodded.

"I hope you take my willingness to cooperate as a sign that maybe you should do the same."

He didn't reply, just opened the precinct door for her, and Sam walked in without a thank you.

Officer Peyton Reynolds sat at his usual desk outside the holding cells. The officer appeared to have lost a few pounds over the summer in an apparent effort to shed the merciless office nickname. His hair neatly combed and beard trimmed, he looked a positive contrast to his usual disheveled, droopy-eyed, and sullen self. Still, he was quite heavy, his belly resting atop his desktop as he perused a magazine propped up by his stomach.

Sam could only imagine what the man had been through in Texas. She'd tried to learn about his traumatic ordeal to find out more about how Bruce had died, which had led to her helping him land a job at the precinct. Sam didn't want to think about telling him what Frank believed—that Wainwright might be in their backyard—and what that might do to him and the progress he seemed to be making, his slow climb back from hell.

"Hi, Officer Reynolds," Sam greeted, slowing her pace and taking the time to smile genuinely. "How's everything?"

"You know, started a new diet." He smiled sheepishly, a bit of rouge coming into his cheeks. "I met someone." He dropped the magazine and sat up straight, the smile vanishing. "Things are good. You?"

"Good, good. We're here—"

"We?" Reynolds threw an arm over the back of his aluminum chair and shifted to look behind her.

Frank hovered a few feet back.

"Agent Spinney!" he said, a bit too exuberantly, before a wave of darkness washed over his face. He cleared his throat and pasted back on his smile. "Always good to see you—far from Texas, that is. Back again so soon?"

"Yeah. It's good to see you too," Frank said softly. "Just visiting the detective here. Keeping her out of trouble."

Reynolds snorted and his belly shook. "Good luck with that."

Sam narrowed her eyes on Frank, noticing how close to the vest he was keeping his business there from Officer Reynolds, even more

so than he'd been doing with her. An awkward silence started to settle between them.

Sam faked a cough. "We're here to see Harlan Bowes."

"That lunatic? Guy was raving all night, screaming to be let out.
He says he's got some kind of medical condition. The officers you had
look into him didn't come up with nothin' suggesting any medical
conditions, but—" He pulled open his desk drawer and removed a
manila folder. "—they did leave this for you." He dropped it on the
desk.

Sam leaned over the desk, resting her palm on the folder. "Great,
thanks. How's he behaving now?"

"Sedated. We called the hospital to check whether he was treated
there. A doctor came by to evaluate him and gave him something to
help him sleep. She tried to have him released into her custody, but
we told her she'd have to talk to you about that." Reynolds shrugged.
"That woman did us a huge favor, shutting him up." He glanced at his
watch. "That was hours ago, though. He'll probably be ranting and
raving again soon, I'm sure, but at least I'll be off duty."

"Did you get the doctor's name?" Frank asked, jumping at the
break in conversation. He leaned into the desk, flicking his fingertips
against his thumb the way he did when he was anxious.

What's got you so nervous now, Frank? Sam studied his expression, in effect sending the question telepathically to the FBI agent.
Frank stiffened, then noticeably relaxed, likely a trained response, his
shoulders drooping and his easy smile returning to make him appear
worry-free.

Reynolds tapped his meaty forefinger on the folder. "All her info
should be inside here."

Sam picked it up. "Thanks. Can you have Bowes transferred to
Interview Room A?"

"Royo's in A, but B's available."

"That'll work. Thanks." She tucked the folder under her arm and led Frank into the room adjacent to Interview Room B. The room was dark and empty, save for a desk, a couple of chairs, and a camera that faced a one-way mirror.

"What was that with Reynolds?" Sam asked as soon as she was sure they were out of the officer's earshot. "Keeping quiet about why you're here?"

Frank shuffled his feet. "I didn't want to scare him is all. The man's been—"

"No." Sam fixed her gaze on his. Something in his words didn't ring true. She squinted. "It's something else." Her chin dropped as she thought, then raised again as his motive slowly dawned on her. "You're worried about a mole?"

Frank clenched his jaw. "You're the only one here I can trust on this. Wainwright has help on the inside. Of that I'm certain."

Sam groaned. "Yeah, inside the agency, not here. Or at least not freaking Reynolds. You of all people know what that man has been through."

"I know not to underestimate Wainwright or his power to turn *anyone* to his cause."

"Including an FBI agent like you, Frank?" Sam crossed her arms. "Maybe it's your mysterious CI—"

"Ha!" Frank's head rocked back as he laughed.

Heat rose in her cheeks. She had no idea what she might have said that could have been so amusing.

"My CI's loyalties are beyond question." Frank composed himself. "Like I said, you're the only one *here* I can trust."

Sam shook her head, then leaned into the hallway and watched Reynolds as he read his magazine. Her frustrations rising, she snapped back into Frank's space. "Will you work with me here?"

Frank just sighed. After a moment, her anger subsided. The thought was absurd. *Not Frank. Not Reynolds. Soon, I'll be looking at Michael with suspicion.* Until the possibility of Wainwright coming back into the picture, she hadn't realized she still harbored some lingering resentment toward Frank for his involvement in Bruce's death. And that was all it was—something she needed to let go. But as her dad used to say, the Irish were best at two things—drinking and holding grudges.

On the desk beside Frank was a small console with a few levers and buttons. Sam pointed to it. "You know how that works?"

Frank nodded. "Flick the switch and sound comes in through the speaker." He pointed to the black box mounted in the corner to the left of the mirror, close to the ceiling.

Sam walked over to the camera and set it to record. "The camera's on already. Let's not advertise your involvement here by having you come into the room with me. The brass might have something to say about it. If there's something you think I'm missing, just come over and knock. I'll come out."

He opened his mouth as if he wanted to say something, and Sam stared at him with arms crossed. When he didn't speak, she turned to the mirror. An officer had led Bowes, who looked half asleep and possibly drugged out of his mind, into the room and had handcuffed him to the metal rings on the desk. He slumped forward onto his arm, a stream of drool sliding from the side of his mouth and pooling on the table.

Sam rolled her eyes. "This should be fun." She stepped into the hall, closing Frank in darkness behind her. As she passed the officer who had escorted Bowes into the interview room, she lightly touched his arm. "Have two coffees, black and as scalding hot as you can make them, brought over to B."

The officer nodded and walked away. Sam entered the room.

Crinkling her nose, she sat across from her suspect. Bowes stunk like stale sweat and stained linens. He probably hadn't showered in days. His breath was worse—chemical-induced foulness, the odor carrying on his every breath. His eyes were bloodshot and his grayish tongue lolled as he looked up at Sam and giggled. Spit bubbles popped at the corner of his lips. If he'd been ranting and raving during the night, he'd been struck dumb by morning.

"T-t-ten lith-thel Injians... st-standing in a lingh. One t-tottered home... gyahh." Bowes hawed, farted, hawed again, and slumped forward on the table.

Just what in the hell did that doctor give him? Sam turned to the mirror and shook her head. She wasn't able to see Frank, but knew exactly what he was thinking—maybe she should try again after Bowes could sleep off his obvious intoxication.

Maybe the coffee will help. A wisp of a smirk formed on her mouth before she could subdue it, and she glanced over her shoulder to see if either the camera or Frank had caught it, sense soothing her as she realized that even if either had, they would have no way of interpreting it or connecting it to what she would do next. She wasn't proud of the plan she intended to execute, but even though she knew it to be wrong, she had no problem taking a shot at one who'd shot at her.

Sitting in the chair across from Bowes, she crossed her arms and legs and stared at his slumped form. As if sensing her gaze, Bowes lifted his head, his mouth slack and eyes bloodshot, and looked at her languidly, then rested back down on his arm.

Sam opened the file to a copy of the man's driver's license. *Harlan Bowes, forty-three years old. Brown hair, brown eyes, five-foot-nine.* She studied the squat, unimposing man in front of her for a moment then glanced back at his file. "No priors. Nothing in the system anyway. Nothing to suggest a violent bone in your body. You're even an organ donor. Yet you tried to kill me yesterday. Why?"

Bowes didn't respond and showed no sign of even listening. It didn't matter. The question had been voiced as much for Sam as it had been for her collar. She pressed on. "It says here that you work as an assistant athletic director for Bishop O'Connell High and that you coach your daughter's softball team. Or at least you did last year. Married with two kids—" She peeped up from the file. "Why isn't anyone looking for you?"

Her attacker's eyes were closed. She thought she heard the low rumble of a snore building. *Where the hell is that coffee?*

A knock came at the door. Sam got up and opened it to see the officer she'd sent on her errand back with a tray in his hand. Two Styrofoam cups filled nearly to the brim with steaming hot liquid sat in diagonal cup holders.

"Thanks," Sam said, taking the tray. She closed the door and returned to her seat.

"Mr. Bowes?" Sam carefully pulled one of the cups from the tray, the liquid sloshing regardless. A drop spilled on her finger and she winced. After putting the cup down on the table, she sucked on the raw flesh. Slowly, she pushed the cup toward her suspect, angling in her seat to keep her back to the camera.

"Mr. Bowes? I got you some coffee to help clear your hea—" Sam knocked the cup over. "Oh, shit!"

Its contents spilled all over Bowes's left hand. His eyes burst open, and he screamed in pain. He jumped from his seat, only to be yanked back into the table as the chain on the cuffs went taut. He tried to wipe his hand on his pants but couldn't reach, then shook it in the air and tried to blow on it. "What the hell? What is this?" Bowes was instantly an entirely different man. His panicked gaze darted about the room as he tugged on his cuffs.

Sam used her own sleeve to dab his hand, the skin raw and blistering.

He jerked his arm away. "Don't touch me!"

By then, the coffee was still hot but tolerable through the fabric. "Oh, God. I'm so, so sorry," she said, trying to sound convincing. As of yet, no one had burst through the door to assist, so she assumed Frank had seen what she was up to and had thrown interference.

She studied Bowes closely, having anticipated the burn would sober him up a bit, but now he looked as if he'd never been drugged at all, like a little pain had snapped him out of a spell. *Okay, maybe more than a little pain.*

Slowly, he returned to his seat, his eyes twitching in their sockets as he glared at Sam, mind scrambling for understanding. "Where am I? What's going on?"

"Detective Samantha Reilly, at your service. I'm the one you tried to shoot yesterday."

"Tried to shoot?" Bowes searched her face. "What the hell are you talking about? Is this some kind of joke? Oh for the love of—" His eyes filled with anger. "You! I remember you! You brought me..." He took in his surroundings once more. "I'm in jail? I thought that was just a nightmare."

Bowes pulled at the chain binding him to the desk until his face turned purple from straining. "Help! Help! Let me out of here! Help!"

Sam leaned forward, palms spread out on the table. "Mr. Bowes, look at me."

When Bowes continued to scream, Sam slapped the table and stood. "Look at me!"

Bowes shrunk away, face ashen, clearly terrified. "I don't know what this is, what any of this is all about." He raised his hands to protect his face. "Please, don't hurt me."

Looking at this scared little boy in a man's body, Sam didn't see a killer. Two decades on the job had trained her to recognize bad men, and Bowes showed no signs of being one—no hint of violence behind his eyes, no malice burnt into the bends of his lips, no evil to be found in his soul. But Bowes *had* tried to kill her. Something wasn't adding up.

"I don't want to hurt you, Mr. Bowes, but you tried to shoot me yesterday." Sam sat down, tried to make herself less threatening by uncrossing her arms and pushing her chair back. "I have you dead to rights. You're going down for attempted murder. Unless—"

"I didn't try to kill you! Why would I do that? I don't even know you. I don't even own a gun." He buried his face in his hands and started to cry. "This can't be happening. Wake up, Harlan. Wake up."

Sam sighed, not knowing what to make of Bowes's reaction. "Okay, let's say for a moment you didn't try to kill me."

"I didn't!"

"Then tell me—what *did* you do yesterday?"

"I..." Bowes's mouth dropped open as he searched for words. His head slowly shook, his eyes scanning the desk for answers that weren't there. Finally, after several seconds of thought, he looked up. "I took a sleeping pill and got into my car—the passenger seat—and had my wife drop me off at the hospital while I slept. You see, I have this condition—"

"Let me guess." Sam scoffed. "Messes with your memory."

"No." Bowes frowned. "No. It's called agoraphobia. After a softball game, I was walking back to my car with my daughter. We were mugged." Tears flowed down Bowes's cheeks. He squeezed his eyes shut. "That bastard put a knife to my daughter's throat. I couldn't breathe. I couldn't help her. I couldn't do anything. And that feeling of helplessness hasn't gone away."

If he was telling the truth—and Sam could confirm it easily enough—Bowes might be worthy of her pity. It didn't exactly add up to innocence, not even close, but something in Sam's gut told her he might be just as much of a victim as she was. A twinge of regret twisted her stomach at the thought of the coffee stunt she had pulled.

He looked up. "So you see, I couldn't have shot at you. I can't leave the house. I can't even work to support my family. I admitted myself yesterday to try and get help." He lurched forward, fingers shaking. "You should have records of all of this. Call Brentworth Hospital. They'll confirm everything."

"Are you willing to sign a consent form releasing your medical records to us?"

"If it will help get me out of here, yes." Bowes's hands trembled as he tried to raise them to his face, once again blocked by the chain. He stared at the table, eyes shimmering with the last of his tears. "I'll sign whatever you want."

Sam rolled her finger on the table. "And you have no recollection of how you got here?"

"Other than you dragging me in here and throwing me into a cage? No." He lifted his head, his face contorted into a pitiable mask of desperation, a tiny glint in his eyes seeking her out for a spark of hope. "Please, let me go. I just want to see my family."

After a few minutes of more prodding, a knock came at the door. Annoyed, Sam took a deep breath then got up to answer it. Frank stood outside, looking as if he'd just swallowed a tarantula.

"What is it?" She stepped into the hall and closed the door behind her.

"I just made some quick calls, first to the hospital. They've confirmed that Harlan Bowes was a patient there but wouldn't say what for. I've got a guy on the inside who could get access to medical records—"

"You've got an undercover agent at Brentworth? What for? And with access to medical records? That's a violation of—"

"I'll explain later. And before you question my tactics, don't think I believe for one second that that coffee spill was an accident." Frank stepped closer and lowered his voice. "Look, Bowes did check into Brentworth yesterday."

Sam knew there was no way Frank could have made those calls in the minute or two that had passed since Bowes had mentioned Brentworth. *He must have started in as soon as I left the room, after*

Reynolds mentioned that doctor coming by. She growled, her frustration festering for the worse because she sidelined it. Instead, she diverted her focus to the more immediate question. "Frank, this is the guy who shot at us. We caught him red-handed. Of course he couldn't have been checking himself in at the hospital then."

"I know that. Let me finish. He actually checked in three months ago, and according to his family, my second call, he's been there ever since. But the hospital has him listed as being there for only a few days."

"So what are you saying? He walked in for treatment three months ago then disappeared? Where's he been for the last three months?"

"That, I don't know."

"But you suspect something's up with the hospital—where I was attacked, where I bring Michael to see his friend regularly." She crossed her arms and seethed. "And you suspected it even before I started in on Bowes.

"Come on, Frank! When were you going to let me know? You've got some nerve." She shook her head in disgust. "You know what? If you aren't going to share information with me, then get the fuck out of my precinct!"

"We wanted to be sure. We didn't want to bring you into this if we didn't have to. You have a boy now, and you've been through so much—"

"Spare me the bullshit. I want to know everything you know, and I want it now."

CHAPTER 11

"Here we go again," Dylan said, laughing and throwing a thumb over his shoulder at the detail following behind them as they began their walk home from school. He still wore his North Face jacket but had opted for a T-shirt and jeans for his second day at Carnegie High. With his styled hair and All-American good looks, he still made even that look fashionable.

A twinge of jealousy flashed behind Michael's eyes, based on an assumption that his new friend's fine looks meant he'd had a fine life. Then he remembered how Dylan had skipped from place to place, never really staying in one area long enough to develop strong friendships or even keep those that he'd made.

Another assumption. *What was it Sam had called that?* He looked down at the ground for a rock to kick. *Projection.* Just because he'd been tossed from home to home without ever making any friends didn't mean Dylan had been in the same boat.

And yet, he felt a kinship with the boy. *Strangers in a Strange Land.* He laughed, remembering the title of one of the books the fat guy at the library was always trying to get him to read since they both liked the same graphic novels. Michael kept turning him down, preferring to keep to books with pictures, but for some reason, he liked that title and felt it applied somehow to him and Dylan despite having no idea what the actual book was about.

"Everything okay, Badass?"

"Huh?" Michael looked up to see what appeared to be genuine concern in Dylan's expression. The boy had narrowed his eyes on Michael, brow furrowed, lips pressed flat.

"Oh, yeah... I'm okay. I just daydream a lot."

Dylan stopped and fixed Michael with a grave look. "Something on your mind? Not to sound stupid or anything, but, you know... I'm happy to listen."

Michael shrugged. "Thanks, but really, I'm good. Sometimes, I just overthink things."

Dylan chuckled. "Sounds serious. Fortunately for you, Dr. Dylan has the solution." He nodded at the cop car trailing them. "But we've got to ditch your entourage first."

"Entourage?" Michael scrunched up his nose with distaste. "Really?"

"What?" Dylan laughed. "Too big of a word for you?"

"I *know* what entourage means. I just don't think I've ever heard it used in a sentence before, and I'm sure no one has ever used it to describe the one or two people who don't even remotely want anything to do with me. Those two"—he jerked his head at the police cruiser—"are getting paid to follow me around."

"Okay, bodyguards, then. Shoot me." He threw his palms up. "On second thought, I shouldn't say that to you since you're in with the cops and could probably have me shot." He laughed again, and this time Michael laughed with him. "I have to say, though. They sort of make me feel important. Like I'm a senator or something, and they're my personal protection."

"You look like a politician."

"I'm not sure what you mean by that, but I sense some negativity in your tone." Dylan placed his hands over his heart, frowned, and sniffled. "That hurts, Badass."

Michael snorted. "Yeah, I'm sure you're real torn up inside."

Their conversation lulled as they walked toward the first short-cut. Michael huffed. He knew he couldn't ditch them. Sam would have a fit. But a stubborn pride rose within him. *I'm friggin' fifteen years old. I don't need a babysitter.*

He sighed, the pride subsiding. *Don't be stupid, Michael.* Even though Dylan had seemingly let it drop, he felt he owed his friend an explanation. "I can't. Sam would kill me."

"Hey, man." Dylan smiled warmly. "It's cool. Not trying to pressure you. I just have this awesome spot I really can't let your bodyguards know about." He shrugged. "No biggie. We can go when you're off home arrest or whatever. In the meantime"—he punched Michael in the shoulder—"I may have to stop calling you Badass, though."

He stopped, and Michael turned to see him staring at his butt.

"How's *Fatass* sound?"

"Fuck you," Michael tried to say angrily but trailed off in a giggle. He punched Dylan back in the arm.

"Hey, easy, man! That's assault! The cops are my witnesses. Why aren't they arresting you?"

"Actually, it's battery. The assault is putting you in apprehension of an attack, but Sam says sometimes it's different in civil law versus criminal."

"Good to know, I guess." He pointed ahead to the stone wall at the back of the lawn. "So are we still taking the shortcut?"

Michael scowled. "Where's this place?" The question came out before he could stop it. Dylan hadn't pressed him, he didn't think, but the change in nickname somehow felt like a challenge.

"No, it's cool, buddy." Dylan shook his head. "I'm not trying to get on your mom's bad side—"

"Where is it?" Michael blurted, that stubborn pride returning. Dylan sounded genuine, but everything he said had the effect of making Michael feel anything but badass. He liked the nickname, but Dylan was right: his actions weren't earning it. Still, logic told him he was being stupid. He didn't even know his new friend's last name. Plus, the detail was assigned for a reason, though since he'd been back, it hadn't seemed valid.

The man attacked Sam. The cops should be following her, not me.

Dylan smiled mischievously. "Come on. I'll show you." The two darted across the lawn to the stone wall, where Dylan halted. The police car had already turned around and was speeding away to meet them on the other side of the shortcut.

"Now, we double back," Dylan said, a glint in his eye. He reversed direction and ran back the way they'd come.

Michael followed. He knew what he was doing wasn't very smart, but his accelerating heartbeat made him feel... *good*? It felt good to be bad, to throw caution at the wind, to do something that *felt* dangerous, even if he knew there was very little danger in it. No one was or had been out to get him.

"Won't they come back this way?" he asked.

"Most... likely not," Dylan said between panting. He took a right down Courtney Street, which ran parallel to the street on the other side of the shortcut, following the direction the police car had gone. "We need to find someplace to hide."

Michael scanned the neighborhood for a quick and convenient hiding spot. The houses were modest, one-story homes, most having equally small but fenced-in front yards. In the nearest driveway, a large black F-150 was parked. As he heard an engine drawing nearer, Michael pulled Dylan by his sleeve over to the pickup. They crouched beside the rear wheel and slowly circled the back of the truck as the police car passed. Once the cruiser had turned, the boys stood.

"They'll be back," Dylan said.

"What are you kids doing to my truck?" shouted a man from the front porch.

Laughing, Michael and Dylan took off running, farther down Courtney Street, taking a right then a left until they were heading in the direction of Brentworth Hospital. They were nearly there, too, when Michael slowed to a stop.

He bent over and placed his hands on his knees, his breaths quick and shallow. "Wait!"

Dylan, who'd already slowed to a trot, halted and turned around. "I doubt we've lost them yet, but we're really close."

Michael winced at a stitch in his side. Still breathing quickly, but consciously trying to take longer, deeper breaths, he asked, "Where are you taking me?"

"I told you—to my spot. Don't worry. You're going to like it."

"Is it at Brentworth?"

"No. Why? Is that a problem? I thought you go there all the time?"

Michael didn't want to explain to a kid he was just getting to know that his detective foster mother had been attacked the last time they'd been there. The many reasons not to ditch his detail, play with strangers, or go anywhere near Brentworth flooded his thoughts like a tidal wave, and his legs wobbled as if they might give out. But to turn back then, without any real, tangible reason for fear, would just be stupid. Cowardly. And worst of all, he might damage his chances of actually making a new friend.

"Okay. I-I just don't want to go to Brentworth."

Dylan's braces twinkled in the late afternoon sunlight. "Just come on. We won't be going anywhere near that place."

As it turned out, "near" meant something entirely different to Dylan than it did Michael. After following his new friend for another half mile, they stopped in front of Brentworth Hospital. A sprawling complex, Brentworth was an old brick and mortar structure that looked more like an Ivy League college dormitory that had been left unattended for half a century than a healing center. Though Michael wasn't born until after Brentworth's heyday and had always known Charlton Memorial Hospital as the place to go if you were hurt or sick, he'd learned all about Brentworth when he found out Tessa would be sent there.

Michael hadn't been born yet when Brentworth was the city's only hospital. After the more advanced Charlton opened, Brentworth had become the home for several specialties, a walk-in clinic, and run-off emergency services when the load on Charlton became too much. But most people, Michael included, thought of the place as the "nuthouse." Though his tune had softened a bit when he started going there to see Tessa, the massive hospital always intimidated him. It had three stories at its center and wings sprawling out in all directions, kind of like his high school. But much of it went unused and neglected like it was two steps removed from being a fine location for a horror film.

As they approached, the hospital looked alive. People in street clothes and scrubs entered and exited every few seconds. An ambulance was silently waiting out front, red lights swirling. A car that looked like Sam's was parked a little ways behind it in a tow-away zone.

"I thought you said no Brentworth?" Michael asked, more annoyed with Dylan's deception than anything else.

"Relax. We aren't going in there." He pointed to the lane that led to the back entrance. "We're going behind it."

Before Michael could protest, Dylan marched ahead. Michael shuffled his feet, wondering whether to follow. His hesitation came with anger, a spark at first that ignited an ever-growing flame. He was so tired of being afraid—afraid of being bullied at school, of what the other students thought of him. Afraid of what he might see if he held hands with a girl or, God forbid, let someone hug him. Of living his life in fear of all the crazies in Sam's and, to be fair, the crazies that he'd found all on his own. He just wanted to be normal, to do normal kid things with other kids.

So he wasn't normal. Fine. But that didn't mean he couldn't or shouldn't have a taste of it now and then. The world was a dark place, but living in fear left no room for light. Or friendship. Or fun. It had left him with no real life to lose.

He clenched his jaw and ran to catch up with his friend. "So, what's your last name, anyway?"

"Jefferson," Dylan said. "I'm sorry. I thought you knew that."

"You know mine?"

Dylan poked him in the arm. "You mean it's not Badass?"

"That's my middle name." Michael frowned. "But seriously. It's Turcotte."

"I know." Dylan smiled. "I paid attention during roll call."

Michael squinted. "Ms. Alvarez did a roll call? I don't remember that."

"Like I said, *I* paid attention." Dylan laughed and Michael joined him.

They continued to walk down the lane toward the hospital's rear entrance. There, the parking lot had gone unmaintained, its surface riddled with long cracks and uneven pavement. Weeds shot up through the asphalt like tufts of stray feathers on a plucked chicken. Smaller trees lined the back of the lot, their larger brethren beyond them, a massive army standing at attention, spanning into darkness.

Michael remembered the lot well. He'd been there only six weeks ago, wielding an ax to save Sam's life. The memory came to him vividly, and he scanned the tree line for any sign of the man in the Indian mask. He clenched his teeth and balled his hands into fists. *I'm not afraid of you.* As much as he wanted to be brave, the lie crumbled to dust under wobbly knees and hesitant feet.

"Come on!" Dylan called from the lot's edge. He was heading into the forest. "It's just a little ways through here."

"Aren't there, like, ticks or something?"

Dylan turned and shrugged. "Probably. You coming?" Without waiting for a response, he stepped past the first row of trees. A few more steps and Michael could barely see the blue of Dylan's jacket.

Michael again examined the trees for anything suspicious, then the back of the building and the remainder of the lot. He saw no one. Nothing stirred. He was alone. The hairs on his neck stood on end, and the temperature seemed to drop ten degrees. That was when he realized the extent of his idiotic pride and his desire to be normal. It had left him alone and at risk. And though he saw no one, he felt as though a hundred eyes were on him.

He ran after Dylan. "Wait up!" As he sprinted into the woods, he could no longer see his friend. He looked left and right but saw nothing but telephone-pole-thin firs, some black and rotting. Their needleless lower branches reached out like skeletal hands to claw at his face and arms as he ran. Roots and twigs, half-covered by moss and underbrush, tried to knock his feet out from under him, but he recovered from each stumble before they could succeed.

About a quarter mile in, he skidded to a halt and looked back, not sure if it was the direction of the hospital. Everywhere he turned, the forest looked the same. Panic rose within him as his heartbeat pounded in his temples. Sweat dripped from his forehead and down his spine. *Where are you, Dylan?*

"Over here!" Dylan was barely twenty yards away, diagonally to Michael's right, as easy to see as the trees directly in front of him. He was waving his arm over his head. How Michael had missed the boy he could only explain as a result of his minor bout of hysteria. He sighed, his eyes welling as he plodded slowly through the brush to Dylan, giving himself as much time as possible to regain his composure.

Dylan beamed as if he hadn't a care in the world. "Welcome to my home away from home, Badass." He swung his arm back, directing Michael's gaze to a thick trunk with wooden rungs nailed into it. The planks that weren't cracked entirely appeared to be splintering, and all could only loosely be described as horizontal, but Michael understood their intent. He looked up.

"Wow," he said, hiding his enthusiasm. "I doubt that thing's up to code."

"It's sturdy enough." Dylan dropped his backpack beside the tree, reached for a rung, and began to climb. "Come on!"

Michael gazed at the treehouse, a plywood box perched on forking branches that, from thirty feet or so below, didn't look much thicker than his calves, which Sam referred to as his chicken legs. The wood appeared weatherworn and maybe even termite infested. He watched Dylan climb as gracefully as a monkey, without the slightest hesitation or misstep. Michael wished he could be like that, and not just in climbing shifty ladders.

He sighed, tossed his backpack near Dylan's, and grabbed the rung just over his head. But when he tried to step up, his sneaker slid right off the plank. His shin banged into it as he slipped, causing a stabbing pain to shoot up his leg. He groaned and cursed, then studied the rung, realizing his error almost immediately. Each rung was wider than the base of the tree. Stepping on the end of the rung would allow him to use the ball of his foot to climb rather than just his toes.

Placing the middle of his sneaker on the end of the rung, he tested his weight on it. He and Dylan were roughly the same size. If anything, Dylan was slightly taller. *If it supports him...* Michael began to climb.

He was about halfway up and becoming comfortable with the climb when one of the rungs spun vertically as he planted his foot on it. He gasped and threw his body against the tree, the scare quickly passing as his other three grips remained firm.

He yelled up to Dylan, pissed his friend hadn't warned him. "Some of these ladder rungs are shit!"

"Oh, yeah. Sorry!" Dylan called back from somewhere beyond Michael's sight.

Michael shook his head and continued without further incident. At the top, he pulled himself up to a landing that served as a sort of porch without railings for the treehouse. Cautiously rising from his knees, he took in the view and immediately wished he hadn't, his legs going shaky again on what might have been less-than-solid footing. He'd never been afraid of heights, but just knowing how easily he could fall from getting dizzy or the slightest careless bump from Dylan, and the treehouse's interior seemed all the more welcoming.

It was much bigger than it appeared from the tree's base, and the branches supporting it were much thicker. It still looked like a box made of rotten wood, and in contrast to the haphazardly constructed shack the rest of the thing was, it had saloon-style doors that swung on double hinges.

"Howdy, partner," Michael said as he ducked his head and pushed through the doors.

Save for two folding chairs, one of which Dylan sat upon, the inside lacked any adornments. Small windows were carved into the sidewalls, facing what Michael thought was the way back to the hospital and the way deeper into the woods. Facecloths were thumbtacked over each window, probably to keep out bugs and weather. The window facing Brentworth was clear, its facecloth folded and tacked above it. Under that, a pair of binoculars leaned against the wall.

Dylan spread out his arms. "Pretty amazing, huh?"

Michael didn't know how he felt about it. Warmth flushed his cheeks. Maybe he was way too old for a treehouse. It seemed like something younger kids did, normal kids—not like him. He'd never been in one before, and he guessed... yeah, that did make it kinda cool.

"I guess." He shrugged, downplaying his elation, then took the seat beside Dylan.

"Let me guess," Dylan said, leaning forward, resting his elbows on his knees. "You're thinking we're too old to have a treehouse?"

"It might've crossed my mind. You build it?"

"Nope. Found it."

Not knowing what else to talk about, Michael watched as a nasty-looking bug emerged from the crack where the wall met the floor. He grimaced as the thing, possibly an earwig, scurried toward his foot. He lifted his sneaker and slammed it down hard on the bug, then froze, the branches below him creaking and groaning in protest.

"Don't do that." Dylan's face had gone a lighter shade. He laughed nervously. "Besides, the bugs up here aren't so bad. Especially the roaches."

Dylan reached over to the wall and retrieved a small lumpy white cylinder that looked like a cigarette without a filter. "You smoke?"

Michael had never smoked weed before, but he knew it when he saw it. He thought about lying to make himself sound cool, but Dylan would probably see right through him, so he stuck with the truth. "I've never had it before."

Dylan reached into his pocket and pulled out a lighter. He put the joint to his lips and inhaled as he lit the already blackened end. As he breathed in the smoke, the end of the joint brightened. Michael found the light sort of pretty and then thought himself weird for finding it so. Dylan removed the joint from his mouth and appeared to be holding his breath. After a moment, he blew out a cloud of smoke that tingled against Michael's face. Then Dylan held the joint out to him.

Michael leaned away. "I shouldn't. I'm probably giving Sam enough to worry about right now."

"Which is exactly why you should. You seem like the type that's always worrying about other people, what they think, and what they feel about you. So high-strung. This will help with that. It's medicine for your soul."

Michael scoffed. "Medicine for your soul? Where'd you hear that bullshit?"

"I don't know." Dylan laughed. "But it sounded good, didn't it? It's cool, though. It doesn't usually work the first time anyway."

The boys laughed together, and Dylan took another hit. Michael would be lying to himself if he said he didn't want to try it, curiosity getting the better of him. With it being legal for adults in Massachusetts, he expected half the students at his high school had already tried it. *Hell, half of them are probably high* at *school. How bad can it be?*

"All right." He held out his hand. "Pass it over."

"Badass!" As Dylan passed him the joint, he explained how to grip the end and take a hit so Michael wouldn't close it off. Michael put the joint to his lips and did as Dylan instructed, inhaling as deeply as he could.

"Now hold it in," Dylan encouraged.

Michael coughed. Smoke exploded out his nostrils before he opened his mouth. A coughing fit ensued that lasted over a minute. Every time he tried to speak, a tightness would return to his chest, and he'd start coughing all over again.

Dylan apparently found the whole thing hilarious. Between bouts of laughter, he said he would have offered Michael some water but had forgotten to bring it. He shrugged and raised his palms. "Sorry!" He laughed some more before taking another hit himself.

When Michael was able to talk again, his own laughter prolonging the attempt, he said, "I pegged you as a quichebag, dressed like you were the first day. I never expected I'd be ditching the"—he made finger quotes— "*entourage* and smoking weed with you in a treehouse behind a mental hospital on day two. What's on the agenda for tomorrow? We gonna steal a car?"

"Yeah, that cop car that's been following you. Er, *was* following you." Dylan blew out a puff of smoke. "What in the hell is a *quichebag*?"

"You know, like a goody-two-shoes."

"What the heck is that?" Dylan burst out into laughter.

It was infectious. "A choir boy?"

"Now that, I understand." Dylan's face went deathly grave, and he fixed Michael with a stare that unnerved him. "There's a lot you don't know about me, Badass. Like where I buried all the bodies."

Michael stared back at him in silence for another second before both boys exploded into laughter. Michael had tears in his eyes by the time he'd finished. "Give me that," he said, pointing to the joint.

Dylan handed it over. "Go easy, now."

But Michael didn't want to go easy. He took a long hard hit that resulted in another coughing fit, but he didn't care. It felt good to hang out and have fun, to let his cares go. To not be a burden on anyone else for once and be where someone actually wanted him to be.

After passing the joint back to Dylan, he pointed at the binoculars. "What are those for?"

"Well..." Dylan leaned over and grabbed the binoculars in his free hand. They appeared to be high quality, like something hunters or the military might use, not those cheap plastic things you could get at a dollar store. "That's so I can see who's coming. As you probably know, we aren't supposed to have this."

He handed Michael the binoculars. "Go ahead. Take a look. You can make out the back door to Brentworth if you aim it just right."

Michael took another hit, returned the joint to Dylan, then grabbed the binoculars. He kneeled in front of the window and peered out it, but everything he saw through the lenses was blurred. His fingers adjusted the small gear on the top of the binoculars and cleared the resolution.

"Wow!" He scanned the top of the trees and could see well beyond the start of the forest. "I can see like a mile with these things." But he couldn't see Brentworth, the trees standing much taller. With minute movements, he lowered his gaze, lower and lower until—

He shrieked, dropped the binoculars, and scuttled back from the window.

"What?" Dylan asked, reaching out to help Michael up. "What is it?"

Michael's lips trembled. He was so stunned that he couldn't get out the words that were terrorizing his mind. Instead, he pointed at the window.

Dylan stubbed out the joint and picked the binoculars off the floor. Gazing out the window, he again asked, "What did you see?"

"Th-Th-Three," Michael stuttered, "maybe, f-four men... w-wearing Indian masks. Looking this way. Looking right at us."

"Where?" Dylan continued to look out the window. "I don't see anyone."

"Toward Brentworth, b-b-but in the woods."

Dylan looked again. After a moment, he said, "Well, there's no one there now. And if anyone was there—"

"They were there!"

Dylan took a deep breath. "And if anyone was there, there's no way they could have seen us. Are you sure the weed's not making you paranoid? It does do that to some people."

"I'm not being paranoid." Michael spat out the words as if there was no contesting them, but he had to consider the possibility he'd imagined those figures. He'd only seen them for a second. Maybe the drug had caused it, but as far as he knew, weed didn't make people hallucinate. "We should go. It's getting dark."

"Go where?" Dylan began to pace, head tucked so he wouldn't scrape it along the ceiling. "Let's say I believe you. Wouldn't we have to walk right into them? Either that, or we'll just end up lost in the woods." He nodded in the direction of the back wall. "I don't know what's out there."

"Do you know any other ways back?"

"No." Dylan ran a hand through his hair. "Mike, you're freaking me out. Is this the reason the cops are following you? I thought you said it was just one guy?"

"It was just one guy!" Michael's heart thudded in his chest. His lungs hurt as he sucked in air, wheezing out the last remnants of smoke.

"Okay, okay." Dylan stopped pacing. "Let's just stay calm. Here's what we'll do. The sun's going to set any minute now. We wait for that, then we quietly creep back to the hospital, where I'll get my dad to drive us home."

"But we won't be able to see them."

"And they won't be able to see us."

Michael nodded and forced himself to breathe deeper, unsure if he was panicking for nothing. He knew what he'd seen—four people standing side by side, each wearing that same plastic Indian mask Sam's attacker had been wearing six weeks earlier. But that day, there had only been a single man in a mask. And Michael hadn't smoked.

Am I high? He didn't know what being high felt like to know whether he was or wasn't. *I hope I'm not just being paranoid, for Dylan's sake.* He chuckled despite his fear, wanting more to have not lied to his new friend than to actually not have any real threat in the first place.

"What's so funny?"

"Nothing."

Dylan tugged on his chin. "Well, we should get down after all. We're sitting ducks up here."

Michael exited the treehouse and crouched on the landing outside, readying to climb down.

Dylan patted his shoulder. "Not that way. Too slow, and what are you going to do if halfway down you see someone waiting at the bottom?" He pointed to the far side of the treehouse. "Watch me."

On the outside of the structure, someone had rigged up a rope and pulley system. "Now this, I built," Dylan said, a big metallic grin on his face. He tugged on one end of the rope, the other end attached to a tree far below like a clothesline rigged between two tall buildings. As Dylan tugged on the upper rope, the wheels on each end of the contraption squeaked. Michael glanced nervously over his shoulder to see if the noise had attracted any unwanted attention but saw no one. A bucket rose slowly from the base of the tree, affixed to the upper rope. Something shiny twinkled inside it in the dying light.

Hand over hand, Dylan drew the bucket up. "When I let go of the rope, the bucket will automatically go back down. I'll put the grip back in it, but you'll have to pull it up just like I did."

Letting go of the rope with one hand, he removed a silver bar with a doughnut at its center. It looked like a giant eye bolt with two arms or something to work out his arms at a gym. It might have been the handlebar from a scooter. Dylan shuffled past Michael to the tree's trunk, where he reached up to clasp the bar to a cable Michael hadn't even noticed.

"Always put it on this way," he said, holding the bar over the cable. Then he pressed until the wire squeezed through a small break in the doughnut's center. "If you do it upside down, the hole in the bar is up, and you and it go straight down."

He winked and grabbed both arms of the bar. "But don't worry. It's perfectly safe. Just like in the movies. Lift your feet and make sure you let go before you slam into the tree at the other end. And whatever you do, don't grab the cable to try and slow down. I'll put this back in the bucket when I land."

Michael mouthed *wait*, but Dylan was already zipping down the cable. When he let go of the bar, he hit the ground with bent knees and tumbled head over heels until he was back on his feet, no worse for wear. The bar hit the tree with a *twang* that made Michael cringe. He hoped he and Dylan were the only people in those woods who'd heard it.

Dylan ran over to the bar and dumped it into the bucket, then gave a thumbs-up. With a deep breath, Michael began pulling the rope. It seemed like the wheels squeaked louder with each tug. When the bucket reached the top, Michael swallowed hard as he reached over the drop to grab the bar. It was much heavier than he'd anticipated, and he teetered on his toes over the ledge for a panicked second before regaining his balance. Heart in his throat, he connected the bar to the cable, took the grips in his hands, and prayed to any god who would listen.

Then, he closed his eyes and jumped. He whipped toward the ground at a much faster speed than he thought, and his instincts screamed at him to slow down. Halfway down, he forced his eyes open and glanced up at his hands. One grip was much lower than the other, the bar venturing vertically and probably to disaster. Without thinking, he released his higher hand and grasped for the cable.

Fiery pain ripped across his palm and he cried out, letting go with both hands and crashing onto his feet. He heard a crack as he landed, either snapping bone or twigs, as more pain shot through his ankle. His momentum pitched him forward, and he slammed face-first into pityingly soft, damp earth.

He looked at his hand as he laid in dirt and pine needles. His glove and the flesh under it were shredded, the muscle beneath raw and sticky.

"That was close." Dylan grabbed him under his arm and helped him to his feet. He gestured at a tree, only a half foot or so from where Michael's head had landed. "Can you walk?"

Michael tested his ankle. As he put more weight on it, he found it sturdy enough to limp on. It was probably just a mild sprain. He nodded.

"Good," Dylan said, still propping him up. "Sun's nearly set. We should start heading back."

Together, the two crept quietly toward the lot as the sky turned from lavender to deep purple. The woods fell into night. Dylan's shoulder served as a crutch until Michael's pain dulled enough for him to walk on his own. Every now and then, Michael would freeze and throw a finger over his mouth, swearing he saw a face in the dark, only to look again at where it was and find nothing. His hand hurt, his ankle hurt, and he'd scared the hell out of his new friend, and for what? Weed-based paranoia? Dylan never saw anyone Michael thought he saw.

They were no more than a few feet from the lot when another face rose from the shadows. It rushed at him.

"Now, I've got you, you little bastard!" a female shouted.

"Wait," a man said, his voice filled with alarm. "Don't touch his—"

A cold hand clasped around Michael's neck. He began to seize.

CHAPTER 12

Tessa felt good. Like, *really* good.

She'd seen a new doctor that morning, and in just one session, the new treatment had sapped away all her negative energy, turned misery into acceptance, and a nightmare into a dream. And afterward, she slept deeply and soundlessly as a baby swaddled in her sheets, comfort and warmth like she'd never felt before hugging her body closely.

When she awoke, it was already late afternoon. She stretched her arms out to the ceiling, her shoulder popping as she did. Her mouth was dry, tongue thick and numb as she pressed it against her teeth. She picked the crusties from the corners of her eyes and hopped out of bed. Without changing out of her pajamas or even putting slippers on her feet, she headed to the bathroom. There, she urinated for what seemed like an hour, then went to the sink and turned on the cold water. Craning her neck, she stuck her mouth under the faucet and drank long and deep the cold liquid. When she'd had her fill, she smiled into the faux glass mirror above the sink, wet hair plastered to her face and water dripping from her cheeks and chin.

Her body was light as air as she glided over the floor, out into the hall, and toward the adult rec room. On her way, she spotted Nurse Francine heading in the opposite direction and stopped to say hello.

"Why, hello to you, too, Tessa," the nurse said, smiling wide. "And don't you look lovely today?"

Tessa giggled. "Thank you!" Elated by the compliment, she nearly skipped to the rec room.

That late in the afternoon, it was mostly empty. The bridge club dealt out another game, and Tessa pulled up a chair to watch. But not understanding how the game was scored, she soon lost interest. She headed over to the bookshelf and grabbed what appeared to be a brand new crossword puzzle book, *sans* dick pics. *Score!*

She snatched up a few brightly colored crayons and headed with the book over to the small plastic table, where she pulled up a chair. Flipping to the first puzzle, an easy one, she began to complete it. The answers came to her lightning fast, her intense focus and clarity no longer hampered by her old prescriptions. In fact, the doctor had said she wouldn't need them anymore. And that was just wonderful!

She completed the first puzzle and was a quarter way through the second, pondering a six-letter verb to make someone or something more lively, when someone spoke behind her. She jumped, and the crayon flew from her hand. But the briefest flash of annoyance was dead and gone before she could even catch her breath. She just felt too good to let such a little thing bother her.

"Where have you been all day? I've been looking all over for you."

A boy about her age with red hair circled the table then sat across from her. He was kind of cute and looked sort of familiar. She frowned, trying to remember, then shrugged, deciding she must have just seen him around the hospital.

She smiled and teased, "Not much for manners, just sitting down there uninvited."

The boy gave her a quizzical look, an eyebrow raised and eyes unblinking, as if *she* were the weird one.

She scoffed. "What?"

"Are you okay?"

Tessa chuckled. "Who wants to know?"

"Tessa?" The boy leaned forward. "What's going on? I woke up, and you were gone. I've been worried all day that something might have happened to you."

Icy fingers tickled Tessa's spine, and she glanced about nervously. The Bandage Man watched them from a chair in the corner. She met his scowl with one of her own then stuck her tongue out at him. Her gaze returned to the stranger in front of her, who she'd just about been ready to dismiss as a confused patient. But the fact that he knew her name caused her pause.

She thought back to last night, trying to remember what she'd done. "I... I went to bed early last night."

The boy leaned forward and whispered. "You spent the night with me. Don't you remember that?"

"I..." The words vanished from her mind. She ground her teeth and began to fidget. Her nose crinkled. "Is this some weird trick to get me into bed? I think you should go away now, or I'll call Jeb over there." She pointed over to the orderly the kids called the Missing Link on account of the size of his head. *Kids can be so mean.*

"*Tessa.*" The boy reached out and grabbed her hands.

"Don't touch me!" She tore her hands free and exploded to her feet. Cute or not, whoever this boy thought he was, he had no right to put his hands on her.

Jeb looked over and snorted. He made no move to come to her aid, but the Bandage Man was on his feet. He stormed over, his scowl contorting into an outright snarl. Tessa didn't know who she should fear more—the man or the boy.

Though the Bandage Man was wiry, he grabbed the boy's shoulder, pinning him to his seat despite his squirming. The boy winced and tried to break the grip, swatting at the man's hand with no success.

"Listen to me." The Bandage Man leaned over and growled low into the boy's ear, but Tessa could still hear him clearly. His voice was scratchy and gravelly as if his vocal cords had been treated with sandpaper. "Leave here now. Stay away from the girl, or you'll be next." He yanked the boy up and pushed him toward the door.

"Tessa," the boy whined. "It's me, Jimmy. Don't you remember me?"

Tessa shook her head, her eyes downcast. She refocused on the crossword puzzle as if it might make the boy and the Bandage Man go away. She'd been having such a good day. If she could only get back to her puzzle—

"Go," the Bandage Man said, loud enough for all to hear. He gave Jimmy another push toward the door.

Jimmy clenched his fists and puffed out his chest, meeting the Bandage Man's stare. Tessa thought he might take a swing at the man, but after a tense few seconds, he skulked out of the room with his tail between his legs. The Bandage Man nodded at Jeb, who nodded back then yawned as if the whole scene had been a bore to him. The older patient returned to his seat.

Whether he continued to stare at Tessa, she didn't know. After only a few minutes, she lost herself in her puzzle again, the feelings of tranquility soon returning.

"Two little Indians fooling with a gun," she muttered softly. "One shot the other and then there was one."

CHAPTER 13

Sam stood at the reception desk for the psychiatric department, a fiberglass partition separating her from some prim and proper Barbie doll with the personality of a sock, who calmly told Sam exactly what she did not want to hear. "I'm sorry, Detective, but we can't give out any information about our patients."

A flush crept up her face, and Sam had to pause before she responded. She'd had about all she could stomach of bureaucracy and red tape—the Feds kept their secrets while she and Michael were hung out to dry—having gotten little more out of Frank. The FBI was investigating the hospital for experimental, possibly illegal and even unconscionable, treatment methods, unexplained disappearances, and suspicious deaths, as well as possible ties to Carter Wainwright and the so-called Four Pi. They had a man undercover inside the hospital, but beyond that, Frank remained tight-lipped.

She scowled at him as he stood beside her, eyes downcast and hands stuffed in his pockets. The FBI agent was hiding more than he was sharing, and even that didn't seem to check out. As far as Sam could tell, Brentworth was a state-funded facility being investigated for criminal activity under *her* jurisdiction, unless the hospital's acceptance of federal grants or some other bullcrap she didn't really understand brought them under the FBI's radar. Even so, the FBI never sent just one or two guys to investigate an operation of this size. Where were the surveillance vehicles, geek squads, posted operatives, and endless parade of black suits with earpieces?

No, Frank was working something off the books and on his own. And he didn't trust Sam enough to bring her all the way in on it.

She took a breath, reached into her coat's inner pocket, and withdrew a sheet of paper. Unfolding it, she palmed it against the partition. "I understand your policy and have received the proper consent." Her frustration began to subside. She had everything she needed. Cooler heads would surely prevail. "Harlan Bowes has granted us full access to his records."

The receptionist's Botoxed lips parted, and she stared blankly as if she'd disappeared into some inner happy place. After a moment, she blinked, tilted her head, then smiled. In a pacifying voice bordering on condescending, she said, "Let me call his doctor."

Sam sighed as the receptionist picked up her phone, dialed an extension, and explained to whoever had answered that two detectives were badgering her for Bowes's medical records. As she hung up the phone, the corners of her mouth twitched. "The doctor will be out to speak with you in a moment. Please, have a seat."

Sam suppressed a smile. Bowes's medical records were only half the reason for her visit. Speaking with his doctor was the other half. She turned to face the reception area. Over a dismal green rug, chairs lined the walls of a sadly empty room. A monitor propped in a corner was tuned to the news, the sound off but closed captioning appearing on the screen in a broken form that couldn't keep up with the actual dialogue. Not that anyone was there to read it.

Sam's anger lessened as she collapsed into a seat, thinking how sad and lonely it must have been to be inside a place like Brentworth—visitor-less, friendless, hopeless. Frank sat two chairs away from her and kept his mouth shut, apparently content to let her run her investigation. *So long as it furthers his.*

They passed the time in silence, except for the *tick tick tick* of a plastic clock on the wall. Finally, when Sam had had just about all she could take of waiting, a buzz sounded. The door to the inner sanctum opened, and an elegant brunette wearing a white lab coat with the confidence of a lioness prowled through the doorway as if on the hunt. She was beautiful in a statuesque sort of way—hard, cold, and chiseled with seemingly perfect symmetry. Just over six feet tall in a modest heel, she wore a loose-fitting gray tunic under her coat that failed to hide her muscular frame. With every movement, the fabric of her shirt and slacks clung to her thick biceps and developed thighs as if they were spandex. The doctor clearly adhered to a strict diet and cardio and weight training regimen that put Sam to shame. She couldn't deny the twinge of jealousy in her gut between the fluttering butterflies.

Frank bit off a hangnail, stood, then put his hands on his hips. He appeared ready to discuss business, neither attracted nor intimidated.

The doctor extended her hand. "Hello, detectives. My name is Mira Horvat, staff psychiatrist. To what do I owe the pleasure of your visit?"

While the doctor's English was clear, it came with a slight accent that Sam couldn't quite place. The word "visit" almost sounded as if it had begun with a W. Perhaps it was Ukrainian or Croatian, but Sam wasn't up enough on her Eastern European dialects to know. Still, it gave Dr. Horvat a greater air of mystery to add to her beauty, and the sharpness in her eyes suggested a great mind behind them.

"Dr. Horvat." Sam shook the doctor's hand. "I'm Detective Samantha Reilly, and this is—" She paused but only for a split second. "—my partner, Detective Fred Spinner."

Frank smiled and shook Dr. Horvat's hand without missing a beat. "Nice to meet you, Doctor."

Dr. Horvat knitted her brow. "I understand you have a consent form for Harlan Bowes's medical records. May I see it? And may I also ask why you wish to see his records?"

"I'm sorry, Doctor, but we can't disclose details of an ongoing investigation." Sam handed over the document, confident it would produce what she needed. The signature was legit, and everything about the document was one hundred percent genuine. So, as Dr. Horvat took her time reading each line, Sam swallowed her impatience as best she could. The longer the doctor took with it, the more Sam thought she was about to hit a roadblock.

"Hmmm..." The doctor turned the paper over, though nothing was written on the back.

"Is there a problem, Doctor?"

Dr. Horvat smiled softly, her proud lioness features shifting to innocent doe as if by the flip of a switch. "I'm sorry, Detectives, but I'm afraid I cannot provide you those records based on this. You'll need a subpoena and a court order to enforce it."

Sam's jaw dropped. "I don't understand. Bowes has every right to his medical records and to grant that right to anyone he wants. Surely you're well aware of that."

The doctor's placating smile didn't waver. "Normally, I'd agree with you, Detective. But I saw Mr. Bowes last night in your custody and tried to get him released into my care as a matter of fact. He was clearly in no condition to consent to anything. Though the officers wouldn't tell me what he was arrested for, it was abundantly clear that he was not in a rational or sane state of mind and can't be held responsible for his actions. He should be here, at Brentworth, where we can attend to his psychological needs."

"Oh, that's a load of bull—"

Frank held up a hand. "Can you tell us when he checked in here?"

Dr. Horvat puckered her lips and glanced at the ceiling. "I don't see any harm in that. About three months ago."

"Thank you," Frank said, matching her smile with one of his own. Apparently, he was of a mind that honey caught more flies than crap. At least he'd gotten something out of the doctor, albeit something they already knew. Detective Spinner was locking her into a story. "Did he stay long?"

"No." Dr. Horvat frowned and scratched her chin. "And we were making so much progress so very quickly. My methods are... perhaps more progressive than most. What's the expression? Like going cold turkey? You know, instead of gradual steps."

She shrugged. "Anyway, I guess he felt he'd healed enough. We had no reason to commit him since he came in voluntarily and wasn't a danger to anyone or himself."

Sam stepped closer to Dr. Horvat. "Not a danger..." Sam shook her head and chuckled, then raised her palms. "Not a danger? That man tried to kill me yesterday!"

Frank touched her shoulder, but she shrugged away from his hand. "And you know something? Bowes thinks he was here yesterday." She ground her teeth. "Something not right is going on here, and I will get to the bottom of it. Mark my words. If you have no part in it, it would probably be in your best interests to show us a bit more cooperation."

Dr. Horvat didn't so much as flinch, though her smile vanished. In its stead was a consistent look of indifference. "His attack on you is all the more reason why Mr. Bowes should be released into my care. As I said, when he came, it was voluntarily, and he left equally on his own volition. We could do little more than recommend he stay for additional treatment, but if he's done as you claim, I feel he should be committed." She handed the consent form back to Sam. "Now, I believe I've already said more than I should. If you'll excuse me, I have—"

The entrance doors exploded open. Sam spun around, hand instinctively going for the gun at her hip, every muscle in her body tensing and ready to draw. When she saw two uniforms, she stood a little straighter, hand still by her side but fingers no longer flexing. The male officer looked familiar and carried someone in his arms.

"Tag?" Sam scrutinized the officer in a split-second, her mind taking in every detail. Officer Tagliamonte had been assigned to watch over her foster son. Her stomach dropped when she saw who was in his arms. "Michael!"

Tag gently laid the boy on the floor. "We need a doctor."

"What happened?" Sam crouched beside the unconscious teenager, taking Michael's gloved hand in hers.

Tag looked her in the eyes. A rookie at the time, the officer had been one of the first responders to the murder-suicide scene where Michael had been found. His father, Mark Florentine, had killed his wife, her lover, then himself, and an infant Michael had been found rocking against a wall with a gun between his legs, blood on his naked thighs. Tag was also one of the few people Sam trusted with Michael's condition and how it could be triggered.

Tag gave her a knowing nod. "Alison—Officer Paltrow—touched his neck."

"Step back," Dr. Horvat commanded with such absolute authority that Sam rose and backed away before she even knew what she was doing. The doctor put two fingers against Michael's neck as Sam reached out to stop her. She pulled back when she saw no reaction from Michael. Her son remained unconscious, not delving into another seizure.

"His pulse is elevated but not dangerously so." The doctor stood and crossed her arms. "Would someone like to tell me the nature of this boy's condition so that I might properly assist?"

Tag opened his mouth to speak, but Sam jumped in before he could. "He's my... he's family. He's prone to seizures. He must have forgotten to take his medication." She renewed her position by Michael's side, scooped him into her arms, then sat him up.

His eyelids began to flutter. He smacked his lips. "Where... where am I?" His eyes exploded open, and he scuttled back from Officer Paltrow. "You! Where am I? Where's Dylan?"

"It's okay, Michael," Sam said low. "You had a seizure."

"You don't understand." His face pale, he stared pleadingly at Sam. "They're out there—those Indians—and Dylan's still out there too. He's not safe."

"What's he saying?" Frank squatted beside them. "Out where, Michael? The hospital?" He fingered the holster on his belt.

Sam glowered at him. "He just had a nightmare, Frank." Her words came out in a low hiss. "We'll talk about it more when we get him home."

"No," Michael blurted. "We have to help Dylan." He placed his palm against the floor to push himself up then cried out in pain and slumped.

Sam took his hand in hers and turned it palm up. The glove was in tatters, and the flesh beneath it was raw and red. She glared at the officers who were supposed to have been protecting her boy.

"That wasn't from us," Paltrow said weakly.

Sam returned her attention to her boy. "Who's Dylan, Michael?"

"A friend... a friend from school."

"He's been hanging out with a classmate after school these last two days." Tag pressed his lips together. "They like to try to ditch us, and today, they almost succeeded. We didn't see anyone else out there, though."

"Michael, what's your friend's last name?"

"Jefferson. His father works here, actually."

"Find him," Sam snapped. "And call in for backup. That boy could be in trouble. Check with his father here, his home—you know the drill. And Tag, call me as soon as you know something."

Tag and Paltrow exchanged a look then turned on their heels and left.

"Is someone going to tell me what's going on?" Dr. Horvat tapped her foot, her arms crossed. "This boy may need medical attention." She sniffed the air. "Though from the look and smell of it, I'd say it's pretty clear what we're dealing with here."

"Oh yeah, Doctor?" Sam rose. "What's that?"

"Bloodshot eyes, the distinct odor of marijuana—I'd say this boy was smoking and perhaps was overcome by a touch of paranoia." She chuckled. "Quite common for a boy his age, particularly now that it's legal."

"Not legal for him," Sam said. She squinted down at Michael, and the overpowering, skunky aroma finally hit her. Worry dissipated into disappointment. She helped Michael to his feet. "I'll take him home, doctor. We know what this is and have it under control."

She sighed, softening a little. "All right, at least let me get someone to clean and dress those wounds on his hands. Come on back." She smiled warmly at Michael. "We'll get you all patched up."

Sam nodded but held Michael by the arm. "Send someone out to look at it right here."

"That's not really how we do things here, Detective."

Sam rubbed her temples. "*Just...* send someone out, please."

"Very well." She again smiled at Michael then, almost flirtatiously. "It was nice meeting you, Michael. Detectives."

She bowed slightly then turned and walked toward the doors leading farther into the hospital. After the receptionist buzzed her in, the doctor disappeared through them.

Sam led Michael to the chairs, and she and Frank each took a seat beside him. With her eyes, she signaled a camera mounted in the corner. "We'll talk about it on the way home," she said with a hand over her mouth. The three sat in silence as they awaited Michael's medical attention. Twenty minutes later, a nurse with nylon gloves cleaned and dressed Michael's hand.

"WHAT WERE YOU THINKING?" Sam slammed her palm against the steering wheel and glared at Michael through her rearview mirror. With the three of them safely on the road, all her worry and stress and love for him came boiling to the surface. And it came out all wrong, pride and disappointment getting in the way when all she wanted to do was hold him tightly. "Why in the hell would you ditch your protective detail? To smoke weed? Of all the stupid, stupid things—"

"I'm sorry, okay?" Michael sulked. He crossed his arms and averted his gaze from the mirror. Then, much lower but not quite under his breath, "It's not like I asked for them."

She'd only been trying to protect him. *How dare he treat me like I'm the bad guy?* Her hackles up, she knew she was heading toward making a bad situation worse but couldn't stop herself. "They were there to protect you, and for good reason, it seems. I thought you were smarter than this."

"I wouldn't need protection if I wasn't living with you."

Sam gritted her teeth and was about to bite when the sting of his words pierced her. Brow furrowing, she let out a breath, her eyes starting to tear up until she remembered Frank sitting beside her. She sniffled and wiped her nose with the back of her hand. "We'll talk about it later. For now, tell me about the Indians."

Frank shifted in his seat. If he'd been pretending not to listen, he wasn't pretending any longer.

"I'm sorry." Michael slouched. "I didn't mean it like it sounded. It's just, why does everyone else get to have normal, fun lives, but I've gotta have these stupid visions and people trying to use me or kill me all the time?"

"Michael, I—"

"It doesn't matter. I know it's not your fault or your problem."

"Your problems are my—"

"Anyway," Michael cut her off and scooted forward, "shouldn't you be focusing on finding Dylan?" He stared at her reflection in the rearview, hurt and anger in his eyes. "They could have him right now. Don't you care?"

"Of course, I care!" Sam growled, then bit her tongue. "Officers Tagliamonte and Paltrow—and probably the whole freaking department—are looking for him as we speak. If he's still at Brentworth, they'll find him and report."

She didn't know if that were true, but she would check in on their status as soon as she got Michael home safely. Tag wouldn't let her down. She tried her damnedest to make her voice even and asked, "Could you tell me what you were doing at Brentworth with your friend?"

"Just hanging out."

"Smoking weed?" Again, Sam couldn't help herself despite the little voice in her head telling her to go easy on him.

"Yeah. I wanted to try it. So I did. Is that so terrible?" He gave her a smug grin. "Can't be any worse than bringing a minor to the house of a murderer."

Her face flushed with warmth, this time from shame rather than anger. "Please, Michael."

Frank shifted in his seat again. He cleared his throat. "May I suggest—"

"No!" Michael and Sam said in unison.

Chided, Frank folded his hands on his lap and faced forward.

Sam considered what to say. Michael had hit below the belt. Though Jonathan Crowley hadn't technically murdered anyone—his ex had been tied up in his basement, still breathing when they'd found her—Sam had still used Michael's unique gift to help her solve a crime. She'd put him at risk and had broken a long list of ethics regulations in order to put a bad man away. She'd been a different person then, willing to take down criminals at any cost—before she'd realized that Michael meant more than the job.

She squeezed the steering wheel until her knuckles turned white. "Just tell us what happened."

Michael sighed. "You know what happened. We ditched the cops you had following me and went into the woods behind the hospital. I know it was stupid, but Dylan has a really cool hangout spot back there. And yeah, we smoked a joint, but we didn't go back there for that. We just went to hang out. You know, do kid things, which is kinda hard to do when your only friend is an adult *and* a detective." Michael choked up on those last few words.

A lump formed in Sam's throat. Whatever anger she'd felt had drained from her like water down a sink.

Frank turned in his seat. "Inside Brentworth, you mentioned seeing someone out there, that it wasn't safe. What did you see?"

Sam sneered at Frank, but Michael sat up straighter. "Indians. Well, not real ones. Dylan had binoculars, and I was looking through them at Brentworth when I saw—or at least I *thought* I saw—three or four people wearing those same stupid masks the guy who attacked Sam had on. They were there one second, gone the next."

Sam caught Frank's grave look and knew he was hanging on to Michael's every word. Whatever had happened out there, he certainly believed Michael. His conviction brought home the danger even more so for her.

"Anyway," Michael continued, "Dylan said it might have been the weed making me paranoid—he never saw them. But I was scared, and we ran back toward the hospital. I twisted my ankle, and Dylan carried me, like, the whole way. That's when Officer Paltrow grabbed me by my neck. I don't remember anything after that except my vision and waking up with you two hovering over me inside Brentworth."

"You ran back to the hospital, *toward* the people you saw?" Frank asked.

"Yeah, I know." Michael shrugged. "It doesn't make much sense, but it was getting dark, and we were afraid if we ran any other way, we might get lost. So we took our chances with the hospital. Dylan's father works there and could've helped us once we got inside."

Michael stared at the floor and sighed. "The more I think about it, though, the crazier it sounds. One guy attacked you, and I saw—or maybe I *imagined*—at least three of them. Like I said, Dylan never saw them. Maybe the pot went to my head like he and that doctor said."

Sam's jaw tightened, but she didn't say anything. Marijuana did tend to make some users paranoid, but hallucinations didn't seem likely unless that Dylan kid's joint was laced with something. But Michael seemed lucid enough, if a bit tired. Still, she didn't want to worry him by sharing where her mind was wandering. More than one masked moron was not a comforting thought.

Bowes's chant played through her head. *Ten little Indians standing in a line. One toddled home and then there were nine.*

Frank tugged on his seatbelt, loosening it so he could turn around and face Michael. "So you didn't see any more of those people in masks on your way back?"

"No." Michael leaned forward between the seats. "Well, yeah, actually, but that was in my vision."

Frank raised an eyebrow. Sam glanced over at him to try and get a read. He'd never commented on whether he believed in Michael's ability or not, never so much as brought up the subject. He opened his mouth to speak, but Sam jumped in, afraid she might not want to know his thoughts on the topic. "What did you see, Michael?"

Michael shuddered. "It was awful. Officer Paltrow's head just exploded." He tapped Sam's shoulder. "You have to warn her, Sam. I don't have much to go on, but I know there's at least one Indian guy out there. He shot her like really close range, blew her freakin' head off. I'm sorry I went nuts when I saw her."

"Can you tell us anything about the shooter?" Sam asked, her attention constantly shifting between Michael and the road.

"Not really, no. Just that he was wearing one of those stupid masks."

"Was he fat or thin, tall or short?" Frank asked. "Were his hands white or black? Any tattoos that you could see? Any other features that stood out?"

"No, nothing like that." Michael slouched back in his seat. "Dark hair, I think... maybe. I'm sorry. It was dark outside, nighttime I think, with lots of trees, but I couldn't tell where and it was like I was standing right next to her when it happened. All I could make out were the mask and her face, like my screwed up mind wanted to see it all happen up close and personal, way zoomed in." He took a deep breath. "I couldn't even say for sure if the shooter was a man or a woman. Officer Paltrow... she never even saw it coming." He buried his face in his hands, which reminded Sam of his injury.

"What happened to your hand?"

"Oh," Michael collected himself. "That was just me being stupid. Unrelated."

Sam sensed there was a lot more to that story than she probably wanted to know but let it slide. "Okay," she said softly. "That's enough for now, Michael."

They rode the rest of the way back to the precinct in silence. The more Sam tightened her muscles to try and prevent her shaking, the more she shook. Her gut told her that Michael hadn't imagined anything. There was more to the hospital, those masked Indians, the stonewalling Dr. Horvat, and maybe to Michael's new friend than she could determine from the facts she then knew. She chewed on her thumbnail, lost in thought and not snapping out of it until she found herself pulling up beside Frank's car.

Frank forced a smile and opened his door. Before closing it, he said, "We'll pick this up tomorrow?"

"Sure."

A pained expression came over him, and he leaned in closer. "Hey, is everything all right? I mean, between us?"

Sam nodded once and pulled her ravaged nail out from between her teeth. The skin around it was bleeding.

Frank pulled away, looking unconvinced. "See you, Michael." He waved.

Michael grunted, then got out and took Frank's seat. He closed the door behind him then dropped the seat back as far as it would go.

WHEN THEY GOT HOME, Michael plodded up the stairs to their apartment like a zombie. Once inside, he turned to Sam with heavy eyelids. "I'm zonked out. From the weed—or the vision. Probably both." He sighed heavily. "I think I'm just going to go to bed if that's cool. But wake me if you hear anything about Dylan. I'm really worried about him."

"Of course." Now it was Sam's turn to force a smile. "I'll see you in the morning."

He turned and shuffled toward his bedroom. Within a few minutes, she could hear him snoring. She doubted he'd done any of his homework and would probably have him take a sick day in the morning. Standing at her kitchen counter, she brewed herself a pot of coffee, then sat down at the table to be alone with her thoughts.

A knock came at her door, and she snapped out of a daydream. She looked at her watch and couldn't believe it was already nine thirty. She ran her fingers down her face, trying to wipe the tired away. *How long have I been sitting here?*

Her gun still at her hip, as comfortable there as if it were an extension of her body, Sam crept to the door and peeked through the peephole. Tag, still in uniform, stood outside. She relaxed and undid the chain lock, unlocked the deadbolt, then opened the door.

"Officer Tagliamonte," Sam said, amused by her over-formality. She sized up the clean-cut, tightly built, and decade-younger officer she'd always found physically appetizing. "What brings you to my humble abode at this late hour?" She was trying to be funny with the archaic phrasing but only felt silly when Tag didn't so much as crack a smile.

He took off his hat, his thick dark hair pluming in its freedom. "I just got off duty." He fidgeted with his hat in his hands. "May I come in?"

Sam stepped back and waved him in. "You want some coffee? Beer?" Tag stepped into the apartment, and she closed the door behind him.

"I'm good, thanks." He walked over to the kitchen table and put his hat down on it then turned to face Sam as she stepped closer. "I just wanted to apologize for today. I know how much that kid means to you, and I feel really bad that I let you down. I have a kid sister—I mean, she's twenty-four now, but I practically raised her—and if anything were to happen to her, I'd..." His chin quivered, and he looked away to hide the powerful emotions that had come over him. It was an endearing side of the officer Sam had never seen before.

Tag cleared his throat. "Well, let's just say I know the lengths someone might go to protect the ones they love. If anything happened to Michael on my watch, I'm not so sure I could live with myself."

"He'll be all right." Sam crossed her arms but the wall she put up started to crack. She had no idea Tag felt that strongly about Michael or... *about me?* "Don't worry about it. Really. He told me he was trying to ditch you. With that other kid. Did you find him?"

Tag seemed to appreciate the change in subject. He sucked in a breath and became the same sturdy officer she could always rely on, though a hint of something—*Grief? Worry?*—remained behind his eyes. "Yeah, he's fine. When he saw us, he didn't know what to do, so he hid and went inside the hospital when the coast was clear. His father works there. We've looked into the boy and his father. Everything checks out. He said he was sorry he bailed on Michael. Sounded like he meant it."

"Good." Sam sighed and stood beside him at the table, resting her fingers on its surface. "Thanks."

She considered waking Michael to tell him the news, but the rhythmic rumble coming from his room made her think better of it. She frowned. "I'm happy to see him making a new friend, but... ditching you guys and smoking weed? That isn't like him at all."

Tag chuckled. "I bet you smoked pot before you were his age."

Sam snorted. "Jesus! If he did half the shit I did before I was his age, I wouldn't be able to handle him." She smiled. "He's such a good kid."

"Maybe you should go easy on him?" Tag reached for his hat. "And hopefully me too."

His finger brushed against hers, just the slightest touch, but it sent a pulse through her body, a spark that ignited a fire. All her stress, all her bottled-up frustration, demanded right then for a release. She slapped his hat out of his hand, drove him against the counter, and pressed her lips tightly against his.

He threw his arms up, not resisting exactly, but not immediately accepting either. He started to say something, but Sam cut off any protests with her tongue. And when she felt his hand on the nape of her neck, pulling her closer, his tongue flitting with hers, she moaned. Chest to chest, she could feel the warmth of his body, the excitement in his touch, and his heartbeat quickening. She knew she was wanted. A finger over her lips, she led him to her bedroom.

AFTERWARD, THEY LAY sweating on opposite sides of Sam's bed. Her body was warm and tingled all over, but some of the tension in her muscles had eased. And she felt young. As fit as Tag was, and she did enjoy the sight of him, it was he who'd had the harder time keeping up.

She took a deep breath. Tag was fun, but their intimacy had to be a one-time deal. Although she wasn't in his direct chain of command, he was still a subordinate. Such relationships were frowned upon, if not outright prohibited. She glanced sideways at him, his goofy grin reminding her just how young he was compared to her. For a second, she thought of Frank, as though she'd somehow betrayed him. But she dismissed the thought easily. She'd needed it, had enjoyed it, and she wouldn't regret it.

"I guess this means you forgive me?" Tag said coyly, adding to the boyishness she already sensed from him.

She fixed him with a hard stare. "It goes without saying that this stays between us."

"Of cour—"

"*And* that this was one night only."

He grimaced. "If that's the way you want it. But I like you, Sam. I've always liked you. And I think, deep down, you've always known that, or else tonight wouldn't have gone down the way it did."

She rolled her eyes. "Let's not make a thing out of it, make anything awkward. Let's say it was just sex." Then, to placate his ego, she added, "Good sex."

He turned to face her, propping himself up on his elbow, his strong arms gleaming in the moonlight. A twinkle came to his eyes, a wry smile to his mouth. "All the more reason to do it again sometime."

Sam pursed her lips. She couldn't argue with that logic. "Maybe. But for now, you should go. I don't want you to be here when Michael gets up."

Tag begrudgingly rose out of the bed then shuffled around the room to pick up his scattered clothes. Sam drew the sheet over her naked form and watched him dress. As he pulled on his pants, he reached into them and took out her underwear that had somehow ended up inside them during their athletics. He tossed them to her.

As she put them on under the sheet, she re-erected her wall. "Lock up behind you."

Fully dressed though a wrinkled mess, Tag opened the bedroom door to leave but stopped when Sam called to him. "His father... what does he do for Brentworth?"

Tag shook his head. "Always the detective, huh? He's on the board or an administrator or some shit. Pretty high up. I can find out more if you'd like."

"Yes, do. And Tag?"

"Yes?"

"What's his last name again?"

CHAPTER 14

Something wasn't right with Tessa.

Unable to sleep, Jimmy paced his room, his mind repeating how she'd treated him that afternoon. *She didn't even know me.*

He had to admit, he'd found her suspicions a little far-fetched. Then Link came looking for her in his room. *He might have been looking for her because she wasn't where she was supposed to be.*

He shook his head, frustrated that he couldn't see the whole picture. Whether he was dealing with some wicked conspiracy or the delusions of a poor, troubled girl, he couldn't decide. Yeah, Link had appeared menacing, but with looks that had earned him the nickname "Missing Link," how could he seem anything but?

Then there was the Bandage Man. Jimmy rubbed his shoulder, still sore from where the mummified patient had grabbed him, his skin bruised in the shape of fingertips. What had he said? *Stay away from the girl, or you'll be next.*

Next for what? Despite her strange memory lapse, Tessa had seemed much happier. Maybe her treatment had some side effects, but if it helped her feel better, to manage that place, then he supposed it was all for the greater good. A fleeting pain, spawned by a sudden but powerful flash of selfishness, stung his heart and caused his breath to hitch. He wished she'd remembered their short but meaningful night together.

She's sick, Jimmy. He sighed. *Probably delusional. Heck, maybe it's all the meds they're pumping into us.* His thoughts seemed logical, but the Bandage Man's threat, that had been real. And so he circled back to something not being right with Tessa. *They* had gotten her and had done something to her. And if that mummified douchebag was to be taken seriously, Jimmy had to play it cool or he might be next.

He paused, a moment of clarity breaking through all his doubt like rays of sunlight parting the clouds. It didn't matter whether Tessa was delusional or not. He had promised to help her. And Jimmy had every intention of keeping that promise. If he could just get to her room, talk to her, and try to get a feel for how much *they* had tampered with her.

He took a deep breath and approached the door, listening for sounds outside it. Hearing nothing, he opened it and stepped into the hallway. The dim lighting cast shadows where none should have been. The pungent smell of disinfectant, perhaps masking the underlying stink of unwashed bodies, made his nostrils tingle. Yet, he saw no one and heard nothing.

Just a quiet night in the loony bin. He relaxed a little, thinking he would use the excuse that he couldn't sleep if someone caught him wandering. As he walked down the hall, his feet would now and then stick to the stained carpet and pull away with a slight pop. He wasn't sure which room was Tessa's but knew the general direction, hoping he'd guess right when he knocked.

As he made it to the corner, he peeked around it. An arm clamped around his neck, another under his arm. He couldn't breathe, couldn't scream out for help as his assailant dragged him backward. Kicking his feet and throwing out elbows, he tried to shake free of his attacker. He hadn't even heard the person behind him. Jimmy had let his guard down, oblivious to the man's approach. *Am I going to die?* He struggled harder. Wheezing, he was losing air fast. His blows lost their strength.

His foe turned, backed them onto the hard wooden floor of the nearest room. There, he tossed Jimmy onto the bed, closed the door, and turned to face him.

The Bandage Man.

"I'll kill you," Jimmy snapped, his face filling with the warm gush of rage. Panting, he hopped onto his feet and raised his fists. He'd be damned if he was going to let some sick pedophile have his way with him without fighting to his last breath.

"Easy." The Bandage Man held out his hands.

"Fuck you." Jimmy charged at the man, swinging wildly and missing with his first punch. The second connected with the Bandage Man's ribs, who grunted but swayed with the blow, hooking his arm around Jimmy's. He tugged on the pinned arm, pulling Jimmy closer, then hooked around his other arm.

Jimmy tried a headbutt, but could only connect with the taller man's chest. His upper body useless, he did the only move left he could think of—he rammed his knee as hard as he could into his enemy's balls.

The Bandage Man groaned and collapsed onto his knees. Jimmy seized the opportunity and ran around him to the door. The Bandage Man grabbed Jimmy's pajama leg, but his grip was weak. Jimmy easily pulled free after landing a right hook to the man's face. The bandages shifted, revealing a patch of purple skin beneath.

"Wait," The Bandage Man croaked as Jimmy headed for the door.

The doorknob twisted in Jimmy's hand. He only needed to open it, and he would be free.

"I'm FBI."

CHAPTER 15

Home sick on his third day of school. A masked man shooting at Sam. More of them possibly assembling behind Brentworth. *We should have stayed on vacation.*

Michael stood at the threshold of Sam's room, tracing circles in the doorframe as he thought about some of the horrible things he had said to her last night. Sam's job came with certain baggage, but he couldn't believe he would have been better off had she not plucked him from that crime scene that he was thankfully too young to remember. She'd been someone constant, and eventually, someone more. She'd even given a home. He'd seen what had become of another with his gift, what he himself would have probably become had not Sam been in his life. And he had treated her as if she were the cause of all his problems.

And now, he was wishing Sam were home, if only to tell her that he was sorry. She'd already gone to work for the day. She'd needed to check something out and had warned him to stay inside with the door locked and bolted, to let no one in except her. As if their flimsy plywood door would make him feel safe. At least she'd told him Dylan was okay.

He stepped over dirty clothes and past the unmade bed to a window partly covered in grime. Looking out, he saw the patrol car right where it was supposed to be. From two stories up and forty yards away, he couldn't recognize the officer in the driver's seat sipping hot coffee out of a Styrofoam cup. He waved, but the officer wasn't looking his way.

Still in his boxers and the wrinkled T-shirt he'd slept in, he went back to his room and threw on a pair of jeans and ankle socks. He didn't bother putting on his gloves, gearing up for a boring weekday alone with Netflix.

He sighed and plopped down on the couch with a massive bowl of chocolate cereal. His feet up on the coffee table, he reached for the remote, scrolled through his recommendations—mostly true crime documentaries based on Sam's inability to distinguish between their profiles—then settled on an anime. *Let the binge-watching begin.*

About midway through the seventh episode, a knock at his door made Michael jump. The empty bowl tumbled from his lap onto the carpet. Slowly, he pulled his feet off the coffee table and placed them silently on the floor. Hitting the pause button on the remote, he listened for sounds outside his apartment.

The knock came again.

"Yeah?"

A muffled but familiar voice came through the door. "Hey, Badass. It's me. Just wanted to make sure you were okay."

"Dylan?" Michael got up and walked to the door. He looked through the peephole and saw Dylan picking at his braces with his tongue. Something black was stuck in the top row.

Michael unlocked and opened the door. "What the heck are you doing here?" He leaned over the threshold and checked the stairwell. Seeing no one else, he crossed his arms and scrutinized his friend. "Where'd you go last night?"

"Man, you ran right into those cops before I could stop you. And as you may recall, we'd been smoking. No sense in both of us getting caught."

"So..." Michael's eyebrows pinched together. "You bailed on me."

"You were on a sinking ship, Captain Ahab."

"Who?"

"Wow, you really aren't reading it, are you?" Dylan chuckled. "Ms. Alvarez will not be happy."

Dylan shuffled his feet, trying to peek around Michael and into the apartment. "Well, aren't you going to invite me in?"

"What are you doing here?" Michael kept his arms crossed and leaned on the doorframe, blocking entry. "Why aren't you in school?"

"Same reason as you, I'm guessing. I didn't exactly get to my homework." He fake coughed into his hand. "Called in sick. Heck of a cold going around."

"A twenty-four-hour one?"

"You know it. Anyway, I just wanted to make sure you were all right. I thought I'd check in on you—actually, it was my dad's idea, if I'm being honest. I told him about what happened when that lady cop touched you, and he suggested it. I guess that's what friends do, huh?" He shrugged and offered a grimacing smile. "Anyway, if I'm bothering you, I'll just..." He turned to leave.

Michael let his arms fall to his sides. "No. It's cool. Come on in."

"You sure?" Dylan raised an eyebrow. "I don't want to get you in trouble or anything."

Michael stepped out of the way and ushered Dylan in, then he closed and locked the door behind him.

"Sam was pretty pissed." He walked around Dylan and plopped back down on the couch. "I mean, we were pretty stupid."

"Yeah, I know." Dylan sat beside him. "My dad was furious. I thought he was going to hit me. Anyway, I'm really sorry."

"Not your fault." Michael raised his thumbs to his cheeks. "This badass gets into trouble all by himself."

"So we're cool?"

"Yeah, we're cool."

Dylan let out a breath so melodramatically that he sounded as if he were deflating. He pointed at the TV. "What were you watching?"

"Some cartoon."

"Any good?"

"Pretty stupid, but amusing. Lots of swears and bad voice-overs."

"I like swears. Not sure about the dubbing. Play it."

Michael gave Dylan a sideways glance, having yet to hear so much as a "shit" or "damn" out of his prim and proper friend, never mind the dreaded F-bomb. But Dylan didn't notice, instead leaning forward on his elbows and watching the TV intently even though it remained paused.

Michael hit play, and the low-brow comedy continued. It soon had them both laughing, distracting Michael from the nagging thought forming in the back of his mind. The episode ended, and the silence allowed him time to think.

"Hey, Dylan?"

"What's up?"

"How'd you know where I live?"

Dylan laughed. "Opposite direction of Brentworth, remember? It was easy to find it. Just look for the place with the cop car out front."

"I could have been on the first floor."

"Yeah, you could have, but no one answered when I knocked down there."

"How about the cops outside?" Michael studied Dylan's face. "How'd you get by them?"

Dylan's smile vanished. He shrugged. "I don't know. I just walked right in. Makes you feel really safe, huh?"

Michael searched Dylan's expression for any sort of tell despite not knowing how to read one if he saw it. When he didn't respond,

Dylan tilted his head and frowned. "I'm not sure I understand all your questions, Mike. You don't think—"

"No!" Michael blurted, his overexuberance likely making him more suspicious. "No. I just—I'm like this magnet when it comes to attracting crazy or dangerous people."

"You sure that's you or the fact that you live with a homicide detective?"

A long creak came from the stairwell—on the same step Sam never asked the landlord to fix for the very reason that it told her someone was coming.

Michael put a finger over his lips. "Shhh." He squinted at Dylan, who'd somehow managed to avoid the creak like he'd known it was there. He shook off the suspicion and focused on the immediate concern, thinking Sam's cynicism was wearing off on him. *He probably just stepped over it.*

As he snuck to the door, he heard another creak. *Two of them? The cops checking in?* Shadows flitted under the door. He grabbed his sneakers and quickly popped them on his feet, the shoelaces tied loosely so he could slide them on and off. Then he peeked through the peephole.

He fell backward onto his butt as something solid swung toward him. The blade of an ax pierced the wood right where his face had been. Whoever held it wrestled it free from the splintering door, only to slam it down with another *whack*. Gasping, Michael leapt to his feet, catching a glimpse of a cigar-store Indian mask through the newly made gaps in the door. He turned to Dylan, who was already on his feet, backing away from the door.

"What do we do?" Dylan asked.

Heart racing, Michael fought to stay calm enough to think. "Fire escape! Through the middle bedroom!" The boys sprinted across the living room, Michael plowing through the cracked-open door of the unclaimed room. He skidded to a halt. A woman in a loose lumberjack shirt and baggy jeans stared in at him, a crowbar in hand and that same stupid mask on her face.

"You see them, right?" Michael shouted. "I'm not just losing it?"

"Of course I see them!" Dylan shouted, grabbing Michael's sleeve and pulling him out of the room. "We need to get out of here!"

Glass shattered behind them. Dylan dragged Michael into his bedroom. He ran to the window. "I don't see anyone." Another *thud* and a loud *crack* came from the front door. "We have to jump!" Dylan struggled to open the window, but it wouldn't budge.

"The locks!" Michael ran up beside him and flipped two levers atop the lower window. Together, they raised it as high as it would go.

"Climb out, hang, and let yourself drop," Dylan said. "It's not far. We should be fine."

"Maybe you should go fir—"

"Go!"

Michael ducked under the raised window and straddled the sill. As he brought his other leg out, his lower half dangled over the ledge. His stomach pressed hard against the frame, making his already fluttering gut roil. Slowly, he slid a little farther back, the sharp pain rising to his ribs.

His feet dangling below him, toes scraping against the side of the house, Michael froze. "I don't think I can do it."

Dylan smiled, but his wide eyes told another story. "Sure you can, Mike. You're a badass."

A masked man wielding an ax and wearing a police uniform appeared at the room's entrance.

"Behind you!" Michael gasped before slipping. He fell then hit the ground feetfirst, jarring his already sprained ankle as he toppled onto his butt. Ignoring the pain, he scrambled to his feet, looking up in time to see Dylan swinging his leg over the window sill. On the fire escape, the woman with the crowbar was staring down at him. She ran for the ladder.

"Run!" Dylan yelled. He tried to say more, but a hand covered his mouth as he was dragged back into the apartment.

Michael hesitated, wanting to help his friend but helpless to do so. This momentary lapse was all the time the woman with the crowbar needed to descend the fire escape. They locked eyes. Michael held his arms out, awaiting her next move.

As she turned her head to the side, dark, matted bangs flopped over her mask, revealing a bald spot with a purple scar that looked like a varicose vein. "Eight little Indians gayest under heaven. One went to sleep, and then there were seven."

"Seven little Indians cutting up their tricks," the man in the cop costume said from the fire escape. He tapped the ax handle against his palm. "One broke his neck, and then there were six."

The woman giggled and charged. Michael ran. Around the front of the apartment complex, he spotted the police car. Even as he raced to it, he knew something was wrong. The officer in the front seat was slumped over the steering wheel. Glass lay shattered on the cement by his door.

Still, he ran toward it. He'd seen Sam use her radio a hundred times. *If I can just get to it...*

Footsteps clomped on the road behind him as he tried to yank the door open. His sweaty fingers slid off the handle. He spun to see a crowbar plummeting toward him, then he dropped into a crouch. The swing was high and wild. It smashed the light on top of the car. Michael rolled forward onto his feet. He took off down the street, his ankle screaming in pain while he did all he could not to listen. As he started to cross the road, a car slammed on its brakes, stopping just in time before it collided with him. The driver yelled some curse words, but Michael pushed off the hood and kept running. When he made it to the other side, a horn blared behind him, followed by a loud thud. He turned to see the woman with the scar hit the ground and roll onto the sidewalk.

With a shaking hand, she removed her mask. Michael stared at his attacker, a young woman with long bangs, bloodshot eyes, and trembling bluish lips.

She looked around then down at herself in confusion. "What happened?" She reached out a hand to the driver of the van that had hit her, a middle-aged man in an electrician's uniform. "Please... help me. I'm hurt."

At the same time, the masked man wearing the police uniform approached his fallen partner. Her eyes pleaded for help. They widened as if realizing her peril when the man lifted his weapon.

"Seven little Indians cutting up their tricks" the man drove his ax down with a sickening squelch— "One broke his neck, and then there were six."

The nearby electrician threw his hands up and tried to back toward his van. As the ax-wielding maniac shifted his attention to him, the man turned to run. Michael watched in horror as an ax came down on the bystander's spine. The car that had almost struck Michael sped away. The ax wielder pulled his blade free and turned to face Michael. His weapon dripping blood, he chanted, "Seven little Indians cutting up their tricks. One broke his neck, and then there were six."

Body racked with fear, Michael ran for his life.

CHAPTER 16

The crowd in the rec room was light. The Bandage Man sat by himself, arms folded over his chest, a perpetual scowl on his face. As instructed, Jimmy tried not to even look in his direction but found himself giving the man an almost imperceptible nod. Almost. Not that there was anyone else around to notice.

Link was absent. Nurse Francine was nowhere to be seen. Not a single staff member was present. But there were cameras, and according to the Bandage Man, *they* were always watching. Jimmy was careful not to look in their direction either.

The bridge club was short a member—a woman in her fifties, the youngest of their ilk—and looked as if they'd opted to play some form of rummy. Dizmo, the guy with multiple personality disorder, and Monica, who was always scribbling away on her sketch pad, were also noticeably missing, and poor Harriet sat at her chessboard, silently waiting for Jordan to arrive.

Of course, Dirty Terry was there, hand down the front of his pants as he read another sleazy romance novel. So was Manny. And Tessa, who sat working through a crossword puzzle. Jimmy might have dismissed the Bandage Man's story as pure lunacy had he not seen Tessa's transformation with his own eyes.

The Bandage Man. Jimmy scoffed. He didn't even know the man's real name. The undercover agent thought it would be better if Jimmy didn't know, to help keep his cover, as if Jimmy was dumb enough to let the name slip. The agent claimed to be investigating a criminal organization akin to the mob but much worse—evil for the sake of evil. He'd been trying to worm his way into the fold but hadn't been enlisted or taken at night like so many others.

Like Tessa.

Nurse Francine and Link were part of it, as was a female doctor who Jimmy had not met. He didn't know who else, but they were recruiting from the patient population. What for, the Bandage Man wouldn't say, though Jimmy got the impression he knew a lot more than he was letting on. He couldn't even explain why the recruits were being taken from prerelease and not the violent and already criminally insane inmates of Ward D.

What does he expect me to do now? Jimmy clenched his jaw and grabbed a magazine from the shelf. *Just sit here and wait for them to take me?* He didn't like that option but could see no others open to him.

So sit and wait he did. He sat down across from Tessa.

The Bandage Man cleared his throat, which Jimmy took as a warning not to go near her. He ignored the man. Federal agent or not, he didn't owe the Bandage Man squat.

Tessa didn't look up from her puzzle, but he felt a curious tingle on his skin as each time she nibbled her cheek, considering the page. A strand of her strawberry-blond hair hung over one of her eyes.

I promised to help you, Tessa. He flexed his fingers. *I remember that, even if you don't.*

Tessa's lips started to move, forming words too soft for Jimmy to hear. He leaned closer.

"Two little Indians fooling with a gun. One shot the other, and then there was one."

"What's that?" Jimmy smiled and rested his arms on the table. "Is that a nursery rhyme or something?"

Tessa looked up and blinked four times as if she'd just awoken from a trance and finally noticed him sitting there. "Huh? What's what?"

"Nothing." He put out his hand. "Hi, I'm—"

"I know who you are." Tessa slapped his hand playfully, none of the distress she'd shown earlier at being touched detectable. "We met yesterday, remember?"

"Oh yeah, yesterday." Jimmy slid back into his seat. "Sorry about that. I was confused."

"You sure were." She tittered and returned to her crossword puzzle, disappearing into it as if she'd forgotten he was sitting in front of her.

After searching for something to say, he blurted, "Do you like it here?"

Tessa beamed as if she'd been waiting for him to ask that very question. "I love it! I can't remember ever feeling this good before." She put down her crayon then grabbed Jimmy's arm, rubbing it with her thumb. "You know, Dr. Horvat has really turned me around. I feel like I'm ready to face the world again. I really hope you get the chance to see what she can do. It's like... magic!" She balled up her fists under her chin and smiled big. Then as if a switch had been flipped, she picked up her crayon and concentrated again on her puzzle.

Nurse Francine came crashing through the double doors, her brow sweaty and her clothes disheveled. She beelined to the table where he and Tessa were sitting. The nurse smoothed out her dress and took deep breaths. "Good morning, Tessa," she said, failing to suppress the edge in her voice. "It's time for your next session with the doctor."

"Oh?" Tessa stood.

"If you'll just follow me." Nurse Francine glowered at Jimmy then forced a smile as ambiguous as the Mona Lisa's.

Tessa waved at Jimmy. "Well, it was nice meeting you... again." She laughed and turned to follow Nurse Francine back out the way she'd come.

Jimmy watched her go, determined to help her but not knowing how. The Bandage Man had told him to be patient, that help would come. But Jimmy didn't know the federal agent and had no reason to trust the man. With the population of the ward apparently dwindling, he didn't know how long he could wait.

With or without the Bandage Man's help, he was getting out of that place. And somehow, someway, he was getting Tessa out with him.

CHAPTER 17

Frank wasn't at her office when Sam arrived that day. She had no messages from him and made no effort to call him. Whatever Frank's game was, he was on his own until he started treating her like an equal. She had her own investigation to run.

Still, she wanted to ask him what he thought about the boy's last name. The man who'd terrorized Fall River all those years ago as Carter Wainwright was born "Darius Jefferson." And lo and behold, a new friend popped up in Michael's life with the same last name after—at least according to Frank—Wainwright had returned to the area. Right or wrong, she was suspicious of anyone befriending Michael, his track record enough cause for concern. Tag had had the presence of mind to take a picture of the kid and had texted it to her that morning. The fair, almost effeminate features of Dylan Jefferson bore no resemblance to Wainwright's original appearance or subsequent transformations, nor did it appear as though the boy had had any work done.

And Jefferson is a common name. Sam didn't know of any personally, but that didn't mean there weren't plenty of Jeffersons out there. In any event, Michael was staying home from school that day. He wouldn't be seeing Dylan Jefferson. She rubbed her temples, thinking for the umpteenth time that perhaps she should be home with him. Sam thought the best thing she could do for Michael was to find their attacker or attackers as soon as possible, and as narcissistic as it might sound, she didn't trust anyone else well enough to leave that solely to them.

She walked out to the bullpen and found Tag sipping coffee with Officer Paltrow. His feet were up on his desk while she batted her lashes at him like some floozy.

Sam frowned. "Who's watching Michael today?"

Tag pulled his feet under him and sat up straight. "Lennox and Dubront. They had the early shift. We're due to replace them this afternoon."

Sam nodded. "Dylan Jefferson—you said his background checks out?"

Officer Paltrow stood. "He spent time in private schools all over the South before moving out of the country. His transcripts from his previous schools were necessary to determine his placement at Carnegie High. They appear legitimate, though I'm admittedly no expert in South American school documents." She chuckled. "And they all coincided with employment records for his father, Walter Jefferson."

Sam glared at her, and Paltrow's smile vanished. She swallowed hard.

"Make some calls. Compile for me the exact addresses for where they lived, went to school, and worked, together with anything else you can find. I want as much detail on the kid and his parents as you can get." She turned to Tag. "You said his father works at the hospital? An administrator?"

"Yes, ma'am."

Sam knew she was being catty, unfair even, and tried to rein it in. She'd never been the possessive or jealous type, but the man she'd slept with the night before calling her "ma'am" was enough to put a sour taste in her mouth, particularly when he was partnered up with a much prettier younger woman. She grimaced. "Well, I'm off to see if I can't meet the man now. If you see Agent Spinney, let him know where I went."

"Will do," Tag said. Officer Paltrow nodded.

Sam turned to leave when she heard Paltrow say softly, "Um, Detective?"

"Yes?"

"People say that... that your boy *sees* things when someone touches him." Eyes downcast, she twiddled her thumbs. "Bad things. I was wondering if he saw something when I touched him."

Sam sighed then leaned in so she could speak in a hushed voice to the two of them. "Listen to me closely. If you see anyone with an Indian mask, do not engage them. Just stay on high alert and stay the hell away from them. And maybe stay out of the woods for a while too. All right?"

Paltrow nodded.

"And you—" Sam pointed a finger at Tag. "Be careful. Watch *her* back."

All cattiness aside, Sam hated having to share that with Paltrow. Telling her exactly what Michael had seen would have been too much, made Paltrow spend the rest of her life looking over her shoulder in fear of what might never come true. As she walked out to her car, scared for the woman and queasy from having put a scare in her, her hands shook. She considered having Paltrow go on leave, but, not really understanding how Michael's visions worked, she didn't know if she would be preventing or causing the peril. From her experience, the visions always found a way to come true, and the best Paltrow could do was recognize the danger coming and react first. Knowledge was power, but foreknowledge was awareness. *Best to give her the warning and pray her extra caution will prevent the future from happening.*

She thought about Paltrow the whole way over to the hospital. There, she drove around the building to the back entrance, hoping to have more luck with the staff than she'd had with Dr. Horvat. She needed an in, to see what was happening behind the scenes. Frank had his man, but neither of them were talking—at least not to her.

She needed to find something that would get her a warrant. *Maybe another round with Bowes would help.*

But Bowes was at Ash Street, charged with attempted murder and denied bail. He wasn't going anywhere. She considered talking to Tessa or Jimmy to see what they knew. Sitting in her parked car, engine idling, she shook her head, pressing a palm into her temple. *And risk endangering them? I can't do that.* Then again, maybe they already were in danger. She scanned the parking lot before heading inside Brentworth.

Sam grumbled to herself when she noticed the Barbie receptionist behind the glass, chewing on a massive wad of gum like a cow chewing its cud. She bet the woman rolled out of bed in the morning looking like a ten when everyone else needed a little work and a pot of coffee to get going.

The eye roll the woman gave Sam as she approached let the detective know that the disdain was mutual. "How may I help you?" the receptionist asked without the slightest amount of helpfulness in her tone.

"I'm here to see Dr. Horvat."

The receptionist checked her monitor. "Do you have an appointment?" She blew a bubble then popped it with her teeth, only to continue chewing the gum with her mouth open, her lips smacking loud enough to be heard through the divider.

Sam huffed and crossed her arms. "Just buzz the fucking doctor."

The receptionist chewed her gum much slower at that, like a camel wadding up spit. "One moment please."

She hit a button on the base of the phone, grabbed the earpiece, then turned her back to Sam, speaking to whoever had answered in hushed tones. Sam caught a few words here and there, a "that detective" and "her away" and maybe even a "bitch." But that was all right with Sam, so long as the bitch in front of her got her Dr. Horvat.

"The doctor will see you now," the receptionist said, donning a false smile. "Someone will be here to escort you to her office shortly." She turned to her monitor and pretended to read something.

"Thank you." Sam's own smile was as smug as she could make it.

A buzz sounded from the door, and she could hear its locking mechanism whirring. Finally, Sam was getting someone's attention.

That someone was a fair-skinned fellow with a slightly upturned nose, closely cropped dark hair, and an inviting smile, easy on the eyes if not a little too *GQ*. He wore light-blue scrubs that looked brand new. Sam was unable to find a wrinkle on them or his face, though the number of grays over his ears suggested either he was graying prematurely or older than the thirty-something he appeared to be. The name tag pinned to his chest read *Curtis*.

For a roadblock, he greeted Sam pleasantly and offered his hand. His handshake was as firm as the rest of him looked. "Curtis Smales, orderly extraordinaire. How may I be of assistance?"

"She's meeting with Dr. Horvat," the receptionist whined.

"Oh." Curtis smiled, the only one of the three who seemed genuine about it. "Follow me, Ms...?"

Sam placed her hands on her hips, pushing back her open coat to give him a clear view of the badge clipped to her belt. His gaze lowered to it. "I assume you are here in a professional capacity, officer—"

"Detective."

"Detective, then." Curtis chuckled and threw up his hands as if in apology, the pads under his fingers calloused either from plenty of hard labor or hours in the gym. They seemed the only part of him that wasn't perfectly kept up. He turned and walked back through the door. "Right this way, please."

Sam followed him down a white hallway cast in yellow light. Both floor and walls shined as if covered with enamel, and her loafers squeaked if she didn't walk exactly heel to toe. The hospital hall was immaculate, unvarnished and unblemished, until she looked closer.

Thin cracks and chipped paint hid in plain sight. She wondered what else—or perhaps *who* else—at Brentworth might reveal flaws under closer inspection.

Averting her attention back to Curtis, Sam noticed a line of discolored skin—purplish-black, almost like a stretch mark—about an inch long where the orderly's left ear met his scalp. A similar line ran behind his right ear. *Scars?* They gave him an air of mystery, somehow raising the level of his attractiveness. She let her eyes linger on his ass. *Hardly a reason to condemn him.*

They reached a nurse's station where a dark-skinned woman sat behind a computer. She didn't even glance up as they circled it and headed down an identical corridor. Every fourteen feet or so, they passed a small office with a window on each side of the hall, usually with its shades drawn. Sam noted the nameplates on each door but didn't recognize any of the names.

Curtis stopped. "Dr. Horvat's office is just up ahead on the right," he said, ushering her toward an open door.

When he started to go back in the other direction, Sam called out to him. "Do you have an administrator or doctor here by the name of Jefferson? I'd like to speak with him when I'm done with Dr. Horvat."

"There are no doctors here by that name." Curtis tapped his chin. "As for administrators, I'm not sure, but their information should be on the website. We don't schedule appointments with them here. You'll have to call them or their assistants directly."

Sam threw a softball to check Curtis's veracity. "Do you know anyone here whose last name is Jefferson?"

"No, I don't think—" Curtis scratched his chin. "Wait, I think there might be a kid working in the daycare by that name. I'm not sure, though. I don't know everyone who works here."

"Does that boy's father work here?"

"That, I don't know. I don't think so."

Sam reached into her coat pocket and pulled out Bowes' signed medical record release form. She handed it to Curtis. "Can you pull these for me while I'm in with the doctor?"

Curtis took the form from her and scanned it. "I'll have to check with the head nurse, but this looks to be in order. I'll see what records I can pull together and make you copies. If it's light, I should have them for you by the time you're done with Dr. Horvat."

Sam checked her enthusiasm. Someone at Brentworth was actually going to cooperate with her. "Sounds good. Thanks."

Curtis disappeared into the hospital's inner sanctum, the consent form in hand. Sam headed to Dr. Horvat's open door.

She paused in front of the window, watching Dr. Horvat as she sat behind her desk, penciling some notes onto a legal pad. The doctor was dressed in an airy white blouse, her long straight hair resting over her shoulder. As if sensing Sam's presence, she looked up, smiled, and stood, beckoning Sam into her office with a wave.

Dr. Horvat pushed back her seat, bumping a closet door behind her in the cramped space. Maneuvering with the grace and flow of a figure skater, she came around her desk to meet Sam. Beaming, the doctor extended her hand. "Detective! It's so nice to speak with you under less chaotic circumstances."

Sam's phone vibrated in her pocket, momentarily distracting her. She reached in and hit a button to silence it. "Uh, thank you for taking the time to speak with me today, Doctor."

"Please, Mira is fine. And Samantha, is it? May I call you that?"

"You can call me whatever you'd like so long as you answer my questions."

"Where are my manners?" She pointed at the chairs opposite to her own. "Please, have a seat. I trust you found your way here all right?"

Sam moved one of the chairs closer to the front of the desk and sat across from Dr. Horvat. "Yes. Thank you. That Curtis is... a delight." Her phone buzzed again in her pocket, and she pulled it out. Frank's name appeared on the screen. Huffing, she sent him to voicemail and pressed down hard on the Power button, then she returned the phone to her pocket while listening to Dr. Horvat.

"Oh? I didn't send Curtis." Dr. Horvat cleared her throat. "Yes, I suppose, if you're into that sort of thing. To be honest, I hardly even notice him anymore—too wrapped up in my work.

"Anyway, how is the boy doing? Michael, right? Such a nice young man." She propped her elbows on her desk and leaned in conspiratorially. "I know I shouldn't say this, but if a little marijuana is all he's into, it could be worse. It's not the stepping-stone drug we used to think it was. Please let him know I'm sorry if I got him in trouble. I don't always have the bedside manner I should have."

Sam stared down her nose at the doctor. "It's against the law. He knows better."

"Sometimes we do a little crime to prevent a bigger one." Dr. Horvat offered a wry smile, then continued as an afterthought, "The benefits of marijuana with respect to anxiety management are undeniable. A new school year is bound to come with many new stressors. What is he? A freshman? Sophomore? If he needs to talk to someone, I offer after-hour—"

Sam snorted. "No. He's fine, Doctor." When her phone vibrated again, she ripped it from her pocket and powered it down, holding it extra long to make sure it shut off that time. Clenching her jaw, she leaned forward, unable to mask the tension in her tone. "Why do you know so much about Michael?"

The wry smile didn't waver. "One of your officers filled me in while we helped them locate Michael's friend." She ran her finger across a desk calendar, her eyes following. "Anyway, I'm sure you're not here to discuss the medical applications of marijuana or even *your* boy." She looked up as she ended her sentence, a glint of challenge in her eyes.

Sam squinted, sensing an implied threat, but unsure if she was just being paranoid. After all, she'd been assaulted outside that very hospital. She had a right to be on edge.

"I have a session in a few minutes, so I suppose we should get right to it. I presume you're here for information on Bowes. I haven't seen a subpoena, and I doubt you could have received a court order already. I'm sorry, Detective, but I cannot just parcel out patient—"

"Let's hold off on Bowes for the moment." Sam clasped her hands in front of her. "Tell me about yourself, Doctor."

Dr. Horvat's eyebrows arched. "What is it you wish to know?"

"Who are you, Dr. Horvat? For starters, you clearly weren't born here. Your accent sounds Eastern European, if I had to guess. How'd you end up in a shithole like Fall River?"

"I don't think any of the doctors here are from Fall River, and many of us have accents, which is probably the case in most hospitals across the U.S." She blew out a sigh. "But I'll humor you. I was born in Lithuania. Most of my childhood was spent there before a family crisis bounced me from one place to another. But you are correct—Eastern Europe, and I presume my accent is a hodgepodge of several dialects I picked up along the way."

Dr. Horvat stopped to point to the framed degrees hanging on the wall. "But as you can see, I am trained in American medicine in both adult and pediatric psychiatry."

Sam scanned the wall, noting documents from John Hopkins, NYU Langone/Bellevue Hospitals, and Brown. Horvat was also apparently a Diplomate of the American Board of Psychiatry and Neurology, whatever that meant. "Looks impressive," she muttered half-heartedly.

"I've devoted my life to treating mental illness in all of its ugly forms. So in a way, we are on the same side, Detective, except I hope to prevent crimes *before* they happen by curing the disease before it festers."

"Is that what you do here, treat mental illness?" The answer was obvious, but Sam wanted to hear it anyway, to keep her talking and see if any nugget of truth would drop. Something shady was happening behind those walls, and it had been Horvat who showed up to treat Bowes. Perhaps she'd been sent by someone else, was an unwitting pawn, but Dr. Horvat seemed too shrewd to be used in such a way. No, whatever the reason Bowes, a man with no history of violence and no evidence of gun ownership, would take a shot at her—*actually, several shots*—the doctor knew something about it. Police work was like poker. Every player's story had to add up. *Find a few gaps and you unravel the bluff. But first, you have to get the story told.*

"I and three other doctors in the Psych Department treat all who are sent here, some on a rotation basis while more difficult cases are sorted against our skill sets. Also, one doctor here focuses entirely on pediatric care and another entirely on adult care, while myself and the fourth treat both." She glanced at her watch. "So, as you might imagine, we all have very busy schedules. I really must be—"

"Who treated Harlan Bowes? You?"

"I can't answer that with any certainty, Detective. We see hundreds of patients every year, not all court-mandated. But I believe the answer is yes, that I treated Mr. Bowes, at least primarily." She rose, smiled, and waved to someone behind Sam. "Now, if you'll excuse me—"

Sam stood and stepped in front of the doctor while glancing back to see Curtis standing in the doorway, a manila folder tucked under his arm. "If I could just ask you a few more questions—"

Dr. Horvat placed her hand on Sam's arm and gently but firmly pushed her aside. "I'm sorry, Detective, but my commitment to my patients comes first. That said, I am happy to continue our conversation at a more convenient time. Please set up an appointment with the receptionist. Book as much time as you need, and I promise I'll be all yours."

Lightly stroking the orderly's arm, she said, "Curtis, will you please escort Detective Reilly out?"

Curtis nodded and faced Sam. He waved his arm and smiled. "Detective."

Sam followed him back out the way they'd come in. On the way, he handed her the folder, which felt as empty as she knew its sparse contents would be. "Here's all we had on that patient. Sorry I couldn't find more, but it looks like he wasn't here very long."

"Thanks," Sam said flatly. She stopped, an idea exploding like a firework in her mind. "Hey, do you think I could speak with a patient? If you just point me in the right direction, I promise I'll be quick—"

"You know I can't let you back there. The patients are kept secluded from the general public for everyone's safety. Any form of stress or anxiety you carry with you in there may be extremely detrimental to their treatment or the progress they've made."

Sam crossed her arms and pretended to pout, playing to his machismo with what hopefully passed for a damsel-in-distress routine. "Come on, Curtis."

The orderly shook his head. "The doctors are already committed to their rounds and don't have time for interruptions except in the case of absolute emergencies. I'm sure I don't have to tell you about HIPAA and other laws protecting the patients and requiring us to always conform to a professional standard of care."

"Please?" She let her arms drop by her sides to appear softer. "I'm a cop, so you know I'll be discreet. Five minutes. That's all I'm asking."

"I'm sorry, Detective, but my hands are tied."

"Screw it." She huffed. "Brentworth's blocking my access to information relevant to an ongoing investigation, refusing to provide me with Harlan Bowes's medical records—his *real* medical records—despite my having his signed consent, and are stonewalling law enforcement in every way imaginable. Can't you see how incredibly suspicious that makes this place look?" She sighed. "Look, I know you're just doing your job. Maybe there's someone higher up I can speak with?"

Curtis kept his inviting smile. "I'm sorry, Detective. I'm just the low man on the totem pole. You can speak with anyone here, by appointment."

Sam had no choice but to relent. She fumed silently as they walked into the waiting area, planning to come back with enough warrants and court orders to fill a filing cabinet. Before Curtis could turn to leave, she tried one more tactic, betting on having better luck with the orderly than the bitchy Barbie behind the front desk. "Okay, so when are visiting hours today? I'd like to set up a time to speak with a patient."

The orderly's gaze narrowed. "Are you a friend or family?"

"Friend."

"Patient's name?"

Tessa or Jimmy. Tessa or... "Jimmy Rafferty."

Curtis faced the receptionist, who gave him a nod. "Very well. We can bring Jimmy to one of our meeting rooms. Visiting hours today are between three and five."

Sam looked at her watch and rolled her eyes. It was just a little past eleven. She would have asked for an exception if the request's futility wasn't written in the lines on Curtis's forehead. Buttoning up her temper to prevent a stomping foot or anything else that would make her look like a petulant child, she grunted, "I'll be back at three," and headed out to her car, letting loose a long string of expletives under her breath.

As she sat behind the wheel, she pulled her cell phone from her pocket and powered it back on. There were three missed calls and nine missed texts, all from Frank. She read the top one. *Where are you? You need to call me or the precinct ASAP!*

She hit the info button and pressed her finger down on Frank's number. It only rang once.

"Sam!" Frank's voice was loud and excited. "I've been trying to reach you. There's been a multiple homicide."

Sam breathed, keeping her own voice steady. "Okay, I'll be right there. Location?"

"Outside your apartment."

CHAPTER 18

Michael's lungs felt as though they'd been scorched. His chest swelled in heaving breaths, only to shrivel again as the air rushed out of him. A side stitch forced his hand over his ribs. It was as if some invisible crab was twisting and wrenching his muscles in its pincers. His feet stopped running on their own, his body telling his mind that a break was needed.

His breathing slowed as he trotted languidly toward the curb on his right, his mind finally slowing enough to take stock of his surroundings. Glancing over his shoulder, he saw no one behind him. The street was quiet.

To his left, the high school, in front of him, Brentworth, and beyond that, the police department. *Sam.* It seemed an impossible distance after his all-out sprint. He was starting to see the value of joining cross-country.

Sam! He groped in his pocket, searching for the cell phone she'd given him, that she'd told him to always carry. His heart stopped when he found his pocket empty.

He stumbled, suddenly dizzy. *Maybe one of these houses will let me use...* His eyes rolled back, and for a moment, he thought he was going to fall. Squeezing his eyes shut, slowly recovering his breath and his balance, he rested his hand against a silver car. Its alarm blared, and he jolted upright. His gaze darted in every direction. Hands covered his ears. A dog barked. A man unseen yelled, "Get away from my car, asshole!"

A siren whooped then boomed continuously as tires screeched around a turn. Michael turned to face the police car speeding his way.

He raised his arm to flag it down, all at once thankful for the protection Sam had placed on him and the cavalry that would take him to safety.

His smile faded, and his mouth went dry when he saw the cigar-store Indian staring back at him from the driver's seat, an identical mask riding shotgun.

He hesitated, trying to determine where to go, but he couldn't think straight under the pressure. The school was closest, his best option. But the police car's engine roared louder as he made to dart across the road. Michael kept to his right and quickly built up to a sprint, getting onto the curb as soon as he saw a break in the parked cars. He could hear the cruiser following—the siren was off but the engine revved occasionally as if to taunt him. He felt like a cornered mouse, the cats *whoop-whooping* their siren, playing with their trapped prey.

He ran another mile, at least, cops in tow. Cars passed without a care, their drivers turning their heads with curiosity before continuing on their way. He thought to flag one down, but knew it would be certain death for whoever stopped. He wondered if any of them would report what they saw when Michael's picture ended up all over the news, when they found his body. *If* they found his body.

Michael didn't dare look back, even as fear and strain brought tears into his eyes. *Just keep running. Just keep running.* But even in his panic, he knew he couldn't outrun a police car.

Another siren came from the opposite direction. Michael lost all hope then. The cops, sworn to serve and protect, were after him. He wondered how many had been corrupted and what made him so damn important to them. *Why me?* God, how he wished Sam were with him. But she had no way of knowing where he was. No, he was on his own.

Before the second car came into sight, Michael slowed and crouched, slumping against the front wheel well of a pickup. Over the hood, he could see the cop car pull up alongside it, engine idling. He needed to rest and regain some of his wind while he let them make the next move. The tenement house to his right looked inviting enough. He considered sprinting for the front door to beg for entrance. But the cops would get him, arrest him in front of whoever opened the door, acting as if they were just doing their jobs, as if *he* were the criminal.

If he even made it to the door.

He glanced back at the cop car as the second sped toward them. The officers had their masks off. The passenger, an old gray-haired man with skin hanging loosely from his face, stared straight ahead at the approaching vehicle. Michael thought he was way too old to be a cop and tried to look past him at the driver but couldn't get a view of him. The second car sped by, a black Toyota Camry.

Sam? Michael jumped up, waving his hands. "Sam!"

He started to run into the street, in front of the police cruiser that had followed him. That car's tires screeched as its siren *whooped* again then blared. The driver ignored Michael. The car whipped around and followed after Sam.

Purple spots appeared before Michael's eyes, and he let out the breath he hadn't known he'd been holding. He felt like he might faint. But those cops, they were after Sam now. He thought to start running again, after her, to help her. But his legs wobbled as he took a step. He would never make it to her in time, even if he tried.

And what if they come back? What if there are more? Sam would want him to hide. He turned around, studied his surroundings, and found himself only a few yards from Brentworth. It was as if fate had driven him there. The police station still a few more miles away, he had a choice to make. Take the ready-made place to hide, or take his chances with an obviously infiltrated police department and all the many steps it would take to get him there.

The whole thing was crazy. He was just a kid. He didn't know anything about those sickos—what they were about or why the heck they would want anything to do with him. When the Suarez gang had kidnapped him, it had been because of Jimmy. In some sick sort of way, that at least made sense. But *this* seemed to have something to do with Brentworth. He wondered if Jimmy had told someone inside something about him and his visions. Or maybe Tessa had.

And he was moving closer to the place. It didn't seem smart, but at that moment, he couldn't feel as though he could trust anyone but himself—and Sam. But she was on her own, just like him. A tear ran down his cheek as he prayed for her safety.

Then, he headed into the woods.

CHAPTER 19

Sam squeezed her steering wheel as she sped home, her fears and frustration bubbling up and boiling over into a roar. Her mind was not on the road where it should have been, her body driving the route by reflex. *What does Wainwright want with Michael? What could he possibly want with me?*

Sure, she despised Wainwright and his ilk, but she'd never even been face-to-face with the man, never done anything that would warrant his special attention. Bruce and his former partner had chased Wainwright out of town before Sam had even made detective.

She burped to stop the vomit from rising. *What was it Frank had said about the bastard? Chaos for chaos's sake?* She screamed with rage before gagging on self-revulsion, knowing she would turn a blind eye to every evil deed Wainwright had done and ever would do if he would just leave her and Michael alone. Maybe even Bruce's murder.

She sniffled then snarled away her tears. The sting of a promise she'd made and never kept—to hunt down Wainwright when her partner no longer could—a duty owed to a fallen friend and mentor that she let go by the wayside. It wasn't as if she hadn't tried. Wainwright disappeared after Texas. No trace. The man might as well have been a ghost, and for all she knew, may have been dead. Still, she couldn't help but wonder how things might have been different had she only tried a little harder.

But circumstances had changed since she'd made that promise. Michael had been in her life, but he hadn't become her son yet—her responsibility. She owed more to the living than to the dead, yet she always seemed to be dropping the boy in harm's way.

Her car skidded to a halt in the middle of the road, a few houses back from her apartment. The street had been cordoned off and was awash in swirling red and blue lights. At least two ambulances and half the force were there.

She swung her door open, hopped out of her car, and sprinted her way through the barricade. Frank stood just outside the caution tape, the gravity of whatever knowledge he held weighing down the skin on his face, making him look old beyond his years, haggard even.

"Where is he?" Sam passed him, taking his sleeve and ushering him past the tape as she lifted it. It caught on his chest, but he somehow managed to limbo under it. "Where's Michael?"

"I don't know," Frank said, following her as she hustled to her front door. "He's not here."

Sam pushed past the officer posted at the entrance to the tenement and took the steps up to her apartment two at a time. Sergeant Rollins, his pro-wrestler biceps crossed over a broad chest, waited for her at the top near the splintered remains of her door.

She nodded for him to lead her inside, tapping his arm as they walked. "Talk to me."

"Quadruple homicide, the vic—"

Sam hushed him by holding up her index finger. "First, Michael."

Sergeant Rollins frowned and shook his head slowly. "We don't know. But the witness who called it in said he almost hit a boy. The description he gave matches Michael's. We believe he got away."

"Then why hasn't..." She yanked her phone out of her pocket. No missed calls or texts except for those from Frank. She'd told him to call at the slightest sign of trouble. *Why hasn't he?*

"Stupid!" She screamed at herself, though both Frank and Sergeant Rollins took a step back. She hit her recent call list, found Michael's number, then called it. A ringing came from his bedroom.

She ran toward it and saw the phone lighting up on the floor beneath an open window.

"All right." She breathed so quickly she sounded as if she were panting. "Okay." Her head spun, her hand going out by her side for balance. She sat on Michael's bed.

"Are you okay?" Frank asked, stepping closer.

"Of course I'm not okay!" She glared up at him, her anger clearing the fog in her mind. "What does he want with us, Frank? Why would he be after *us*?" Her nostrils flared. "Why isn't he after *you*?"

"You're asking me to explain why a homicidal maniac does what he does?" Frank pursed his lips and knitted his brow. "I can't do that, Sam. I do know that you're way too close to this now. Maybe one of the other detectives should take point on—"

"Oh, fuck you, Frank!" Sam stood, her fist clenched, wanting nothing more than to take the smug SOB down a peg. "This is *my* case, and with Michael gone, the only way anyone's taking me off it is over my dead body."

Frank threw up his hands in defeat. "Okay. I'm sorry." His chin dipped against his chest. "We—I wanted to keep you out of this, you and Michael. Truly, for your own protection. You have something, *someone* to lose, whereas... I don't. God, Sam, if anything were to happen to you because I screwed up..." He choked up, then cleared his throat. "Anyway, I see shielding you from my mess is no longer possible. Perhaps it was a mistake from the start. I'll tell you everything I—"

"Later." Sam fixed him with a gaze that probably seemed more hostile than she intended. "Our first and only priority is finding Michael." She turned to Rollins. "Sergeant, can you walk us through what happened?"

Rollins pulled a notepad from his back pocket and flipped it open. "According to Arthur Tellier of 3044 Damascus Avenue, he was driving northbound on Wilshire just before eleven in the morning when a boy matching Michael's description ran out in front of his car. He honked and yelled at the boy, who continued on to the other side of the street."

Rollins turned to the next page. "As Tellier was shouting at the boy, he heard tires screech and a loud thud then saw a van stopped on the other side of the road and a woman lying by the curb with a strange mask. The man driving the van, identified as Cormac McCaffrey of 197 Cheshire Street, exited his vehicle to provide assistance. At this time, another individual wearing a police uniform and a mask similar to that of the injured woman approached from the west—that is, from around the side of your building—carrying an ax. Tellier saw the individual, who appeared to be male, say something to the woman before burying the ax in her head."

Rollins paused, apparently expecting questions. When he got none, he cleared his throat and continued. "Tellier froze but regained his senses when the man with the ax turned on McCaffrey as he tried to flee, and a third masked individual approached from the front entrance—from your apartment—holding a knife to a boy's throat."

Sam gasped. "How do you know—"

"The description, though incomplete, matches that of Dylan Jefferson, according to Officers Tagliamonte and Paltrow."

"Where is the boy now?" Frank asked.

"Not here." Rollins sighed. "Presumably taken by the masked individual or individuals. As you can see by the number of cars out there, we have many officers canvasing the neighborhood for other witnesses. I mean, this happened in broad daylight. Even the people in this city can't deny they saw or heard something. We hope to have more information on the perps and the boys' whereabouts shortly."

"You said quadruple homicide. The officers on protective duty, Dubront and Lennox, they're..."

Rollins nodded. The muscles in his jaw tightened.

A twinge of guilt tickled Sam's throat in response to the relief she felt that it hadn't been Tag that shift or Michael who'd been taken. "So... after one of the masked perps was struck by the van, another one of the masked perps killed her?" Sam rubbed her forehead. "That doesn't make any sense."

Frank tapped his chin. "Perhaps he was afraid she'd be taken into custody and didn't want her to talk."

Sam squinted, not liking the sound of that. "Any information on the dead perp?"

"Nothing yet. Other than a crowbar, the deceased suspect had nothing on her—no identification, no money, no jewelry, no nothing."

"Were they wearing gloves?"

"No." Sergeant Rollins might have smiled had it not been her son that was missing. "Potter is dusting the doorway now. He'll work his way through." He shrugged. "Medical examiner's got the bodies, too, though the cause of death appears to be fairly obvious."

"Order a toxicology report on the dead woman anyway," Sam said.

"You thinking she came from Brentworth? Like Bowes?" Frank looked down his vulture-like nose at her, which wasn't really his fault since she was still sitting on Michael's bed.

She stood. "You're not? The compounds found in Bowes's system weren't exactly your garden variety. A match here would strongly suggest a connection between him and the dead woman. And if Brentworth links the two of them, we have our probable source of the pharmaceuticals. Obviously, this is all on top of the fact that they all were wearing the same damn masks."

She glowered up at Frank. His silence spoke volumes. She knew Frank was thinking the exact same thing as her. And that pissed her off even more. He probably knew all about Brentworth from the start. Had he only filled her in from the beginning, they might have prevented the attack on Michael.

But he hadn't. And if anything happened to Michael, she was going to take it out on him—violently.

She closed her eyes for a second, trying to still the rising storm. "Sergeant, the scene is yours. Let Potter finish up and tell him to discount any fingerprints from yourself or Officer Tagliamonte."

Frank raised an eyebrow at that but said nothing. She wondered if he questioned her exclusions or the fact that he wasn't included in them.

Addressing the sergeant, she said, "Don't let anyone in—eh, you know what to do. If Michael returns or anyone else finds him first, I know you'll give me a call right away."

Rollins nodded, and Sam turned to Frank. "You coming?"

"Where?"

"Michael's hidden at the school before. We should try there first."

Frank offered what she thought was supposed to be a reassuring smile, but it collapsed into something weak and ugly. "Right behind you."

CHAPTER 20

Michael winced and wagged his injured hand in the air. His bandages had caught on a nail and tore away as he climbed up to the treehouse. Every subsequent rung pressed into his raw, exposed wound, sending shockwaves of pain through his arm.

Reaching the top, he allowed himself a moment to relax, the first time he felt even the slightest bit safe since an ax had split his apartment door. He'd taken the high ground, and though there were two ways down from the treehouse, there was only one way up. He thought he could defend the ladder if he had to. *I wish I had a bat.*

Trying to keep his wound clean, he slapped the dirt and splinters from his hands, squealing but enduring the pain. Hand over hand, he shimmied the handlebar up the pulley system to have it ready should he need it. Then, he headed into the treehouse, grabbed the binoculars, then knelt before the window. His watch would be vigilant. At least it had been for an hour or so.

Fear slowly transformed into boredom, and adrenalin depleted into exhaustion. Still, there was nothing to do in his little hideaway but sit and watch. He had only the binoculars and Dylan's copy of *Moby Dick* discarded on one of the chairs to keep him company.

He sat on the empty chair beside the book, picked it up, and flipped through it. He read the first page before tossing it back onto the chair. *Talk about being vigilant. That'll put me to sleep.* He sighed, crossed his arms and his ankles way out in front of him as he slouched, and listened to the sounds of the forest.

"I knew you'd come here."

Michael jolted upright, fist raised. He turned toward the saloon doors to see Dylan freeze partway through them.

"Woah! Easy there, Badass." Dylan creaked the door open the rest of the way and stepped inside.

Slowly, Michael brought down his arm, eyeing the boy from head to toe, looking for weapons without realizing he was doing so until a few seconds later. Dylan's hands were empty. His pockets were flat. Still, he could have had a knife tucked in the back of his pants or something worse hidden outside the treehouse, beyond Michael's view but not Dylan's reach.

Hands still balled up but at his sides, Michael kept what little distance he could from Dylan. He dared not blink, scrutinizing his friend's every movement and expression, always on guard. "I saw them grab you. How'd you get away?"

Dylan pointed to a gash on his neck that Michael hadn't noticed despite its conspicuousness. Smeared blood stained the skin beneath it, and dried flakes fell like scraped rust from his T-shirt's collar as he ran a finger along it. "Wasn't easy." He shrugged. "I guess they were just more interested in you. I saw the other two going after you. The one that had me seemed old and out of shape, kinda had a wimpy grip on me. When I saw the one with the ax go completely psycho and you take off, I stomped on my guy's toes as hard as I could. It worked. He let go but cut me as I slipped free."

Michael's gaze narrowed further. "You sure have a funny way of showing up right before those Indians do."

Dylan's eyebrows shot up, his mouth dropping open. "You think I have something to do with them?" He puffed out a breath. "Maybe you're used to this crap, but that guy had a knife to my throat! I lived in a lot of places, some of them a lot more dangerous than Fall River, and nothing like that's ever happened to me before. I thought I was going to die! And all I could think was how embarrassing it would be to be found dead if I pooped myself. Being friends with you, well... it's never boring, anyway."

Michael shrank into himself. "I—" he sighed, his head suddenly too heavy to hold up. "I know. I'm sorry. I get it if you—"

"No, man. Forget it. None of this is your fault. It's not like you asked for this crap." Dylan touched around the wound and winced. "I don't think it's deep. Can you tell?"

Michael leaned closer. "Doesn't look too bad."

"Anyway, I tried to follow you, but damn! Who would have guessed you could run that fast? And on a hurt ankle? You should definitely consider track this year."

Michael exhaled. His shoulders drooped, and he sat back down. Dylan picked up his book and sat beside him.

Michael punched him in the shoulder.

"Hey!" Dylan whined. "What was that for?"

"Sneaking up on me. I didn't even hear you coming up. I could've killed you." Michael didn't really know how he could have done that last part, but it sounded like the way he would be expected to finish his gripe. Or perhaps it was all his fault Dylan had gotten the drop on him. He didn't remember falling asleep, but the last few hours had passed so quickly they blurred at times. Other moments had moved so slowly he could describe their every detail. Though the day had certainly been too real, his wearied mind and body had left him so detached from himself that he felt like an outsider looking in, a spirit watching from an ethereal realm. A lot like he felt when he had a vision.

Dylan chuckled. "I can't help it if I'm a ninja. Also, I didn't exactly want to let the whole world know we were here." He nudged Michael with his shoulder.

Michael giggled softly. The more he tried to stifle it, the louder it became.

The smile vanished from Dylan's face. "What the heck could be so funny right now?"

Michael laughed harder, warmth flushing his face. "Did you really think you were going to *poop* yourself? I mean, *poop,* not shit."

"Oh, fu—" Dylan huffed. "Fudge you."

They burst out into a laughing fit that. Though grossly exaggerated, it let out some of the stress Michael had been harboring and relaxed the tension between them. He laughed until tears formed in his eyes. Wiping one with the back of his hand, he gazed over at Dylan, who had gone quiet. Apparently, his friend couldn't laugh away the madness so easily.

Dylan grimaced. "So, what do we do now?"

Michael chewed on his cheek. "I don't suppose you have a phone?"

"Sorry. No."

"I thought everyone had a phone?"

Dylan shrugged. "Left mine in my bag. Not like anyone's calling."

Michael puffed out his cheeks and blew out air. "Then I guess we wait for Sam. She'll find us here."

"I believe you, Badass." Dylan dropped to his hands and knees and peered out the window. "I just hope those nutbags don't find us first. This is so messed up."

Michael buried his chin against his chest. "I'm sorry, Dylan. For getting you into this." He glanced up but could only see Dylan's back. "Sam will find us. She's a really good—"

"Shhhh!" Dylan hissed. "Someone's coming."

Michael cocked his head and listened. Dead leaves crackled and twigs snapped as feet plodded through underbrush. The sounds grew louder.

"Michael?" a familiar voice called. "You up there?"

"Sam?" Michael leapt to his feet as Dylan signaled with his hands for him to slow down. "It's all right. It's Sam!"

After bursting through the double doors, Michael watched from the platform as Sam, Frank, and Officers Tagliamonte and Paltrow approached the base of the tree. He might have cried, he was so happy to see her, had he not been too damn tired.

Sam smiled up at him, her eyes wet. "Michael! Thank God you're all right."

"I'm okay," he called down to her. "Dylan's okay too."

"Dylan Jefferson is with you?" Sam glanced over at Frank, and they shared a look Michael couldn't decipher from thirty feet up. "That's great, Michael. Come on down, so we can all go someplace safe."

Home? For a second, Michael thought it odd Sam hadn't used the word. But home wasn't safe anymore. No, they wouldn't be going back there, and he wasn't sure he wanted to. *Is anywhere safe?*

Michael turned to his friend, who stared back expectantly. "It's Sam. We can trust her."

Dylan smirked. "If you say so." He ducked his head under the threshold and grabbed the bar for the zip line. "But I'm taking the easy way down. See ya!" He chuckled as he hustled over to the cable, snapped the bar onto the wire, then jumped off the platform.

"What the..." Frank said, circling the base of the tree and heading to where Dylan had landed. Sam and the two officers remained at the base of the tree, staring up at Michael. He sighed and began his slow descent.

At the bottom, Sam pulled him into a hug. Her hands only touched the back of his shirt, and her arms, covered by her long coat, prevented contact with his. But she almost pressed her cheek against his before apparently remembering herself. Instead, she leaned it against his clothed shoulder.

Behind Sam, Officers Tagliamonte and Paltrow watched in silence. Warmth rose in Michael's cheeks. Down on the ground, it was much darker under the canopy of trees than it had been up above. Sam was whispering something to him, but he wasn't paying attention. Then the hair on the backs of his neck prickled.

"O-officer—" His mouth dropped open, and he stuttered, struggling for the words. "Officer Paltrow! Look out!"

As if he'd materialized from tree bark, a masked figure dressed like a cop appeared behind her back. He raised his arm as she turned to face him. Michael heard the slightest chirp, and the back of Officer Paltrow's head exploded. Her body dropped to the forest floor, glassy, dead eyes staring at Michael accusingly. A rivulet of blood trickled down her forehead where a third socket had formed. Then, he was falling.

Sam had thrown him to the ground as she drew her gun. Officer Tagliamonte went for his as well, but froze when another masked person pressed something to the back of his head.

"Don't," the person said, a woman's voice.

Still holding her service pistol, Sam raised her hands. She glanced around, then at Michael, her eyes begging for forgiveness. Behind her, more masked figures circled.

Michael stayed put, hands smeared with cold earth. He looked anywhere and everywhere but Officer Paltrow. He counted at least half a dozen in the strange group, men and women of varying shapes and sizes, even one with the frame of a child. Nothing indicated their connection beyond the identical cigar-store Indian mask each wore. Most of them were chanting, each something different, but he couldn't understand one over the other. *Something about Indians?* That they were crazy, Michael was certain. And there was no telling what they might do next.

A tall woman with an athletic build stepped out from behind her brethren. "Take them," she said with the trace of an accent, pointing at Sam then Michael. He tensed as they approached, but he didn't fight the two pairs of hands that pulled him to his feet. Two others were on Sam, taking her gun and cuffing her hands behind her back.

The woman behind Officer Tagliamonte pushed him forward. "Five little Indians on a cellar door." She cackled, then pushed the officer harder. "*One* tumbled in and then there were four."

The Amazonian woman held up a hand. "Easy, Laura. *He* doesn't want that one. You know what to do. But just shoot him. No knives. Return to your room when you're done here and await further instructions." She nodded, then signaled something to the others. Michael lurched forward, pushed by rough hands. Behind Sam, he was shoved in the direction of Brentworth.

He heard Officer Tagliamonte whimper a soft, "No... no."

But Michael didn't want to look back, not even when a gun fired and a body dropped. He'd seen enough of death that day and was sure he would see more soon enough.

CHAPTER 21

"Jimmy," Nurse Francine called after knocking on the door, her irritating singsong voice driving his drowsiness away. "You have a visitor."

Jimmy sat up in bed. He never had any visitors, and to come on a Saturday morning when he was allowed to sleep in was just rude. The clock on the wall read eight in the morning. Breakfast hour had just ended, which left him with no solid reason to get out of bed. Still, his curiosity nagged at him like a toddler tugging on his sleeve. But the hollow pang in the pit of his belly told him that no good would come from it.

My parents? His mom had come to see him once after he'd been arrested and without his father's knowledge. She told him how he'd embarrassed the family, soiled the Rafferty name. As if the Rafferty name had ever stood for more than domestic violence, alcoholism, and degenerate gambling—things they could hide behind closed doors, mouthwash, and revolving credit cards. But she'd cried as she'd spoken the words—his father's words, reiterated in a letter that practically disowned him after the Suarez mess—and he knew she still loved him. His baby sister, too young to even understand what Jimmy had done, was kept away from him entirely. It was as if his sole act of violence, retaliation against a boy who'd done terrible violence to him and so many others, was infectious and could corrupt sweet innocent Tabitha with its poison. He hoped he'd see her again some-day, probably aged well past her crescent pigtails and deeply dimpled pudgy cheeks. Smiling but only for a moment, he touched the divot in his own face before it could fade. *Then again, maybe not.*

He changed from his pajamas, pretty much a T-shirt and sweat-pants, into his day clothes, another T-shirt and sweatpants—the kind with an elastic stretch-band waist. Jamming his feet into slippers, he headed for the door.

"Jimmy?" Nurse Francine knocked again. "I'm coming in."

The door opened and the raven-haired nurse entered, looking quite beautiful that morning except for the sharklike quality of her smile. She gave him a once-over. "You need some time to get ready?"

He'd thought he was ready but nodded anyway as he bounced on his feet. "Just gotta brush my teeth and... you know."

She smiled and nodded back. "I'll wait for you here."

Jimmy hurried to the restroom and let out a stream so pleasant his eyes rolled back. Finished, he flushed, washed his hands, then doused cold water on his face and neck. Drying off, he tried to flatten his curly, reddish hair, which was deeply in need of a razor or maybe some hedge clippers. He was starting to look a bit like Ronald Mc-Donald.

After brushing his teeth, he met Nurse Francine in the hallway. "Come on," she said, putting an arm around his shoulder.

Though her touch was gentle and kindly, he flinched a little before he could stop himself.

"He's waiting in one of the private meeting rooms," she continued without seeming to notice his apprehension. "Right this way."

He wanted to ask who his visitor was but thought better of engaging a possible threat to his existence. His brow furrowed, and he glanced back down the hall behind them. No one was following. The hallway was empty, eerily quiet except for the sound of his and Nurse Francine's footsteps.

What if she's bringing me to the same doctor that fixed *Tessa?* His shoulders stiffened, the nurse's touch no longer seeming so warm. *What if I'm one of the ones who doesn't come back?*

He could run, break away from Nurse Francine and raise a huge stink up and down the halls, but that would probably only result in getting himself tackled by Link and poked with a thick needle. They'd probably still drag him knocked-out to the doctor and do that old-fashioned lobotomy-thing for the mentally ill to make him into a drooling obedient dog.

Nurse Francine buzzed them through a door. The hallway on the other side looked pretty much the same—faded, snot-colored carpet, hotel-like walls lined with doors with square windows. The windows were lined with what looked like chicken wire, but he could make out the rooms on the other side. In the second one on the left, a tall man in a dark suit with short graying hair stood with his hands in his pockets, back to the door.

Nurse Francine ushered Jimmy into the room, and the man turned. He buttoned his suit jacket as he did, then extended his hand. "Jimmy Rafferty? Special Agent Frank Spinney." He glanced at the nurse, then added, "I'm doing some follow-up on the Suarez case and was hoping for a moment of your time."

Jimmy sensed this last bit was meant more for Francine's benefit than his own.

"Well—" Nurse Francine smoothed out her uniform and winked at Jimmy. "I'll leave you boys to it. When you're finished, just hit the intercom by the door and someone will come get you."

Jimmy let the agent's hand hang in the air. He circled the small desk to the seat on the opposite side, wondering why the agent hadn't done so himself before Jimmy had arrived to make things easier on them both. Apparently, the man preferred his back to the door, where someone could sneak up on him, maybe wrap some piano wire around his neck.

Jimmy snickered, then shifted in his seat, waiting for the agent to sit down and get to it. Instead, the agent paced the eight feet or so between the side walls, apparently taking in the scenery or noticeable lack thereof. Jimmy, too, looked at the blank white walls, the linoleum floor, and those cheap Styrofoam-looking ceiling tiles like in school, wondering what the FBI guy saw in them. Jimmy had been in rooms like that many times before. Sure, they had different names—interrogation room, interview room, meeting room—but they all served the same purpose—someone wanted information. And the guy expected Jimmy to provide it.

Frank Spinney, that's what Francine had called him. He studied the man, growing more uncomfortable with the agent's pacing. His gaunt features—pointed nose, high cheekbones, and sharp chin—made him almost look like that Guy Fawkes dude, or the mask that was supposed to look like him anyway. Maybe Jimmy might have learned about him in history class had he not been expelled.

But there was something else about the lanky agent, something familiar. Aside from the wrinkled suit, stubble, faint aroma of sweat, and sunken eyes that made him appear as if he hadn't slept in weeks, Jimmy could have sworn he'd met the man before. He leaned forward to study him more closely, then slapped the table, pleased with himself for having remembered where he'd last seen the agent but not so pleased with the memories that flooded in with it.

The blood of the youngest Suarez brother, Luther, not even twelve, had covered Jimmy's hands as he'd tried to comfort him in his final moments. Sometimes, he thought he could still feel that sticky warmth on his skin. He hadn't been remotely responsible for Luther's death, but he hadn't been able to stop it either. The agent and Mikey's detective friend had found Jimmy like that, covered in blood. His reward was Detective Reilly shooting him. *To be fair, I was holding a gun.*

The *bang* Jimmy's hand made on the table seemed to snap the FBI man out of his thoughts, and he took a seat. Still, he just sat there, staring silently at Jimmy while he scratched his chin as if the fate of the world would be determined by his next words.

At last, he leaned forward and whispered. "I am not, in fact, here to talk to you about the Suarez case." His eyes twitched in the direction of the intercom as he pulled a small black mechanical device from his pocket and flipped a switch. "Scrambler of sorts," he said, tapping the device. "There's a camera in the corner that's not supposed to be recording audio, but I am sure they've got this room bugged every which way to Sunday even if it isn't. This should allow us to talk freely, but we should still keep our voices low and our mouths facing away from the camera."

Jimmy folded his hands and slouched. "Okay." If the agent expected Jimmy to do his work for him, he was sadly mistaken. "Why am I here?"

"Can I trust you, Jimmy? May I call you Jimmy?"

"Yes. And I don't know, can you?"

"Right. Assuming you answered those questions in reverse order, I've gotta know I can trust you before I tell you what I have to say." He tapped his fingers on the table. "When I say peoples' lives might depend on it, people you know and may even care about, I am not just slinging bullshit."

This is serious. Jimmy sat up straighter. "All right." Figuring he'd throw the agent a bone, he lowered his voice. "Well, your agent inside here trusted me enough to tell me his secret."

Agent Spinney's eyebrows raised long enough for Jimmy to catch his surprise before he slipped back to his robotic government mode. "You see, Jimmy. That's exactly the type of secret I wouldn't want you to just leak to a stranger in a psych ward."

"Interview room." Jimmy scoffed. "Anyway, this isn't the first time we've met. You're a friend of Detective Reilly's, and she's done right by me. At least, she's always kept her word, and since she owes me less than nothing, I think that's probably just about as much as I could ever expect from her."

"Good, you remember me, and I remember you trying to help that little boy. That took courage and showed character. A whole lot of it." Agent Spinney tented his fingers. "What I'm going to ask you to do will take both. In addition, you help me out, and I will do everything in my power to make your stay in a place like this as short and as comfortable as possible."

"Mine and Tessa Masterson's."

"What?" This time, Agent Spinney didn't let his eyebrows fall.

Jimmy surprised himself with the ask, which had sprung from his mouth without the slightest forethought. But now that the ask had been made, there was no going back. "Tessa Masterson and me. You make both our stays here as short and as comfortable as possible."

The agent smiled briefly, the skin under his eye twitching as the smile fell away. He extended his hand again. "Deal?"

Jimmy shook it. "Deal. Now what do you want me to do?"

"I have an agent in here. You might know him as—"

"The Bandage Man. Yeah, I told you, we've met. Real friendly fella."

Agent Spinney didn't ask how Jimmy knew his colleague. Instead, he curled back his lips and gritted his teeth. "I need you to get a message to him. I'd do it myself, but I'd blow his cover. Tell him they've got Sam and her boy somewhere in here. We need his help. *Sam* needs him."

Jimmy's forehead crinkled like an accordion as he squinted at the table. "Sam and her boy? You mean Detective Reilly and Mikey, don't you?"

Agent Spinney hushed him.

"Wait," Jimmy said, lowering his voice. "How do you know this?"

"I saw them being led into the building at gunpoint."

"And you just let that happen?" Jimmy's nostrils flared. His muscles tightened as he leaned over the table, glaring.

"I had another boy to protect and a police officer in need of saving, and they hadn't seen me yet." He huffed. "It's complicated. And by the time I'd taken one of them out and convinced the officer to get the kid to safety and not to charge into the hospital with guns blazing, they'd sealed up the entrance they took Sam through. It's like it was never there in the first place, a hidden door or..."

When the agent trailed off, Jimmy snapped his fingers. "Who are *they*? What do they want?"

"Honestly, probably the less you know, the better. Needless to say, they are bad people. Some of the worst. Their ringleader is like Hannibal Lecter, Darth Vader, and Richard Nixon all wrapped into one. Anyway, we don't really have time to go into it. They could be anywhere in Brentworth, doing all sorts of nasty things to our friends."

"Or they could be long gone."

Agent Spinney stroked his chin. "It's possible, but I don't think so. I've been following their leader a long time, and the one advantage we have is his cockiness. He likes to let you get close, really close, just so he can show how much smarter than you he is." He gritted his teeth. "No, they're here. I'm sure of it. And by now, they must surely have noticed one of their own didn't report back in last night."

He folded his hands in front of him and fixed Jimmy with an earnest, hopeful stare. "Sam and Michael need our help, Jimmy." The agent's hard features might as well have been chiseled in stone. "I'm counting on you. *Michael's* counting on you."

"Woah, hold on a second." Jimmy pushed away from the table. He shook his head. "This is crazy! If these people are as bad as you say they are and they've got innocent people for hostages, why don't you call in the National Guard or the Army or whoever else you need to sweep through this place and take them all out?"

Agent Spinney's gaze fell, boring a hole in the table. "I can't." The agent seemed to deflate. "My colleagues won't come, not without a confirmed sighting of my target. You could say my business here is... unsanctioned. And even if they did come, my guys would call Detective Reilly's team and let them know what's going down on their turf. But Detective Reilly's guys are compromised. So calling them—"

"Might get Mikey and the detective killed?"

Agent Spinney nodded slowly. "Not *might*." He collapsed into his chair, flopping over himself like a bouncy house that had been popped. "I wouldn't be asking this of you if I saw any other way of getting Sam and Michael out alive. I know how this guy works. Any whiff we're on to him, and he'll kill them immediately, if not for any other reason than the sheer enjoyment of it all. Then he'll disappear before we even get through the door."

Jimmy shivered then steeled himself against the fear threatening to take hold.

Agent Spinney ran his fingers down his face. "If my man can't find them fast enough, I'll have to do just that, anyway—send in an army. He's got three hours. We'll have the place surrounded, the whole damn city blockaded, in less than two."

Jimmy took a deep breath. A chance to save Michael was a chance for redemption. He set his jaw and nodded. "Okay. Tell me everything I need to do."

CHAPTER 22

Sam took a deep breath through the canvas-like material over her head. It clung to her face like a plastic bag as she sucked in air, only to balloon back out as she exhaled. She could make out a pixelated display of blacks and grays through the covering, darkest by the floor where everything below her knees sank into an abyss. Above, sun through a skylight cast shadows in a sparse room. *Daytime? How long was I out?* She recalled being prodded into a big garage, a sharp pain in her neck, then nothing.

The outline of a figure stood only a few feet in front of her, the outline of their lower half spilling out like tentacles merging with a sea of black. The figure nodded. Rough hands dug under the collar, cinching the hood over her head. Jagged nails scraped over her skin. For a moment, the cinch tightened, and she couldn't breathe, a jolt of panic sending an impulse into her arms. She tried to lash out, her panic heightening when she felt plastic biting into her wrists, her hands bound behind her. Panic gave way to pain as the hood was torn away from her head, scratching her lips and bending back her nose hard enough to make her tear up. The hood stung her scalp as it caught in her hair and was yanked free. The light dazzled her eyes, and she blinked rapidly as her vision adjusted. All the while, the figure—a woman—stood as motionless as a support column.

Her eyes clearing, Sam glowered at the woman while subtly testing the binds around her wrists and ankles for any slack. Her captor stepped closer. The tall, Amazonian build was overtly muscular yet apex feminine, a match for only one person Sam knew—Dr. Mira

Horvat. The doctor wore the same cigar store Indian mask as her cohorts, who stood somewhere behind Sam and—

Michael grunted as an older gentleman wearing that same idiotic mask and a police uniform—a legitimate one, or at least a good copy, but not bearing all the call signs of a Fall River Police Department uniform—ripped off Michael's hood. The man stepped backward, beyond her sight. She stared at Michael as his eyes fought to adjust, herself fighting to hold back the torrent of emotion that came with the sight of him in danger and the feeling of helplessness. She yearned to help him but was powerless to do so. Even as the skin beneath her eyes twitched with fear and rage, she clamped her jaw tightly shut and reminded herself she was no good to him if she didn't keep it together.

She learned what she could about her own binds by studying his. Michael's wrists were zip-tied together through the back of an aluminum folding chair, his ankles strapped to the chair's legs. The chair itself did not seem to be held in place by anything other than Michael's weight. Assuming the same was true for hers, she might be able to slide the chair up and out of the binds around her ankles if she leaned forward and shifted her weight onto her feet.

She glanced at the floor, a sprawling area of hard cement. If she fell forward onto her knees—or worse, her face—she might have more severe pains to complain about. Black patches stained the floor. They looked slick, oily, the light reflecting purplish, swirly patterns here and there on their surfaces. An insect or spider walked stilt-legged over the ridges in the poorly poured concrete, dragging something in its wake. The walls were bare, save for cobwebs and a few rusty old tools that might have looked menacing as torture devices if they didn't appear as though they'd crumble to dust at the slightest touch.

Above was just the one light, hanging from a high ceiling in a protective, bullet-shaped metal cage. Beyond it, a flat ceiling with tracks that appeared to be for rollers, doors that opened vertically. Sam wondered if she was in an abandoned ambulance port or perhaps a loading bay from back when Brentworth was Fall River's only hospital. If that were the case, the parking lot and freedom were right outside, just beyond a single wall.

As she looked back at Michael, Sam's heart sank again. She teetered on the edge of despair despite what that would do to their chances. He was watching her closely. His body trembled, but he kept quiet, trying to be brave. His eyes remained dry, wide and unblinking, as his chin quivered. He winced when she looked back at him, having probably seen the terror in her own eyes, the hopelessness she was trying to fight.

Dr. Horvat stepped forward, flicking the tip of a syringe Sam hadn't seen before. "Thanks for waking, Detective Reilly. We are all very busy. That said, I want you to know that none of this is personal." She made no attempt to disguise her voice or remove her accent. She put her free hand on her hip. "At least, not for me."

"Why are you doing this, Horvat?" Sam spat. "What have I or Michael ever done to you?"

Dr. Horvat lifted her mask and propped it on the top of her head. She smiled softly, sadly even. "It is regrettable. Your boy—he is a means to an end. I'm just a simple scientist, content to continue my work with those at my disposal. And you could be so much help to me, to the world even. I must admit, having someone as strong-willed as you will be the true test of my formula, but the boy, a shame, really." She clicked her teeth and shook her head. "It leaves... how do you say it in America? A bad taste? I'd let him go if I could, but..."

Sam leaned forward, her fight draining. "Then please, let him go. If it's me you want, you have me. Just... just let him go. I'll do whatever you want."

"That's just the thing, Detective." Dr. Horvat stepped forward, her expression soft, even compassionate. There was a flicker of doubt flashing behind her eyes, hesitation before she could take another step, followed by almost sad resolve. She sighed, closed the distance between them, and aimed the needle at Sam's neck. "You *will* do whatever I want."

"No."

A man's voice spoke from somewhere behind her. Footsteps approached, heavy-heeled shoes clomping on the cement. A tall man with dark hair cropped close to his skull and pale skin stepped into view, his nose slightly upturned. The expensive, tailored shirt and designer jeans went with his clean, preppy look, and at once she knew who he was and who he'd pretended to be. "She'll do whatever *I* want."

"Curtis?" Sam cursed. "And I thought you actually might be one of the good guys. Some detective I am."

"I really wouldn't know about Curtis," the man said. He turned to the doctor. "Honey, have we enlisted him yet?"

"No. Not yet."

Though his cheekbones were higher and his skin bleached somehow, his slightly widened eyes shimmered with a zeal that could not be altered or counterfeited. Wondering how she could have been so easily duped, she thought back to all the photos she'd seen on Bruce's wall, in the case folders, and in Frank's countless computer files. So much was different but his eyes—those hadn't changed a bit. The eyes of a monster. She was looking at Carter Wainwright.

The realization must have shown on her face. The man offered her a slow clap. "It looks like you've got it all figured out. Bravo! It's nice to be recognized and to be able to play with my food directly. Friends, accomplices, whatever—they're all well and good, but things are always done best when you do them yourself, don't you think?"

Sam shook her head and looked away, hope a distant memory. With the exception of Officer Reynolds and one or two others, people kidnapped by Wainwright were generally never seen alive again. Worse, their bodies evidenced all sorts of horrors enacted upon them while the hearts were still beating. Death would come slow and hard.

"Why?" she muttered under her breath, tearing as she thought only for Michael.

"Maybe I wanted to see if you were as good an adversary as your former partner. That man would go to amazing lengths!" Wainwright laughed, showing off his two rows of long pearly teeth. "Given your current predicament, however, it would appear not."

He laughed again, then took Dr. Horvat's free hand and twirled her as if they were on a dance floor. The doctor blushed and tucked in her blouse when he let her go.

"Or maybe I just have a flair for the dramatic." Wainwright waggled a finger in front of Sam's face. "Relax, Detective. Not everything is about you, you know?"

He turned and stepped toward Michael, who flinched at his approach. "And who do we have here?"

Sam lurched forward, rattling her chair. "If you touch him, I'll—"

"You'll what, Detective?" Wainwright sneered at her through gritted teeth, eyes sharp as daggers, stabbing into her courage and bursting it with a pop. He squeezed her neck, his fingers pressing deep, nails like shovels into graveyard dirt. Sam writhed, trying the squirm away from the pain. But as quickly as his rage had exploded, he released her. A calmness settled over him as if he'd always been the picture of serenity. Wainwright glided over to Michael.

"Ah, yes, I remember you now." He ruffled Michael's hair as the boy jerked in his seat, then tapped Dr. Horvat on the arm. "You remember, dear? He was the kid I told you about—the one who stopped me from getting her the first time."

The killer tugged on his chin and smiled as if he and Michael were old pals. "The way you swung that ax back then, you were definitely trying to take my head off!"

He turned from his victim to Dr. Horvat then wrapped an arm around her waist, pulling her in close. He kissed her with a vibrancy that might have been passionate if not for the fact he was a sadistic psychopath.

What is she, his mad scientist lover? But Dr. Horvat didn't seem mad. Maybe she could be reasoned with. Sam was grasping at straws, but she had to try something. *When the moment is right.* She fought back her tears. *If it ever comes.*

As Wainwright kissed Horvat, he groped in the pocket of her lab coat. She kept the needle in her hand tilted away from her lover's shoulder. When they finally stopped their unnecessary display, the killer faced Sam and Michael, holding a syringe of his own. Dr. Horvat straightened her coat and adjusted the mask on the top of her head.

Wainwright prodded the needle's point under Michael's chin, forcing the boy to look up into his eyes. "You should have let me have her, kid. You probably wouldn't be here today if you had."

Cold sweat dripped down Sam's brow. Wainwright's fingers were dangerously close to touching Michael's skin, a shit-eating grin plastered across his face.

"Soooo, you each get a needle. The good doctor will give you hers, Detective Reilly, a nice little concoction she invented that includes sodium thiopental, midazolam, a little ar—oops, that's proprietary information, actually. Let's just say that her chemical expertise combined with hypnosis has yielded some rather amazing results."

He raised his arms in a what-can-you-do gesture. "Personally, I like gaining a following the old-fashioned way. You know, with charm and charisma. But since Texas, I just haven't felt like my old self. *C'est la vie.*"

He brushed back Sam's hair. She snapped at his fingers with her teeth.

Scowling, he backhanded her. "Knock it off!"

Stars appeared before Sam's eyes, blackness in the peripherals.

"Oh no, you don't," Wainwright said, tapping her face gently. "I've waited long enough to add you to the team, and I'm not a patient man. The first dose already put you out for hours, but if the doctor says it's necessary, so be it." He leered at her, his eyes scanning her every curve. "But don't worry. No one touched you while you were out. We're all gentlemen here, and my wonderful woman wouldn't have approved."

He rolled his eyes. "Anyway, since Ten is in jail and Eight is dead—" He raised an eyebrow at Dr. Horvat. "Is it Eight who's dead or Seven? Eight? Seven?"

Dr. Horvat frowned. "I keep telling you, you can have as many as you'd like."

"True, but that would spoil the whole motif."

Dr. Horvat sighed. "We already have more than ten, if you count me, you, and—"

"The motif!" Wainwright glared at the doctor. "Besides, you're confusing the chiefs with"— he crossed his arms and nodded at Sam—"the warriors. Assuming we get Ten back eventually, we need someone to replace the dead one." His smile widened, and he rubbed his hands together, the needle twirling between his palms. "And who better than a detective?"

"Let the boy go," Sam's voice was low. "I'll do whatever you want."

Wainwright clicked his teeth and shook his head. "You know, for a detective, you don't pay attention very well. I've places to go and people to kill. The boy gets a needle full of air, which has to be the cleanest way I've killed anyone in ages." He shot a finger gun at Michael, whose eyes were beginning to tear. "You're welcome."

Dr. Horvat stroked the killer's arm. "Do we have to harm the boy? I'm sure he wouldn't be so stupid as to talk while we have the detective under our control. And even if he was that dumb, I could make him more pliable, join him in the ranks—"

"No!" Wainwright seethed and looked like he might take a swing at the doctor.

Horvat didn't flinch.

"No," he said again much softer. "I'm sorry, dear, but you know I need this."

"But he's just a ki—"

Wainwright snapped. "A kid that knows too much!"

As before, the rage came and went. He massaged Dr. Horvat's shoulders. "Honey, he's seen our faces, has a pretty good idea what's going on here, and is a perfect pawn to sacrifice in this chess game with the FBI. It's my move, and it's time I made it."

The doctor sighed and hovered over Sam. As Sam's eyes filled with tears, and as she strained to rip her arms free of the zip ties, a sharp pain bit into her neck. Horvat had injected the strange concoction as lithe and quiet as a cat on the prowl. Sam's eyelids flickered and her head began to reel. A crash came to her right, and Michael was on his side, his body thrashing so violently that he was bound to wrench a shoulder out of its socket or cut through to his ankle joint if his binds remained intact. Foam spewed from his mouth.

"I barely even touched him," Wainwright said as he watched the boy flop.

Sam slung her head onto her shoulder, her every movement an effort. "Ung... ung-tie him."

Dr. Horvat crouched beside Michael, a scalpel appearing in her hands. She cut away his binds. "The boy appears to be epileptic. I attempted to treat him for a similar seizure not two nights ago." She turned him on his side and lay down beside him, scooping his head under her arm as if she were cuddling with him.

"What are you doing?" Wainwright stood over her, his face awash with amusement.

"Making sure he doesn't crack his skull against the floor."

"What's it matter? I'm just going to kill him anyway."

Sam giggled. Drool spilled from her mouth. "Not a... not a seigshure. Vishions. He shees futshures." She cackled, unable to stop talking, the words spilling out before she could focus on what she was saying. "More value than me, that's for shh... shure."

CHAPTER 23

Michael has experienced enough visions to recognize them from the beginning. There are two types—visions in which his future self is present and those where he is not. Both start like waking from deep sleep, his sight blurry as it adjusts to light, his other senses dull from lack of use. Time accelerates faster than an airplane, his sight coming into focus with it at an almost heightened state. But in the visions where his future self is not physically present, so, too, does Michael lack the sense of touch—a ghostly watcher of wicked deeds, trapped in an ethereal plane others can neither see nor hear, unable to impact the events fate or God or his own subconscious deems necessary to show him.

Those visions are actually less terrifying. In the other, he is an unwilling participant. While he can move as if in possession of his own, albeit somewhat older, body. He can feel everything, do anything, be responsible and harbor guilt, or hurt and be hurt. Which is why he momentarily confuses the latter with the former.

Michael can't move. He thinks he might be paralyzed. The thought sends a chill up his spine, raising all the hairs on his neck. Panic threatens to whip his thoughts into scrambled eggs. His appendages are useless. He can't even wiggle a toe, never mind lift his head off the dewy grass. His eyes move in their sockets, but on his side, he can't see a damn thing out of his left eye beyond spears of thin green grass and the water droplets clinging to them. The scent of damp earth fills his nostrils, not unpleasant, fresh like a field after a summer rain. The only sound belongs to cicadas chirping out their nightly mating song.

What good can I do with this if I can't see anything? But his right eye can see more. He focuses on learning what he can about his environ-

ment, and his pulse ticks down half a beat. Unfamiliar bleachers, painted white and wooden, with those dangerous gaps between each row that Michael didn't think existed anymore; a starless night sky lit up by stadium lights too bright to stare into; a scoreboard standing to the right of the bleachers, Go Sabres or something similar written on it. Much closer, a line of chalk runs at a diagonal out of sight.

A thump and a groan silences the night critters. A slap follows, then bodies crashing only a foot from Michael's face. Two people, both with short white hair, each with hands around the other's neck, strangle each other. The bigger man on top has better leverage and position. He digs his thumbs into the other's neck, likely crushing the Adam's apple and windpipe.

The slender figure below him wheezes, head turning toward Michael. He gasps, seeing no man at all but Sam. Her hair is cut short and styled up in an unfamiliar rounded coif. And the color is as silver as a coin, making her look older than her years. Her face, too, shows signs of aging, with wrinkles where she never had them before. Whether they are due to exertion or the passage of time, Michael cannot tell.

He tries to reach out for her, tries to scream for help, but he can do neither. Sam rakes at the man's eyes then throws punches into his jaw, but for all her efforts, she cannot break his hold. Michael can only watch as Sam fights on, much longer than he thinks possible, dragging out the inevitable with every last bit of fight she can muster.

He cries as her hands fall by her sides. Her face tilts toward him, lips parted as if to let her soul escape, eyes open and filled with the knowledge of what is to come—for her and for Michael.

The man grunts and rises to his knees. His face is not immediately recognizable, yet as he glowers down at Michael, it is somehow familiar. Sweat drips from his temples. He wipes his hands on his pants and shuffles toward Michael. Resting on his forearms and breathing heavily, he plops down inches from Michael's face. So close that, for all the differences and only meeting the man once before, Michael knows who he has to be—the man with the needle, the man who must have touched him. The man with a city burning in his eyes, a vision he yearns to make reality.

But on recognizing the killer in a vision in which he himself is present, Michael's fears actually begin to retreat. Although disabled, he knows he cannot be dead, and he couldn't have been killed any time between his capture and this moment, whenever the events are supposed to occur. This realization comes with a bittersweet sense of hope—he will survive whatever is happening to him at Brentworth, if only for a little while.

His teeth chatter, and he bites into his cheek. A pain in his shoulder rises with a sob in his throat.

The needle man smiles. "Oh, don't worry, my little shit stain of a friend. I won't do you nearly as quickly."

CHAPTER 24

"So..." Jimmy stared at the mummy-wrapped face of the federal agent he knew only as the Bandage Man. "Do you actually need that face get-up, or do you just have a toilet paper fetish?"

The agent scoffed. "Quit wasting my time, kid. You said you needed to talk, so talk."

Jimmy crossed his arms. He had important information. He knew stuff this idiot would want to know. *Valuable* information, which he would share in exchange for his and Tessa's improved conditions.

"I met with a friend of yours earlier—Special Agent Frank Spinney."

"That—" The Bandage Man threw up his hands and growled. He started to pace the length of their meeting place, the same room the Bandage Man had dragged him into the night before. The empty room was the agent's hiding place near the kids' hall, a fact that only added to his creepiness.

"Is he trying to blow my cover?" He jabbed the tip of his finger into Jimmy's sternum. "Is he trying to get you killed?"

"Michael Turcotte's in trouble." Jimmy pulled down the tail of his shirt. "Detective Reilly too. I'm not sure if you know these people, but—"

"Sam?" The agent grabbed the front of Jimmy's shirt and balled it in his fists, wrinkling everything Jimmy had just straightened. "Sam's in trouble? And her boy? How?"

Jimmy knocked the Bandage Man's hands away. "Your partner said *he's* got them. He said you would know who *he* is."

The Bandage Man resumed his pacing, stroking his chin and muttering to himself. "Where?" he blurted. He looked as if he might grab Jimmy again but didn't. "Did Frank say where he had them?"

"Here... somewhere. They were captured in the woods out back. He wasn't able to see where they took them, but he doesn't think they've been shipped out."

"That's impossible." The Bandage Man muttered to himself like a proper psych ward resident. His pacing became feverish. "I've been over every inch of this place, and I still haven't seen *him*. Not once. I know he's here, but-but-but I need more time, I need more—"

He froze. His Adam's apple bobbed as he swallowed. As he straightened, all his nervous energy seemed to evaporate. "I have to help Sam and her boy, even if that means all this time has been for nothing."

Then he grabbed Jimmy's shoulders and locked eyes with him. "Did Frank tell you what he planned to do?"

Jimmy frowned. "He said he was going to send an army in here and level the place, but he knew what that would mean for Sam and Michael."

The Bandage Man didn't need to ask what Frank had meant by that. The shake that ran through the agent's body confirmed that he'd inferred the same thing Jimmy had when Frank had told him the plan.

"How much time?"

"He said he'd give you three hours while he locked this place and all roads out down, then he's lighting Brentworth up. Said you were his only option for anything stealthy." Jimmy shrugged. "Whatever that means. He said he left you supplies and a new burner phone in the usual spot."

"All right. Thanks, kid." The Bandage Man took a deep breath, then he crept past Jimmy toward the door. "You ready?"

"Ready?" Jimmy's brow furrowed. "Me? Ready for what?"

"If I get caught, they're going to easily tie my actions to the fact that an FBI agent came to see someone here today. You're no longer safe here. I'm sorry, kid. Frank should not have put you at risk, but I'm sure he wouldn't have if he wasn't truly desperate." The agent cracked open the door and peeked out. "So, you're coming with me."

"Where?"

For the first time in the short while Jimmy had known him, he saw something almost resembling a smile form in the crease between the bandages. "We're busting out of this joint."

Jimmy frowned. "How?" The idea sounded great, in theory. Security inside their ward was perhaps criminally lax, the hospital obviously not caring if the whack jobs tore each other apart. But every door leading to the main building or outside was either badge-accessed or guarded, sometimes both. And though Jimmy knew from their little skirmish the other day that the Bandage Man was stronger and scrappier than he looked, the two of them were no match for some of the gorilla-sized security guards and orderlies that stood between them and freedom.

The Bandage Man reached down the front of his pants then pulled out a laminated ID badge. On the front was a picture of the Missing Link. Printed beside the photo was the name Jeb Abercrombie.

Jimmy shook his head. "I guess there weren't too many places for you to hide that, huh?"

The Bandage Man shrugged. "Not where I could keep it handy. Anyway, we've got to move quickly. Frank will have left me a care package. We know Sam and Michael aren't being held anywhere we have access to, so we'll have to sneak into the back rooms. Not all of the staff can be in Wainwright's employ, but we'll stick out like sore thumbs traipsing through areas we don't belong. If anyone sees us—" He shook his head. "Best not to be seen at all."

Jimmy shifted uncomfortably as the Bandage Man groaned then continued talking, more to himself than Jimmy. "We're outnumbered. Outgunned. I don't like this, Frank, but what choice have you left me?"

He gazed at Jimmy with eyes that seemed to tremble, and the uncertainty sent a chill through Jimmy. "If we don't find them, they're as good as dead. We'll have to pray we get lucky, find them, and hole up somewhere until the cavalry arrives."

He grabbed Jimmy's wrist, his grip tighter than a collar, then yanked him into the hallway. "Stay quiet, stay close, and stay behind me."

Jimmy wrenched his arm free. "I got it, man."

The Bandage Man grunted, then hurried down the hall in a half crouch, stopping at every intersection to make sure the coast was clear before proceeding. When he reached the men's room, he gently pushed open the door and stepped inside. Jimmy checked the hall both ways then crept into the bathroom behind the agent.

Checking each stall, the Bandage Man cleared the restroom before dragging an aluminum trash can underneath the room's only window a little more than six feet up. After laying the trash can on its side, the agent kicked off his slippers then balanced on the cylindrical surface like a lumberjack in a logrolling competition. The can rocked and crinkled under his feet, and the cover shot off with a loud din.

Both he and Jimmy froze, listening for any response in the corridor. After a moment of bated breath, the Bandage Man opened the window four inches, as far as it would go. Vertical bars striped any escape that way anyway, though the window sat at ground level, knotted roots from the hedges in front of it partially obstructing the view to a grassy lawn.

"We aren't going out that way," Jimmy said, stating the obvious in a hushed voice. He hoped the agent would explain what they were doing in the bathroom in the first place.

But the Bandage Man just groaned as he stretched his arm through the bars, his fingers clawing at the dirt. "Got it!"

He turned, smiling at Jimmy as he showed him the frayed and dirt-stained end of a nylon rope. Jimmy saw the agent's smile vanish before he heard the door swinging open behind him. He turned and looked up into the eyes of Jeb Abercrombie, aka the Missing Link.

For a second, no one moved. Then Link reached for the whistle that hung around his neck. Jimmy reacted without a thought, rushing the much larger man. He slammed his shoulder into Link's stomach before he could blow the whistle. It shot out of the Neanderthal's mouth with a *whoosh* of air, emitting the slightest chirp as it fell back against his chest.

Link doubled over but snapped back up, a sneer curling up his mouth, nostrils flaring with rage. As Jimmy backpedaled, his mind grasping for his next move, Link's hand, large enough to palm an overinflated basketball, wrapped over his skull. The hand thrust Jimmy's head left, and his body followed. He flew to his side and crashed into a urinal, insult added to the sharp pain shooting through his shoulder because it was the second time he'd been intimate with the inside of a piss pot. The anger filled him with energetic hate, and he gnashed his teeth as he again charged the much larger Link.

His fist flew out wildly, and he hit his foe with at least half a dozen solid body shots. But the orderly shrugged them off as easily as if they were flea bites. He spun Jimmy around, hooked his arms under Jimmy's, and locked his hands behind Jimmy's neck in a full nelson. Pain shot through Jimmy's collar bones. It hurt even more when Link used it to lift Jimmy off his feet. He tried to struggle free, kick his heels against his captor, but every movement caused stabbing pain in his neck and shoulders. Lifting his head in spite of the pain, he could just raise his eyes enough to see the Bandage Man standing roughly eight feet away, arm raised and holding a gun.

"Put it down!" Link roared, but both his arms and his voice trembled. Whether it was fear or the strain of his hold, Jimmy couldn't tell. "Give me the gun, and we can forget this ever happened."

The Bandage Man tossed a ziplock bag with a rope looped through it into the sink. Something was still in the bag, but Jimmy couldn't tell what it was. It thudded against the basin as it hit. The gun the Bandage Man had obtained from the bag—a gift from Agent Spinney, Jimmy assumed—had obviously been the more pressing item.

"I don't think so." The Bandage Man stepped closer. His hands showed no sign of infirmity as he aimed the gun at Link's face. Jimmy assumed he had a clear shot. Link towered at least a foot and a half above him. Sure, Jimmy, lifted as he was, shielded much of Link's body, but that mega pumpkin-sized head must have been an easy target at such close range.

"Shoot him!" Jimmy grunted. He squealed as his neck wrenched forward and the pressure against his shoulders amplified.

"What's your role in all of this, Abercrombie?" The Bandage Man took another step forward. "I haven't pegged you as the brightest bulb or even a good guy, but brainwashing and murder? How'd you fall so low?"

"What are you talking about?" Link's grip tightened and he laughed, but the question came out shakily. "Murder? I haven't killed anyone. Crazy talk from a crazy man. I'm just here doing my job. I'm not the one holding a gun and ranting like a madman. How'd you get that in here anyway?"

"I'm a federal agent investigating the criminal activities of this hospital and the mass murderer behind them. Dr. Horvat—"

"Now, I *know* you're crazy. You? A federal agent?"

Link took a step back toward the door, shrinking a little behind Jimmy. "And Dr. Horvat? A mass murderer?" He scoffed. "She's like the nicest lady in the world. She's helped so many people, me included. I used to be a chain smoker. Not anymore."

He took another step back. His shift in weight told Jimmy he was leaning against the door.

"Not another step," the agent said. "Or I'll have to shoot you." He moved closer. "The way I see it is, you have two options—you can either let the kid go, get on your knees, and hope I'm a whole lot less crazy than you think I am, or I can just kill you now and be done with it. But if you move even one more inch, I'll know you've gone with option two."

Link let out a breath. It whistled through his nose and tickled Jimmy's scalp. After about five seconds with no one doing anything, Link lowered Jimmy to the floor and slowly released his hold on the boy. He pushed Jimmy forward, maybe intending to push him into the gun, but the distance was too much. Instead, Jimmy staggered in front of the first stall and slid inside it to get out of the line of fire.

"Good," the Bandage Man said. "Now, on your knees, hands behind your head."

Jimmy could hear Link's heavy breathing and assumed he was complying. He wondered what the Bandage Man's plan was. They couldn't exactly arrest Link, walk him right out the front door, then haul him off to prison. They had people to save and killers to stop. He looked around for a solution.

"Did she hypnotize you?" the Bandage Man asked.

"Yes, and I haven't smoked a cigarette in like three months. She helped me with... another thing too."

"And you never saw anything wrong with her taking people out of their bedrooms late at night and giving them off-the-books treatment?"

"Yeah, I know her methods are not normal. But she's helped so many people. Like you and those bandages. You don't need them anymore. Why you are wearing them still, I can't figure out, but after she hypno—"

Jimmy broke the back cover of the toilet against Link's forehead. The orderly toppled over then lay unmoving, blood trickling from a fresh wound.

"What the hell did you do that for?" The agent checked Link for a pulse, then sighed when he apparently found one.

Jimmy shrugged. "What else were we going to do with him?"

The Bandage Man rose and went to the sink. From the bag, he withdrew a small black phone, two ammo cartridges, a shiny badge that looked little different than a costume gag one might find at a thrift store, and a pair of handcuffs. He twirled the cuffs around a finger. "I could have used these."

"Still can." Jimmy smiled. "At least this way, he won't be hollering for help for a little while. Or"—he yanked the whistle over Link's head— "blowing on this thing." He threw it in the toilet and flushed.

The agent sighed. He patted his clothes for pockets and places to stuff his equipment. Finding none, he kept it all in the bag except one of the cartridges.

"I guess I should thank you," he said, loading the gun. "Not sure what he might have done had he known the gun was empty."

Jimmy held out his hand. "Maybe you should give me that."

"Like hell, kid." The agent snorted. "Why would I do that?"

"You heard Link. You've been hypnotized by the doctor. You could be one of them, like Tessa, and not even know it."

The agent's brow furrowed. He tugged his lip. "I... I don't remember that." He seemed to consider handing Jimmy the weapon, then shook his head. "No, no. That didn't happen. Anyway, if they got to me, they could have gotten to you too. And even if I am compromised, I'm not at the moment. If I think for a second that might change, you'll be the first to know. And kid, if I start helping them, you'd better shoot me."

Jimmy nodded. "Will do."

The Bandage Man studied the unconscious man lying at their feet. "Well, looks like my cover is definitely blown." He stuck out his hand. "Agent Matthew Pike, FBI. Nice to officially meet you, Jimmy."

Jimmy shook his hand and nodded.

Agent Pike moved toward the door. "You ready for round two?"

Jimmy crept up beside him. "Let's just find Mikey and get the hell out of here."

CHAPTER 25

Michael blinked the sleep from his eyes. He awoke on a cart with plastic side rails under a high loft ceiling, his restfulness and comfort shattered by his strange surroundings and the memory of what had happened. The space was about the size of a studio apartment, but the walls and floor were bare, exposed wooden husks of pest-riddled wood. Besides another gurney to his left with Sam apparently unconscious upon it, Michael saw no furniture or anything of note except for a bucket in the corner. After seeing enough movies where people were taken hostage, kidnapped, or imprisoned in dirty shacks, he didn't have to guess what the bucket was for, though he hoped they'd at least been courteous enough to leave him a TP roll.

He sat up. Aside from a thick steel door, which looked like it belonged on a submarine rather than affixed to the dying wood straining to support it, and the skylight letting in a hazy gray overcast, he saw no means of escape.

He checked his hands. Someone had put gloves on him, the stretchy plastic kind that cops and doctors used. His skin prickled as he wondered how they'd known to do that. His captors must have been confident in their ability to keep him locked up; they'd removed his wrist and ankle restraints. Sam stirred on the cart beside his. He hopped off the gurney and hurried to her side, where she thrashed as if in the throes of a nightmare.

Michael shook her arm, and her eyelids fluttered, briefly exposing blank white sheets. She groaned and rolled onto her side, her back to him. Sweat flowed in streams from her hairline down her face. He started to place his palm on her damp forehead but felt the heat emanating from Sam through his glove even before he made contact. She was burning up or burning *off* something, likely a side effect of whatever they'd injected into her.

His lips trembled. *Come on, Sam. I need you.* He thought about Dylan and Agent Spinney and Officer Tagliamonte, none of whom had been taken prisoner. A lump formed in his throat. The last he'd seen of Officer Tagliamonte, a masked woman had placed a gun against his head. As for Dylan and Agent Spinney, he didn't know. Maybe they were alive and safe. Maybe they'd escaped and would bring help.

Maybe.

He jumped as a slot in the steel door slid open with a *shick*. It closed before he could see whoever was looking through it. Then the door opened. He sat beside Sam, taking her hand in his, eyes fixed on the person entering.

Dr. Mira Horvat was alone. Michael scanned the room for weapons, his mind formulating vague plans of escape even as the door closed tightly behind her. He fidgeted where he sat, his gaze still darting around the room for any symbol of hope and finding nothing. The doctor looked strong enough to take on four or five of him, but she was still just one woman. If he could get past her, get help—

"Even if you managed to escape," Dr. Horvat said as if reading his thoughts, "he would only take it out on her. And although I mean no harm to her or you, my Carter would not be pleased. I would hate to see additional harm happen to either of you."

Michael slumped forward. "Additional harm? Your boyfriend tried to kill me." He sneered. "Somehow, I doubt he'll stop before he succeeds."

Dr. Horvat smiled and stepped closer. "True, he can be somewhat... unpredictable."

"Unpredictable? He's insane."

"He can't help it, Michael. He's sick, like all the folks here in Ward D, some of whom have extremely violent proclivities. Imagine if we can help them to live normal lives. But I'm not there yet.

"Believe me, I'd rather be testing on them than those in prerelease, but the more unstable the brain, the harder it is to reconfigure."

Michael knew a bit about how treatments worked from his own brief conversations with psychiatrists, mostly to check up on his mental well-being after being nearly killed and taken hostage and injected with heroin. Depression could sometimes be treated through the patient's efforts to almost restructure the way they thought with the help of therapy or a combination of drugs and therapy. So he had some idea what Dr. Horvat meant. Talking to strangers had never worked so well for him, and he was glad Sam hadn't pushed the issue. But if it was no help to him, he found it hard to believe someone like Carter Wainwright could be "fixed" through a few casual chats. "You can't fix that level of crazy."

Dr. Horvat frowned. "True, those with more severe forms of psychosis can sometimes be managed the same way, but it's not easy. To truly help them without a lifelong dependency on treatment? We're working on that. You'll see—Carter Wainwright will be my crowning achievement someday. I'll make him better. But it's as you Americans say—baby steps. It's so hard not to sprint for the goal line once you see it within reach."

Michael scoffed. "I don't think that man has any interest in getting better."

"The sick can't always tell what's in their best interests." The doctor sat on the empty gurney. "Anyway, he no longer wishes to harm you. And I'm doing my best to keep him thinking that way. It's different now that he knows what you could do"—she pointed at Sam—"or at least what she claims you can do. I have to admit, I'm skeptical. But if there's one thing my studies have taught me, it's that the extent of what the human brain can do and how it can be manipulated are well beyond the capacity of most of my simpleton colleagues to understand." She grinned and blushed. "My Carter... at least he has an open mind."

"He's a psychopath."

"I can see why you might think that." She sighed. "And you're not entirely wrong. But there is more to him than he lets the world see. And would you discard him so easily due to a disease inflicting his mind? Would you turn your back on your foster mother or your friends if they were similarly afflicted?" She didn't wait for an answer, and Michael had no intention of giving one.

The doctor folded her hands in her lap. "He *is* sick. Plus, most only see his methods, not his end goals. His ideals are grandiose. If you could only see the bigger picture..." She sighed again. "We are both slaves to our ambitions, he and I. Most visionaries are misunderstood at first."

Michael rolled his eyes and grunted his disgust. "Visionary? You think he's a visionary." He scoffed. "Well, then you're just as batshit crazy as he is."

Dr. Horvat stared at her hands. "Crazy?" She stared into space as if considering the notion for the first time, then summarily dismissed it a moment later. "No, not crazy. And we don't use that word around here. I'm not mentally ill, either. A little naïve, perhaps—" She straightened. "No, that is just my insecurities talking. We've accomplished so much already. So much. I just need to be patient."

Dr. Horvat stood and produced a needle from her coat pocket. She raised it before her eyes to check the level of the solution inside. Michael shrunk back, but she circled to the opposite side of Sam's bed and gently grabbed her arm, prodding her inner elbow with gloved fingers, searching for a vein.

Michael bounced on his toes and clenched his fists, but before he could summon the courage to make a move, Dr. Horvat had found a vein and was depressing the plunger. She seemed not to notice his feeble opposition.

"This will counteract some of the aftereffects of the initial dosages I gave her. The second stage is always a little volatile, but no worries. It just gives her flu-like symptoms and causes no permanent damage. She will be fine by nightfall, and we can move into the next phase."

Michael winced at the thought of a next phase, whatever that might entail. "Why are you doing this?"

Dr. Horvat fixed him with a not entirely unsympathetic gaze. But any feeling that exuded from her pursed lips and softening demeanor was undone by the lifelessness that came over her eyes. "We are not monsters, Michael."

Still holding the needle, she circled the bed then sat at its foot, while Sam moaned and kicked in her sleep. "I don't wish to harm you. In fact, I'd love to *help* you, if you'd let me."

"The last stranger who wanted to help me shot me up with heroin. And with that needle in your hand, you'll have to forgive me when I say I think you're full of shit."

"I know how this must all seem to you, and I can't blame you. But our work here is so important. With Carter's funding, we are so close to achieving the impossible. None of this could have been done through the usual channels, at least not in my or even your lifetime. Too much red tape—clinical trials, bureaucratic approvals from small-minded, risk-averse cretins, etcetera."

She gently reached for his arm. The gesture was harmless enough, but Michael retreated nonetheless.

She tried again. "I know all about you, Michael. Our work here would have prevented people like your father from doing what he did to your mother and himself, maybe even kept your birth mother from having her affair in the first place. Imagine all the pain and heartache of your life avoided at its outset, allowing you to grow up in a more positive, nurturing environment. A happy one."

Michael wondered how she'd found out about his childhood, but it didn't matter. His brow furrowed. "You don't know me, and you've got no idea what I've been through."

Her eyes glazed over for a moment, and she blinked. "You see, I was orphaned at a young age too. My father suffered a psychotic break when I was a mere girl of seven. We were a happy family of five with the means to live comfortably in Lithuania. Father had been diagnosed as bipolar and was on medication for it. He was the kindest, sweetest man until one day, he wasn't. He caved in my mother's skull with a tire iron and my little brother, too small and weak to defend himself, he beat to death with his fists. Newborn Alyssa, still swaddled in her blanket, he threw into the fireplace. Hearing their screams, I hid in a closet until a police officer pulled me out the next morning."

Dr. Horvat again stared blankly into space, a slight quiver to her lips. After a moment lost in her thoughts, she took a breath and rose. She tapped Sam's other arm and splayed out her fingers, palm up. Giving Michael no time to react and no hint at what the second needle might contain, she injected its contents into a thick blue vein.

"Anyway, my father was arrested, calmly drinking vodka at our dining room table. He claimed the government had ordered him to do it through a device they had wired into his jaw. His teeth—the antennae, he claimed—sat on the table beside his glass with the pliers he'd used to pull them out. Said he was okay then, that he'd taken care of the problem."

Michael listened, mouth hanging open with horror. Cold indifference had reestablished itself behind the doctor's eyes as she stared at him. She seemed suddenly bereft of humanity, a soul, or anything resembling a spark of life.

He sat on his gurney, all his wind gushing out of him, taking his strength with it. In a hushed voice, he asked, "Why are you telling me all this? Do you expect me to care about you?"

"No, child. I wouldn't expect you would. I suppose I just want you to understand, not only that I mean you no harm, but that I want to help you and people like you. You've seen enough in your own life that makes me believe you want to see people made better—the people who have hurt you, and your friends in here. It's a hard, cruel world we live in. Sometimes, difficult choices must be made if we want to improve it. Sadly, if you live long enough, you'll see that the springs of hope run dry with the fall of youth. The remaining drought dampens only with blood and tears."

"Very poetic? Who said that? Dr. Seuss?"

Dr. Horvat clicked her teeth and cast him a motherly, pitying look that stripped him of his defenses, tempered his cynicism, and left him feeling like a small boy with a bruised knee. "Anyway, after what happened to my family, I lived with my uncle—a safe life but not a good life. We moved around a lot—Russia, Ukraine, Georgia. We even spent some time in what is now Montenegro. He sent me to university, and I continued my studies through multiple doctoral programs." A flicker of a flame appeared in her dead eyes, enough to alight her entire face.

"But my true passion, my *raison d'être*, is to bring about the complete eradication of mental illness through agile psychological treatment, behavioral readjustment, hypnotherapy, and chemical—"

"By brainwashing people to be normal?" Michael squinted. He thought he was getting the picture. Those people in masks—they weren't necessarily bad people. They were just victims, brainwashed by Dr. Horvat and that whackjob, Carter Wainwright. And their *experiments* had gotten at least one good person killed.

"In a simplistic sense, yes." She smiled like a proud teacher. "It's no different than using subliminal messaging to bring about desired behavior, conditioning like that of Pavlov and his dogs, and using hypnotherapy to eliminate nicotine or sugar cravings. With my formula, I can make the subject vastly more susceptible to suggestion, outright behavioral correction even. And I am on the verge of a complete breakthrough. Can you imagine the implications? No more violent personality disorders, no more homicidal thoughts or tendencies, delusions, hallucinations—hell, no more depression. Beyond that, no more racism, hate, bigotry, evil, which means no more war, needless death, genocide. Every undesirable behavior can be corrected in every individual. We are marching toward a future that will be nothing short of a utopia!"

At the last point, she shook her fist in the air. Michael had seen this sort of zealousness before. Victor Suarez had explained away his gang's violence as acts of social justice or some other bull Michael hadn't cared enough to grant his full attention. Dr. Horvat was just another misguided idiot using the greater good as an excuse to justify her wicked deeds.

"I've seen the future, and believe me, it ain't pretty." He snorted. "If you want to eliminate mental illness, killing yourself and Carter Wainwright would be a hell of a start."

She raised a hand and gritted her teeth, then stopped herself from lashing out. "I don't expect you to understand now. But someday, when the naivety of youth gives way to the cynicism of experience, you will. For now, let me simplify it for you. I believe you Americans have an expression about making eggs—how you have to break the shells to do it?"

Michael closed one eye and wrinkled his brow. "You can't make an omelet without breaking some eggs?"

"Yes! You see? Though unorthodox, Carter has given me a place unrestricted by the usual limitations and unburdened by regulation with an open pool of subjects on which to test my formula and techniques."

Michael closed his eyes and shook his head in disgust. "They're not subjects. They're people."

Dr. Horvat crossed her arms. "They're eggs. And I will break as many as needed to make the perfect omelet. Forty years from now—not even, *twenty*—I will be hailed as a genius for my work. The world will not remember the eggs but only the omelet I create." She scowled at Michael. "And if you be a good little egg and do whatever Carter asks of you, you may just live to see it."

Sam moaned and rolled onto her back. Her eyelids began to flutter.

"She'll be waking up soon. Carter will want to speak with you both before we decide what to do with you." Dr. Horvat walked to the door and knocked on it. "Open."

As soon as the door closed behind Dr. Horvat, Michael tore apart his bed. He examined every corner of the room for something to kill Carter Wainwright and his mad scientist groupie. The psychopath was coming, and Michael would fight his damnedest to make sure only one of them left that room alive.

CHAPTER 26

"Two little Indians fooling with a gun. One shot the other, and then there was one." Tessa didn't know where the rhyme had come from, but saying it over and over again filled her with serene joy. It was as if all her troubles, all the bad things she'd faced in life, were scrubbed clean of their griminess, leaving her unburdened and unblemished. And yet, every now and then, her thoughts would wander to that cute, curious boy. When he'd approached her, she'd felt a nagging tug at the back of her mind as if she might know him from somewhere.

But the thought always passed quickly, Tessa content to be left without an answer. And she was happy—happier than she'd been in all her years with her stepfather, happier than she remembered being in the years before even, when she and her mother had lived a close, quiet life filled with love. She flinched at the thought of her dead mother, but that pang in her heart, too, passed quickly. She focused on the crossword puzzle on the table in front of her with almost zealous exuberance. She thought that maybe the world would be an amazing place if she could just work on an endless stream of crossword puzzles every day. As it was, life in the nuthouse lately had been better than it was cracked up to be.

"Where's Jeb?" A high, tinny voice called, snapping Tessa's concentration. Francine marched by her table like a soldier hungry for war. Her body was stiff and straight, her walk brisk, and her cheeks flushed.

Tessa offered Francine a wave and a smile, then shyly let her hair fall over her eyes as the nurse failed to notice her. After all, Francine was busy and had lots of patients to care for. Even if the nurse hadn't seen her, Tessa knew Francine would be there for her if she needed her. Those nights Francine had checked on her in her bed and eventually brought her to see the doctor—Tessa had been a real jerk to the nurse, not understanding that she was just trying to help. And Francine and Dr. Horvat were her champions. They'd helped her see light when all around her was darkness. They were more than caretakers. They were her friends.

Not like that dirty Bandage Man. A chill ran through her at the thought of how he'd grabbed her and pulled her into a room, made her believe all sorts of lies about her friends. She cast her head down, a rush of shame welling up in her for having been so easily fooled.

How she'd needed a friend. But the scowl Francine was wearing then unsettled Tessa, and her fingers began to fidget. "Two little Indians fooling with a gun," she muttered in a barely audible voice. "One shot the other, and then there was one."

Repeating the phrase on silent lips, she watched as Francine moved inches away from the bodybuilder orderly—Curtis, according to his nametag—a three-hundred-pound monstrosity with a surprisingly delicate touch. Of the hospital's staff, he paid her and the other patients the least amount of attention. In fact, he didn't seem to do anything but read magazines or play on his phone unless someone told him to do something or a patient needed help or restraining.

Curtis shrugged. "Haven't seen him."

Francine jabbed a finger into his chest. "That's exactly my point—nobody has. Dr. Horvat sent him for a patient, and now both he and the patient are missing. That new boy, the kid with the red hair, he's missing too."

The meathead shrugged. "Well, I don't know where they are. I just got here. Maybe they both just needed to take a—"

"Find them, Smales! And bring them to the back office when you do. We can't have them running around unchecked. Besides, Dr. Horvat asked if someone could push her desk back, closer to the far wall, so do that, too, will you? Oh, but wait at least twenty minutes. I think she's meeting with someone right now."

"Dr. Horvat's jacked." The orderly huffed. "Can't she do that shit herself? I mean, how hard could it—"

"Just do it, Smales." She softened, put a hand on her hip, puffed out her lips, and stepped closer. "Please? To be honest, I was supposed to, but I have to do some, uh, damage control."

"Ooooh, that sounds ominous." Curtis chortled. "But you need to practice those feminine charms on that officer you've been chatting up. If you were going for sexy, I read constipated."

When she scowled at him and started to speak, he threw up his hands and said, "But yeah, I'll do it. Relax."

A *clack* came from the entrance doors, and Tessa turned toward it. She thought she saw a patch of red hair duck under the window and out of sight.

Curtis, who'd been facing the doors the entire time, hadn't seemed to notice. "I'm sure they're fine." He chuckled. "Jeb probably just got that massive head of his stuck up—"

"Go!" Francine pushed his arm.

The orderly barely budged.

"Find them. Now!"

Curtis rolled his eyes but finally headed toward the double doors.

Without so much a glance in Tessa's direction, Francine walked toward the staff-only door at the opposite end of the rec room. Although Tessa wasn't sure, she assumed that door led to the other wings of the hospital. Francine held her badge over a device beside the door handle. It beeped, and a small red bulb flashed green. She opened the door and stepped through it.

"Hey, aren't you—"

The big orderly's sentence hung in the air just outside the double doors, immediately followed by a loud *thump* that rattled the floor and fluttered the doors. The red-haired boy—Jimmy, if she remembered correctly—pushed through one of them, and behind him, the Bandage Man followed.

"Whew!" Jimmy said. "I thought for sure you'd have to shoot him, or at least whack him a few times. Did you see the size of that sucker?"

"Of course you need to hit them hard, but placement of the strike is key," the Bandage Man said as he tucked something behind his back. "They don't really teach you that at the academy."

"Tessa!" Jimmy sprinted toward her and grabbed her arms as she stood to meet him. "You have to come with us!"

She smiled sheepishly and twisted on her toes, her gaze retreating floorward. The edge of a plastic bag scraped along her bicep but she couldn't see what was inside.

"Are you crazy?" The Bandage Man stared at the boy and placed his hands on his hips. "We can't take her with us. We've gotta keep moving. That nurse could be telling her boss about us as we fart around here."

"We have to take her," Jimmy said. "She's in danger."

Tessa had no idea what danger Jimmy was referring to, but she admired his passion. That said, she had no intention of going anywhere with them. She was exactly where Dr. Horvat wanted her to be.

"She's a liability," the Bandage Man snarled then paced. "We have to keep moving."

"What? You mean like you? Or me?" Jimmy frowned. He reached for Tessa's hand. "Come on. We're leaving this place."

Tessa recoiled and fixed Jimmy with a pointed stare. She wasn't about to be bossed around by him. "I'm staying here."

"Jimmy," the Bandage Man hissed. "We don't have time for this!"

Tessa tilted her head as the boy's expression contorted into one of overwhelming concern, worry lines appearing in droves. All that feeling, all that fear... *Is that for me?* She blushed and bit her lip, unable to keep her gaze above his knees. Though she wouldn't be going with him, some deeply rooted part of her longed to.

She dismissed the thought. Dr. Horvat knew what was best for her, far better than any silly boy could. A bead of sweat tickled her cheek as she tried to keep her smile from wavering. A soft *crack* came from her hands, and she looked down to find her crayon broken.

Jimmy's gaze darted from her to the Bandage Man and back again. He balled up his fists, stiffened, and let out a grumble of frustration. Then he did something Tessa would have thought completely unlikely had it not just happened—he kissed her. It was light and on her cheek, but it made her stomach gurgle as if it were hungry. She stepped backward, her hand over the spot his lips had touched, not knowing what to say or do.

"I'm sorry, Tessa." He had the big-eyed, sad look of a neglected puppy. "We need to go, but I will keep my promise. You'll see. We'll come back with help—for everyone stuck in here."

He left at that, heading for the door with the bag in his hand, which appeared to be holding a cell phone and something metallic and shiny. He ran to the Bandage Man, who was pressing a keycard over the reader at the staff-only door. None of it made any sense to her, but her mouth uttered a word as soon as it had formed in her mind. "Wait."

But Jimmy didn't hear her. He passed through the doorway, letting the door swing shut behind him. Tessa sprinted for it, lunging forward with her foot to block the door from closing all the way. Something told her she needed to follow them. The boy seemed kind, and for some unknown reason, she worried about him. Maybe it was the Bandage Man, filling Jimmy's head with lies about Dr. Horvat. Did that nasty man mean to harm the doctor?

The door's weight pressed hard against her slipper as she debated what to do—stay put and be good, as the doctor wanted, or follow the Bandage Man to make sure he didn't hurt Dr. Horvat. *Or the boy?*

She slid forward onto her trapped foot, wrenched open the door, then stepped through it, a pinging in her subconscious spurring her on despite her better judgment.

CHAPTER 27

"Ugh!" Sam sat up then fell back onto the gurney. She closed her eyes again. "Someone please stop the room from spinning."

"Sam!" She heard Michael shout, his voice like an air horn blasted in her ear. He scrambled to her, which meant he wasn't tied up. In a moment, he was at her side. She tested her arms and legs, raising and lowering each slowly to keep her head and stomach settled. Neither met with resistance.

"Sam!" Hands groped her sleeve and jostled her. "You need to get up!"

White lights flashed under her lids. Sam forced herself to open them, squinted, then closed them again.

"Hurry!"

"I'm trying!" she snapped, her throbbing skull provoking a more venomous response than she'd intended. "It would be easier if you'd quit shaking me and stop yelling."

"Sorry," Michael said, barely a whisper. "But they're coming back. You need to get up now. *I* need you. We've gotta do something."

"Okay." Sam forced herself up again then slid her feet off the bed. She stood up, her body shaking as if her blood sugar had taken a nosedive. She froze, vomit threatening to explode from her mouth, but she swallowed it down, its bitterness worse than sucking on a lemon. Her face puckered and she groaned, but struggling through the burning tang helped clear her head.

The sun coming through the skylight failed to illuminate the room, but even its meager rays stabbed like daggers into Sam's brain. She squinted then snapped her fingers.

"The skylight," she croaked, her voice sounding more like that of an eighty-year-old chain smoker than her own. "Maybe we can get out through there."

She grabbed her gurney and half-rolled, half-slid it into the center of the room, pausing only once to keep from puking. With it directly under the skylight, Sam still wasn't sure she could reach the potential exit. The room's cathedral-like ceiling put it at least ten, maybe twelve, feet up.

"Hold it steady," she told Michael as she climbed atop the gurney. He tried several grips on the rails before he had it. He tightened his grasp, planted his feet, and grit his teeth, his determined expression aggressive, almost savage.

Sam nodded as she rose from her knees to her feet, the gurney shifting and wheels squeaking as it trembled despite Michael's efforts. The shaking, though slight, was enough to make her head reel and stomach churn all over again. Taking deep breaths, she reached for the latch securing the skylight, stretching out her arms and rising on her toes. "I... I can't..."

She let out a sigh and slouched. "I could probably jump up and undo the latch, but I'm not sure if it's a crank, or a push will open it... if it even opens in the first place." She studied Michael, estimating his weight in her head. "Maybe if I lift you up, you could get it open."

Michael raised his eyebrows and slowly removed his hands from the rails. "I'll try." But as he slid his knee onto the mattress, Sam heard voices talking outside. She thrust out her palm.

Michael's gaze darted between her and the door. "What do we do?"

"Shhh!" She crouched on the gurney as if that would somehow make it easier to hear the approaching voices. She needed a moment to think. Maybe two with the way her head was spinning. If she had just a little more time, she was sure she could think of some way out of there. Only one idea came to mind, and she acted on it.

"Quick." Sam jumped off the gurney. "Help me push this in front of the door."

Together, Sam and Michael hurried to block the entrance, making it to the door and tipping the gurney on its side just as the viewing slot slid open and a pair of dark eyes peeked through. "Goooooood," Wainwright's smarmy voice said. "You're both up. Step back, please."

Sam bolted forward and jammed the railing underneath the door handle. She crossed her arms and stepped back, allowing herself a moment of satisfaction as she took in her makeshift barricade. Michael mimicked her, stepping back from the gurney. Wainwright would have had no trouble assessing their lack of weapons or defense from his vantage point.

He tried to open the door. The lever clanked against the gurney's rail then returned to rest. When it moved again, it stayed pressed against the rail. The door pushed open in a smooth gait, the gurney sliding away with it.

Wainwright clicked his teeth as he stepped over the threshold. His doctor girlfriend followed.

Sam rushed him, fist raised. She threw a haymaker that would have leveled King Kong had it connected, but Wainwright effortlessly bobbed away from the blows with speed a man his age should not have had. He was faster than anyone she'd faced before. And her own movements felt slow, hampered by both intoxication and nausea.

She brought her arms back to guard her face, but before she could execute the series of punches she had in mind, the doctor, as strong as Wainwright was quick, kicked her in the side. Sam groaned and folded over the fresh injury. She'd instinctively deflected it with her elbow, but had the kick been a little higher, she would probably have suffered a few broken ribs. A ruptured kidney, though, didn't seem much better.

Still, it was far from her first beatdown. She took in a breath and tried to stand tall, readying for her next offensive against two opponents. As she gritted her teeth and charged, Wainwright drew a pistol. Its nozzle indented her forehead before she could swing, stopping her in her tracks.

"Come now, Detective," Wainwright said, his wry smile returning. "We're all civilized here." He laughed uproariously as if he'd made the world's greatest joke then abruptly stopped.

"There's nowhere to go, Samantha." He lowered the gun to his side. "That's a lovely name, Samantha. Do you mind if I call you that?"

Without waiting for a response, he continued. "Do you remember what you told me while you were under the good doctor's spell?" He paced in front of Michael then back in front of her. "You said the boy here could tell the future."

Sam stiffened. "I have no idea—"

"There's no use denying it, Samantha. You said it. Whether it's true or not remains to be seen, but if there's one thing I know about my darling Mira's serum, it's that if you said it, you meant it." He peered at Sam with calculating eyes.

Unable to talk herself out of what she might have said while under the influence, Sam said nothing.

"Hmm." Wainwright scratched his chin. "Well, I believe you, and you believe you, but Mira here... she's too hard on herself. She thinks perhaps her formula needs a little more tweaking, that maybe you were just too high to think straight."

"She *is* the doctor here." Sam scoffed. "That doesn't make any sense to you?"

Wainwright frowned, and Sam took satisfaction in the small win. His dark, shining eyes, like oil spills aflame, lost some of their twinkle. "Well, your little disclosure is what's keeping—" He jabbed his finger into Michael's cheek with enough force to make Michael grimace. "—him alive."

Sam let out a breath when Michael didn't begin to seize at the touch. Wainwright, however, wasn't done with the boy. He snarled and grabbed the front of Michael's shirt. "Let me ask you, boy. Is it true? Can you see the future?"

Michael gaped at Sam, eyes widening.

"What are you looking at her for?" Wainwright sneered. "I'm asking you. What's the matter? Don't have the balls to speak for yourself?"

"I-I-I," Michael sputtered, then faltered.

"Leave him alone!"

Wainwright let go of Michael's shirt at Sam's voice. "I've dabbled in the occult for many years, seen and done things that you wouldn't even believe possible. So I have a uniquely open mind on the subject. But the people I collaborate with, they've engaged many so-called psychics, and none of them could even predict that I would kill them if they lied. So much for seeing the future."

"It..." Michael's gaze fell to the floor. In a low voice, he said, "It doesn't work like that."

"Oh, so the boy *does* speak!" Wainwright raised his arms to the ceiling as if in exaltation. "Tell me, then. What did you see when I touched you?"

Michael squinted, his face contorting as if he were in pain. "I saw you strangling her." He turned to Sam. "I'm sorry, but it wasn't here. It wasn't now."

"Ho!" Wainwright's head cocked back, and he chuckled. "So all I have to do to prove you a fraud is to kill her right here and now?" He glanced over at the doctor. "What do you think, Mira?"

"You'd be losing a potentially valuable asset." Dr. Horvat shook her head. "*We* would be losing one. She'd be an added layer of protection in allowing us to continue what we started here."

Wainwright rolled his eyes. "Oh, we have plenty of layers for that. Where's your sense of adventure?"

The doctor rested a hand on her hip. "One of us needs to remain pragmatic."

"And that's why I love—"

"All you'd be doing is changing the future," Michael said softly, "which doesn't prove anything."

Wainwright leaned in closer to him. "What's that?"

Michael met his stare, the corner of his upper lip twitching. "I said, that wouldn't prove a fucking thing! People who know what's going to happen can change it."

Wainwright turned to Mira. "I like this kid. Did you know he swung at me with an ax?"

"You might have mentioned it—"

"A fucking ax! I've gotta say, that was a first, and I don't think anyone else would have lived long enough to get a chance at a second try." He shook his head. "Still, the language on someone so young." Wainwright puckered his lips. "*He'd* be a more valuable asset if what he says is true, don't you think? Any ideas on how to test it?"

Dr. Horvat stared up then scrunched up her nose. "I could put him under, and we can find out what predictions he made that came true. A little research should be able to verify what he says. Of course, that assumes my serum is working."

"It's working, honey!" Wainwright pecked her cheek. "Your serum is amazing, and you're amazing!"

Dr. Horvat smiled and blushed. She coughed and straightened her lab coat when she caught Sam staring.

Wainwright tucked his gun in his pants then clapped. "All right. We'll do that, then. We'll keep Samantha alive until we know for

sure, and if he's lying, we'll kill them both as gruesomely as possible."
He clapped again. "Sounds like a plan. I'll send in a few squaws to
help—"

A woman wearing a nurse's uniform nearly stumbled through
the open doorway. "The agent and the boy..." she said through heaving breaths, her mouth twisted with worry. "We can't find them."

"Really, Fran?" Wainwright dropped his hands and brushed his
thighs, sighing loudly. "You had one job."

The woman shrank back at his stern tone, but Sam thought she
detected a hint of a smile on his lips.

"The *Grand Chingon* will not be pleased." Wainwright said the
words as if the Grand Chingon was part of some private joke. He
shook his head and chuckled, somehow amused by the turn of
events, a challenge presented in what to him seemed all some vile
game.

He shrugged. "Well, nothing short of an army is probably on its
way then. Time to exit stage left."

"But my work..." Dr. Horvat crossed her arms and probably did
what was as close to a pout an automaton like her could manufacture,
looking instead as if she were sucking on a lime. "We've accomplished so much here."

"We'll find you a new lab and fresh lab rats *tout suite*, my dear."
Wainwright ogled Sam and Michael, his excitement exuding through
his pores. A glistening near the corner of his mouth might have been
drool. "But first, we have to take care of the supporting cast." He
drew a *Mad Max*-caliber blade from a sheath at his hip. The knife
had teeth more jagged than a crocodile's, with spikes jutting out of
it at odd angles—crafted more to look savage than for any practical
use. Sam wondered if it was anything like the sacrificial weapon he'd
used to remove the hearts of his victims all those years ago, nothing
more than a silly movie prop sharpened to work like the real thing.

Silly or savage, Wainwright's intent for it remained the same. Sam raised her arms in front of her and hoped her training would come instinctively as she executed her defense.

A man, face covered in bandages, stepped behind the nurse as silently as a cat on the prowl. "Don't move."

The man pressed something into her back, and she yelped as she arched away from him. A red-headed boy in pajamas stood in the doorway behind him.

"Jimmy!" Michael shouted, his whole face shining with fresh hope.

Sam put an arm out to hold him at bay. The man appeared to be armed and had not made his intentions known. He wore sweats similar to Jimmy's, so he may just have been another patient at Brentworth, but whose side he was on and how he'd gotten a weapon, Sam couldn't know.

In a scratchy voice, louder and somehow familiar, he said. "Agent Matthew Pike, FBI. You're all under arrest." He slid what he held over the nurse's shoulder—Sam knew a Glock when she saw one—and pointed it at Wainwright. "Anyone moves, and I shoot you first."

Sam scrutinized the eyes behind the bandages, a cold metallic blue that reminded her of clear water on the verge of freezing. She knew those eyes, tried to remember where she'd seen them. Frank must have brought Agent Pike along on the Wainwright ride when he'd stolen her partner away from her. Perhaps that was the reason her mind was invoking images of Bruce.

The agent flexed and curled his fingers around the Glock's grip. "You have no idea how long I've waited for this, Wainwright." His index finger twitched over the trigger. His breaths came shorter, quicker. "There's no way I'm letting you get away this time."

"Shoot him!" Jimmy urged from the threshold. "Before it's too late."

The agent's hand shook. His jaw worked back and forth underneath the bandages as if he were mulling over his next action. Sam knew some men who wore the badge would think themselves heroic for taking a shot at someone as evil as Wainwright, think they'd be doing the world a favor, and Sam wasn't so sure she disagreed with that line of thought. But this man had a stronger moral code—Sam could see him caught between the hate in his words and eyes and the uncertainty and hesitation in his posture. The man who claimed to be FBI was suffering some deep, internal conflict.

Jimmy stepped forward, hand out. "Give me the gun. I'll do it."

For the first time, Wainwright's face lost a bit of color, and his shit-eating grin fell away. However well he'd thought he had things under control, the killer had evidently not considered Jimmy. And Jimmy, poised and steady, looked like he could easily do what the agent could not.

"I said stay behind me, kid." Agent Pike snarled. "I'm not like him. I can't just... Anyway, he needs to answer some questions. The boy? The inside man?" His voice cracked as he shouted. "It's over, Wainwright. No more games. Tell me everything!"

Wainwright's hands rose. "I could, but I'm not sure you'd like the answers I have to give."

Agent Pike roared and threw the nurse aside. He charged at Wainwright with the ferocity of a bear, clobbering the killer with the butt of his gun about the head, over and over again. Wainwright squealed, dropped his weapon, and crouched with arms up to shield the blows.

After ten or eleven strikes, the agent at last relented. Breaths heaved in and out of his chest, which pulsated like a heart. Wainwright had managed to fend off half the strikes with his forearms, but his hair was matted in places where the skin had split, and his right eye was swollen closed. With one hand planted on the floor and the other draped over his knee, he glanced up at his lover, raising his un-bloodied eyebrow. "Well?"

"Oh, shit!" Jimmy hurried to Pike's side.

Her voice calm and monotone, Dr. Horvat said, "Four little Indians up on a spree."

The agent froze. The doctor's words, nonsensical as they seemed, had stilled the bandaged-faced man right down to the tremor in his trigger finger. He stared blankly forward, Glock still raised as Jimmy chopped it from his hand. The gun spiraled and clattered onto the floor. Sam and Jimmy started for it, but the sound of a gunshot froze everyone in place. Sam whipped around to face the shooter.

Wainwright dropped his arms to his sides, knife hanging loosely in one hand, a freshly fired pistol in the other. His wicked grin had returned despite his injuries. "I could do this the easy way, or—" He pointed the gun at Sam, the agent, and finally Jimmy. "Who the fuck are you, kid?"

Jimmy said nothing. He slowly raised his hands.

Wainwright took a deep breath and tilted his head, wheels spinning. "It doesn't matter, except now you've gotten yourself into something you probably wish you'd stayed out of. I was going to kill those two"—he pointed at Sam then Michael—"or use them then kill them just to further fuck with you and your bumbling FBI agent friend. But this? *This* is too good an opportunity to pass up! I couldn't have asked for a more amusing scenario than what you've hand-fed me."

He handed the gun to Dr. Horvat. "Honey, would you be so kind as to clean up the mess should our favorite Fall River detective fail? By now, good ol' Frank's gotta have the building surrounded. I'm going to make sure our escape route hasn't been compromised."

He hesitated as a boy called to dinner who wanted nothing more than to stay and play. "I do so hope he lives, though. Such a wonderful plaything he's been! But lately, things have been just a little too easy. Perhaps it's time to kill off some of the mice in the maze. Oh ho! Imagine his face when he realizes we made him kill his own partner?" He kissed the doctor's cheek. "I'll want details!"

Dr. Horvat scowled, the gun hanging from her limp-wristed grip as if she found its feel distasteful. As far as Sam could see, she was both the brains and the stability behind the duo, yet for some reason, she'd decided to play second fiddle in his mad opus and did as she was told.

"Fran," he called, waving the nurse to his side. "You're with me."

"Yes, sir."

Just as Fran stepped up to him, he jabbed his knife into her stomach. He twisted it as he pulled it back. The squelch it made as it slid out of her belly turned Sam's stomach. Other than a slight *umph*, the nurse made no other sound. She slowly dropped to her knees, hands clutching the front of her uniform as blood seeped between her fingers. To Sam's right, Michael gurgled, his face porcelain white.

"Just saving the Grand Poobah or whoever some effort." Wainwright waved his hand flippantly. "Ah, who am I kidding? I just really needed to stab somebody." He waggled his fingers, turning his back on the dying woman. "Ta-ta."

As he exited, he shouted cheerfully, "Kill them, Bruce! Kill them all!"

CHAPTER 28

"Four little Indians up on a spree." Agent Pike thrust his arms around Jimmy as he and Sam scrambled for the gun. "One got fuddled and then there were three."

With her hand on her hip and cheek pinched, Dr. Horvat watched the action unfold with disinterest. She raised her pistol slowly to fire on whoever came up with the weapon. With Jimmy held back, Sam became her target. And with Francine dying on the floor and Wainwright gone, that left no eyes on Michael.

Did Jimmy come to save us? He had so many questions, though it did seem like he and Sam had gained at least one ally. And they were all fighting to survive, while he just stood there doing nothing. He seized his chance and charged.

A second later, he skidded over the dirty floor, Dr. Horvat's backhand knocking him aside and emblazing his ear. He pushed himself up, a little dazed but pissed and primed for another attack. But before he could get to his feet, the doctor had him by the hair and was bashing the butt of her pistol against his ear. "Do you know what this setback will cost me?"

The sound of her voice was muffled on one side, replaced by a soft but persistent ringing. He staggered to his left, suddenly off-balance, dizziness and shakiness overpowering his pain.

He was no match for the strong tug on his scalp, which kept him standing. "Hold still, child," Dr. Horvat grunted. "Carter may like his games, but I have no time for this."

"Let him go!" Sam shouted from the far wall. She held the gun out in front of her in a two-handed grip, just like she'd taught him.

But the business end of the Glock seemed to be pointed directly at Michael.

Hard, hot metal pressed into his temple. Dr. Horvat crouched and pressed her breasts against his back, the feel of them making Michael blush despite his peril. Her breath tickled the hairs on his neck and sounded like a hurricane in his damaged ear. As he stared at Sam and her gun, he immediately understood the doctor's intentions—she was using him as a shield.

"Shoot her, Sam." He hoped he'd sounded more confident than he felt. He knew he was shaking and hoped Sam—or Jimmy, for that matter—didn't see it. But Jimmy was facing his own problems, his arms pinned inside a wiry-armed bear hug, the agent's muscles taut as he squeezed the life out of the boy. Jimmy thrashed and sucked in air, but the agent seemed immune to Jimmy's constant kicking, his eyes glazed over as if he were lost in a daydream.

If I had just stayed out of the way. A tear ran down Michael's cheek as he chided himself for ruining Sam's clean shot, preventing her from doing her job and saving them all. Even when he tried to help, he just made things worse. He was such an idiot, a loser, and was always going to be a loser. He closed his eyes, pushing out fresh tears, no longer knowing who he wanted Sam to hit. "Just do it, Sam."

Sam raised her arms, gun pointing at the ceiling. "Wait. Just... wait." She crouched and placed the gun on the floor, then slowly stood back up. "You don't have to do this."

Dr. Horvat trained her gun on Sam. "Sadly, I do. Believe me, I wish I didn't, but I do." She roared out her frustration. "And *he* knew I would have to."

"You could walk away. Just lock us in here and leave." Sam took a step forward. "You don't have to kill us, or at least not the boy." Her voice cracked. "Not Michael... please."

Without the gun, Sam was a sitting duck. "Please," Michael whimpered. "I really do have visions. I can help you, help him. Just let her and Jimmy go, and I'll do everything you want."

"I'm sorry, child," Dr. Horvat said softly. "I'm afraid there's no getting around it. You've both seen too much. The detective will never stop coming after me, never let me do my work in peace, much like that persistent agent over there." She flicked the gun toward Agent Pike, who was still squeezing the life out of a poor wheezing Jimmy.

"He's just using you, you know." Sam groaned. "You're an intelligent woman. You must see that!"

"We both have our uses. My interests in him are purely scientific and economical... well, mostly, anyway. A woman has her needs, and Carter is nothing if not exciting." Dr. Horvat let out a long exhale. "I'm sorry, Detective. Not so much about you, but for the boy. My hard work is intended to help people, not harm them. But if it's any consolation, my contributions to society will, in the end, far outweigh any harm I may have caused."

"Wait! Let's talk about—"

"Play it again, Sam," the doctor uttered in that same calm robotic voice she'd used when she'd spoken to Agent Pike.

Sam frowned, squinted, then blinked a half dozen times. "What?"

Dr. Horvat growled. She repeated the phrase more loudly.

"She's trying to brainwash—"

A hand clamped over Michael's mouth. Sam's forehead grooved. Her head cocked, and she shook it as if she were trying to get water out of her ear. Then she took a step forward. Straightening, she stared unblinking at the doctor like an obedient dog awaiting a command.

Dr. Horvat snickered. "You're faking. You think I don't know when a subject is under?" Her arm slid across Michael's throat. "I do *not* have time for this!"

"Don't hurt her!" a familiar voice shouted. Someone hurled herself from the doorway just as Dr. Horvat snapped out her arm to fire at Sam. Michael bit into the doctor's sleeve, teeth clamping through the thin fabric of her top. The gun went off as he, the doctor, and the stranger tumbled to the ground in a rolling mass of limbs.

Michael struggled to his feet. As Michael pressed his palm against the floor, something wet coated his skin. Rising, he glanced at the red liquid dripping from his plastic glove, then held his breath as he hastily checked himself for wounds.

"Freeze!" Sam said, looking more herself and standing only a few feet away. She stared intently at Dr. Horvat. Nodding over her shoulder to the agent who was still crushing the life out of Jimmy, she said, "Drop the gun and make *him* stop."

Dr. Horvat, still holding her gun at her side, smiled insincerely, her brain working behind that sinister grin. She was weighing her options while Jimmy was dying.

"I said, drop it, and make him stop." Sam stepped forward, her gun still leveled at a spot between Dr. Horvat's eyes. "Now!"

"I-it's good to see you again, Michael," the stranger said in a shaky voice.

Michael had nearly forgotten about her, his focus on the standoff and Jimmy's limp frame in the agent's arms. He turned to face Tessa, his heart jumping with elation despite the heartache around it, then plummeting into despair as he took in her ashen face and bloodied shirt. A gun clattered at his feet, but Michael hardly noticed it. "Tessa! How? What are you and Jimmy doing here?"

"Are we still in Brentworth? I feel... dizzy." A smile flickered across her lips as she reached up with a bloody finger to touch his face. "I... missed... you."

Michael flinched back from the touch. Every word seemed a struggle for Tessa, each much lower than the one before it. Tessa's eyes rolled back. She fell to the floor.

"Shit!" Sam said, making it to Tessa's side almost as quickly as Michael had. "Apply pressure to the wound. Both hands!" Sam's fingers searched Tessa's neck for a pulse, her other hand still aiming the gun at Dr. Horvat.

With Sam's attention divided, the doctor made for the door. Sam fired. The bullet exploded the wood in the wall beside the exit. Sam bolted after her, stopping the door from swinging shut and locking them in.

But Sam didn't continue after her. She turned and roared. "Fuck! Tend to her while I help Jimmy."

"Why are they here?" Michael whined. He looked at the open door, seeing an escape from the madness around him, wanting at that moment to be anywhere but there. Sam would get them out, would keep them safe. She had to. Even as two of his only friends died around him. "Why is this happening?"

"Michael, you need to help Tessa. Now!"

The sharpness in Sam's voice incited purpose. Michael sniffled and searched Tessa's top for the entry hole, but so much blood had soaked it that he couldn't tell where it was coming from. Her chest no longer rose and fell, but a slight hiss between her lips kept him hopeful. He yanked up her shirt and found blood bubbling from a dark patch just over her left breast. Placing both hands over it, one overlapping the other, he pressed down hard.

"Don't die, Tessa." His eyes blurred. "Please don't die."

He heard a *thump*, then Sam shouted. "Shit! He's not breathing. Shit! Shit! Shit!" A thump on the floor came with every word. "Beginning CPR. How you doing over there, Michael?"

Michael blinked. He watched his tears fall against Tessa's bloodied chest. "Not good." His nose ran, and he sniffled. "Not good."

"Just... keep applying pressure. The Fed is out cold, but if he's who he says he is, I'm sure help is on the way. Hold on, Michael."

Even while pumping Jimmy's chest in a cadence that seemed to match the pounding of the heartbeat in his head, Michael could see through the lie in her words. He leaned forward, hovering his wet cheek a fraction of an inch over Tessa's mouth. The faint hiss of air was gone.

A sob escaped him. Wails tightened up his chest and suffocated him. The blood smearing his hands was cooling, congealing. Tessa's body under it was still. His friend—no, she was so much more than that—someone with whom he'd shared a bond of loneliness, of freakishness, of kinship, and maybe even of love—was gone.

And it was all his fault.

CHAPTER 29

J immy gulped in air as he sat up, the splintering pain in his sides as his lungs expanded a terrible reminder that he was still alive. He took in his surroundings, everything coming back to him quickly. Detective Reilly crouched beside him.

"Agent Pike!" he sputtered. God, how it hurt to talk.

"Easy," the detective said, her face contorted with what looked like genuine concern. She pointed to her right. "He's over there."

Jimmy's eyes widened as he saw Agent Pike lying prone and not moving. "You didn't—"

"No. He's just unconscious. Whacked him pretty good with his Glock, so his head's going to be ringing something awful when he wakes. But listen, if you're okay, I need—"

"That jerk! I told him—" Jimmy groaned and blinked, his head still a little fuzzy. Pressing his knuckle into his forehead and making small circles. "He should've just given me the gun. Asshole tried to kill me!"

Detective Reilly snapped her fingers. "Jimmy? Are you listen—"

"Phone! I had a phone!" He scrambled to his feet and began looking for the bag he'd brought in with him. Detective Reilly gave him a confused, maybe annoyed, look, but he paid her no mind.

Scanning the room for the plastic bag he'd been carrying, he spotted Michael crying and squatting over a limp form. His breath hitched. "Mikey?" A chill ran through him. "Is that... Tessa?"

Hands grabbed his shoulders and spun him back around. Detective Reilly's pained expression communicated the gravity of the crap he'd awoken to, her soft, almost sickly look casting a vibe through

Jimmy that rattled his nerve. "If we don't do something soon, she'll die. You said something about a phone?"

Jimmy tried to focus. *She looks like she's dead already.* He started to turn, but the detective shook him. Stern eyes met him as he faced forward again.

"The phone, Jimmy. We need that phone!"

"I-I-I must have dropped it when the Bandage Man, er, Agent Pike grabbed me." He took in the room again then ran to the doorway where he found the plastic bag. Inside was the burner phone and Agent Pike's badge, which was apparently jostled out of his arm and knocked over there during the melee. He muttered a thank you to the Almighty as he bent to pick it up, grateful neither the doctor nor that crazy killer had seen the bag while retreating.

Wasting no more time, he ripped open the bag and powered on the phone. He dialed the one number he found programmed into it, and as it rang, he hurried back into the room.

"Matthew?" Agent Spinney spat after one ring. "What's your status?"

"Uh... Agent Spinney, right? This is Jimmy. We—"

Detective Reilly stole the phone from his hand. "Frank? Is that you?" After a split second, her shoulders dropped a little away from her ears. Even then, she looked wound up tighter than a lug nut. "Oh, thank God. He's okay. *We're* okay. But listen—"

Detective Reilly winced then frowned. "Your agent? The fucking guy tried to kill us. But, Frank—"

The detective huffed as Agent Spinney apparently interrupted her a second time. "*Brainwashed?*" The word came out of her mouth as if it were the stupidest thing anyone had ever said to her. She paused a half a second, breathed, then said, "Okay. Maybe. It doesn't matter. We need a bus stat! Civilian down. Plus—" She stomped her foot. "I know we're at a hospital, but those lunatics are still here somewhere if they haven't already made their escape, and who knows how many other *brainwashed* people they've got here to do their bidding? So get off your ass. Get us hospital staff you can trust, lock down this place and the entire damn city, and do all of that right fucking *now*!"

She cocked her head, scowling as she listened, then handed the phone to Jimmy. "Here. Tell him how to get to us."

Jimmy placed the phone against his ear and did his best to explain to Agent Spinney the circuitous route that would lead the cavalry through the rec room and into an unused portion of the hospital to the dungeon of a room where he stood.

Jimmy held the phone loosely by his side and turned to Sam. "He put me on hold."

Sam rolled her eyes. Shouting came from somewhere far off inside the hospital.

"What's all that screaming?" he asked.

The detective, Michael, and Jimmy searched the walls as if the voices came from somewhere within them. No one said a word.

"Jimmy!" Frank's voice bellowed through the phone's speaker, and Jimmy pressed the phone back to his ear. "You have to get out of there. They're all out. All the most violent offenders from Ward D. It's a madhouse in there."

"Shit!" Jimmy spat. He looked at the detective then Michael. Both gazed at him, expressions expectant as if he might be able to give them good news, some hope, or at least a false promise that help was on its way. He looked down. Instead, he could only tell them that things had gone from bad to worse.

"They're killing staff and other patients alike," Frank said. "Get out of there! Get out now!"

The line went dead. He could see in Michael and Detective Reilly's wide eyes and bloodless cheeks that they'd just heard every word and felt a modicum of relief at not having to be the one to tell them. He waggled the phone at Tessa. "We can't just leave her."

Detective Reilly took a step toward him. "We have to. Jimmy, she's already—"

"I'll carry her." Agent Pike was on his feet, surprising them all. Jimmy nearly dropped the phone as he jumped.

All eyes were on the agent as he walked over to Tessa and crouched near her limp form. With the gentleness of a loving father, he scooped her into his arms and stood. "Let's go."

CHAPTER 30

"We need to get a move on before someone finds us." Agent Pike nodded at the gun in Sam's hand. *His* gun. "Sam, you take point. I'll guard the rear."

Sam didn't trust the stranger and supposed FBI agent who'd just tried to kill Jimmy to watch her back. A little voice inside her head, growing louder, screamed at her to shoot the man for whom he pretended to be. It couldn't be, *shouldn't* be him. Not after all those years of silence, of letting her believe he was dead. A betrayal like no other. *How can I trust him now?*

She put it out of her mind, tending to what needed to be done, but she couldn't keep the nagging question at bay any longer. Her voice quivering, she asked what her heart had already answered but what her stubborn brain refused to accept. "Why did he call you Bruce?"

"You know why, Sam," the agent said, his voice quiet, filled with shame. "When we get out of here, we'll have a lot to talk about. But first, we need to get these children to safety."

Sam bit her lip, but she nodded. Slowly, she crept to the door, the pistol by her side pointed at the floor. Michael followed behind her, then Jimmy, then the agent—*no, then Bruce*—carrying Tessa's dead weight. Sam's heart went out for the girl, but it was too late for her. And by the sounds of screaming and mayhem happening in the direction they were headed, she could use another able-bodied person at her side, not one encumbered by the fiction of hope.

They exited the room into darkness. The corridor outside was like an abandoned subway tunnel, cool and desolate. Despite having a fixed beginning and no offshoots that she could tell, it was unnavigable in its utter blackness. One of the boys trotted up beside her, lightly brushing against her elbow.

"It's this way," Jimmy said. "Just follow the wall. There are a few steps up to a door at the end of the corridor. There should be light on the other side."

They walked the hall as quickly as caution would allow. Banshee wails echoed around them as if they were at the bottom of a well, making it impossible for Sam to determine which direction they were coming from. A *bang* sounded ahead of her, and she reached out for Jimmy, her heart skipping when she couldn't find him.

He grunted. "Found the stairs."

The squeak of a turning doorknob and the creak of a door hinge brought light flooding into Sam's eyes. When her vision adjusted, she saw another mostly empty hallway with a few cardboard boxes stacked along the right wall. This corridor, though, had many offshoots and rooms to boot.

She tugged on the back of Jimmy's shirt, pulling him behind her. "Which way?"

Jimmy pointed. "Second left. That hallway should lead to the rec area inside the prerelease ward. From there, I'm not a hundred percent sure how to get out. But I can get us to the visitation area. Patients come from one direction while the visitors always come from the other, so..."

Sam nodded. It was as good a plan as any. If they passed by the offices where she'd met Dr. Horvat earlier, she could get them out from there. But having spent most of the last twelve hours drugged out of her mind, she couldn't even venture a guess as to where the psychopath and his deranged girlfriend had deposited her and Michael. Resuming point and keeping her weapon at the ready, she stalked down the hall past sparsely decorated rooms with separating curtains and rusted gurneys. Anyone could have been hiding behind those curtains or in hidden corners. She halted and listened.

A shriek came from somewhere up ahead, muffled by plaster and partitions. Unfortunately, it seemed to come from the very direction they were heading. To her right, a shadow shrank into a room.

She aimed her gun at the doorway. "Police. Show yourself!"

A giant hand, raised in surrender, emerged from around the wall. A massive frame of pure muscle in scrubs and the unfamiliar face of a dark-skinned young man appeared. Pinned to his chest was a nametag that read *Curtis*. "Don't shoot! We're unarmed!"

"We?" Sam held up her hand for the man to stop moving. "Who's in there with you?"

"A few of the patients—Manny, Terry, and Harriet. Good people. Please, help us. The place is overrun, inmates from Ward D killing everyone they see. How they all got out is beyond me. It's a bloodbath out there. We were in the rec room when we were attacked. One of them had a scalpel and started slitting throats."

"How'd you escape?" Sam kept her gun trained on the orderly. She'd already been betrayed by one Curtis.

"The staff-only door. You need a badge to get in through here, so those psychos couldn't follow us. They only stopped pounding on the door a few minutes ago. Hopefully, they've given up. The screams don't seem as close anymore."

"Okay," Sam said. "Step out slowly, all of you, and line up against the wall."

A woman in her seventies with knobby, arthritic fingers but a shrewdness in her eyes followed in the wake of the hulking Curtis. Behind her came a pudgy middle-aged gentleman whose shirt was a little too short and tight to cover the hairy spare tire hanging over his waistline. Finally, another man with a full head of thick gray curls came staggering out, face as white as clean linens. His neck was wrapped in medical tape, a dark-red stain blotting a compress under it.

"Manny took a pretty good slice in the melee," Curtis said as he nodded toward the last man's injury. "I did what I could for him. I'm just an orderly, but I'm going to nursing school, so I've had some training."

"Really?" Jimmy stepped between Sam's gun and Curtis and tugged at the orderly's sleeve. When the man didn't budge, Jimmy pointed at Tessa and said, "You've got to help her!"

"Jimmy, can you vouch for these people?" Sam had almost asked for Bruce's opinion, but that would have meant acknowledging her late partner's continued and inexplicable existence. She wasn't ready for that.

"Yes. Portuguese Guy, Chess Lady, and, uh, Dirty Terry. They're all fine, I think. Who knows who's been brainwashed in this place."

"What about him?" She waved her gun at Curtis.

"If he helped all these people, I'm guessing he's okay." Jimmy dismissed Sam, again tugging at Curtis. "Can you help her? Please?"

Sam nodded, and Curtis slowly let his arms fall. He walked over to the girl cradled in her formerly dead partner's arms. He froze when he noticed who was holding her, then cocked back his fist. "I oughtta kill you for—"

"Enough!" Sam shouted.

The orderly shook his head and let out a breath, then he examined Tessa.

Bruce straightened. "I'm a federal agent. Undercover. Sorry about earlier. Like the boy said, it's hard to know who we can trust in here."

Curtis looked around incredulously, but when no one disputed the man's claims, he just shook his head. "This day just keeps getting weirder and weirder."

He put two fingers against Tessa's wrist. "I'm not getting a... Wait. It's there, but it's faint." He hurried back into the room. "Bring her in here quickly."

Bruce carried Tessa into the room and laid her upon a dusty old gurney. It squealed beneath her weight.

Curtis shuffled about the room. "There's little I can do for her except maybe stop the bleeding." Whatever he'd grabbed to fix up the one called Manny, he carried over to Tessa. Without hesitation, he ripped open her shirt and doused the wound with what appeared to be hydrogen peroxide. Sam bet it would have hurt like hell, but Tessa didn't budge. Sam didn't have much hope she'd survive. And the longer they stayed there, the longer the rest of them remained in danger.

"She was shot?" Curtis's eyes searched each of them in turn for an answer.

"Yes," Sam said.

Curtis lifted Tessa's shoulder. "I don't see an exit wound. I can clean and stitch her up and stop the bleeding, but the bullet will still be inside her. She will need it removed and probably several blood transfusions if she's to have any chance at survival. We need to get her to the ER ASAP."

Without another word, Curtis hastily went about caring for the wound as best he could with the few tools he had to work with. When he was done, Tessa appeared just as lifeless as she did before he'd started, her chest falling and rising almost imperceptibly.

"Spinney!" Jimmy shouted into the cell phone. "Are there ambulances outside?" Jimmy began to pace. "Okay. Got it. We'll find a way." He hung up the phone.

"He says the doors are barricaded. Everyone who could be evacuated has been, but doctors are on standby. The police have the building surrounded and are rounding up most of the residents who tried to flee. But several patients still inside have blocked the entrances and taken hostages. They can't barge in without risking innocent lives."

"So, we find our own way out?" For the first time, Sam looked Bruce in those glossy blue eyes she knew so very well.

He met her stare. "Looks that way."

"I don't recommend moving her," Curtis interjected.

"You go," the old woman, Harriet, said. "I'll stay with her and Manny." She pointed at the curly-haired gentleman slumped in the corner, rocking with his hand pressed against his neck. "I'm too old to be fighting off sick men with scalpels. I'll only slow you down." She patted Tessa's hand and grabbed Manny's. "At least here, I can provide some comfort."

Sam's uncertainty in leaving Tessa's care to a psych ward patient must have shown in her face because Harriet looked her dead in the eye. "Not all of us here are crazy. Most of us are just tired and beaten, worn down by a world that never had much of a place for us in it. The girl will be fine with me. I'll keep her safe."

Sam nodded slowly. "Curtis, do you know another way out of here? If the entrances are blocked—"

"It doesn't make any sense." Curtis scratched his scalp, taking a moment to breathe. The direness of their circumstances seemed to be finally catching up with him. "I mean, how could they have gotten out? And gotten weapons?"

"This hospital has at least a few sick fucks on staff, Dr. Horvat and Carter Wainwright among them." Sam ground her teeth. "But Curtis, listen to me—"

"Carter Wainwright, the serial killer? Here? And Dr. Horvat? That—"

"Curtis!" Sam yelled, then checked herself. "Do you know any other ways out of this place?"

The orderly shook his head. "No, but... you said Dr. Horvat has something to do with this? It may be nothing, but I was given the oddest instruction from Francine just before this asshole"—his eyes shifted to Bruce—"clubbed me in the back of the head."

The agent grunted in apology.

Curtis shrugged. "Anyway, Francine wanted me to move the desk in Horvat's office, but not until twenty minutes into my shift. When I went to Horvat's office, I was wondering if maybe she got her instructions wrong, 'cause otherwise, I'd be blocking a closet door. So I peeked inside to see if Horvat kept anything important in there, and it actually led to the basement, but not the one we use—the old section. Couldn't find a light though, so I don't know what's down there. But now I'm thinking, even if it's not a way out, it could be a great place to hide."

"Take us there," Bruce said.

Sam studied what little she could of her former partner's face, unable to read his intentions. She wondered if he cared more about catching Carter Wainwright than leading the children to safety. Having no other means of escape that didn't involve facing down violent psych ward inmates, she assented.

"I should stay with the injured and Harriet," Curtis began. "Take Terry—"

"Show us!" Bruce snapped. He let out a breath. "We don't have time for discussion."

"We'll be okay, Curtis," Harriet said softly. Her soft wet eyes shimmered with something far short of confidence.

Curtis sighed. "Okay." He set his jaw and looked at Sam. "I hope you know how to use that thing."

Sam followed him left to the hall that Jimmy had indicated. There, they walked quietly toward a door at the end.

Curtis put his ear to it. "I don't hear anything."

Sam closed her eyes as she listened for any sound, near or far, within the hospital. All had gone quiet. The screaming had stopped.

Curtis hovered his keycard near the card reader, his other hand gripping the door handle. "You ready?"

Sam flexed her fingers around the grip of the pistol, spread her feet apart, and nodded curtly. She held her breath as the door swung open. Seeing no immediate threat, she let out some of the tightness in her shoulders. Then she took in the room. The air tasted of copper, and the smell was that of emptied bowels. "Michael... just, uh, try not to look."

"When you say that to someone, what do you think will be the first thing they'll do?" Michael crept up beside her. "Anyway, hanging with you, I'm sure I've seen..." His mouth dropped open.

Sam stepped in front and turned to face Michael, shielding him from the worst of the carnage. In her quick assessment, Sam had seen four dead. A security guard lay not far from her feet, his uniform riddled with small punctures and caked blood, his face—well, Sam didn't really know how to describe it other than *missing*. Someone had removed the skin and muscle to reveal his smiling skull, the unlit room making it look as though it was coated in barbecue sauce. Sam's eyes were drawn to the only light in the room, seeping in around drawn shades.

"The windows!" Sam ran to one and peeked out. Her spirit dampened at the sight of the bars behind the panes.

"They're all like that in here," Curtis said. "We'll have to get out of the ward before we can use a window to escape."

"Then we keep moving," Bruce added. He placed a hand gently on Sam's arm to lead her away from the window.

She recoiled at his touch, slapping his hand away. But her flash of anger quickly waned as she took in the room in the window's light. The bodies around a small card table—one slumped over it and two others on the floor nearby—looked like human pincushions. Their clothes and skin were carved like jack-o'-lanterns, strange symbols cut into their forms as if they were some twisted artist's new medium. The art extended beyond the bodies to the walls, where smiley faces and a mathematical symbol had been painted in blood.

Pi. Sam wondered if the violent inmates truly had any part in the carnage, or if it had all been the work of the Wainwright, Horvat, and their warrior natives. Sam wouldn't have wasted time checking each for a pulse, but she had to hand it to Curtis—*this* Curtis—as he went about the room and confirmed each was dead.

The one called Terry took shaky steps toward a book rack that had been toppled over. He picked up a paperback with a bare, broad-chested man on the cover and rejoined the group, his eyes glazing over. He appeared to be in shock.

Sam put her arm around Michael's shoulder. His face was pale and he looked like he might vomit. "You okay?"

He nodded shakily but kept it together. She snuck a glance at Jimmy, who was fishing through the security guard's corpse. He looked so unfazed that he could eat a rare steak dinner right there amid the bloodied cards. But Sam couldn't really fault him for it, her stomach grumbling at the thought.

She crossed the rec room, the others in tow. The door at the other end was ajar. She softly pushed it open. The dull-yellow fluorescent lighting beyond was just enough to see down the windowless hallway lined with rooms—sleeping quarters.

"The office area is to the right," Curtis said, keeping his voice low.

A sound like teeth scraping over shells came from ahead. A wiry man with a crooked smile and sparkling eyes stepped out of a room down the hall. His skin appeared melted and loose like he was suffering from leprosy or had experienced several bad skin grafts. His orange T-shirt and matching gi-like pants were smeared with blood. A scalpel carved a line in the wall as he approached. As he neared, she could see his face was some sort of mask. *No, he's wearing someone else's face.* She swallowed as she recalled the dead guard in the rec room.

Across the hall, another man emerged, this one bald, shirtless, fat, and tattooed with swastikas, lightning bolts, iron crosses, and God knew what else all over his face and body, but with the same orange pants as those of his face-wearing buddy. He began to rap a baton on the wall opposite of the scalpel man.

"Stay where you are," Sam said, aiming her gun at the neo-Nazi, the closer of the two. He kept coming slowly, then disappeared into an open doorway. The scalpel man did the same on the other side.

"Move!" Sam wasn't sticking around to play. She ushered Michael down the hall to the right, keeping an ear primed to any noise coming from behind. Allowing Curtis to take the lead, she followed with the boys at her side and Bruce at her heels as he shuffled along a nearly catatonic Terry.

After a few turns through silent and euphorically empty corridors, Curtis raised his badge to a card reader before noticing that the door had already been broken open. He pointed to it then put a finger over his mouth as he slowly pushed it open. A *thump* followed by a *twang* came from somewhere inside. They entered the spacious area containing an L-shaped nurse's station with several monitors and file cabinets off to the left. To the right were three examination rooms like those Sam had been in for every physical, with those paper-covered chair-bed things. Manila folders and stationary speckled the floor. A scale lay on its side a few feet in front of her.

The *thump twang* came again like a meat cleaver chopping through a side of beef and striking a metal tray beneath it. Movement behind the nurse's station caught Sam's eye. A pattering of feet came rushing toward them from her right. Sam whipped around to aim.

"Curtis!" A boy who couldn't have been much older than seven came running at the orderly. Sam lowered her weapon as the snot-nosed, teary-eyed boy wrapped his arms around Curtis's leg. A shy girl, about the same age as the boy, sprinted out from their hiding spot behind a trash bin in the corner to hug the same leg. The thumping stopped.

Curtis hugged the children close, his massive arms like anacondas swallowing their whole frames. "Grady, Valerie... you're safe now. I've got you." He grimaced, his face reddening as he looked up at Sam's weapon, but he kept his voice calm and soothing. "Where's Helena? Colleen? Jeb? If they just left you here, I swear to God, I'll..."

The little boy pointed to the nurse's station. At the same time, Bruce stepped forward to investigate the sound, which had stopped. Out of the corner of her eye, Sam saw the orange Ward D linens. A patient charged at Bruce with an aluminum chair raised over his head. Sam raised her weapon and began angling for a clear shot around Bruce. He raised his arms to defend himself as the man reared back to swing.

In a blur of movement, Curtis was between Bruce and certain pain, catching the chair in his hands before it could connect with the formerly dead man. Curtis ripped it out of the inmate's hands as easily as if he were snatching it from a toddler, then planted it sidelong through the man's face. With a sickening crack and horrible twist of his neck, the man dropped to the linoleum floor.

Sam had only a moment to think how happy she'd been that Curtis hadn't been made an Indian when she heard a squelching noise behind her. The neo-Nazi scumbag had Terry's arms pinned behind his back, the docile patient still holding onto his book as Skin Mask Man plunged his scalpel repeatedly into his neck.

Jimmy and Michael rushed the children to Curtis's side, out of harm's way. Sam aimed at the face wearer and had a clean shot, too, but the fat Nazi shoved Terry into her as she fired. The shot went wide as she staggered back from Terry's weight, letting him fall to the ground as she struggled not to fall herself. As she regained her feet, the Nazi was already charging. She unloaded into his chest and stomach, emptying the magazine into his bulbous form. He dropped inches from her feet, but Skin Mask Man had ducked in behind him, out of sight until it was too late. He swiped at Sam, cutting deep into the soft skin under her eyebrow and sending a waterfall of blood into her eye.

Out of her good eye, she spotted Michael and Jimmy circling the man. Before she could object, they each dove in for a leg and pulled so hard it sent the man horizontal. He smacked down hard onto the floor, his mask knocked askew.

"Catch!" Jimmy shouted as he threw what looked like a cartridge at her. She tried to grab it, but her blinded eye screwed up her depth perception. Bruce caught it for her and shoved it into her hand. She released the spent cartridge and reloaded just as the man snapped up to his feet. He raised the scalpel but fell dead before he could strike, a bullet hole in his forehead, slightly off-center.

As Sam pawed at the blood in her eye, Curtis pointed behind the nurse's station. "One of my coworkers, Helena... she's there." Curtis shook his head. His voice cracked. "She was trying to protect them."

Curtis's gaze found Terry, who lay prone on the floor, unmoving. He ran over and checked for a pulse. He shook his head then massaged his brow. "Am I the only one who thinks this is all so fucking insane?" He stood, grumbled, then regained his composure. "Sorry, kids, I shouldn't have used that word."

"We're all insane in here," Valerie muttered.

"No, you're not." Curtis hugged the children. "Don't ever say that, okay? You guys are the best darn kids I know."

"We should keep moving," Bruce said, not unkindly. "We don't know how many more of them might be loose in here."

Curtis rose. "There might be other... other patients and staff members who need our help."

"Bruce is right." Sam put a hand on Curtis's shoulder. "We risk the lives of these children the longer we stay inside here. We don't know who might be left inside or where they might be, but we'll be able to gather that information and reinforcements once we make it outside."

Curtis took a deep breath. "Okay. The office suite is just ahead, but whether we can get out through the basement—"

"It will lead out." Bruce fixed him with a cold stare.

"If you say so." He took off at a jog. "This way."

As they circled the man who'd done in Helena with an aluminum chair, Jimmy gave him a swift kick to the groin. The man moaned in a semiconscious state. Sam frowned.

"Sorry." Jimmy shrugged, a mischievous smile worming over his lips. "Couldn't resist." When Valerie copied him, he just shrugged again.

They made it into the office area without further incident. Dr. Horvat's door was locked, but Bruce kicked it in on his first attempt. Horvat's degrees had been removed from the wall, but other than that, the office looked undisturbed. Sam noticed the door behind the desk just where Curtis had said it would be, though she hadn't recalled it. Likely, she had picked up the detail on her earlier visit and quickly dismissed it as unimportant.

Curtis circled the desk. "Stand back," he said, as he heaved it forward. As he opened the door behind it, the odor of compost, wet leaves, and fertile soil rose from the darkness below.

"Great. Another dark tunnel." Michael sighed. "So, who wants to go first?"

Curtis started down the steps, but Sam put her hand on his shoulder. "I'll go. I've got the gun."

She licked her fingers and wiped the now-crusting blood off her eyelid. Then she took the first step.

"Be careful," Bruce and Michael said in unison. They exchanged a look Sam couldn't read. She lost all sight of them as she descended into a cold, damp grave.

Her feet touched down on what felt like cement. The basement wasn't very deep, maybe eight or nine feet. It was easy enough to stand up straight but she wouldn't dare jump, wary of low cross-beams or whatever else might be lurking in the dark. Beyond the stairs, a wall blocked passage. Using it to guide her, she felt along to her right then to her left before ducking under the stairs. She passed through a horde of cobwebs then found two more walls at right angles. They left her with only one direction to go.

"I suppose it would be too much to ask for a flashlight or a lighter?" she called back to the others above.

After a moment, Bruce's voice came back. "Sorry."

"It's okay." She squinted through the dark. A hazy cloud, a gray in the field of black, seemed to come from what could have been twenty feet or half a mile ahead, impossible to gauge in that underground tomb. Something squeaked and ran by her foot. *Just a mole or a field mouse*, she told herself, knowing she was probably right but still imagining red-eyed, opossum-rat beasties devouring human flesh all around her. Focusing on the task at hand, she started forward, calling over her shoulder, "I think I see a way out."

After she'd walked about twenty more steps, the ground softened. The transition was immediate. It felt like she had stepped from what had once been a basement floor onto spongy dirt, dry enough thankfully not to be mud. An ammonia-like odor, as if mulch had been stored down there and never turned, wafted her way. Her skin tingled as if covered in ants, followed by the disorientation of claustrophobia, the air short on oxygen and unclean, the room no more than a crypt where sick and wounded animals went to die. Anyone could be down there, hiding in darkness, waiting for just the right moment to—

She jumped as someone grabbed her sleeve then fumbled down to her hand. "It's me," Michael said. "We've all joined hands, the adults between the children, right behind you."

Michael's hand in hers renewed her strength. As her tension waned, she wished they hadn't been so hasty, but what was done was done. With Michael following closely, she crept forward. Step by step, they inched onward. At one point, someone behind her stumbled, but the others picked whomever it was up and continued on their way. One of the two young children sniffled quietly, but otherwise, they were faring as bravely as the rest. Sam was sure she had Curtis to thank for that.

The hazy cloud she'd spotted earlier had grown and brightened. Soon, Sam could see a line of light gleaming through what appeared to be a steel cellar door. The light spilled over the top few steps of a staircase leading up to it. She let go of Michael's hand, sliding her feet forward like a cross-country skier until her toe hit against the bottom step.

After scrambling up the stairs then throwing open the heavy metal doors with a bang, she caught a glimpse of the sky and the shadow of a person before ducking down again. Pine needles fell atop her head as the scent of Christmas filled her nostrils. A blast, followed by a further smattering of pine needles and dirt, made her duck lower.

"Six little Indians, all alive," a haughty female voice sang, sounding like Robin Williams's in *Mrs. Doubtfire*. "One kicked the bucket, and then there were five."

"Knock it off, Matilda!" a man's voice yelled. He groaned as if he were wrestling with the woman. After a moment, the man's voice came again. "It's okay. You can come up now. She dropped the gun."

Sam looked back at the others, brow furrowed. She wasn't ready to take another look. Slinking farther down, she ushered everyone back.

Curtis approached. "I think I know what this is." He started up the steps, Sam urging him not to, but he shrugged her off. Near the top, he called, "Dizmo, is that you?"

"Yeah," the man said. "It's me. Who are you? And what are you doing down there?"

"It's Curtis. I'm coming up. Are you alone?"

"Yeah. Matilda was here, but she's gone now."

Curtis turned. "Matilda is one of his personalities. Dizmo suffers from dissociative identity, uh, multiple personality disorder. The Dizmo personality is most common, and he's harmless. But generally, *all* of his personalities are pleasant. I can't imagine why he'd have a gun and be shooting at us, but this whole day has been kind of crazy, so... why not?" He climbed the staircase.

"Hi, Curtis," the man, presumably Dizmo, said.

"Hey, Dizmo. I've got some friends with me, but don't be alarmed. No one here means you any harm." After a second, Curtis appeared over the opening. "You can come up now. It's safe."

Sam looked at the others, then went up. Curtis stood beside a chubby man who looked to be in his thirties. He watched with apparent disinterest as she made it topside. Curtis handed her a pistol, grip end toward her.

As the rest of the group filed up, Sam took in her surroundings and found she knew them well. A dumpster, overstuffed with garbage bags, blocked the view of the basement door from the back lot. Another twenty or so garbage bags were strewn around the basement's exit. Sticks poked through some of the black bags. Sam picked one up, not surprised to find it as light as a couple of loaves of bread. She ripped it open to find it half stuffed with dry leaves, branches, pine needles, and other forest waste.

"They must have used these to cover the door," she said to no one in particular, then tossed the bag against the wall. She looked up and to her right, searching the treetops for Dylan's treehouse. It was probably less than a few hundred yards away.

A rustling came from a bush nearby, another to her right. She handed the new gun to Bruce, and together, they scanned the woods around them.

"Lower your weapons!" A man in full SWAT fatigues and carrying an AK-47 said as he broke cover. "You're surrounded!"

A quick glance to her left and right, and Sam saw that it was true. Persons with bulletproof armor and semi-automatic pistols and machine guns, all aimed their way, had them encircled.

"Don't shoot!" Sam shouted, throwing her hands in the air, while Bruce encouraged the others to do the same. "I'm a police officer."

"Lower your weapons!" A familiar voice repeated, but this time it was the officers around Sam who pointed their guns at the ground.

Frank stepped into the clearing. But Tag rushed past him and into Sam's arms. "Thank God, you're all right. I wanted to go right in, but that asshole wouldn't let me. I'm so sorry, Sam. So—"

"It's okay, Tag," Sam whispered, touched by the sentiment but embarrassed by the scene.

Tag seemed to pick up on her discomfort. He straightened and backed away, then he scanned the group and swallowed hard, a look of nausea invading his face. "Is this everyone? Any other survivors inside? We need to get back in—"

"We will, son," Frank said, placing a hand on the officer's shoulder.

Tag's face flared with anger, but he bit his tongue and stepped back, while Frank looked as solemn and as wrinkled as a basset hound. A hint of feeling shook his mask as he took in Sam. His lower lip curled under his upper, but only for a moment.

"As you probably guessed," Frank began, "the Ward D commotion was a diversion to allow for Wainwright's escape. When we heard banging and a gunshot over here, we moved in. Now we know how he got out. How the heck did we miss this?"

"It wasn't on any of the building plans we reviewed, sir," a man wearing a helmet and a bulletproof vest said. "This shouldn't be here."

Before Frank could retort, Bruce stepped between the men. "There may be more survivors inside." He roared and shook his fists. "Damn it, Frank! How could you let him escape?"

"Easy, Bruce." Frank sidestepped the accusation, then Sam's own anger blossomed.

He knew about Bruce? Of course he knew! Frank avoided looking Sam's way, probably ashamed of the momentous secret he'd kept from her.

Frank smiled shakily. "We've got the whole city on lockdown, and we know where to look for him next." He pointed out to the woods. "As for survivors, most of the inmates are accounted for, and most of the prerelease patients, children, and staff got out. We've broken down the barricade and sent in a clean-up crew." He smiled warmly at Grady and Valerie. "With these two here, only two children remain unaccounted for."

Jimmy and Curtis both stepped forward. Jimmy deferred to the orderly. "Please, sir. We have injured patients inside, in the unused hospital rooms in the old section behind the adult rec area." He handed over his keycard. "Hopefully, they are still safe behind that door. If so, they'll need immediate medical attention."

"One of them is Tessa!" Jimmy blurted. "She's been shot... right here." He pointed to his chest. "She needs help fast." His gaze fell to the earth.

Frank radioed his men to apprise them of the injured inside and their location. After that, he looked from Sam to Bruce to Michael. "Now, what should we do with the three of you?"

CHAPTER 31

O nly three days had passed, and Michael was ready to pull every hair out of his head. Instead, he suffered in silence and tried to stay out of everyone's way. He'd even taken to reading *Moby Dick* to busy himself and was slowly getting into it once he started skimming over the endless particulars of whaling. He particularly liked Queequeg, though he had no idea how to pronounce his name. The irony of rooting for the tattooed cannibal wasn't lost on him, given that his kidnapper had supposedly practiced cannibalism in Fall River before Michael had been born. But based on the beginning of the novel, he was pretty sure his favorite sailor was going to bite it.

But Wainwright was no Queequeg. *If only I had a harpoon...*

The safe house Frank had landed them in was in a downtrodden area just outside the financial district in the "redevelopment area," as the mayor preferred to call it. Despite all the heavy construction equipment lying around the neighborhood, the projects remained unchanged as far as Michael could see.

On a sofa with stained cushions that weren't infested with bedbugs but made him itch every time he thought they could be, he turned the page of his book, excited to find himself on chapter forty-nine. He dog-eared the page then flipped toward the end. When he discovered the book had more than one hundred thirty chapters, his enthusiasm faded.

Looking up, he saw Sam, tapping her foot and chewing on a thumbnail in the middle of the room. Her gaze bore a hole through the wall. Agent Matthew Pike, truly the late Detective Bruce

Marklin, sat still as a statue in a mismatched chair in the corner, his head buried in his hands. Neither said a word.

Michael sighed and returned to chapter forty-nine. "'There are certain queer times and occasions in this strange mixed affair we call life,'" he read aloud, "'when a man takes this whole universe for a vast practical joke, though the wit thereof he but dimly discerns, and more than suspects that the joke is at nobody's expense but his own.'" He looked up. "Huh." He chuckled. "I guess the joke's on us."

Neither Sam nor Bruce paid him any attention. He went back to reading, though distracted by the others' silent presences sucking the air and life out of the room.

The safe house—more of a safe *studio apartment*—didn't leave him much space to be on his own. And with Bruce and Sam sharing the cramped space, he never knew when the fireworks would erupt.

They hadn't yet, and that was almost worse. It appeared neither Sam nor Bruce were ready for the blowout, apparently content to let their tension fester until it swallowed up everyone and everything around them. Michael did his homework diligently for the first time in his life, having little better to do, his assignments coming from Dylan and Robbie through Officer Tagliamonte and one or two other officers Sam trusted with their location.

The silver lining was that Michael had found a genuine friend. Sam had received birth certificates verifying both Dylan and his father, Tobias Jefferson, who worked as a med-tech buyer for the hospital, as well as a host of employment documentation, references, and proof of residencies that supported the man's long career in the field. Officer Tagliamonte himself had visited their home, recorded the interview for Sam, and triple-checked the Jeffersons' whereabouts against Carter Wainwright appearances, finding no link—and sometimes hundreds of miles—between them and the killer.

Still, neither Dylan nor Robbie were allowed to see Michael or even know where he was. Other than the trusted officers, only a few key persons at the FBI knew about the safe house. But there was no doubt Wainwright's cult wouldn't hesitate to torture them to find it. These strangers and the threat they posed kept Michael in a constant state of unease. Rest didn't come easy. Not for anyone, it seemed, by the sullen looks and darkened eyes of his... *foster parents*? Bruce and Sam *did* seem a lot like passive-aggressive lovers in a tiff. He chuckled at the thought.

Bruce never laughed. And he never took off his bandages, so Michael assumed they weren't part of his undercover identity. But what unnerved Michael most about the man, beyond his constant scowl, contemptuous gaze, and standoffish demeanor, was the fact that he always carried his gun. He thought the man must sleep with it at his hip. It made him wonder if Bruce knew something they didn't.

It had been a few days, and Frank's team had found little—unless he was hiding something from them, which Michael doubted. Together, they'd made a list of potential Indians, piecing together their individual and group encounters with the masked puppets. Three were in custody and undergoing extensive psychological evaluation: Harlan Bowes, the man who'd first shot at Sam and Frank; Dizmo, who voluntarily surrendered to the orderly, Curtis; and Laura Vark, a young lady who'd been a patient at Brentworth but had supposedly been released a couple of weeks prior. If not for Frank, she would have ended Officer Tagliamonte's life in the woods outside the hospital, but he'd managed to sneak up on her and subdue her while she'd dawdled with a knife in her pocket.

A fourth Indian, Monica Berube, was dead, killed by another brainwashed cohort. The other two who'd attacked Michael and Dylan were still at large, disguised as police officers and apparently in possession of an actual police cruiser, though Fall River records showed all vehicles accounted for. FRPD was looking into decommissioned vehicles as well as bulk mask sales as possible leads into the whereabouts of Wainwright's crew, but if they had found anything, Sam hadn't shared it with Michael.

Tessa and Bruce rounded out the party of Indians. The former barely clung to life, unable to breathe without the assistance of a respirator. Though not predicted to pull through, she had no one to sign off on pulling the plug. The latter had been sidelined for no other discernable reason than that a madman got off on using him as a plaything and befuddling his mind. By Michael's count, that left a minimum of four Indians to complete the "motif," as Wainwright had put it.

Michael frowned. If the orderly they'd found gutted in the bathroom had been one of Wainwright's Indians, the Ward D patients had eliminated him from the playing field. Wainwright himself had taken out that nurse, Francine. And Jimmy had been relocated to a halfway house, apparently no longer considered a flight risk after exhibiting no signs of Horvat's brand of hypnotherapy, while the powers that be decided where to send him next. Only a handful of staff and patients remained unaccounted for.

So there were anywhere from two to four Indians, plus Horvat and Wainwright and whoever had helped them escape. According to Dizmo, actually named Scott Collins, there had been no one else except a kid with them. At his tip, Frank's team had found an abandoned cabin where the fugitives had rested briefly before driving off over uneven forest trails. The tire tracks they left belonged to two Jeep Wranglers that had purportedly been left waiting for them at the cabin. The tracks had ended at the street, with just enough dirt left on the pavement to indicate the direction they'd turned. Where they had gone from there was anyone's guess. They had avoided all CCTV cameras, at least as far as the footage the FRPD had reviewed could reveal, which had been a lot. Wainwright and Horvat were in the wind.

Checkpoints remained at all ins and outs of the city. Everyone whose opinion apparently mattered believed Wainwright was still somewhere in Fall River, lying low and forcing Michael, Sam, and their grumpy old roommate to do the same. Michael wasn't convinced but had no real reason to doubt their assumption.

He finished his chapter and dropped the book open across his chest. He thumbed back a few chapters to a line he liked so much he'd highlighted it: "I know not all that may be coming, but be it what it will, I'll go to it laughing." He sighed, wishing he could be like that—to face whatever might come, no matter how grave, with a light heart. Maybe the problem was that he knew more than most what would come. He sighed again, loud enough for the others to hear him, turned to where he'd left off, then started into the next chapter as he waited for one of his roommates to explode.

Finally, the bomb went off. "You know something? You're such an asshole!" Sam pushed Bruce, sending him staggering back against the wall. "How could you? How could you not tell me a damn thing?"

Michael raised the book to just under his eyes. He blushed and would have left the room had there been another room to go to. He supposed he could hang out in the bathroom—

"I'm sorry, Sam," Bruce said meekly, and at once Michael understood that all of the man's hostility and detachment had been born of his own failures. He didn't hate them. He hated himself.

"You're sorry?" Sam pushed him again. "Is that really all you have to say for yourself? We were partners, and all this time..." She gasped and covered her mouth with her hand. Her eyes shimmered in the incandescent light. "You let me believe you died that day!"

"I *did* die." He reached for the bandages around his face, tentatively tugging them at first, but soon tearing at them feverishly. It was as if he'd finally decided to shed his false persona, his lies and deceit, to face up to who he was and what he'd put her through. "My heart stopped half a dozen times. I was confined to a hospital bed for months. Then came the physical therapy." He raised his right hand. "My fingers were melted together like a damn flipper! If it weren't for my hate, my desire for revenge, I would have given up and stayed dead."

More gauze and bandages fell to the floor as he thrashed. "Look at me, Sam! Look what that man did to me!"

Sam swallowed, but she didn't look away.

A tear fell down the left side of his face, which looked much like it always had, if not more wrinkled and sallow than the picture Michael had seen of Bruce. On that side of his face, color came to his cheek, and he stared at the floor. On the other side, no tears or color appeared. Uneven, hairless flesh was mottled with parts burned pure white, others charred, but mostly blotched with varying shades of purple that might have resembled a birthmark if not for its leathery texture. His eyelid was missing, the scar tissue climbing up the side of his scalp and over a curled, blackened cauliflower of an ear.

Michael studied him over the top of his book, slightly repulsed but more fascinated than anything else. Bruce would never be called handsome, but he was no Phantom of the Opera either. He looked more like the comic book villain, Two-Face, but even that was an exaggeration. Still, it might be a good origin story if the agent turned out to be one of the bad guys. Or maybe even one of the good guys, like Deadpool or Darkman. Michael studied him closely. Hero or villain, the verdict was still out on Bruce.

He chewed on his lip. *When did my life become so much like a comic book?*

Sam softened, but just a little. "I'm sorry for what happened to you," she said quietly. At least she'd stopped pushing him. "But it doesn't excuse letting me think you were dead all this time."

"No." Bruce shook his head. "I know. We thought it was the only way for me to go undercover. I'm a special agent with the FBI now, on the books as Matthew Pike. Only Frank and one or two of his superiors know who I really am. We needed it to look convincing, and we needed you and others to help sell it. The best way to do that was to make you believe it was true."

"Damn it, Bruce. I went to your funeral. All three of your ex-wives went to your funeral."

"Then I guess I wasn't all that bad, after all." He chuckled.

Sam crossed her arms. "None of this is funny."

He showed her his palms. "I know, I know. I'm sorry. But if I'm being honest, I'd do it all over again if it gave me another shot at Wainwright."

"Yeah." Sam scoffed. "Some shot that was. He knew who you were all along. Probably got it right from your own lips when he had his doctor bimbo brainwash you. Frank's been looking for a mole this whole time. And come to find out, his *inside man* is a double agent." Sam laughed then, but there was no mirth in it.

"And that's not the worst part." Bruce looked away and began to pace. "Don't you see? *I'm* the reason he came back here. He just wanted to play another game with me, show there were so many more ways he could still get to me. Had I just walked away after Texas, he may never have set up base here again, targeted you and Michael—"

"Stop." Sam clenched her jaw. "I don't and I won't blame you for the actions of a psychopath. I—"

A car backfired somewhere outside. Bruce's hand hovered over his gun.

Sam frowned. "Can you cool it with the gun, Bruce? You're keeping everyone on edge." Then softer, she said, "He's just a kid. He's been through enough already."

Half of Bruce's lips curled into a sinister grin, the burned half remaining in its perpetual scowl. "Well, if he's smart—if *you're* smart—you'll be ready. There *is* a mole, Sam, and I'm pretty sure

Wainwright has already found out about this place. He'll send his lackeys soon enough, and when he does, I plan on capturing one and having him lead me straight back to Wainwright. And this time, I won't hesitate."

Michael dropped the book at that, springing up to a sitting position. "So we're what? Bait?"

"That's not funny, Bruce." Sam crossed her arms again. "You're scaring Michael. Frank would never use us like that."

It was Bruce's turn to scoff. "He thinks like you do—that I was the mole. But I never knew Michael was living with you. I couldn't have been responsible for the break-in at your apartment. Someone else must have told him that."

Sam rolled her eyes. "Or he had someone follow me home, got it out of Tessa, etcetera."

"Believe me or don't. Just be ready. Might want to give the boy a piece too." He glared at Michael, a wildness in Bruce's eyes that reminded him of the maniac he'd just escaped. "Just don't kill them all, kid. I need one of them alive."

CHAPTER 32

J immy didn't know what to do with his newfound freedom. Residing at the halfway house under an assumed name, he wasn't supposed to leave. But the parole officer, Weston something-or-other, had taken a liking to him, had even gone so far as to call him a hero. Without disclosing his identity, the newspapers had run several stories concerning events that took place at Brentworth three days earlier, including the terrifying ordeal of three brave teenagers who fought their way through a hallway of deranged lunatics to escape with the help of police, saving three other patients in the process. *Only two, once Tessa dies.* The papers had left out the parts about the innocents they'd failed to save—Terry, that nurse who'd had her head bashed in, and the four dead people in the rec room. Those facts were too troublesome to add to a feel-good piece.

Anyway, Weston must have put two and two together and guessed Jimmy had been one of the teenagers mentioned in the articles. Jimmy saw no sense in denying it, particularly if it curried him favor with the warden of his new prison. Weston allowed him to come and go as he pleased, practically encouraged him to do so, so long as he was back before the evening meal and curfew.

Jimmy had stayed inside on the first day. On the second, he went for a walk, feeling like a stranger in his own city. Everything seemed different somehow. But Fall River was the same as it had always been. *He* was the one who'd changed. Everything since he'd shot Glenn Rodrigues, which seemed like a lifetime ago, had shaped him into a new person. A man, he supposed, and maybe not a good one.

One newspaper had told his story as one of redemption—the teen with a "troubled past" rising in the face of adversity or some other garbage. But if helping Michael and those children escape Brentworth had made up for all the terrible things he'd done, then he couldn't figure out why he still felt so dirty—like he could wash his skin under scalding hot water for hours, scrub it with wire mesh until a layer grated off like parmesan cheese, and still never remove the constant stain. The blood on his hands.

But it wasn't guilt. No, the people he'd hurt had deserved it. Every last one of the sons of bitches. The cloud over him wasn't placed there by himself but by society and by allowing his eyes to see himself as others might see him.

He slunk back into the home after only being out an hour. And when he woke the third day, he couldn't think of any reason to step out again. He thought about visiting his parents, who upon seeing him, might put things together the same as Weston had. But he wouldn't know what to say to them and felt like they owed him an apology for thinking he owed them one. There was Michael, too, somewhere out in that city, maybe lost to him as a friend. And then there was Tessa, dying if not dead already and probably off-limits to visitors.

His body felt like a hollowed out tree. Tessa had taken a bullet for Michael, for Sam, for him. He decided he would try to see her anyway.

Getting to Charlton Memorial had taken him nearly forty-five minutes on foot, and that had been the easy part. Sneaking into the ICU had been only slightly more difficult. He had arrived during family visiting hours and followed a couple while they signed in, entering behind them as if he were their son. When he broke away from the pair, he walked by nurses and doctors with his head down, all of them much too busy to give him any real notice, until he found Tessa's room.

The only truly hard part of his visit was seeing Tessa lying as she was, her every breath a struggle, clinging to life through various tubes and apparatuses connected to her every limb and orifice. Machines beeped and whirred. Other than the heart monitor, Jimmy didn't know what any of them did. He wanted to reach for her hand and hold it, to be there for her when she left their world for whatever came next. He'd been raised Catholic—like all good Irish children, his mother would say. But somewhere along the way, he'd stopped believing. Nevertheless, he sent up a prayer for Tessa's sake.

And so he sat there in the dark on the floor beside her bed, remembering the night not too long ago when they'd done the same beside his. Lost in thought, he didn't notice the man in the lab coat and surgical mask until a gun was pointed at his face.

CHAPTER 33

An uneasy silence fell over Sam, Michael, and Bruce as they each claimed a corner of the room and refused to make eye contact with one another. She took inventory of the many emotions fighting for control of her body—melancholy, anger, anxiety, and even compassion battled to be king of the hill. In the end, a combination of fear and disgust won, and she sneered at her former partner, a man actually willing to use them as bait to catch a killer. Tears filled her eyes. *Something I would have done with Michael not even a year ago.*

Disgust turned to shame, and she hid her face in her hands. *What am I doing with my life? With his?*

A knock came at the door. Bruce's hand went for his gun.

"It's me, Frank." The deadbolt snapped back. "I'm coming in."

Sam stepped behind the door, gun in hand, unable to see who'd entered until the door swung closed. The tall, slender figure of Frank Spinney was unmistakable. He was alone.

She holstered her weapon and stepped around him slowly so as not to startle him. "Any news?"

Frank's gaze fell. "Nothing." He glanced at Bruce, his eyes lingering half a second too long on the burned, unbandaged face he likely hadn't seen in ages before noticing Bruce's trigger-happy gun hand. "You can relax. I haven't been compromised."

"One can never be too sure," Bruce said, but his hand did fall loosely by his side.

"How can there be no news?" Sam huffed, tucking her hair behind her ears. "These patients can't be in a constant state of hypnosis. They must be hard to keep wrangled. Not only that, Wainwright and

Horvat's faces are all over the news. They have to pop up sooner or later."

Frank sighed. "I'm guessing they're already long gone."

Bruce snickered and began to pace.

Sam shot him a glare. She had no time for his stupidity. "You got something to say, then say it."

"I told you, he'll come for us." He stopped pacing and stared at Frank. "You know this guy like I do. He never finishes a game unless he's won. I think this time, that means me dead. Maybe all of us dead."

He scratched his chin. After a pause, he added, "Well, maybe not Michael. He'll catch and release him so he has someone to toy with later."

Sam slapped him. It felt good, deserved even, but the feeling quickly passed as she noticed the sickly pallor in Michael's cheeks. And at that moment, she pitied them both—her son, who would live in fear until they caught Wainwright, and her former partner, who'd lost something deeper than skin in battle.

Bruce's face reddened from more than just the strike. "Oh, wake up, you two!" He jabbed a finger in Frank's face. "You! You know better!" Twirling to Sam, he added, "And you, you I taught better! He *will* come for us!"

"Well, if he does, then that can only mean one thing—the mole is one of us." Frank rose to his full height, his cheeks flushing. "And I, for one, am not ready to believe that one of us could ever be that evil. He used you, Bruce. Played with your head. And we never even knew he was doing it. You're angry. You have every right to be. Hell, I'm angry! But the only people that know about this place are the four of us, Tagliamonte, and—" He held up a finger. "Do you hear that?"

Bruce frowned. "What in the...?"

Sam cocked her head and listened. A low rumble, like the beginnings of an earthquake, rankled her nerve. The sound grew louder and with it an indefinable dread, like eyes watching from the shadows while walking through a dark alley. The menace quickly amplified as the entire building shook.

"What's happening?" Michael rose from the couch, hands out at his sides.

Glasses rattled on shelves. Car horns blared outside. A sound like dynamite blasting a tunnel through a mountain came from nearby, then another happened just outside. Every hair on Sam's neck stood on end.

"Sam?" Michael called, just loud enough to be heard over the din.

"Get down!" she shouted as she dove to cover Michael.

A deafening roar came from behind her as splinters of wood and plaster bombarded her back. She hugged Michael closer, shielding his head. Powdery dust filled the air, stinging her eyes and making her cough. She tried to hold her breath, which only made her cough worse.

Slowly, the roar died to a whimper. The dust began to clear. "You okay?" she asked, rising off of Michael.

He nodded but stayed right where he was, gaping.

Sam stood and turned. Her head spun as she took in the wreckage. Where the left front of the safe house had been, open air filled the space. She swatted dust away with one hand as she coughed into the other. Bruce helped Frank up and out from under the front door. She followed the direction of the noise.

Gasping, her heart thumped angrily against her ribs. A wrecking ball the size of a bus ricocheted off another building as it spun like the Earth on its axis, slowly teetering to the end of its pendulum swing. Sam struggled for words. "It-it-it's coming back!"

"This isn't him," Bruce muttered, a fresh cut on his forehead. "He likes up close and personal."

"You hear me?" Sam shouted. She grabbed Michael's hand and pulled him toward the steps, or what remained of them, leading out of the building. She pushed Bruce toward them as she passed. If the door had given him a nasty hit, Frank snapped out of his stupor and ushered Bruce along.

Missing their railing, the stairs creaked underfoot as Sam hurried Michael down them. But they held firm, Sam skipping every other one to race down the three flights to safety. As she busted out the building's double front doors, a circular shadow the size of a manhole cover swung toward them, gaining speed and growing bigger.

She started to her left as a bullet splintered the brick inches in front of her face. Whipping her neck to her right, she tried to spot the shooter when she should have been seeking cover.

"They're here!" Michael shouted, his hand slipping from her grasp. "Quick, back inside!" He pushed past Bruce and Frank, who'd drawn their weapons, and yanked open the right door as the one beside it shattered.

"Michael, no!" Sam reached for him but was far too late. Two men in police uniforms and cigar-store Indian masks approached, still firing and apparently oblivious to the giant wrecking ball careening toward them all. Sam charged for the entrance but barely made it a step before Bruce and Frank each had an arm under hers and were toting her in the opposite direction.

She fought and thrashed and screamed but still was driven away as the wrecking ball hit pavement behind the older man in the police uniform. It continued its forward momentum through him with a sickening crunch. Attached like a fly stuck to a swatter, the unknown brainwashing victim smashed into the building with the wrecking ball. It leveled the bottom of the structure, collapsing what remained of the upper floors on top of the devastation below. On top of Michael.

CHAPTER 34

J immy didn't recognize the kid, who couldn't have been more than seven or eight, standing next to that murderous psychopath. If he'd been a patient at Brentworth, Jimmy had never met him. He might have spat at Wainwright for enlisting someone so young if his mouth hadn't been duct-taped shut.

"I knocked down the building just like you asked me to," a young boy said, beaming with pride. "It only took me, like um... one and a half tries!"

"That's impressive, Mitchell," Wainwright said, tussling the boy's hair. "I'm shocked, really. I didn't think you could do it, even with Number Eight's help."

The boy bristled. "I did it all by myself!"

Wainwright chuckled. "Well, hopefully, you saved at least one or two of them for me." At that, his smile wavered, but only for a second. "And you made it back here, which is more than I can say for the others. We'll give them another half hour. Did they let you drive?"

Mitchell pouted. "No, they only let me use the controller thing." The boy could not stay sad. "It was so much fun!"

"Did you say the line?"

"Why?"

"Because it makes Dr. Horvat happy. You want to make Dr. Horvat happy, don't you? She gets so upset when she thinks you're not part of the team, you know."

Jimmy groaned. *They're brainwashing the kids too.*

Mitchell crossed his arms. "It's so stupid. Three little Indians out on a canoe. One tumbled overboard and then there were two." He threw his arms up, exasperated. "It doesn't make any sense. There wasn't even any water anywhere near us."

"Yes, you're too smart for your own good." Wainwright laughed. "We'll make you a star within this business yet."

He walked over to Jimmy, whose wrists were handcuffed to a pipe running along the ceiling, and shook his head. "Almost makes up for your mistake at the hospital."

"Jordan said you said to grab whatever boy showed up to see the girl." Mitchell pointed at Jimmy. "That's who showed up, so that's who we got."

"Did you kill the girl?"

"Uh... were we supposed to?"

Wainwright frowned. "Mira, who's this boy again?"

"Jimmy Rafferty," a woman's voice came from another room. "He's a patient at Brentworth. Or at least, he was."

Wainwright leaned forward, his breath warm and pungent on Jimmy's cheek. "Well, kid, you're part of this now. I didn't think much of you showing up with my old pal Bruce and might have left you alone. Bigger fish to fry, as they say." He sighed. "Alas, here we are. I don't suppose you're psychic, too, like the other one?"

Wainwright tapped Jimmy's cheek, waiting for an answer. Then he ripped the tape from his mouth. Jimmy's face stung and his eyes teared, but he didn't respond. He had no idea what the bastard had planned for him, but he wasn't about to make anything easy for Wainwright. From the sound of things, it looked like Jimmy might just have been in the wrong place at the wrong time.

"Should I kill him?" the sick bastard shouted to the doctor.

"I could try to make him an Indian," the doctor called back. "He seems like a good candidate—reasonably stable-minded. And our ranks have dwindled quite a bit."

"She makes a good point." Wainwright tapped his chin. "Still, I'm partial to watching your intestines slide out of your opened belly like spaghetti through a wet paper bag."

Jimmy sneered. "Why would you have spaghetti in a wet paper bag?"

"Touché." Wainwright smiled broadly. "I like this kid," he said to Mitchell, who looked up and smiled back.

Returning his attention to Jimmy, he said, "Well? What would your vote be? Do we kill you or induct you?"

Jimmy started to open his mouth to speak, then thought better of it, looking for the trap behind the words. Even if there was no trap, he wasn't sure he wanted to live if it meant he was someone else's puppet even part of the time. "Why don't you take—"

Wainwright punched him in the stomach. "Just kidding. You don't get a vote." He took a step toward the young boy. "I guess that means it's up to you, Mitchell. Do we kill him or induct him?"

Mitchell curled up his cheek. "What does 'induck' mean?"

"It means we make him one of us."

"Oh?" Mitchell's face lit up. "You mean like another Indian. Yeah! Let's do that!"

Wainwright tucked his chin against his chest and quietly laughed. "Well, I guess there you have it." He patted Jimmy's cheek again. "It looks like you have a fine future ahead of yourself within our little organization. We've got a high turnover rate, but that just means there are a lot of opportunities for promotion. Welcome to the team!"

CHAPTER 35

M ichael's vision vacillated in and out of focus. A high-pitched
tone resonated through his skull, drowning out all other
sounds. He didn't know if he was standing or lying there, what was
up and what was down. His breaths came constricted, a heavy weight
pressing down on him, yet he felt no pain.

I'm paralyzed. His heart pistoned at the thought, causing more
tightness in his chest. *Oh, God. I must be paralyzed.* Grunting he shot
his arms forward, reaching for a square of light. They moved easily,
and *he* moved easily, and that was a mixed bag of relief and anxiety.
Not paralyzed, but... am I...

The last thing he remembered was racing for the safe house's
back door and seeing an *Indiana Jones*-sized boulder racing after
him. A spark of hope as he slammed through the door, the kind with
the push bar that blessedly opened outward. The explosion of wood
behind him. Diving to the ground, covering his head. Praying.

Something had hit him in the back, then another something.
Then a whole bunch of somethings, hitting him about the head and
body. Sensation returned to his extremities as he recalled the bom-
bardment. His head throbbed at a spot just above the back of his
neck. Another something jabbed him in the leg just below his left
butt cheek. All in all, though, his limbs seemed intact. Then he remembered how amputees felt like they could still feel their missing
parts.

Slowly, he pushed up from the pavement, orienting himself. He
crawled toward the light. The brightness grew as rubble over him

shifted and toppled to the ground. The weight on his back lessened. He worked his way into daylight.

Behind him, splintered segments of wall and plaster coated the ground. Obliterated into unmatchable puzzle pieces, the rubble didn't look like it had ever comprised a building. What had been atop him was thin and sparse like fence slats and art canvas. It was strewn about in every direction.

He looked down at his hands, dusted over with black specks of embedded gravel and tiny rivulets of blood. "Sam?" he called out, how loudly he couldn't know. He only heard the word as if projected from somewhere inside his head, fighting to be heard over that vicious finger-stuck-on-the-dial blare a phone made. He shoved a pinky into his ear and wiggled it around before he could think better of it with all the filth coating him.

And not just his hands. His jeans and T-shirt were dusted with what looked like asbestos or anthrax. Michael was sure he wasn't breathing in anything good. Then, very faintly, he heard something. He strained his ears.

Sirens. All at once, the gravity of his situation returned to him. *The cops!* He looked around for Sam but instead saw plenty of other people, a crowd gathered a safe distance away as if he were contaminated and the building was about to explode a second time—gawkers, most likely. But Michael couldn't be sure. Any one of them could be a brainwashed zombie just waiting for the chance to open fire on Michael. His heart thumped faster. *I need to get out of here!*

His neck swiveled left then right as he sucked in his breath. He couldn't wait for the cops. The cops were the ones shooting at him. Bruce had been right all along. There must be a mole, maybe two or more of them, and they were willing to shoot at him in broad daylight, in front of plenty of witnesses, while running the risk of being flattened by an enormous wrecking ball. *They could still be here.* He looked around again, praying he'd find Sam, but saw no one he knew. Which meant she'd either left him there, had been recaptured, or worse.

He cursed at the sky, the skin in his neck tightening around his veins. Everyone was staring at him then—people with their judging eyes, fearful gapes, and closed hands, not one of them offering help, and maybe some of them wanting worse for him. For a split second, he wished they'd all been in the building when it had been speedily renovated. Then he hung his head, berating himself for the thought.

Sam's voice—or was it his lizard brain—was screaming at him to run, but he forced himself to think it out. Run, or search for Sam, which meant going to the other side of the building where the shooters had been. She would want him to get somewhere safe, out of the way, and not make circumstances worse like when he'd tried to fight and ended up with that doctor's gun to his head. Without him in the way, she could do what she needed.

He hoped it was logic and not fear that had made him draw that conclusion, but the growing crowd only fed his need for flight. He didn't trust the crowd. He didn't trust the cops. He took in his surroundings and took stock of where he was—not far from the financial district, if he could call a few banks and the government center that. Charlton wasn't far off to the east, the high school to his north, and a police station much closer than them both.

But the choice for him was simple. *It worked when I had to hide from Masterson.* Without deliberation, he headed toward the high school, the place where he'd once been bullied his only option for safety. School was no longer in session, though all of the sports teams and afterschool clubs would be meeting. Plenty of students would be there if he needed help, plus security guards, metal detectors, and plenty of phones he could use to discreetly search for Sam. Maybe he could get Principal Duluth, if he were still in his office, or the Athletic Director to make the calls for him. He would explain to them the importance of not revealing his location to anyone but Sam. Sure, if

Wainwright's people got the call, they could trace it or perhaps just look at their caller ID, but Michael didn't have to stick around once the calls were made. *Watch from afar. Run at the first sign of trouble.*

He had already run almost the entire mile or so to the high school. Aside from the need to cough out some debris particles when he'd stopped, his legs and lungs hardly felt used. With all the running he'd been doing lately, his body was finally getting used to it.

Standing stoically on the hill in front of him, Carnegie High School loomed like a prison complex minus the barbed wire. It was a sprawling, multi-winged building with four adjacent sports fields and a track and football field surrounded by stadium seating. The shriek of whistles and the bangs, slams, and grunts of team activity carried over to Michael.

On the left side of the main building were the parking lots, tennis courts, basketball courts, planetarium, and even a small amphitheater, which was the one building in Fall River where the taxpayers' money hadn't been misapplied or misappropriated. Amid the crime and drugs, one could still find good parents who wanted the best for their children. Michael didn't have two good parents to turn to, and at that moment, he wasn't even sure if he still had one.

He jogged toward the front entrance, screening the nearly empty street for vehicles and his police escort. He saw neither, and his police detail likely had been dismissed as soon as Michael had been placed in the not-so-safe safe house. In what was probably the easiest thing he'd done all week, he walked up to the door, pulled it open, then stepped inside.

There, he was greeted by the quizzical look of a security guard as he folded the paper he was reading. Michael wasn't sure of the time, but he guessed classes had ended at least a half hour ago. The halls were nearly empty except for the security guard and a boy getting a drink from the water fountain. And although the guard might have been well within his rights to question where Michael was coming from and why he wished to enter the school so late in the day looking like he must have, he instead passed Michael through the metal detector and sent him on his lovely way.

The restrooms were straight ahead, the principal's office down the hall to the west wing and around a corner toward the faculty entrance. Already feeling much safer and guessing he didn't make a very pretty sight, he headed into the men's room to clean up as best he could. He checked his appearance in the mirror over the sink. Dirt, dust, and grime covered his skin and clothes where sweat hadn't washed it off. He looked like a mime who'd been trying to escape a glass box for hours in hundred-degree weather. The back of his T-shirt had a long gash in it, and blood stained the back of his jeans in a small dark patch just under his butt. His hair was tousled and speckled with filth. Even his teeth had caught a layer of film as if they were coated in crap.

As Michael took all of this in, an uproarious laugh shot up from his belly and escaped his mouth. He didn't know why he was laughing but was powerless to stop himself. As it petered out, he turned on the cold water, cupped his hands, then bent over to splash it on his face.

After wiping the cool, clean water from his eyes, he once again looked in the mirror. A small cry escaped his lips as he gripped the sides of the sink. Dylan stood directly behind him.

"I thought that was you I saw come in," Dylan said as he finished a text message. He looked up from his phone and smiled, something green and leafy stuck in his braces. "I didn't know you were back."

Michael slowly turned, keeping his back to the sink as he did. Of all the students to appear out of thin air, Dylan showing up after all that had just happened raised the hairs on his neck. After all, the boy was tied to Brentworth, whether he and his father had been cleared of any wrongdoing or not. "I'm not back, technically. Just here to, you know, pick up some things and talk to the principal for a sec... if he's still here."

"Well, it's good to see you, Badass!" Dylan beamed. "Everyone here is talking about you. You're like a local hero now. Everyone knows how you helped those people get out of Brentworth." He blushed and scratched the back of his head. "I, uh, may have helped embellish that story a bit too. It's all over school. Now everyone knows what I always knew about you—that you're a badass."

"That's... good." Michael glanced to his right, at the only exit, then back at Dylan. Had he had more time, he might've stopped to think about whether any form of fame or notoriety was good at all, but at that moment, all he cared about was why Dylan was crouched over his backpack, reaching inside.

"I guess I should give this to you now." Dylan pulled a notebook from his bag and ripped out a sheet of paper. "We have a couple of essays to write on *Moby Dick*. Sorry to be the bearer of bad news."

"Thanks." Michael took the sheet of paper, folded it up without looking at it or taking his eyes off Dylan then jammed it into his pocket."

Dylan frowned. "Are you okay? You look stressed. I can't imagine all you've been through." He hung his head. "If not for that FBI guy, I would have been right in there with you. I'm sorry I wasn't. I should've let you go first on the zip line. If I had... It's not fair—"

"It's okay. *I'm* okay." Michael eased off the sink and relaxed his shoulders. If Dylan wasn't being genuine, then the school play had just found its new lead. Still, the timing remained... *peculiar*? It kept Michael slightly wary. "Why are you still here, anyway?"

"I was waiting for that officer to show up to give him your homework. Robbie was waiting, too, but he had to go to practice. I said I'd hang out a little longer and was about to give up when look who comes strolling into the high school."

"Duh!" Dylan slapped his head. "That reminds me—Robbie says you're supposed to read chapter three in your math book and complete the exercises at the end of it." He snickered. "*Exercises.* I'm pretty sure he was quoting the teacher word for word there."

"Thanks." Michael tried on a grin. "I wonder if that's really *my* assignment or *his.*"

"Beats me. I'm just the messenger." Dylan laughed and shrugged. "You're going down to see Duluth? I'll walk with you. With Brentworth shut down, it's not like I have anything better to do."

"Okay." Michael waved his arm toward the door. "After you."

He followed Dylan out of the bathroom. Side by side, they walked down the solemn, empty halls of the high school, Michael keeping an arm's length between them despite the assurances of Sam's department—a *compromised* department—and the reasonableness of Dylan's excuse for being there. Their heavy footsteps clomped with such gravity that Michael imagined himself a death-row prisoner taking his last walk.

How stupid... Michael stopped then tapped Dylan on the arm. "Your phone! Can I borrow it?"

Dylan hesitated a half second then smiled. "Of course." He pulled it out of his pocket and handed it over.

Michael stared at the screen. "Shit."

"What's wrong?"

"I don't know Sam's number." He ground his teeth as he stared pensively at the screen. "I don't know *anyone's* number."

He ground his teeth as he stared pensively at the screen. *They couldn't have gotten to the 911 operators, could they?* He groaned. "Screw it."

If Sam could be listening to dispatch, she would be. *She has to be.* Michael set his jaw. Every fiber of his being believed that Sam was alive and okay, which made it all the harder to understand why she hadn't found him yet. His gift hadn't given him much foresight beyond what he could gather through contact, though he'd met others who could use their gifts more broadly. Still, he felt it in his bones that she was out there and searching for him. *I'll just have to pray she finds me first.*

At that moment, the phone vibrated in his hand. He looked down at the screen. Without thinking, he handed the phone back to Dylan, who grabbed it and answered.

"Hello?" A row of lines appeared across Dylan's forehead.

Michael watched as his friend's face slackened. Slowly, Dylan let his backpack slide off his shoulder and plop onto the floor. Still holding the phone to his ear with one hand, he crouched and unzipped the bag with his other, using his knees to hold it in place.

Unblinking, he said something under his breath, his lips moving like a fish out of water, gulping for air. He reached into the backpack's front pocket, muttering something incoherently. The phone fell from his other hand and clattered to the floor. Michael bent to pick it up as Dylan slowly rose to his full height, holding what appeared to be a stick with a pointy tip, its base much too thick to be a pencil.

"One little Indian living all alone," he said, wearing a blank expression.

Michael froze.

"I killed him, and then there were none." Dylan thrust the sharp point outward.

Michael reversed direction with reflexes so quick they surprised him. But he hadn't been able to grab the phone, instead keeping back to dodge the blow and assume a defensive stance. Dylan held the mini spear out in front of him like some evil wand reject from the *Harry Potter* films. Michael's fears had been realized—though just a victim of Wainwright and Horvat, Dylan was brainwashed and dangerous. Michael was beginning to feel like the whole world was against him. And with Sam's whereabouts yet unknown, he was on his own.

His heart thumping, he followed Dylan's eyes, awaiting his next move. He didn't wait long. Dylan shot out his arm, the point aimed at Michael's stomach. As the strike came, Michael sidestepped it and slapped Dylan's arm aside. Dylan's shoulder turned, taking his whole body with it, and Michael took the opportunity to dart past him. He sprinted down the hall, back toward the door he'd entered to the security guard—

Where's the security guard? Michael gasped. *Of all the times to take a piss break!* He ran through the checkpoint and out the double doors, feet slapping tile right behind him.

"Help!" Michael shouted but saw no one who could answer him. Skirting along the front of the school, he hurried over to the track area where he knew there would be a ton of people. No way all of them could be brainwashed. And even if he died there, at least there would be plenty of witnesses to tell Sam who'd done it.

His fear made him angry. He growled. "Can't I just have one normal friend?"

Dylan didn't answer. Still, Michael knew he was following, his breaths coming out rhythmically and controlled.

Pumping his legs so hard they burned, Michael bounded through a group of students in shorts and T-shirts as they stretched on the track, ignoring their funny looks. When he got through the crowd, he glanced back over his shoulder. Dylan was nearly close enough to grab him as they both trampled onto the football field.

"Help!" Michael shouted, racing across the short grass.

At the other end of the field, the football team was running drills. "Hey, you!" Coach Pelletier yelled. "Get off the field, you nitwits!"

"Help!" Michael screamed, his lungs scorching as he inhaled. Nobody moved. He sprinted toward the team, then by it, Dylan hot on his trail.

A rattling of pads and a tremendous *thump* behind him was followed by a chorus of "ohhhhs" from the team. Still running, Michael turned to see no one chasing him. He slowed to a jog then stopped, resting his hands on his knees as he saw a large football player rising from the ground. When the player turned his head, Michael could see Robbie Wilkins's eyes peering out from his face mask. He dusted off his hands as he stood. Only then did Michael see the much smaller boy he had flattened.

"What kind of crap have you gotten yourself into now?" the star athlete asked as he approached.

Michael kept his eyes fixed on Dylan, who wasn't moving. "Same crap. Different day," he managed to say as he caught his breath.

"Well, I hope I didn't just level that kid for no reason."

"No... he was chasing me. Brainwashed." Seeing the confused look on Robbie's face, he added, "It's a long story."

Behind Robbie, Dylan began to rise. He massaged his temples and was slow to his feet, unsteady when he finally reached them. His hands were empty. Assuming Robbie hadn't noticed Dylan's sharpened stick, Michael searched the field for the makeshift weapon and spotted it only ten feet away from Dylan.

"Unless you boys want to serve as tackling dummies, you mind getting the hell off my field?" the coach said with a snarl. He made no effort to assist Dylan. "Wilkins, get your ass back on that line!"

Robbie leaned in. "You good?"

"I'm not sure. Maybe."

"I'll be right there" —he cocked his head to the left—"watching. I'm not sure what's going on, but if you need me to call the cops—"

"No!" Michael blurted much too loudly. "I mean, thanks, Robbie. I'm not sure that's... you hit him pretty good by the sound of it."

"I laid him the hell out." Robbie laughed.

"Wilkins!" the coach snapped. "Get those kids off our field and get back over here! You want to do laps all afternoon?"

Robbie ignored him a moment longer. "Okay, but like I said, I'm right over there." He snapped back on his chin guard and hustled back to the rest of the team while some of his teammates jeered.

"What? Where?" Dylan blinked rapidly, his eyes taking in his surroundings as if he were moving in slow motion. He turned toward Michael. "Mike?"

Michael walked closer to his friend, studying him for any sign of deceit. "Are you okay?"

"Okay?" Dylan spread out his palms. "How'd the heck we get out here? And why do I feel like I got run over by a freight train?"

"I think you were brainwashed like those others. You were chanting that nursery rhyme or whatever it is, like those people that attacked us. Who called you a minute ago?"

"Call? Brainwashed? I..." Dylan's forehead creased, and he frowned. "I don't remember a call or anybody doing anything to me." His gaze rose to meet Michael's eyes, and he gulped. "I-I-I didn't attack you, did I? Oh, God, Michael, I'm so sorry. I—"

Michael's lips flattened into a tight line. "It's okay. I get it. Let's just get out of here before we both get run over." He walked over to the sharpened stick. "But if you don't mind, I'll hold onto this."

CHAPTER 36

Two men had held Sam down as the safe house blew apart around them. She had heard their grunts as debris rained down upon them, their backs shielding her from the blast. And she hated them for it. She had fought like a rabid dog, barely holding back from biting as she thrashed beneath their weight. She should have been looking for Michael, protecting him, getting him help if he was injured.

If he was still alive.

But they had kept her pinned, their combined weight too much for her. They would pay for it, she would make sure of that. And if her boy died because they'd kept her from him, she swore to God she would—

"Help me!" Frank had shouted. "We need to get her out of here."

She at first had slapped away their hands as they'd tried to help her up. She didn't want their help, didn't *need* it, but she'd eventually relented and let them escort her to cover behind a parked vehicle.

Hysterics no longer controlled her mind. Anger had pushed it out, cleared away the clutter. She sat stewing, waiting for her anger to implode. No one was going to stop her from looking for Michael. She would pull her gun if she had to.

"Well, at least no one appears to be shooting at us," Frank said, his levity working its way under her skin. "Yet."

Cursing, Sam leapt to her feet, dumbstruck by wreckage before her. Hand over her mouth, she hurried toward the desolation.

No more than fourteen feet or so away stood a bowl-shaped opening where the front of their building had been. It was as some giant monster had opened its maw and chomped down on the safe house, leaving only its corners rising like bedposts.

Sam walked on shaky legs toward the basement cavity that remained. A hand touched her elbow, but she swatted it away, gaining momentum and strength as she staggered clumsily toward the hole.

"Sam, the shooters may still be..." Frank had started to say behind her, then apparently gave up.

Down below, piles of smashed wood, concrete, and plaster speckled the remains of the building. Sam cried out as she approached. Amid the upturned sofas, dismantled chairs, sections of cabinets, and other somewhat intact or obliterated furniture and personal belongings, a hand jutted from the rubble. She stepped onto the remnants of the floor, no more than broken up wood stabbing at the air like fence pickets. She walked cautiously across it to its end as if being forced to walk the plank.

"Sam!" Bruce shouted from behind. "It's not safe!"

"Is it safer than when you went into that church, Bruce?" She spat, her anger and fear for Michael getting the better of her. "At least this one's already in pieces." She crouched, sat down, then scooted toward the drop. Only about four feet of space hung between her and the pile of debris below. Without knowing how sturdy the pile might be, she lowered herself down gently.

The pile held firm. As she edged toward the hand in the rubble, her arms out by her sides for balance, the smaller debris shifted underfoot, slowing her progress.

Labored breathing came from somewhere above her.

"You, too, Frank?" Bruce's voice called into the sinkhole. "You've both lost your freaking minds. The person who did this, who's responsible for *all* of this, is probably getting away as we speak."

Sam didn't respond. She heard Frank drop down behind her.

"Forget you, then." Bruce groaned in frustration. "I'm going after them."

Frank delicately rested his hand under her elbow. "Here, let me help you."

Sam flinched at his touch, but this time, she didn't bat him away. His strength supporting hers helped her to move faster, and only two seconds later, she was falling on her knees beside the hand.

Tears of joy exploded from her eyes as hope welled inside her. Sniffling, yet almost giddy, she said, "It's not him." She grabbed the hand as if she were going to arm wrestle with it. "See? It's old, veiny... white hairs on the knuckles. Not Michael's."

Frank smiled, but it didn't reach his eyes. "That's good, Sam."

She knew what he thought, that Michael was just somewhere else under the rubble. But she wouldn't believe that, couldn't believe that, until all hope was confirmed lost.

The hand twitched. Sam gasped and fell backward. Frank caught her in his arms. As the rubble shifted below them, he held her close, Sam allowing the embrace. The ground moved like tectonic plates, destroying and reforming the land around them. When it settled again, they were about a foot lower. The face and upper torso of the hand's owner had shimmied to the surface.

Sam broke free of Frank and leaned forward for a closer look. The body looked like a tire that had been popped, left to droop on a warped frame. One of his teeth was poking out of his nostrils. The top of his head looked like a plate of nachos with chili and salsa. And the rest of him wasn't any prettier. He was clearly dead, the twitch probably the result of gas leaving his body or some other deathly function.

Sam would have thought the man unidentifiable, but Frank knew. "Jordan Rockefeller—a patient at Brentworth, and by all accounts, a kind and peaceful man." He rubbed his hand down his face then roared out his frustration. "This case, *that* man! So many lost. Even those we are trying to stop are victims in all of this."

He fixed Sam with a watery gaze, an unusual display of emotion for the usually robotic agent. "We have to stop him, Sam."

She looked at him then and knew he'd been trying to stay calm for her sake. Thinking she would offer some words of comfort or encouragement if she could find them, she faced him straight on and spotted blood on his cheek. "Frank, you're bleeding." She checked him all over for injuries.

"Huh?" He checked his palm and wiped the blood away to reveal no wounds. Then he looked where he had touched her, and her eyes followed his. "Your elbow."

She turned her arm inward to view the gash in her shirt and deep into her forearm. In her frenzy to locate Michael, she hadn't even felt the injury. She must have caught it on the jagged floor as she'd dropped into the basement.

"We need to get that looked at."

She clenched her jaw and fixed him with the coldest stare she could muster. "We *need* to find Michael."

"Sam! Frank!" Bruce's voice bellowed from above. "Get up here quick! It's about the boy!"

Frank slapped his sides. "And how do you suppose we do that?"

"There's a dresser along the back wall. If you can make your way over there, you should be able to climb out the other side." Bruce's shadow briefly disappeared before returning. "I'll meet you over there."

Frank shrugged. Sam nodded. Arm in arm, they carefully navigated their way over the rubble. Aside from Frank slipping into a knee-deep hole and Sam having to pull him out, the two made it to the dresser with little hardship. They climbed up onto the street behind the building. There, a throng of spectators stood gawking at them as they dusted themselves off.

Bruce led one of them over by the arm—an older lady with thick gray curls and a sleeveless floral shirt. "Please, Mrs. Canto, tell them what you told me."

In a heavy Portuguese accent, the woman said, "I saw a boy run away from here after the building fell. Then a man, a police officer, came running after him. I think he was chasing him."

"Which way did they head?" Bruce prompted.

The woman raised a finger and pointed it directly away from the building. "There."

"It's Michael!" Bruce bounced on his toes. "He's in trouble. We need to go after them!"

"Michael?" Sam was slow to process the information, and Bruce's sudden concern for him rankled her suspicion. Still, a boy being chased by a police officer... *Who else could it be?* Though she'd hoped Michael could still be alive, that cynical part of her that made up so much of who she was continuously chimed in to tell her she was dreaming.

"He's alive?" She laughed and more tears of joy sprang from the corners of her eyes.

"He is for now," Bruce said. "But we need to move if we want to keep him that way."

"Sir," a man standing with a woman and a dog called from across the street, apparently having eavesdropped on the conversation. "My wife and I saw a boy, and—"

Sam started to turn, but Bruce grabbed her arms and shook her. "Sam, we have to go now! Your boy is in trouble!"

Sam couldn't think, but after a moment trying to straighten out her thoughts, she nodded. "Right. Michael." She took a deep breath. "Let's go."

The three sprinted after the boy and the cop, Sam hoping they would catch up before they vanished into Fall River's many dark places.

CHAPTER 37

Michael walked side by side with Dylan out the front doors of the high school, having doubled back for Dylan's phone, which Michael kept in his pocket for "security reasons." Michael explained what had brought him to the high school in the first place, all the while watching his classmate for any tell that Dylan already knew what had happened.

For his part, Dylan either showed genuine surprise and concern for Michael or faked it well. As they walked toward the road, Michael never let him move beyond his sight. Although Officer Tagliamonte had cleared the boy of any connection to Carter Wainwright to the point of producing official records that proved his identity and innocence, Dylan still worked at Brentworth. The circumstances that had brought him and Michael together had always seemed a little too convenient, perhaps contrived. Michael had needed a friend. Boom, he'd gotten one. Dylan had survived not one but two attacks by Horvat's brainwashed Indians. And Dylan had been brainwashed himself.

Sam didn't believe in coincidences. Her cynicism was wearing off on Michael. As they reached the road, he turned to face Dylan. "So... where should we go?" he asked, having a sneaking suspicion Dylan would only recommend one place.

"I don't know." Dylan shrugged. "Can't go to the police, right?"

Michael nodded, watching Dylan's facial expressions closely. "Right."

"How about the treehouse? She found you there once. Maybe she'll think you'll go there again."

Michael suppressed his smile. It was the answer he'd suspected, and it made him trust Dylan even less. His friend's suggestion wasn't without any reason—Sam *might* think to look for him there—but so might all the Wainwright douchebags, particularly if Dylan was one of them.

It didn't matter. Michael was tired of running. Without his phone, Dylan wouldn't be able to contact Wainwright, except if he had a backup. Maybe there was even one in the treehouse. But Michael had his main phone, the stick-knife, and the wariness to be ready for even the slightest inkling of bull. Dylan was either a true friend used by a malicious enemy or a malicious enemy posing as a true friend. He claimed to have been brainwashed, and Michael could think of no reason why Wainwright and Horvat would brain-wash a willing participant in their schemes.

At the same time, Michel desperately wanted to trust his friend. Wainwright had had ample opportunities to use Dylan against Michael before that day. *Why would he have waited until then?* On top of it all, and the real reason behind Michael's burgeoning suspicions, was that he couldn't believe anyone would truly want to be his friend.

He kept all these thoughts to himself, letting the doubt fester while keeping his expression level. Outside, he said, "Sure. Sounds good."

"Hey." Dylan frowned. "We're good, right? I hate what happened. It seems just so... unreal to me. I don't want to hurt you. I don't want to hurt anybody. This whole thing is just so freaking crazy."

He rubbed his eyes, and Michael wasn't sure if he'd seen tears. But Dylan took a deep breath and found his composure. "Anyway, you have my phone and that stupid stick. So unless we run into those brainwashing jerks, I don't think there's any way they'll get to me again or that I'll be able to hurt you." He threw up his hands. "I don't think I'll be answering any calls ever again."

"Not your fault, man," Michael said flatly. "I get it. Let's just get out of the open. Sam's probably worried sick about me, and to be honest, I'm worried sick about her."

Dylan nodded, and the two walked in silence back to Brentworth, both taking occasional glances over their shoulders and hiding their faces from oncoming vehicles. They saw no cops and few cars. No one passed that raised Michael's suspicions.

Brentworth was closed off to anyone but the police. Caution tape and orange cones stood sentry over a deserted building. Security patrolled the parking lot, so Dylan and Michael kept inside the tree line at the back of the adjacent properties, a gas station and carwash, working their way behind the hospital.

Michael hesitated only a moment before heading deeper into the woods. Of course he second-guessed his logic in going back to the place where it had all began. But he'd had a vision of the future in which he was still alive and Sam was older, and he trusted that meant they would make it through the day okay. Of course, Sam could be hurt and needing help sooner than later. Moreover, having seen the vision, Michael knew that he might be acting in a way he wouldn't normally act had he not had the benefit of foresight. He could be changing the future without even realizing it.

He was growing tired of the constant battle, his life of fear, helplessness, and loneliness. And he was tired of being pushed around. If he kept running like he always had, he was starting to think he would always be running. Maybe it was time he pushed back.

As they plodded over pine needles without saying a word, Michael thought back over the events of the last several days—the attacks on himself, the people he'd seen die. He thought back to those who'd exploited him for his curse, all the way back to Tessa, whose actions caused her stepfather to murder his last foster parents, and Sam, who'd exposed him to a murderer just to solve a case. He thought of the Suarez gang and Jimmy, who'd sold him out to the brothers. His so-called friends, people who were supposed to care about him, using him like some carnival freak for their own selfish reasons.

Heat rose to his face, and he flexed his fingers. He wondered who his real enemies were. At least with Wainwright and Horvat, he knew where he stood. But there was no hurt greater than that of betrayal. The betrayal of a friend.

He stared up at Dylan as they climbed the splintering ladder to the treehouse. Michael reached for each rung without hesitation, squeezing them as if he wanted to strangle them, his feet marching from one to the next with hostile snaps.

When he reached the top, Dylan was working the pulley. "I'm just going to bring it up, you know... just in case. To have it at the ready."

Michael stood a foot away from him. "Your father's an administrator at the hospital, right?"

Without turning, Dylan continued to draw up the bucket. "Yeah, but he didn't have anything to do with those crazies, if that's what you're wondering. He's been cooperating with the cops ever since everything went down."

"It just seems odd that... I mean, you were just hypnotized by them, right?" Michael pulled Dylan's cell phone from his pocket.

"Yeah?" Dylan worked the bucket closer.

"Well, aren't you even the least bit concerned that maybe he was too?" The cell phone was locked. "What's your password?"

"Three two one... one two three. Why? Who you going to call?"

Michael typed in the password, then scanned the recent calls. The last one had come from *DAD*. He dialed it back and let it ring.

Dylan looked over his shoulder and sighed. He smiled shakily. "Where are you going with this, Mike?" His brow furrowed. "Who are you calling?"

"Don't you want to make sure your father's okay? You haven't even mentioned him or asked for the phone on the entire walk over. Aren't you concerned about him?" Michael inched closer to Dylan. "Or is it that you already know there isn't anything for you to be concerned about?"

The phone continued to ring until, at last, someone answered. A familiar voice said, "Where are you? Are you with that detective's kid?"

"No," Michael snarled. "But I'm with yours." He hung up the phone.

"Michael," Dylan said, starting to turn while holding the pulley in place. With the metal bar at his side, he stepped toward Michael. He raised his hands, confusingly placating and threatening at the same time, as he inched ever closer. "You've got things all wrong. I'm your friend—"

"Get away from me!" Michael saw the raised bar and acted. He threw out his arms, slamming his palms into Dylan's chest.

Dylan cried out. His arms reached wildly for something to grab, finding nothing but air as he plummeted from the platform. His elbow smacked the bucket, tipping it and spilling the handlebar down to the ground with him. He hit earth will a dull thud.

Michael gazed over the ledge. Dylan was sprawled on the leaf-covered dirt below. He wasn't moving. Michael made his way to the ladder and began his climb down, his whole body trembling and working on cruise control. In his mind, reruns of what he'd just done played over and over again.

At the bottom, he circled the tree to check the body of the kid he was sure he'd just murdered. But Dylan was no longer where Michael had pushed him. Indentations in the dirt marked the spot where he had landed. A trail of footprints led away, then turned, circling.

In his peripheral, Michael spotted something metallic swinging toward his head.

CHAPTER 38

Sam hadn't run far before encountering the crane that had been used to destroy Frank's safe house. It sat on a flatbed and appeared to be unmanned. A barrel-chested man in a denim shirt and red hard hat stood next to the machine that had tried to kill them. She drew her gun on him. "Freeze! Police!"

"Woah!" The man's arms shot up. "I-I-I didn't do this! I just came to help!" Apparently, he was just a construction worker.

Beside her, Bruce had his weapon drawn and was examining the cab. She knew Frank was somewhere out of view, watching her back or flank. She kept her weapon raised. "What do you mean by 'help'?"

"Help you, the police!" the man sputtered. "This truck, the crane—they were stolen from our site nearby. When I heard all the noise, I came running. I'm the only guy who knows how to operate it other than Joe, and they shot him."

"You can lower your arms, but keep your hands in front of you. No sudden movements." Sam lowered the gun but kept it in her hand by her side. "Explain."

The man removed his hard hat and used his sleeve to wipe the sweat from his brow. "My name's Phil Dempsey. I'm a crane operator with GXC Demolition. We're working a site about eight blocks that way." He pointed to his right. "Not even an hour ago, two cops, an old guy and a young guy, come on site with a little kid. And the younger guy—at least I think he's younger—is wearing this weird Indian, uh, Native American mask. Says he's wearing it for the kid, for what reason, I don't know. But the two men have badges and they look legit."

He shrugged. "Anyway, they ask Joe—that's Joseph Botticelli—if they wouldn't mind showing the kid how the crane works. Mind you, they ain't got no business being onsite, but them being cops, Joe entertains them. No actual operation, mind you. He just lets the kid play with the joysticks and work the pedals while everything is off."

Phil tipped his head and sighed. "Then they ask Joe for his keys, for the crane, and for the truck. Joe, me, and everyone think they're joking until they pull out their guns. This young cop just smiles and pumps a round into Joe's knee. At that point, the rest of us are keeping our distance, and Joe's down, fumbling in his pockets for his keys. He hands them to the young cop, who shoots him in the face. We all run then. Those cops and that boy, they drive off with the crane."

Sam bounced on her feet, wanting Phil to tell her everything but to do it without mincing words. "Did you get a good look at any of them?"

"The old guy and the kid, yeah. Like I said, the other cop was wearing a mask. And once they drew their sidearms, all the fun and games were over. You know what I mean?"

Sam's mind began to spin. Two out of three obviously hadn't cared whether they would be recognized. Maybe only those two had been brainwashed. *And the third?* He could have been Wainwright. She shook her head. *Questions better left for later.*

Phil raised his arms in exasperation. "We were still waiting on the cops when I heard the noise over here and came running, figuring I might be needed." He looked up at the crane on the bed and shook his head. "It's counterbalanced to support the weight of the wrecking ball, but the outriggers aren't positioned right. The boom could have snagged a streetlight or powerlines, or—" He sighed. "About a hundred things could have gone wrong, tipped this thing over, and injured everyone within range of that four-ton wrecking ball. Though I'm guessing hurting innocent people was the last thing on their minds. It's amazing they even got it to work, unless one of them had experience. I mean, that kid couldn't even reach the pedals..."

As Phil trailed off, Sam searched for a lead on Michael's whereabouts in his story. Finding none, she glanced about for Frank and Bruce. "You guys find anything?"

"No," Bruce said from right behind her, much closer than she'd thought. "I suggest we keep moving."

"They're not here," Frank called from around the truck.

"They came back this way," Phil said. "One of the cops, anyway, and the kid. I saw them coming and hid around the corner of that building." He pointed behind him. "They got into a black Jeep and drove off."

Sam scowled. She turned to Bruce, so mad she couldn't even speak. She wondered if he'd known the kid they were chasing was not Michael but perhaps the missing child from the hospital. She had half a mind to go back to the rubble and start digging, but just because Phil hadn't seen Michael didn't necessarily mean Wainwright's goons hadn't picked him up. *Or may have killed him.* She tried to keep her emotions in check while talking to Phil, who was not to blame. "Did you get a license plate?"

Phil nodded. "Some of it. Rhode Island plate, W F dash nine. There were two more numbers, but I'm not sure. Next one might have been a six or an eight."

Sam met his eyes. "You're sure on the first three?"

Phil nodded again.

She grabbed her portable radio and called into dispatch. "Put out a BOLO on a black Jeep Wrangler, Rhode Island license plate beginning with W F nine. Any sightings, report back immediately to Detective Samantha Reilly. Do not engage."

"We should head back to your car." Bruce grabbed her by the elbow. "Get on the wire and be ready when—"

"Take your fucking hand off me!" Sam's face was hotter than a leather car seat in summer. Whipping her arm away from her former partner's touch, she wheeled on Phil, who jumped.

Nostrils flaring, she asked in a low tone, "Did the men posing as officers say anything to you or your coworkers that could suggest where they might have come from?"

Phil's eyes rolled upward. "Uh..." He tapped his chin. "No, I can't really think of anything."

"Did they say anything at all?"

"Other than what I already told you, no. Not really." He shrugged. "The old cop seemed like he was lost in his own thoughts, kinda spacey and muttering to himself, ya know? And the younger one... well, he was kinda hard to read on account of the mask and all, but he didn't really say much neither. I got the sense he was just there trying to humor the kid." Crow's feet spread from the corners of his eyes. "It was the kid that did most of the talking. He was just so excited about getting to drive another big machine, like it was for his birthday or something. He kind of reminded me of my own boy, actually, except that he didn't seem all that concerned when his dad or whoever shot Joe."

Sam was about to thank the man for his time and head back to the rubble when something he'd said repeated in her brain. "Say that again?"

"What?" Phil squinted. "I just mean that my son is scared to death of blood. He'd be—"

"No, I mean what the kid said, something about getting to drive another big machine."

"Oh! Yeah, the kid was bragging about how he got to drive a train earlier. A real one too."

"Train?" Frank stepped up beside her and Bruce. "There aren't any trains in Fall River. No subway. The commuter rail from Boston was supposed to be extended into Fall River in the next couple of years, but you know how those things are always getting delayed."

"Any chance they've already started work on the station?" Sam asked.

Phil chimed in, surprising Sam, who'd almost forgotten he was there as her mind tinkered with the details. "Yeah, they broke ground on the station, but there wouldn't be any trains there yet. That's a long way off."

"What about an old station?" Sam asked. "Trains must have come through here back in the city's glory days."

"That's even before my time," Bruce said. He stared into space, eyes narrowing on some invisible target. "But I do know where there's an abandoned train depot. Down near Battleship Cove, across from the Port Authority. There's a lot of traffic by there, so it's not an ideal place to hide, but once on the lot, you could probably get lost on it."

Sam looked at Frank, Bruce's voice stirring her ire.

Frank pursed his lips. "It's the only lead we've got right now."

"You two go." Sam spun around. "I'm heading back to look for Michael."

"He could be anywhere by now," Bruce called, stopping her in her tracks. "If he hasn't tried to get a hold of you, he's probably with them. And if he's not with them, the best way to keep it that way is to take the son of a bitch down once and for all."

Somewhere out there was a boy who needed her. But Bruce's words rang true. Michael would need her all the more if he was with Wainwright. With no other clues to where he might have gone, following the one possible lead they had seemed her best choice. Either that, or she could go shift through the rubble, unsure if she would be able to handle what she might find. The thought turned her stomach, so she coerced herself to believe he'd gotten out, that there might still be something she could do for him.

A blue Honda was approaching from the west, rolling slowly forward as the light turned green. Pulling her badge from her belt, Sam held it up as she stepped in front of the vehicle. The car jerked to a stop.

"Sorry, miss, but we're going to need your car."

The twenty-something behind the wheel started to protest, but then she grabbed her purse and phone and stepped out of the car. "But how will I get it back?"

"We'll bring it to you." Sam hopped behind the wheel. Frank, she was happy to see, took the passenger seat, while Bruce slid into the back. Any hostility she'd harbored for Frank seemed a distant memory, overshadowed by the animosity for the man she'd once considered a second father. Squeezing the wheel tightly and wishing it were Bruce's neck, she spun the car around then sped toward Battleship Cove.

CHAPTER 39

Michael dropped to the ground as the handlebar for the zip line swung through the air where his head had been. His side hit earth first, and he barrel-rolled from his back to his stomach. Dirt flew in his face as he pushed himself up, the metal instrument displacing the topsoil only a hairline from his hand. He scrambled to his feet and turned to face Dylan, squaring off with his hands before remembering the stick knife he'd put in his back pocket. Reaching for it, his hand found empty space. He glanced about the underbrush and saw the barbaric weapon inches from Dylan's feet.

Dylan didn't seem to notice it. Blood darkened the skin under his nostrils and outlined his teeth. One hand hung by his side, clutching the handlebar, while the other hugged his torso just under his ribs.

"Stay... back," he said through wheezes, his voice barely more than a whisper. He coughed, and blood ran like drool from the corner of his mouth. "I can't believe... you pushed me."

Seeing Dylan struggling to stand, to even breathe, made his anger leak away, replaced by grief and something akin to shock at what he'd done. "Dylan, you're hurt bad. Put the bar down, and we'll get you help."

Dylan laughed at that, but only before the laughter brought about a coughing fit and more blood from his mouth. His eyelids fluttered, and he bent over. "No way, man... I... I thought we were... friends."

"Give it up, already." Michael snarled, unsure if his anger was toward Dylan or himself. He kept his hands out in front of him. "I checked your phone. Are you going to tell me your own father brainwashed you? Why'd you have to be part of it, Dylan? Is *he* really your father? I don't even know the jerk."

"My father... called me?" Dylan's eyes rolled up. He blinked away tears. "Dad... He can be a real dick sometimes, but... I guess you already know that. Always talking about some sort of... rite of passage, vision quest thing. Taking this Native American thing way too seriously. Before that was some Liberian tribal ritual. Made me eat—"

Michael didn't think Dylan's face could get any paler, but just then, it blanched as if some distant memory had scared the rest of his life out of him. He leaned over, using the zipline grip line as a cane for support. His voice softer, seemingly talking more to himself than Michael, he said, "He thinks... I'm too soft." He raised his hand to his face and studied it, but Michael was unsure of what he saw there. "Maybe I am."

"I thought he wanted to use me." Michael began to circle as Dylan did, the latter still making no effort to raise his weapon.

"Does he? I... I don't know. Stay back!" Dylan feinted to his right, causing Michael to jump, but the braced-faced boy made no move to attack. "I think... he's run out of reasons to keep me around."

"Come on, man." Michael stepped to his left, sneaking a glance down at the stick knife, which was almost within reach. He hoped he wouldn't need it, but he didn't know if Dylan was severely hurt or just playing up his injuries, truly ignorant of his father's games or playing one of his own. "You can stop this, then. He doesn't care about you. He's just using you or trying to like he is me, Sam, that doctor lady, all those masked patients. We're all just pieces in his game. Put the bar down, and we'll get you help. Maybe we could even figure out a way to still be friends."

A sad smile crept over his face. "Ishmael... floats alone... my friend. Maybe... you're Starbuck." The bar fell from his hand. "I'm sorry, Michael." Then, he, too, fell.

Michael hurried to his side. He looked at Dylan's hand, still clutched over a wound spouting dark blood, the tip of a branch poking through his fingers. He tried to pull it out, but between his weakened condition and his hands repeatedly slipping on the blood everywhere, he soon gave up.

Face white as death, Dylan peered up at Michael. He smiled, a smile that was warm and friendly and reminiscent of the first one he'd given Michael—the smile of a friend. "I told—" He coughed several times, his eyelids fluttering once more as he began to sway. "I told you... you were... a badass."

"Get up!" Michael cried. "The hospital, it's only a short walk—"

Dylan's head swiveled slowly to the side, and Michael understood what Dylan must have already known. He was dying. He crouched, tried to pull his friend to his feet, which only spurred more coughing, then sat beside him. Lying there on the cold dirt, his chest expanding and contracting, Dylan seemed to be at peace. Michael's own mind was still too frantic to figure out how to help his friend or even to know whether he should.

"Dylan, please. I have to know." He wiped his eyes with his sleeve. "Were you for real?"

He looked into Dylan's eyes and saw that if the boy had had any answers to give, they would no longer be forthcoming.

CHAPTER 40

Sam, Frank, and Bruce parked in the lot at Heritage State Park among a scattering of other vehicles, hoping to give her quarry no hint she was after them. The park lay just around a bend in the road from the abandoned train depot. From where they sat, she could peek through the chain-link fence into the depot's entrance, her view hindered only by a hodgepodge of disconnected antique train cars in various degrees of disrepair, a carnival of autumn colors and rust. No one appeared to be at home, but she couldn't see beyond the cars closest to her.

Besides the hangar-sized lot itself, several restaurants, small businesses, docks, a city park, a decommissioned battleship, and a submarine called the cove home—not an ideal place for a confrontation if there was to be one. Sam wasn't so confident they had the right place, given the bustling neighborhood and that Wainwright might prefer naval warships to the depot. He was probably insane enough to take a shot at them.

As she and her tagalongs made their way to the enclosed lot's fence, Frank separated from the group to go toward the front. The security hut at the entrance appeared to be empty, their first sign that they might have hit upon the right location.

The second sign came when someone opened fire on Frank. He went down fast out of sight, though he hadn't appeared to have been hit. He must've taken cover behind the security hut. Only when shots sounded from his direction did her concern truly lessen.

She called in backup. Even if a bad apple had spoiled them, as Frank believed, she trusted her department to come through for her.

Bruce, impetuous as ever, was already straddling the top of the fence before the call had ended, muttering something about how Wainwright would just escape again if they waited.

In a voice louder than she'd intended, Sam admonished him—some of the masked shooters might be victims. She hoisted herself up and over the fence and followed Bruce into danger, not voicing but partially sharing his concerns after what had happened at Brentworth.

Train cars dotted the lawn like tombstones in a forgotten cemetery, no rails beneath them. Sam briefly wondered how they'd gotten there as she slid along the side of the burnt husk of a cargo car. Some were rusted and decayed, while several were in relatively good condition despite them being decades, maybe even centuries, old. Some had the logos of railways Sam had never heard of, while others bore the insignia of a circus or railroad shipper. They were lined up like dominos, zigzagging through a weedy gravel landscape home to rats and God knew what else. The broken beer bottles and syringes strewn all about the ground indicated a different kind of rat that would hopefully scurry away upon police arrival.

As she made her way toward the sounds of gunfire, Sam spotted a fancy-looking dining car that appeared to be the source of the cacophony of shots. Bruce signaled with a nod his intent to head around the back of it. She approached from the side, breaking cover and planning to circle to the front in the hope of getting the drop on whoever was still firing at Frank. But as she neared the car, a masked face appeared in the window. Spotting her, it quickly dipped out of sight.

Sam wasted no time sprinting back to cover. Glass shattered and bullets kicked up dirt in front of her. She swung around the end of the car she'd originally approached from, pressing her back flat against it as she caught her breath and steeled herself to fire back.

What sounded like a firework finale came from the back of the train car, and Sam knew Bruce had encountered some trouble of his own. He'd be no help to her, but at least they had the shooters pinned on three sides—so long as all three of the good guys remained standing. She sprang around the corner and opened fire on the spot in the window where she thought her target had been. Her aim had been deadly accurate, except the masked shooter had moved. He let out his own barrage of bullets. They clinked off the metal of the train, dangerously close. Still, Sam held her ground. She fired just one shot at her assailant, causing him to duck behind the relative safety of the car's wall.

She pictured the shooter in her mind. A bald head rose over a mask, so unless they'd decided to give Michael an impromptu shave, the shooter wasn't him. She was still holding onto the hope, believing in her heart that he lived. Having no real reason, she chalked it up to a mother's intuition for lack of a better term. She'd warned the others of the possibility, however unlikely given the amount of time he would have spent in Wainwright's company, of Michael being brainwashed and used against them. She'd likewise warned them she would shoot them where they stood if they even scratched Michael.

So as she waited at the ready for her target to reveal himself, Sam convinced herself that it could not be Michael and dared not think of the consequences might she be wrong. She knew she had the shooter. She might have smiled if not for the gravity of what that would mean for someone likely brainwashed and innocent of any crime. Still, she couldn't risk any of the so-called Indians hurting anyone else. As if playing some twisted carnival game, she scanned the row of windows, trying to guess where the masked head would pop up next. She was one off, but it didn't affect her ability to shoot twice at Wainwright's minion. She crept forward, certain the first had hit its mark, the second shot only a cautionary measure.

"I'm pinned!" Bruce shouted to her left. It sounded as if he was facing a Tommy gun.

With no entrance on the side of the car facing her, Sam had a decision to make—circle to the back and help Bruce shoot his way into the train or head to the front to help Frank. The third option, the wait-for-backup option, certainly seemed the smartest, but she knew backup wouldn't distinguish between killer and confused. They would shoot all equally just as she'd been forced to only moments ago. With a department on edge, she couldn't trust some trigger-happy bozo to not light up anything that moved. As much as she hated to admit it, Bruce was right to move in. The three of them were the best chance any of the patients had of survival. If only they could aim low—something the head in the window unfortunately hadn't allowed for.

Nevertheless, Sam chose the front. If she could get the drop on Frank's shooter, and maybe thereafter Bruce's, too, they all stood the best chance of staying above the dirt. She stalked closer, peering under the car and looking for feet near its entrance. She saw none.

Frank had stopped shooting, to her great relief, and she figured he must have spotted her. But the shooter inside the train kept firing, one or two at a time at Frank's position with long breaks between as if the assailant was losing interest.

She crept to the end and readied for the turn. She needed to act quickly to eliminate hostiles and clear the way for the others.

"Look out!" Frank shouted.

A tall figure, lithe as a gymnast, sprang off the car's outer platform, over the handrail, and smack into Sam. A sting in her arm caused her to cry out. Her gun hand knocked her attacker away, jostling her own weapon free. It clattered onto the gravelly earth. With a shaking hand, she pulled a ten-gauge needle from her arm. Its stopper had not yet been compressed. She held it out in front of her eyes, shivering as she wondered what the murky liquid inside could be.

Dr. Horvat's expression was flat. She assumed a fighter's stance, hands curled into fists and held upright, her right leg slightly forward.

Sam ejected the liquid onto the ground then tossed the needle aside. She barely noticed the gunplay behind and beside her, Frank no doubt trying to keep whoever else was in that train inside.

"You've ruined everything," Horvat said matter-of-factly. "This all has been a huge setback. I might have ended the crime you struggle so vainly against, taking down one criminal only so four more can take his place. And yet, you stand in my way. For what? A few insignificant mentally ill patients, several of whom you yourself killed?"

Sam watched the doctor closely, looking for a shift in her eyes, a clench in her jaw, or the flex of a muscle—any sign telegraphing her attack. She almost respected Horvat for making no secret of the fact that an attack was indeed coming.

"You never cared for them before!" The doctor snarled. She sucked in a breath and stiffened. "No one ever has. No one but me. Yes, I have lost a few along the way due to my benefactor's... *unique* proclivities. But they are nothing when compared to all those I will help, the countless I will heal. People who are hurting in ways standard medicine can never cure. People like your boy, Detective."

"Leave my boy out of this." Sam scowled. The mention of Michael and the doctor's purported diagnosis that he was mentally ill shook Sam. The momentary lapse into thought was apparently what Horvat had been waiting for. She struck with a jab that hit Sam square in the mouth. At once, Sam tasted copper as her head rocked back.

The doctor followed with a left cross while Sam was still reeling. The hit sent her staggering into the railcar, jarring her shoulder, but she pushed off it with almost feral ferocity. She wiped the blood from her lips and squared off against her opponent.

Horvat showed no pleasure in her earlier success, her mouth flat and eyes filled with determination. That she'd had training was evident, but the extent of that training was unknown. Something about the way she moved suggested that kicks were in her repertoire of moves, so Sam guessed some form of MMA. Sam, with her father's boxing instructions and years of judo under her belt, didn't know if she could win a fair fight against the doctor.

But Sam had no intention of fighting fair. She charged at the taller, stronger, and younger woman, unleashing a barrage of jabs and hooks. Aside from a few punches that glanced her sides, Horvat easily blocked the rest with her forearms. The flurry of strikes hadn't been intended to do damage but to move Sam in close, to eliminate the doctor's reach advantage.

Her plan worked to close the gap, but what Sam didn't expect was that Horvat was just as effective with her elbows as she was her fists. Sam took one to the jaw so hard her teeth actually rattled, something she'd previously only thought an expression. She rubbed her chin as she fell to one knee, taking her eyes off her opponent for only a second. And for that second, she was rewarded with a breath-stealing kick to her chest.

Neither paid any mind to the bullets ricocheting off metal around them. Sam was getting her ass handed to her and needed to do something to turn the tides. Her hands clawed at the ground as she pushed herself up, hoping for enough sand to throw into Horvat's eyes but only coming up with a few pebbles. Those dropped back down to the ground as she endured another kick, this one just under her chin and feeling as if it might have enough force to pop her head right off.

Instead, it lifted her into the air. Her back crashed down into the unforgiving ground, knocking what little wind she had out of her.

She clawed at her neck, unable to speak or breathe, hoarse wheezing the only sound emitting from her. Had she had an Adam's apple, she would have eaten it. As it was, she couldn't swallow. Tears filled her eyes, which bulged in their sockets. Unable to get any air into her lungs, she tried to rise, rolling to her stomach and pushing herself up onto hands and knees.

Horvat moved in for the kill. Sam could offer no defense as the doctor wrapped her arm around Sam's throat and yanked her to her feet. Sam flailed weakly against Horvat's chest, the chokehold tightening. It almost seemed superfluous since she was already breathless.

Through her pain and tears, Sam heard a low voice in her ear. "I'm sorry it's come to this, but I can't have you interfering again. Just know, no harm will come to your boy from me." An exhale tickled her ear, a strangely peaceful sensation despite the chaos ravaging both her mind and body. "I'll do my best to keep Carter from harming him, assuming his boy can even bring him to us."

Sam gritted her teeth. *Michael!* Through the din, Sam clung to one idea. Horvat was talking as if Michael were still alive. She'd hoped as much, but whether Horvat's words were truly confirmation or not, Sam took it that way. And there was no chance she was letting Carter Wainwright anywhere near her boy again, not so long as her heart still beat.

At some level, Sam registered that the gunfire at both ends of the train had stopped. Standing her up had been a mistake. The doctor should have locked in her legs in what wrestlers called a double grapevine and stretched Sam out so she had no chance of standing or escaping the choke. Sapped of energy, darkness spreading across her vision, Sam summoned the last of her strength. She shot her hip to the side and slid her arm around the doctor's waist and a leg behind her body. With a roar that sounded like a croak, she thrust her hip in and up, lifted Horvat into the air as she leaned back, then threw the doctor over her body.

In a loud *thunk*, skull met train car. Dr. Horvat fell limp.

Still unable to breathe, Sam clawed again at her throat even as a small boy ran around the front of the train, holding a gun that seemed too big for his hands. He pointed it at Sam, his face contorting into a sulk. "Is she...?"

Sam paid him little mind. She had to get her panic under control if she wanted to live. Concentrating on her breathing, she slowly paced and took in air through her nose, her throat burning and chest exploding in pain as her lungs began to fill. In and out, each time with a little more air. It felt like sucking thick liquid through a thin straw. Amid her pacing, she snagged the gun from the boy's hands.

He ran to Dr. Horvat and shook her. "We were just playing a game," he whined, tears in his eyes. "You weren't supposed to hurt her."

Sam caught a glimpse of Frank approaching, using cover as he did. He made his way toward them, pistol trained on the car's entrance. "The boy," he said, not taking his eyes off the door. "That's Mitchell Lancaster, the missing child from Brentworth. I think," he continued, his voice rising in disbelief, "he was just shooting at me."

"It was just a game." Mitchell cried. "Youse are the ones that ruined it. She"—he pointed at Sam—"she killed Dr. Horvat."

"Is it true, Sam?" Frank asked. "Is Horvat dead?"

Sam was breathing a little easier then, but every inhalation felt as if she'd swallowed a milk jug full of pins. She wobbled over to Horvat and checked for a pulse. "Still breathing," she hissed. "Who's left inside?"

The question hung in the air as they exchanged a look. After cuffing the doctor to the train's undercarriage, she tucked Mitchell's gun in her waistband and picked up her Glock. Mitchell made no effort to move from Horvat's side, so they frisked him and left him there. Sam signaled that she was going to check on Bruce, leaving Frank to cover the front. She headed toward the back of the train, biting down against the pain sizzling throughout her body, fairly certain she was suffering some internal bleeding. After she took down Wainwright, *after* she found Michael, she thought a medically induced coma sounded like a wonderful plan.

A shot whizzed by her, and she groaned.

"Sam?" Bruce called. "That you?"

She couldn't speak above a hoarse whisper, so she did something akin to a jumping jack to get his attention then extended her middle finger. Slowly, he rose then proceeded to her position. By the time he was halfway there, he was nearly skipping. "Is he in there? Do we have him?"

Sam just shrugged. Sirens howled, growing closer. The first of Fall River's finest were arriving on the scene.

A slow clapping came from inside. "Come on in. I'm unarmed."

A flash of anger crossed Bruce's face. He pulled something out of his pockets and pressed it into his ear, then he charged into the train car. "I've got you, you son of a bitch. I've finally got you."

Sam delicately pulled herself up onto the platform, then she stepped into the car. Bruce stood in the narrow aisle several feet beyond the entrance, his back to her and gun raised. Over his shoulder, Sam saw a smiling Carter Wainwright with his hands in the air. She could see no one else alive in the car, though anyone could be hiding between the seats, waiting to spring up at the most inopportune moment.

As for the dead, Sam counted two. Staying on alert, she crouched before a still figure wearing a mask just inside the threshold, who'd evidently been shot in the chest by Bruce. Another masked man lay midway down the aisle, his mask askew and revealing his bald head and half of the dead man's stare. A hollow pang hit her stomach as she realized he was her victim, and the security guard's uniform he wore, together with the absence of any other guard on the lot, made her certain she'd likewise gunned down an innocent.

Thinking she couldn't be so hard on Bruce for taking out the poor puppet at her feet, Sam reached for the fallen brave's mask, hand trembling. She froze, panic rising in her so quickly it made her head spin as her brain tried to process who it was. The shooter's size was so much like Michael's. Then his red hair registered somewhere deep, but it did nothing to diminish her dread. Her shaking intensifying, she slid the mask from his face and gasped.

"Jimmy!" she shouted, finding her voice through the pain. His eyes found hers as his chest rose and fell in almost undetectable shallow breaths. She immediately put pressure on his wounds.

"What?" Bruce asked, his voice inordinately loud as he dared a glance back at her. "What is it?"

"Ten little Indians... standing in a line," Jimmy whispered, the corners of his mouth twitching as if trying to smile as a tear ran from the corner of his eye. "One... toddled home..." His eyes searched the ceiling as if looking there for the rest of the rhyme. They fixed on a spot and went still.

"I'm sorry, Jimmy," Sam whispered, finding it suddenly hard to breathe all over again. She thought of Michael—how easily it could have been him instead, and how easily Bruce would have shot him. Jimmy hadn't deserved that any more than Michael would have. "I'm so, so sorry."

She checked his pulse, first at his neck, then at his wrist, already knowing what she would find but doing it anyway. Crying, she closed his eyes with her fingers. Hanging her head, she rose, her sadness and rage mounting to a boil. Pulling energy as if from the ether, she ran at Wainwright, checking her way past Bruce with the form and grace of a bull. And like a matador, the killer danced aside, spun her around, then caught her in his arms. He had a knife to her throat before she could even move to stop it.

"Ah, and here we are, Bruce, old friend." Wainwright kissed Sam's cheek as she squirmed in his hold. "Now this, *this* is the drama one might say I kill for."

He pressed the knife harder against the soft flesh of Sam's neck. She could feel the warmth of her blood trickling down to her chest.

"I had more plans for you," Wainwright whispered in her ear. "But this is so, so much better, no? Ol' Brucey losing not one but *two* young partners? The only question is, will he shoot you before I slit your throat?"

Sam threw back her elbow, but still winded from her fight with Horvat, only managed a glancing blow. She was rewarded with the blade pressed harder into her neck and much more warm wetness cascading down her skin.

"Will you take the shot, Bruce?" He tightened his grip around her waist, his hot breath on her cheek sending waves of revulsion through her body. "Does your desire to kill me trump the risk you'd be taking with her life? Take the shot, Bruce." He tittered with excitement. "Take the shot."

Bruce's expression never wavered. He stared emotionlessly down his barrel at Wainwright, likely ruminating on whether to take the shot.

Sam nodded. She was willing to take the risk her own stupidity had placed her in. Bruce narrowed his gaze down the barrel of his pistol, aiming. She was going to die, her only consolation being that Wainwright would surely die with her. She closed her eyes.

"He never learns," Wainwright whispered in her ear. "Such A fool. He and I are going to have some fun with you." With a booming, singsong voice, he said, "Four little Indians up on a spree."

Oh no. Sam didn't think it was possible for her heart to sink any further, but it did. Bruce's expression, already fairly blank, remained that way—robotic. And no doubt under Wainwright's spell.

Wainwright laughed. He shifted behind her. "Shoot out her left knee cap."

Bruce didn't move beyond tracing the movement of Wainwright's head with his aim.

Wainwright cleared his throat. "Four little Indians up on a spree. Shoot yourself, Bruce!"

A *click* sounded behind Sam. "You have one second to drop it," Frank said. "One."

The knife fell from Wainwright's hand, and he raised his arms high. Apparently, he was a bit more cautious with his life than he let on.

Frank slammed him down onto a nearby table, yanked his arms behind his back, then cuffed him.

As Frank stood him back up, Wainwright smiled at Bruce. "You should have killed me when you had the chance."

"Huh?" Bruce pointed to his ear and the earplugs he'd jammed into them. Then he punched Wainwright in the stomach.

"Enough," Frank said.

But when Wainwright started to laugh, Sam couldn't help herself. She punched him too.

"Enough!" Frank shouted. He threw Wainwright into a seat, which with the killer's hands cuffed behind him, might have hurt Wainwright more than both punches combined. If it had, the sadistic bastard didn't show it. He just sat quietly, smiling up at the three of them.

AS THE SUN BEGAN ITS descent, the cavalry took up position outside. Frank announced their presence, and they exited the train car with weapons holstered, dragging their prize in tow. They ushered him toward a patrol car then corralled him into the backseat just as three men in black suits made their way past.

Once Wainwright was secure, they turned to see one of the suits reviving Horvat with smelling salts.

"They yours?" Sam asked.

Frank shook his head. "No, but I was afraid something like this might happen."

"Something like what? Who are they?"

The suits removed Horvat's cuffs, stood her up, then secured her with handcuffs of their own. As they guided her toward an unmarked sedan, Sam blocked their path.

"Woah!" She pushed one of them in the chest, enough to make him step back. "Where do you think you're going with her? That's my collar."

The man flipped open his wallet, showing credentials Sam barely even had time to read. "Don't worry, Officer—"

"Detective."

The man nodded. "We'll take it from here, *Detective*." He strung out the word as if its mere parlance on his tongue were distasteful. "This woman is now in the custody of the United States government. All her rights to freedom in this country have been revoked."

Sam started to protest, but Frank pulled her away as Bruce just watched dumbfounded.

"What was that?" she asked again. "What the hell, Frank?"

Frank let out a deep sigh. "People like her, people with certain skills that are attractive to the Department of Defense, Homeland Security, etcetera... they are offered much more hospitable sentences in exchange for their cooperation."

"You mean..."

"It's like what we did with all those Nazi scientists and defectors after World War II." He shrugged. "There's nothing we can do about it. But you can rest assured, they will have her under lock and key—and probably chipped—for a very long time."

She was about to voice her opinion on the subject when Tag interrupted. "Sam, er, Detective Reilly. Michael called 911. He's safe, but he wouldn't reveal his location. Instead, he left you a message. Said he was where he'd go if he wanted to get high."

Sam threw her arms around the officer, not caring at that moment for decorum. Horvat was no longer her problem. Michael was alive and safe, and she knew exactly where to find him.

"You guys okay here?" she asked Bruce and Frank. "I need to go be with my son."

CHAPTER 41

Michael watched in the dark as two figures plodded toward him through the thick foliage. He'd spent the last several hours up in the treehouse alone with his thoughts, turning over the idea that he might be a murderer and eventually coming to the conclusion that he was. Though he hadn't planned it, he'd meant to push Dylan. And he had intended to kill him before because he thought Dylan would try to do the same to him.

But he couldn't be sure what Dylan had intended when he raised his hands out in front of him. He'd had the bar, but he hadn't drawn it back for a swing.

Below, the two individuals were now only a dozen yards or so away. One was the silhouette of a slender woman who appeared to be about Sam's height and might have been her, but the other, beyond being that of an adult male, was a question mark. He waited in silence at the top of the treehouse, while Dylan's body lay below, behind the tree and collecting critters.

"Michael?" Sam's familiar voice called up.

"Here!" Michael pushed his way through the treehouse doors and began his descent, his body alive with excitement even while his heart weighed heavy with what he'd done.

When he reached the ground, he ran to Sam and she to him. They embraced, wet cheek to wet cheek, Michael chancing a seizure and vision—one that never came. He wondered briefly if that was because he'd already seen her future, and nothing they'd done had changed it.

After nearly a minute in each other's arms, Michael pulled away. He looked back and forth between his foster mother and the person with her, Bruce, trying to learn what he could from their expressions. "Is it over? Are we safe?"

Sam sniffled and nodded. "We got him. Bruce is here for backup, you know, just in case, while Sergeant Rollins is managing the scene with Frank's assistance."

She clapped Bruce on the shoulder. "This guy would never have left Wainwright until he saw him behind bars or dead. But since he couldn't stand next to the sicko without wearing earplugs, I forced him to come with me." She smiled. "It's been too long since you last had my back."

Bruce frowned. "What about—"

"Anyway, Wainwright's headed off to jail as we speak. Dr. Horvat's in custody, too, but... well, that's a long story. We also saved the little boy who was taken from the hospital, but two of his other victims, the people he used, died in the shootout." She placed her hands on his shoulders. "Michael... Jimmy's dead."

Michael jerked away. "What? How?" He shook his head as he began to stutter. "It-it's not possible. He was in a halfway house. He—"

"We don't have all the details." Sam exchanged a look with her former partner. "Whether he was brainwashed all along and made his way back to them or was kidnapped or whatever, we won't know until we can investigate. He was masked and shooting at us when we found them, and—"

"Did you kill him?" Michael wasn't sure he wanted the answer to that question, but he fixed his gaze on Sam and waited nonetheless.

But it was Bruce who answered. "I did, son." He winced, and for the second time, Michael saw a hint of vulnerability in a man who'd seemed all anger and hate.

Michael's chin quivered, and he had to look away, trying to board up the dam before it cracked. He fell back against the tree trunk, and he slid down it to his butt, burying his face in his hands. He thought of Jimmy, then Dylan, and the dam burst. Everything just poured on out. "I killed him."

"Huh?" Bruce crouched. "No, son, it was my fault. I should have aimed lower, should have been more careful. None of this is—"

"Not Jimmy... oh, God, Jimmy too." He bellowed a moan that sounded like an animal in its death throes, dying alone at night in the woods. "I-I-I came here with Dylan, and I... and I *killed* him!"

"What are you talking about? Michael, you're not making any sense. Dylan's here? Where?"

"Dylan?" Bruce asked.

Michael ignored them and poured on. "I thought he was faking, that he was really his son, not brainwashed like the others."

"Wait." Bruce stepped closer. "Whose son?"

"Wainwright's or Jefferson's or whoever he is." Michael felt a tingle in his nose and knew it was starting to run. He wiped it with his sleeve and sucked it up. "He attacked me at the school, acting like one of them, but Robbie tackled him, and he started acting all normal again. So I led him here, took his phone, checked his calls, and saw the call had come from his father." He pointed up, his arm swaying in small circles. "I pushed him off the top there."

Sam exchanged a glance with Bruce, then said, "Michael, slow down. Start from the beginning."

"Don't you get it? I pushed him out of the treehouse! I killed him! And I don't even know—"

Sam put a finger over her lips. In a soft tone, she said, "He fell, Michael."

"You're not listening to me. I pu—"

More sternly, she said, "He *fell*, Michael."

"Where is he?" Bruce asked.

Michael threw a thumb over his shoulder as he held back a sob. He hid his eyes with his forearm, resting on bent knees, his heels tucked under him. As Bruce walked around the tree, Sam hugged him again.

"Was he working for his dad?" Michael sniffled. "Or just brainwashed? Was he really my friend?"

"I don't know."

"Sam," Bruce said. "You'd better come over here."

Sam held him a moment longer. "Are you okay to go with me?"

Michael nodded, but he stood up shakily. She led him around the tree. As he saw Dylan's pale, lifeless form, his tears ran anew.

Bruce crossed his arms. "I thought you said you pushed—"

"He *fell*, Bruce," Sam snapped.

"Did he fall onto that branch?" He pointed at the stick poking out of Dylan's stomach then the two pairs of circling footprints. "Looks like he got up, and—"

"He fell, damn it! Or Michael pushed him in self-defense!"

Michael's body shook, but he managed to respond. "He was holding that bar." He pointed to the zip line handlebar on the ground beside Dylan. "I... I thought he was going to attack me with it, but..."

Sam looked him in the eyes. "So you didn't kill him. See? Even if you had pushed him out of the tree, he was trying to kill you with that bar, and you did what you had to do. It was self-defense."

"You say he was Wainwright's son," Bruce said as he removed a cell phone from his pocket and turned on its flashlight. "Why do you say that?"

"It's something we vetted internally because the boy's last name, Jefferson," Sam said. "I put someone I can trust on it. Dylan's the son of someone else at the hospital. Everything checked out."

"Did you vet it personally? Wainwright's people can fake all sorts of documents. Whoever looked into it may have seen only what

Wainwright wanted him to see." Bruce leaned closer to the boy. "But just looking at him, I can tell he's not Wainwright's son, at least not biologically."

Bruce crouched, shining the light into Dylan's face. He went eerily silent, holding that position for several seconds as he ran his fingers down his face.

"Bruce?" Sam said, breaking the quiet. "Is everything okay?"

Bruce stood and turned, his face haggard and ghastly in the light of his phone. In a quivering voice that seemed not his own, he said, "I just can't believe how much he looks like Jocelyn."

CHAPTER 42

Officer Ronald Tagliamonte closed the door to his police cruiser as he settled in behind the wheel, Sergeant Rollins already seated beside him. He sighed, he and half his department having been stuck at the various crime scenes all afternoon and well into the evening. Behind him, separated only by the partition cage, sat the most accomplished serial killer his city had ever known. The FBI agent and Sam had trusted only him and the sergeant, a good man, to bring in Wainwright in Sam's absence. After all, like her, he had lost a partner. *I'm sorry, Paltrow.*

He turned the key in the ignition, shifted into gear, then rolled out of the sea of whirling lights. But when they reached the precinct, he drove past it, instead taking the onramp for I-195 West toward Providence.

"Where are you going?" Sergeant Rollins asked.

Tag threw a thumb over his shoulder. "He killed my partner. I just want to have a little chat with him before we bring him in. It'll only take a minute. No one will know."

Rollins set his jaw. "Not a good idea. Turn around. We bring him in, *unharmed.*"

"And if she were your partner?"

Rollins let out a breath. "Believe me. I get it. You have no idea what's going through my mind right now, what I'd love to do this guy. But we can't, and you know it. So turn around. If it makes you feel better, you can consider it an order. I won't let you jeopardize your career or mine for some payback, no matter how deserved it would be."

By that time, Tag was already crossing the Braga Bridge into Somerset. He shook his head and rubbed his brow, sick with the thought of what he would have to do. "Of course, you're right, Sergeant. I... I just lost my head for a moment there." He passed the exit for Somerset and took the first Swansea exit. "I'll just turn around in the Park and Ride ahead."

But instead of turning around, he pulled into a spot.

"Tag... Ron," Rollins said softly. "Don't do this. I'll drive from here."

Tag ran his hands down his face. He shook like a junkie in need of a fix and pushed the car door open. He jumped out and circled the car, drawing his gun as he rounded the trunk. Rollins was already outside when he fired two rounds into the sergeant's chest. Seeing his fellow officer, his friend, bleeding out, a stunned expression blanketing his pale face, Tag put another bullet in his head to end both their misery. Then he keeled over and dry heaved.

Once he had composed himself, he turned and looked through the back window. Grinning, Carter Wainwright stared back, a deathly visage in the pale moon's glow. Tag opened the door, and Wainwright slid across the backseat and out of the car.

As Tag spun him around to unlock his cuffs, Wainwright asked, "She still doesn't suspect you?"

Tag sneered. "Not in the least. Well, at least not before now."

Wainwright massaged his free wrists. "May I have the gun?"

Tag nodded. He handed his service pistol to Wainwright.

"Good. And the keys?"

The officer pointed to the only other car in the lot, a black Subaru Forester. "Already in the ignition." He choked up. "I've done everything you asked, pretended to be your Indian." He looked down at Sergeant Rollins' lifeless body. "*Killed* for you. Please..." He dropped to his knees, hands folding in front of him. "Please just let her go."

Wainwright cackled. "Oh... all right."

Hopeful, Tag glanced up.

"I *was* going to tell you that I would be keeping her since your position has been undeniably valuable." Wainwright patted the officer's head, treating Tag as if he were his good little dog. "But I suppose you've earned the truth. Besides, your usefulness has likely run out after tonight. So here it is—I never kept your baby sister. I tortured her and killed her months ago."

For a moment, Tag couldn't comprehend what he'd heard. He stared up blankly, the cogs in his head turning slowly, grinding out sparks that bloomed into a conflagration. He exploded to his feet, charging at Wainwright without thought or regard for his own safety.

He heard the gunshot before he felt the pain in his stomach. Tag fell, groaning in pain as his hands covered the wound.

"If you live, that will help you maintain your cover."

"Cover?" Fear had crippled any further aggression, the need to survive trumping all else. His hands remained where they were, but the hate kept him lucid. "You might as well kill me. I will never help you again, you son of a bitch." He tried to spit, but only a little blood trickled down his chin.

"Never say never." Wainwright shrugged. "Your sister may be dead, but your little nephew is still very much alive." He started to walk away.

Tag tried to rise, but the pain drove him back down. He called over his shoulder. "When will you be back?"

"When I'm ready."

"Yeah? Well, I'll be waiting."

The killer waltzed over to his new Subaru, got in, then drove away, leaving Tag bleeding on the pavement.

EPILOGUE

After going through September without stepping foot outside Sam's apartment, Michael finally returned to school and some semblance of a normal life. Well, as normal as he could with an old, severely disfigured man staying with them. Bruce spent his nights in a chair facing their apartment door, a gun in one hand and a glass of Scotch in the other. He hadn't seen Frank since the botched arrest, but Sam said he was doing well, having regained some of his status at the FBI since he had been able to track down the monster and place him into custody. No one blamed Frank for not being able to keep him there, and with Wainwright having become Public Enemy Number One, Frank's intimate knowledge of the killer was too valuable an asset to be ignored.

Officer Tagliamonte had required hospitalization, but so far, only his career had been hurt in the long run. His story about Wainwright grabbing his gun and turning it on him and Rollins raised serious questions that would, in the least, subject him to discipline and likely termination. But with him being the only witness to what had actually gone down, criminal prosecution seemed unlikely. Michael imagined that letting a killer like Wainwright escape was probably devastating enough on the mind of the poor officer. Sam was tight-lipped when it came to Tagliamonte, but Michael noticed his absence on the details that would be forever posted outside the school either until he graduated or Wainwright was caught or killed.

In his period of social distancing, Michael had ventured out with Sam only once, to visit Tessa at her new hospital in Bridgewater. After a couple of flat lines and several blood transfusions, her condition had slowly gone from critical to recuperating nicely. Her mind, too, seemed to be doing much better, excellent even—so much so that it looked like she'd be getting out soon, once they found a place for her. Whatever Dr. Horvat had done to her had been nothing short of miraculous, assuming she'd done more than just repress damaging memories. She seemed genuinely happy, except when he'd told her about Jimmy. Even then, her smile had fallen away only for a few minutes. Her thoughts had turned somewhere deep inside herself while her face had borne the marks of a dreadful, contagious sorrow before the smile reappeared, and she said, "That's too bad. He seemed really nice."

Michael hadn't moved on from Jimmy's death so easily. Nor could he move past his act of what Sam insisted had been self-defense. He wasn't so sure. Samples taken from the body confirmed what Bruce had suspected—Dylan was the son of Jocelyn Beaudette. Even if he was after Michael or part of the so-called Indians—to which Sam had discovered no firm connections other than the familial relationship—he didn't know what chance Dylan had had to be anything but what Wainwright had made him. Michael had deprived him of that chance as well, and in some sick way, given his own violent upbringing, he still felt he'd had more in common with Dylan than anyone else he'd met. He still considered Dylan a friend. And he had killed him.

He hung his head as Robbie, who'd known the day he was returning, and all his football friends clapped and cheered when Michael returned to school that morning. Though he'd been used to people gossiping and whispering as he passed in the halls, he couldn't get used to the salutes and thumbs-up signs he got from complete strangers throughout the day. Apparently, the whole school thought him some kind of hero for killing a killer. Yet no one except Dylan, and perhaps Wainwright, knew the truth.

Walking into his English class immediately before the bell, he stopped just inside the door. It was comforting that so few inside seemed to notice his presence as they hurriedly set up their notebooks, writing utensils, and copies of *Moby Dick*, which the class was then finishing. Three empty seats remained in the room—in the far corner, his and Dylan's, and one unclaimed near the entrance, right next to the girl with bifocals who no one seemed to talk to. He took the seat beside the girl. She glanced at him, swiped her bangs away from her eyes, then smiled sheepishly, averting her gaze.

Ms. Alvarez looked his way and offered a nod, which he took to mean his seat change had been approved. Catching the girl's sidelong glance, he thought to say hi. But then he thought of Dylan, how they'd met in that very class, and how their friendship had turned out. Instead, he opened his copy of *Moby Dick* and pretended to read. He'd read it three times already, trying to figure out how he was like Starbuck, looking for answers everywhere but within himself.

About the Author

In his head, Jason Parent lives in many places, but in the real world, he calls Southeastern Massachusetts his home. The region offers an abundance of settings for his writing and many wonderful places in which to write them. He currently resides with his cuddly corgi, Calypso.

In a prior life, Jason spent most of his time in front of a judge... as a civil litigator. When he tired of Latin phrases no one knew how to pronounce and explaining to people that real lawsuits are not started, tried, and finalized within the 60-minute time-frame they see on TV, he traded in his cheap suits for flip-flops and designer stubble. The flops got repossessed the next day, and he's back in the legal field... sorta. But that's another story.

When he's not working, Jason likes to kayak, catch a movie, travel any place that will let him enter, and play just about any sport (except for the one with that ball tied to the pole thing where you basically just whack the ball until it twists in on knot or takes somebody's head off). And read and write, of course. He does that too sometimes.

Read more at authorjasonparent.com.

About the Publisher

Dear Reader,

We hope you enjoyed this book. Please consider leaving a review on your favorite book site.

Visit https://RedAdeptPublishing.com to see our entire catalogue.

Don't forget to subscribe to our monthly newsletter to be notified of future releases and special sales.

www.ingramcontent.com/pod-product-compliance
Lightning Source LLC
Chambersburg PA
CBHW052239200626

46817CB00025B/308